SEASONAL ADJUSTMENTS

Adib Khan makes his fictional debut with *Seasonal Adjustments*, although he is also the author of a book of literary criticism.

Born in Dhaka, Bangladesh and with a passion for travel, Adib arrived in Australia in 1973 to study at Monash University. He currently teaches English and History in Ballarat, Victoria where he lives with his wife and two daughters.

SEASONAL ADJUSTMENTS

ADIB KHAN

ALLEN & UNWIN

Publication of this title was assisted by The Australia Council, the
Federal Government's art funding and advisory body.

First published in 1994 by
Allen & Unwin Pty Ltd
9 Atchison Street, St Leonards,
NSW 2065 Australia

National Library of Australia
Cataloguing-in-Publication entry:

Khan, Adib.
  Seasonal adjustments.

  ISBN 1 86373 652 2.
  I. Title.

A823.3

Set in 10/13 Palatino by DOCUPRO, Sydney
Printed by Australian Print Group, Maryborough, Victoria

10 9 8 7 6 5 4 3 2 1

For Shahrukh, Aneeqa and Afsana

PROLOGUE

Well Claire, here I am groping among the faint echoes of my beginnings. If only you could see me now, sitting under the shade of a jackfruit tree, painstakingly piecing together the shards of my earliest memories.

How is the lake in the warm weather? Are the black swans as bold as ever? Do you still think of them as the harbingers of your soul's release? Are you sitting on the wheelchair by the bay window, drinking hot water and clutching your decaying dreams of an emerald land you have never stopped loving? Is your migrant's restless spirit tormented by those childhood songs you have never forgotten? Tell me Claire, do you really feel the chilly drafts of mortality in summer's warm calmness, or is it only your febrile imaginings? I miss your company—the cups of awful herbal tea and the gossip about your rich neighbours behind their ivy-covered trellises, the ones who smile at you out of confused politeness and never say 'Hello'. You don't believe me, but I never tire of your ramblings about Ireland where most things, you claim, are controlled by unseen hands.

Are you thinking of me as you said you would? What do the tarot cards say? I am only joking. I am sorry I laugh and sometimes make you angry. But see, I followed your advice.

'Go home, Iqbal, go where you really belong,' you said. 'Go back to your source and find the past. See yourself in its reflection and know who you are. Heal yourself in your spiritual womb.'

So here I am in a landscape dotted by the fragments of a nearly forgotten age, scraping together the remembrances you say will help to restore me . . .

ONE

The first thing I asked to see was the river.

Of course I didn't need Mateen's permission, but it was an appropriate gesture of conciliation, judging by his perceptible annoyance with the way I had slipped into the village without informing him. Mateen would have preferred a formal welcome—musicians with harmoniums and *tablas*, dancing girls sprinkling me with rose-scented water and scattering flowers at my feet, special prayers in the mosque followed by a feast for the entire village. A celebration befitting the return of the wayward Chaudhary.

As it happened, I left the car outside the village and walked to the house to surprise him.

The muddy water of the Dhaleswari gurgles as though alarmed at my presence. It continues to slither away like a restless snake with a voracious appetite for swallowing everything which comes its way. Where I sit, the trees are sickly thin. They struggle to produce a few scaly-skinned fruits hanging droopily like the shrivelled breasts of starving women. The branches are dry and twisted. The ground around me is bare. Even weeds do not flourish here. So far December has been a rainless month, I was told. The powdery dryness of the earth feels coarse against my fingers.

Across the river fishermen cast their nets and wait patiently to catch an evening's meal. The dugouts have not changed since the days we went across. They are calmly steered over the currents by hands and eyes which dull the fear of danger for those who wish to cross. I can hear the delighted squeal of children swimming in shallow waters. On the other side, the unbroken line of trees beckons me with its dark silence. The river continues to flow with a pulsating disharmony.

Nothing is different. An invisible hand has imprisoned time, holding in its palm the idyllic scene of my childhood days.

Memory struggles sluggishly. It is unfamiliar with the depths it is feebly probing.

Self-consciously I take a piece of recycled paper from my backpack. My fingers feel stiff and clumsy. I fold the paper, twist and shape it into a boat. I eye it critically. Not a bad effort considering the lack of practice. I choose to overlook an important childhood ritual. I do not spit my wishes into the boat. I lean forward and float it on the water. Eager currents sweep it away.

Years ago I ran along the riverbank, chanting imaginary war cries, until the boat disappeared around the bend on its way to a land crowded with heroes and happy endings. Now I feel the sadness of a futile journey. Such a land does not exist any more.

The boat was a vehicle of my young imagination. It never failed to return, laden with a cargo of stories. My mother was often alarmed by the fecundity of my imagination. *Hai Allah!* I can hear Ma's despairing shriek. *Kee hohbey? What will become of this boy? What a dreamer he is! He remembers everything he wants to and repeats everything he shouldn't! He spends all his time with this made-up nonsense. What will happen to him?*

I am aware of another presence at a distance on my right. Curiosity compels me to look at him with resentment. He is a heavily built man who threatens the peace of my private sanctuary. He does not notice me as he continues to write furiously in a notebook. His obvious affluence contradicts my initial impression of a PhD student researching for a dissertation on rural sociology. He is impeccably dressed in a grey suit, white shirt and a red tie. My persistent stare interrupts him. He looks up and reluctantly raises his right hand in a salutatory gesture. The rings on his chubby fingers glint in the sunlight. I am immensely relieved by his decision to veer toward the graveyard. I am in no mood for idle conversation with strangers.

I focus on the rippling surface of the river as if my mind's eye were trying to penetrate its depth and locate a secret chamber full of past wonders wrapped in tinsel happiness. Memory begins to create entrances for the reality of the past. Each door creaks open to offer shadowy glimpses of a lost world floating in the mist of a time I once knew. My private universe expands slowly. The past creeps up shyly to claim me with weak, grasping hands. There are silent faces and distant places, snatches of happenings, distorted and blurred, as they come closer to wrap themselves around me. Embracing. Choking. As we merge, memory weakens and betrays me. It allows the present to invade and lacerate me with its shrapnels.

I cannot escape, can I Claire? I am not empowered to let the present flow back into the past and begin again. I have to live through this wretched pain. Didn't you once say the present is a dimension of time to be endured?

Behind me stands a charred brick wall, once a part of an annex to a *zamindar's* house. *Naach ghor*. Dance-house. A place for entertainment and relaxation. The mud bricks are the only visible reminders of my ancestral misdeeds.

For the itinerant visitors a guilty past is colourfully revived by the village elders. They pay scant respect to narrative cohesion or factual accuracy. I suppose it doesn't really matter. The relevance of details becomes insignificant with the distance of time.

I have been briefed about the old men of Shopnoganj as though I have never met them.

Be patient. They are harmless enough.

They have not seen me since I was in college. They expect a visit. A chat over a cup of tea.

Oh, they are very tiresome! They talk too much. Fantastic imaginations! But they mean well. Listen politely without taking them too seriously.

In the gathering darkness of mild evenings, they sit outside the tea shop and swap arcane stories, often pausing to listen to the river flowing with the pained roar of a guilt-ridden madman.

The river comes alive at night. They warn those who bother to listen. It cries as if it were tearing out its own entrails. Thoughtfully they chew *afeem* and refurbish a remote world of *zamindari* opulence and cruel excesses.

The exact nature of the wrongdoings has never been clearly established, not to my knowledge anyway. All sorts of stories have been created, intricately embroidered and circulated for years. The flexibility of the oral tradition has lent itself to an incredible variety of activities among the sepulchral figures who gather near the river at certain times each month for their nocturnal mourning. I can only assume that whatever my great-grandfather did to set loose these restless beings can only be called *criminal* by today's standards. Mind you, the villagers would never dare use such a word to condemn him. To malign the legendary village patriarch would be an unforgivable act of disloyalty. To be disrespectful to a Chaudhary is unthinkable, especially in my presence. Subservient politeness is a genetic conditioning of the villagers.

The custodians of the past are only too eager to tell me about the recent flurry of disturbances near the wall. Movements and weird noises every night for the past few weeks. Sights and sounds dreadful enough to make everyone pray for the village's safety.

On clear nights the lunar effulgence freezes the landscape into a silvery stillness. Animals and insects retreat deep inside the sanctuary of darkness. The wispy jackfruit trees crackle their limbs and stretch to lean over the dark river like bent old hags lost in a baffling maze of their withered years. All is quiet until the midnight hour cracks the fragile silence. Night bursts into life with the dance of writhing shadows.

The stories are wild all right. Positively mind-boggling. What am I to make of dancing ghosts, ululating *pethnis* and singing maidens who glow in the dark? A fiercely burning river where they bathe before dawn? The sound of *shahenies*, ghoulish cries, potent curses and magical chants?

I maintain a diplomatic silence and listen with a growing sense of sceptical amusement. I am uncomfortable here in the village of my birth. I can discern no changes in the years I have been away. Yet there is an unfamiliarity about everything I hear and see. It is like looking at life with borrowed eyes.

I now live in a world where myths are wafer thin and commercialised, without mystery or a multiplicity of meanings. I am neither religious nor superstitious. I am at home in an empirical world of sense impressions. I am enmeshed in the tangible. My life follows a narrow path of seek and gain with predictable consequences. Work . . . money . . . consumerism which dictates the quality of life . . . ceaseless striving for professional success and recognition even as I warn others of the dangers of ambition . . . competition . . . self-induced stress . . . more work . . . periods of emotional drought and mental fatigue . . . spiritual aridity followed by a yearning for a simple life in isolation. I am caught in a self-destructive vortex euphemised as living in the developed world. I never seem to view life from a stationary position. I do not know how to stop and see. I have lost the patience and skill for nourishing dreams. That is not to say I am without ideals. I continue to support the Greenies, argue in favour of land rights for the Aborigines, speak in favour of Amnesty International and express my abhorrence for domestic violence. I continue to vote Labor and gladly plead guilty to the accusation of being a cultural snob on account of patronising the theatre in Melbourne. Relationships play a peripheral part somewhere in my life—colleagues, acquaintances, a few good friends, a rapidly disintegrating marriage . . . a daughter.

I am a changed person, I have been repeatedly told over the last few days. I am firmly entrenched in the self-centred ways of the world I have chosen to live in. I measure time not in terms of people and values but in relation to palpable achievements. I want to conquer life instead of living it.

I must confess I am not used to this sort of idle loafing—listening to far-fetched tales over cups of tea and extending my creative horizons by adding episodic incidents to the supernatural phenomena haunting the village. I see it—no, not as a waste of time but something extraneous to my life, something which has been purged from my system. I am unaccustomed to the energy emanating from primitive imaginations. It is too raw, too concentrated, too alive, even dangerous, for my rationally attuned mind.

I feel trapped between polarised worlds of disenchantment when I consider the circumstances which have brought me back. Once I fled in fear and shame. I have never been intensely patriotic. That was a moral failing, I was sternly reprimanded during the war. I remember expressing my distaste for a photograph depicting a Bangali patriot proudly displaying the severed head of a Pakistani solder. I was made to feel like a traitor. *They began it. We must do the same to them. Our dignity must be restored.* Our acetylene hatred ignited a frenzy of self-righteous revenge against the Pakistanis and later became a volatile catalyst to activate the slaughter of their Bihari supporters. I turned my back on a nation born in agony, its soul deformed by loathing and chose to roam the fringes of a conservative community clinging to a dubious past and becoming increasingly agitated about drifting toward a future waiting to alter its identity.

There are occasions when I regret my exposure to the diversity of cultural radiation which has bleached my individuality. I think I know how a travelling performer might feel in his private moments. Effortlessly I can slip into cultural roles. I am a variable without a constant to measure myself against; a changing shadow whose exact composition cannot be determined. I should be grateful for the stability in my life, people tell me. How secure would I be in a third-world country? I have a house. A job. A country . . . let's say I possess a passport. What I lack is the weight of emotional anchors. There is nothing which binds me to a place.

I am buffeted by a cross-current of conflicting emotions— regret, relief, nostalgia, anger, gladness. Through the confusion a faceless voice persists. It has troubled me before. It mocks and provokes. Doubt is a sharp, shooting pain which strikes without warning. *Where do you think you belong?* It teases and then bursts into a playful laughter as though hiding the answer is a game to be relished and played repeatedly.

I switch back to the men-horses who gallop along the riverbank.

Men-horses? What! That's a new one. Men-horses. My suppressed laughter explodes into a spluttering noise. I apologise for spilling the tea. I do not bother with a parallel explanation of Thessaly and Mount Pelion. Surely they know nothing about Ixion's union with the cloud?

Men-horses?

I ask them about the winter's harvest.

We are sitting outside the teashop, basking under a mild sun. I have been honoured with garlands of marigold and boxes of sweetmeats. A cushioned, cane chair has been especially brought out for me. After all, I am a Chaudhary. Iqbal Ahmed Chaudhary. My surname bears the proud legacy of a Moghul title bestowed on chosen warriors. I come from a family of landowners. *Zamindars*. Tyrants and despots, some would say with justification. The fact that I live overseas gives me additional prestige. I live among white *shahebs* and *memshahebs*. That in itself is a laudable achievement.

The old fellows are perplexed. I speak English but do not live in England. How can that be?

'Australia?' I suggest tentatively.

They scratch their heads and stroke their beards. *'Beelath? Bhadshah* George?'

Obviously Elizabeth II has not been crowned yet.

'Na, na. Australia. Aus-tra-lia. Australia.' An imitation of a kangaroo hop won't help here.

'Aust-tre-leah. *Aacha.* Aushtreleah!' There are grins all around. 'Aushtreleah! Aushtreleah!'

I ask for another cup of tea.

The grim expression of poverty makes me fidget. I prefer to confront it in print and coloured images. This sort of relentless reality, beyond the control of a push-button, cannot be cushioned with platitudes nor made more bearable by fatalistic rationalisation. It jostles the conscience and unsettles me. Humpbacked and skimpily dressed peasants, like neglected beasts of burden staggering under the weight of bulging baskets, shuffle along slowly on bare feet. Naked children, with splotchy skin and distended bellies, balancing tied bundles of wood and dried cow dung on their heads, walk dutifully behind their parents. There is a sustained grimness about life here, an unmitigated sadness which compels me to look beyond myself at the bleeding rawness of bare existence. It is an expansive experience, a forced act of selflessness to be able to reach out and feel a pulse of suffering not my own.

Travelling beyond Dhaka is like taking a giant leap back in time. The countryside is steeped in superstition and quaint customs which fascinate me much in the same way as a museum might strike a romantic chord in a present-day technocrat ruled by the precision of a microchip. The *pucca* roads, radiating from the city like the arms of a starfish, are the only enduring symbols of a marginally successful invasion of modernity into the otherwise impenetrable depths of an ancient way of life.

Shopnoganj is a replica of the thousands of villages which confirm the rural primitivism of Bangladesh. Bamboo shacks crowd the sides of a wide, uneven dirt road which ends abruptly at the northern edge of the village. A raised stretch of a cracked bitumen track takes over for several hundred metres. This is the privileged and exclusive side of the village, clean and uncluttered. The villagers are strongly discouraged from walking here. Surrounded by lychee and mango trees, a sprawling double-storeyed house stands conspicuously like an abnormal growth. Its whiteness makes you think of a mirage. You expect the house to disappear as you approach it. It is an imposing sentry box for monitoring the activities in the village. For the farmers it is an awesome symbol of the Chaudhary empire.

It is the house where I was born.

The day has ripened into noon. Behind the teashop the *krishnachura* trees murmur in unison as a breeze drifts through their branches, carelessly plucking the orange-yellow flowers to carpet the earth. In a wide arc a black kite climbs above the trees, skimming the tightly stretched calmness of a cloudless sky. Suddenly it catches a breeze. There is a fluttering noise. A sharp movement upwards. The kite ploughs furiously through space until the unbeatable emptiness blunts its momentum. It falters, as if in recognition of its insurmountable limitations. It becomes a wavering dot on a blank screen, as insignificant as life itself.

Roshan Ali points in the direction of the river. 'Very dangerous,' he says emphatically. His blindness has not affected his assertive manner of speaking. 'I see the world up here,' he informs me, tapping his forehead. 'I see the past and future

11

the same way I see the present. I can see them all at the same time.' His toothless grin tells me he can sense my disbelief. 'You don't believe me, *Choto Babu*? Do you not understand what I am saying?'

Roshan Ali is the oldest in the trio of tea-sipping octogenarians. He is a formidable repository of my family's history. His imagination is like a tall tree. The roots burrow into the factual soil for nourishment as the trunk grows the other way with proliferating branches climbing without containment. He owned the village's only store when I was a child. I remember him as a sprightly shopkeeper who sold us sweets at an inflated price. He was a cunning man who invariably managed to recover the price of marbles and tops we sometimes stole from his shop.

I should not go anywhere near the wall, he warns me. Those who touch the bricks are plagued with ill fortune. The place was to be left alone, my grandfather had decreed after a heinous infringement long before I was born.

It happened on a foggy January night. Reckless villagers, stuporous on *thari*, plotted to chop a jackfruit tree for firewood. Three Hindus, armed with axes, crept past the wall at the stroke of midnight. One had his toes severed and bit off his tongue in pain. He was found in a semi-conscious state the next morning, never to speak again. Gangrene set in. Death was painful. Another man was found dead under a tree, his head split open by a fearful blow deemed to be beyond the power of an ordinary mortal. The third? His body was never found. Swallowed up by the river, people concluded and went about their business.

The work of evil spirits, thundered the *maulvi* to a cowering congregation at the Friday afternoon prayer in the mosque. Infidels could expect no better. For weeks afterwards the Dhaleswari jumped, roared and raged. Boats capsized. Villagers could neither wash nor bathe. Fishing was impossible. The river was protecting its secret until all evidence was beyond redemption.

'A bad place. Very bad.' Ramzan Mohammad shakes his head ruefully. 'Evil. City people do not believe when we tell them. They joke about it and call us crazy.' He looks at me with a glint of suspicion in his eyes.

I continue to sip the scalding hot tea from a chipped cup. I am careful to avoid the tiny cracks on the rim. The cup bears the insignia of a luxurious city hotel. The village is not entirely without its share of enterprising entrepreneurs.

Sharif Alam cranks up the conversation again. 'The river knows everything that happens,' he says definitively. 'It talks to those who wish to listen. It never lies.'

They nod in vigorous acquiescence.

There are fine scratches at the bottom of the cup. Ten . . . no, eleven. Mateen assured me all the cups had been washed in boiling water. Yet I am unable to escape a slight shudder. A bare movement of the shoulders betrays my sanitary expectations of the world.

I shall have to say something soon. My silence has the unmistakable quality of an unacceptable insolence.

'*Choto Babu*, we don't wish to be disrespectful.' Sharif Alam looks at me with sombre eyes.

'Yes?'

'You have paid your respects to your departed relatives?' There is a polite curiosity in Ramzan Mohammad's voice.

I was dreading this. 'No, not yet.' The truth is, I don't particularly care for the additional depression of a wander in the family graveyard.

'Your presence would please their souls. May they rest in peace!'

'*Aameen!*' Roshan Ali sighs.

'Is Moti Mia . . . ?'

'Still there!' Sharif Alam snorts. 'He can hardly see. He sits under a tree all day and pretends to look after the graveyard.'

'It is our duty to pray for those who are no longer with us, *Choto Babu*,' Roshan Ali persists. 'Candles and incense sticks can be bought in the shop.'

I am saved by the screeching brakes of an old van announcing the global influence of Coca-cola. *Mishti pani*, they call it here. Dogs yelp and hens scatter. A startled goat brushes past our table and rushes inside the shop. There is a clatter of pots and pans followed by a loud obscenity suggesting a rather unnatural relationship between the offender and its mother. Roshan Ali shouts a command for moderation. Ramzan Mohammad and Sharif Alam look utterly disgusted.

The driver, a long-haired young man wearing a pair of torn jeans and a black T-shirt, dumps a crate of bottled coke near my chair. He nods stiffly at me in a grudging acknowledgement of my privileged status as a fellow member of the universal denim club. He leaps back on the driver's seat and makes a spectacular U-turn. Horn blaring, the van roars away. The brief interlude of absurdity leaves behind a lingering haze of dust in the air. A silence of disapproval settles over the table.

A malnourished youngster with lustreless eyes, immune to sadness and suggesting an in-built resistance against any euphoria of happiness, wipes the laminated table with a rag which has rarely made contact with soap and water. A voice barks at him. In slow motion he begins to drag the crate inside.

I am relieved to see Mateen walking rapidly toward us. He is about to rescue me. Mateen is my first cousin. Until this morning we had not seen each other for eighteen years. He has done well for himself. He is now the baronial chief of the village, a position ideally suited to his medieval view of the world where a farmer's existence can only be justified by the menial work he does for the Chaudharies.

The principles of Islamic egalitarianism abound with infinite possibilities for social reformation. But Mateen treats the mere hint of the slightest change as an all-out assault on his *zamindari* privileges. Our morning conversation was dominated by his complaints against the villagers. They are militant, greedy, devious and without the traditional respect for their masters. They need discipline. It was far more satisfactory in the old days when the slightest misdemeanour was punishable by a public thrashing.

Mateen is a devout Muslim. He contemplates the precept of equality within the walls of the local mosque and agrees meekly with the teachings of the Koran. He attends the mosque every day and listens to the *imam* preaching the virtues of social justice. Judging by the bills Abba receives at the beginning of each month, Mateen is extraordinarily generous in the contributions he makes toward the upkeep of the House of Allah. Mateen prays five times a day, fasts rigorously during *Ramazan*, celebrates all the auspicious days on the Islamic calendar, does not touch pork or alcohol and fervently believes that his religious orthodoxy will eventually win him a permanent place in Heaven.

As he proudly showed me around the renovated mosque, I discovered that the prospect of eternal indolence in a manicured garden, graced with gushing fountains and sparkling streams, surrounded by fruit-laden trees and bashful virgins in servile attendance, was a futuristic certainty he never doubted. Without losing his temper, Mateen looked shocked when I teased him about all those untouched female attendants, *fair as coral and rubies*. Is there, I asked, an allowance made for some earthly entertainment, 'a bit of the other,' with a demure maiden of one's choice under the shade of a pomegranate tree?

'*Tauba! Tauba!* What are you saying? It is all spiritual,' he muttered, slapping his cheeks with the palm of his right hand. My playfulness must have shaken the structure of his entire universe and violated the sanctity of his empyreal domain. He managed a sad smile. What could he have said to a misguided family member corrupted by the hedonistic ways of the West? It was an act of magnanimous forgiveness to tolerate my blasphemous facetiousness. Would I like to attend the noon prayers?

'No,' I replied.

He waited for an explanation. I gave him none.

He mumbled something about repentance. The salvation of my capricious soul was bound to feature in his prayers.

Mateen approaches us with aggressive strides. He looks agitated. His rotundity gives him the comical air of a professional clown. He has a porcine face which grossly exaggerates his age. At forty-four he looks about fifty-five, sliding toward sixty. Instead of imparting dignity, Mateen's greying hair hints at a deeply disturbed personality. The top of his head is like a cyclone-ravaged sugarcane field. Strands of coarse hair point in every direction. Some lie flattened on his skull. Others defy the regulative influence of a comb and stand rigidly erect. The combined effect of gluttony, excessive smoking and an abhorrence of any physical exertion has shaped him into a permanent state of fatigued obesity.

His nostrils are flared and he is breathing heavily. He is visibly upset. 'Lunch should be ready,' he pants and flops into a chair.

Farewells are said to the old men with a vague promise of seeing them again. I give each some money sealed in a white envelope. To buy sweets for their grandchildren, I add hastily. I am pleased about remembering the cultural nuances which demand that monetary gifts to older people must never appear to be a vulgar act of condescending generosity. There must be an excuse, a tangential reason so they do not feel humiliated.

They bless me. May Allah bring me many sons and much happiness.

I refrain from saying that happiness and many sons would be incompatible, especially in these times. But then here the

basic laws of economics are not understood to have a corre-
lation with one's well-being.

We walk leisurely and stop in front of a bamboo shack with
sagging walls and without a door. It is the local pharmacy. A
coloured poster pinned on a post has outraged Mateen. Belligerently he steps inside to exchange heated words with the
recently arrived pharmacist, cum quack cum fortune-teller
and dentist, who is probably paid quite handsomely by the
Family Planning Clinic to promote the way to prosperity by
virtue of those little pills which are rarely as effective in these
parts as they are in the city. Now a more sinister dimension
of birth control is being publicised.

I can hear their voices. Mateen is disgusted that the poster
is directed at men. He emerges with a howl of indignation.
He rips the displayed poster off the post with a force that
shakes the entire shack.

The Family Planning man stands near me, smirking.

Mateen launches into an improvised description of a hell
crowded with cindery creatures condemned forever for their
nefarious deeds. We meet monsters with every conceivable
deformity and with an unceasing appetite for human flesh.
We traverse burning plains dotted with overflowing cauldrons
of boiling blood and pus. There are screams for mercy and
cries for oblivion.

I sense a commercial opportunity here. I interrupt Mateen's
gush of words. My suggestion, of making a quick ethereal
fortune by installing a vending machine near the burning
gates to facilitate a final fling with sin and fun before the
unsuspecting newcomers are pronged and dipped into the
infernal cauldrons, is not received with any enthusiasm.

Mateen glares at me. I think I have gone too far.

Not to be outdone, the Family Planning man offers Mateen
a posthumous business proposition.

With a stern, *'Beyahdub!* Be warned!' Mateen straightens his
shoulders and marches off with slow, measured steps, fuming

17

at the impertinent man who is neither repentant nor frightened of the village head.

The versatile, betel-chewing apothecary hurries back inside to fetch a sheaf of coloured posters. He holds up one for me to examine. Against a pale blue background a bulbous index finger, sheathed in a pink condom, points at us. The caption in Bangla reads: YOU ARE ALSO RESPONSIBLE!

We discuss the drawbacks of the advertisement. Most of the villagers cannot read. Very few have ever seen or heard of a condom. Men will refuse to accept the message even if it is explained to them.

'It does not matter Chaudhary *Shaheb*. I do what the head office tells me. I am paid well.' The man winks at me and expectorates vigorously. A glutinous blob of phlegm curdles in the dust near my feet. He shakes with silent laughter. He is under instruction to decorate the entire shop.

He brushes aside my suggestion of taking a vacation. 'My place is here in the village,' he declares assertively. 'I only arrived last week.'

He will be leaving soon. Very soon. If he is lucky.

I quicken my steps to catch up with Mateen. I ask him about Rehana. I met his wife briefly in the morning. She is a shy village girl, hardly half his age. This is his third marriage. His previous wives died during childbirth. He married Rehana last year, and now she is pregnant. Rehana will be sent to live in Dhaka a month before the baby is due.

'This time I must make sure,' he says with fierce determination. 'Best doctor in the best hospital. May Allah favour me with a son.'

I am apologetic about my behaviour with Rehana. I had resisted stubbornly when Mateen insisted that she touch my feet in the established manner of greeting an older relative. It is a Hindu custom grafted into some Bangali Muslim families. The firmness with which I resisted must have upset her. She burst into tears and ran into the kitchen. My insensitivity has made me miserable and contrite.

My stomach growls like angry storm clouds. I long for a salad roll—a fresh wholemeal roll with ham and Top-hat cheese, lettuce, tomatoes, shredded carrots and alfalfa sprouts with a light topping of French mustard. A beer would go down well with the roll.

Lunch turns out to be a veritable feast. Despite my protests, Mateen heaps steaming hot *pilau* on my plate. Placed in front of me is an inviting array of curries. I eye them with some apprehension. I succumb to the prawns cooked in coconut milk.

'Won't Rehana eat with us?' Immediately I regret asking. I should know better. I am no more than a stranger to her. A male. Decorum forbids me to try and establish even a conversational aspect of a friendly relationship. Talking to her for any length of time would be an act of impropriety. She is my cousin's wife. It is a delicate relationship. In the country it is considered to be potentially dangerous.

'Later,' Mateen replies brusquely. 'When she has finished in the kitchen.'

The food is superb. My self-imposed dietary restrictions are forgotten. I do not have to be persuaded into a second helping. Between mountainous serves of *pilau* and meat, Mateen drinks half a jug of water. He points to my untouched glass.

'I am not thirsty,' I lie through tingling lips. I think of the bottle of mineral water in my backpack near the stairs.

Despite my scepticism, I cannot help harping on the old men and their fascinating yarns.

Mateen dismisses them contemptuously. 'They tell good stories,' he admits. 'They make up all these things just to get attention and feel important. They have nothing else to do.'

'But some very unpleasant things did happen,' I insist. 'Even I know that much. I have never bothered with the exact details. What were they? Come on, you know.'

19

Mateen pauses for a drink. He bites his lips in embarrassment as if a child has caught him off-guard with an awkward
question. 'Well, I . . . ' He scratches the back of his head with
his left hand and avoids my eyes. 'Well . . . in the old days
the *zamindars* were fun-loving people. You know how it was.
A little harmless fun in the dance-house. Sometimes they went
a little too far and the villagers heard about a few incidents.
That's how the stories began.'

That is not what I have heard over the years. To put it
mildly, my great-grandfather was a bit of a scoundrel. He
spent his days riding his horses through the fields, looking
for young peasant girls who could be trained as dancers for
his nocturnal revelries. His evenings were spent in the dance-
house with drunken friends and a bevy of young women to
entertain them. I know nothing about my great-grandmother.
I suspect she may have been one of Ishtiaq Ahmed
Chaudhary's concubines who cajoled him into matrimony
during one of his periods of inebriated generosity.

I tell Mateen what I know about the debauchery and the
violence. He winces at my choice of words. Family honour,
izzat, means everything to him.

'There is no proof of what you say,' he mutters stiffly.

I remind him of the incident about the Hindu girl who was
randomly picked up from a paddy field. She was a temple
priest's daughter. A Brahmin. She disappeared for several
weeks before her decomposed body was found floating in the
river. The priest publicly cursed my great-grandfather and his
descendants. The Chaudharies would never know happiness
again. Never find peace. Later that night he poured *ghee*
around the dance-house and set it on fire. The next morning
he was found hanging from a jackfruit tree near the smouldering ruin.

'But no one knows if that is true!' Mateen protests vehemently. 'There is such a story. I have heard it. The villagers
will even tell you that the ghosts of the priest and his daughter

are to be seen near the river. Can you believe that? There are new stories every year. You know how superstitious these people are.' He laughs nervously and spreads his hands in a gesture of exasperated helplessness as if to indicate that such tales are only to be expected from the ignorant. 'It's all rubbish! *Bajey Khotha*. Nonsense! The fire was an accident.'

'There were people thrown into the river with weights tied to their legs.'

'Never! Aha! Where did you hear that? That's another lie! At most they were whipped and allowed to go home.'

A young maidservant holds a silver tray in front of me. I refuse the cigarettes and betel leaves. I feel bloated and drowsy. Mateen stares incredulously when I tell him I usually have a sandwich and a piece of fruit for lunch. I accept his suggestion of an afternoon nap as an excuse to go upstairs. I think we have discovered enough of each other. I need some separate time to prepare for an amicable parting.

The room is refreshingly cool. I am in the old part of the house. This is my room in a very special sense. I was born here forty-three years ago. Every corner is crowded with cobwebbed memories which leap at me with unbounded joy. Their richness gives me a fortifying strength, a meaning which begins to fill the yawning blankness of the present.

The good things from the past can never be taken away. They are a part of you. Don't neglect them. Treat your memories well and they will work for you.

I think I understand, Claire. I think I know what you meant.

I look around the room, taking in each detail as though it were a form of visual therapy intended to lift me out of this trough of hopelessness. *Dhobi*-washed clothes and a fresh towel are neatly folded on a spartan wooden chair. Spread in a corner of the floor is a blue and gold prayer mat. The sheen on the velvet tells me it has been recently purchased. It would make an attractive wall-hanging. On the chunky antique dresser there is a large white porcelain bowl and a pitcher of water. I recognise my grandfather's copy of the Koran bound in brown calf's skin. I finger his sandalwood prayer beads and try to remember some of the names. *The Merciful, the Compassionate, the King, the Most Holy, the Tranquil, the Faithful, the Protector, the Victorious, the Mighty* . . . That's only nine. Oh yes! *The Avenger, the Enricher, the Possessor* . . . I should know a few more . . . *the Eternal* . . . *the Afflicter* . . . The sandalwood has lost its heady aroma.

The linen on the huge double bed near the window is crisply clean. A white mosquito net, with its corners tied to the four posts and its sides neatly folded over the top, hangs like a canopy over the bed where I arrived reluctantly on a stormy night.

I part the green cotton curtains behind the bedhead. The afternoon light bathes the world in a golden haze of fairytale innocence. I can see the wall in the distance. Beyond it the river meanders like a torpid serpent, slowly winding its way through a pristine sanctuary, searching for the primordial weakness of human vanity.

We were forbidden to swim in the river. It was too dangerous, teeming with underwater creatures hungry for little boys. *Stay away*! Khuda Buksh, our family servant, would warn us. *Keep clear! Otherwise it will gobble you up!*

The dense foliage across the river evokes more than a fleeting touch of nostalgia. I feel as though a part of me is permanently alive there. The straw-roofed huts remain as I remember them, like ticks embedded in the thick coat of a furry animal. The paddy fields and orchards are untouched.

The past unfurls with a startling clarity, as if my childhood had left me only yesterday. I can hear myself tiptoeing over rotten leaves and dry twigs. Watching, probing, creating . . . learning.

It was the accepted norm to spend a part of our school holidays in Shopnoganj. In the early days the liveable part of the house was a small section of the grand edifice built by my great-grandfather. I sensed a terrible loss when a sizeable part of the original building had to be demolished and replaced by a number of characterless rooms and ostentatious verandahs.

The house was the family's summer meeting place. Uncles, aunts, cousins, friends, servants, pets and cartloads of luggage arrived from distant parts of the country for a noisy month's reunion. The world was small and simple then; ordered and peacefully structured with few, if any, blemishes.

The house was never quiet in the morning hours. Farmers, with their wives and children, assembled in the front yard to pay their respects to *Boro Shaheb*. The men strolled along the riverbank and discussed business affairs and politics, pausing occasionally to talk to the fishermen. The women preferred to stay inside to sew, cook and gossip. The children wandered through the village with a cockiness we deemed to be appropriate to our lofty status. There was always the opportunity to civilise the locals by teaching them about cricket or asserting our superiority by thrashing them in a game of soccer.

When the hot evening crept across the river and engulfed the house, the family assembled in the lantern-lit front verandah to eat a huge meal and listen to Lipu Chacha singing *Rabindro Shongeet* and *Nazrul Geethi*. As the melancholy sound of the harmonium sank into the night's deep darkness, we were dragged into a primeval frenzy of song and dance that lasted until exhaustion silenced us and we tumbled into bed with the certainty that the next day would be much the same.

I assumed that the summers would keep rolling along endlessly, enabling me to return each year to savour my unguarded hours of freedom across the river. Time and change had no bearing on my life as I drifted through my early years without ever suspecting the cruel finiteness of innocence.

There were three of us in a similar age group—my older brother, Hashim, Mateen and I. My sisters, Nafisa and

Shabnam, were too young to belong to this fraternity. Even if they had been older, the fact they were females would have disqualified them from our adventure treks. We were bound by an unshakeable belief in our masculine toughness which made no allowance for girls and their silly toys. The territories we explored were mined with imaginary dangers—wild animals, pirates, prehistoric monsters, thieves, dacoits and Hindus. They were places for catapults, bows and arrows, tin swords and wooden guns; not dolls and kitchen sets.

We waited patiently until the heat of the day peaked and the adults were in the depths of their afternoon sleep. Surreptitiously we crept to the riverbank and coerced the fishermen to carry us across in their dugouts. The giddy smells of ripe guava and mangoes beckoned us. We shed the mantle of civilised behaviour with imitative cries of Tarzan. An insatiable hunger for exploration possessed us. An element of unpredictability excited our curiosity and prompted us to venture further into unfamiliar territory. Of necessity, Mateen was our leader. Although he attended a boarding school in Shillong, Mateen spent more time in Shopnoganj than we did. His father supervised the farms, collected the profits and kept the farmers ignorant and hard-working. Mateen knew the terrain far better than Hashim or me.

It was in the summer of my tenth birthday that Mateen promised to introduce us to a new jungle game. 'It's silly,' he confessed. 'It is played with a girl.'

Hashim and I looked at him with unbridled disdain. Traitor! He had betrayed the binding principle of our little group.

'We cannot play,' he assured us. 'We can only watch.'

'Why can't we play?'

'Because it is a game for older people. I don't understand the rules. They are too hard.'

'Can't we ask someone? Khuda Buksh?'

'No!' Mateen snapped. 'People get very angry if you ask. You must be very quiet. *Akdum chup!*'

Late one afternoon we hid behind a clump of mango trees and watched each stage of that most fundamental of human games with those subtle and variable rules which made the whole thing even more difficult to apprehend as I grew older.

On this occasion instinct negotiated with consumerism and reached a mutually satisfactory agreement. The horizontal inclinations of a coy, young woman were bribed with gifts of hair oil, soap, ribbons and face powder. An elderly farmer put an arm around her shoulders and whispered words of endearment.

We moved closer.

'*Aami tomai bhalo bashee.*' He kept repeating.

Even after all these years the words reverberate across the river. Now that I think about it, in its context it was a very clever phrase—caring, persuasive and yet without a hint of serious commitment. *Aami tomai bhalo bashee. I like you. I am fond of you.*

We suppressed nervous giggles as he undressed her. On an uneven mattress of wild grass, two wrinkled mounds, like the halves of a worn-out soccer ball, bobbed up and down with a frenzied vigour. Limbs jerked. Twigs snapped. We edged forward, nudging and shoving.

To me it was disappointingly obvious. 'It's a wrestling match!' I observed with a smug assurance. I was slugged on the arms from either side.

The soft sighs and the wild bellows were a bit of a mystery. The man groaned. I strained over Hashim's shoulder for a closer look. I began to have doubts about my initial pronouncement. It just didn't make sense. There was no purpose to it. It looked undignified. This was not the way I wrestled in the school yard.

There was a strange heaviness in my loins. My legs trembled. My face felt hot. Tiny insects began to crawl down the inside of my left thigh. I felt guilty without knowing why. I looked at Hashim. His face was darker and his eyes were glazed. Mateen grinned at us slyly.

The ending was unexpectedly abrupt. Hashim and I understood Mateen's complaint about the difficult rules.

'Who won?' I whispered.

Mateen didn't know.

'The man did,' Hashim said tentatively.

'Why?'

'How do you know?'

'He was the one who moved and made the noises.'

'So?'

'Ssh! Not so loudly. They may play again.'

'He played from the top! He won!'

'So? Why did he make so much hurt noise?'

'Because he was winning. It was a victory cry! Oh I don't know! Maybe it was a draw.'

'It's silly to have a wrestling match with a girl. She could hurt herself and cry.'

'It wasn't a wrestling match!'

'It was!'

'Wasn't!'

Yelling and jostling, we forgot about hiding. The startled couple grabbed their clothes and ran. I ducked as Hashim tried to hit me. His fist caught Mateen on the side of the face and knocked him over. With a howl of outrage Mateen struggled to his feet and, with unsteady hands, fired a barrage of plastic arrows at us. Arms flailing, we swung and missed, kicked and cursed until fatigue subdued us.

I had the final say on the way back. 'It must have been a wrestling match. It must.'

They pretended not to hear me and trudged back to the river without speaking.

Much later, when we were back on speaking terms, we agreed that it was a stupid game not even suitable for girls. It was a waste of time. The rules were too complicated for such a short period of play. We would never stoop to such a game. Never.

Never. That definitive pronouncement of children.

The lazy afternoon strokes a vast silence shrouding the other side of the world. The past may be better off without my presence there. I change my mind about a ride across the river. Reluctantly I draw the curtains.

For the first time since morning I think of Nadine. It is Christmas tomorrow. Her presents will have to be wrapped. Despite my lengthy explanations she cannot quite understand why there won't be a Christmas tree and presents from everyone.

TWO

A pallid light ages the tired afternoon. The leaden sky weeps from its ulcerous wounds. What are these shapes of rattling bones and withered skin that look almost human? They huddle under a soggy cardboard shelter, their eyes riveted on an empty spinning bottle. Who are these that create fear and shrivel compassion? He comes at last! The old woman cackles. We have been waiting for you. Sit here. The mouth of the bottle points toward me. You have won! She cries and claps her hands. They turn to look with marble eyes. Their feet are turned backwards. What do you know about the pain of endless journeys? The nibbling teeth of injustice and the painful grind of slow death? The burden of waiting with a burning revenge? Have you lost anything? My daughter. Have you seen her? The bottle spins again. Can you tell me where I am? Hands point to the bent pole. The letters have been scraped off the twisted sign. The dim outlines of distant monoliths waver like praying figures immersed in water. There are no others. These sights and smells do not belong here. Rat-gnawed cabbages like battered, dug-up skulls. Acrid smell of slow-burning leaves. Pieces of frayed ropes like half-eaten snakes. Blood-splattered blades of knives and torn cigarettes like slashed intestines loaded with faeces. What is that noise from the abandoned carriages behind the wall? Pardon me. The back-seat bunts of loveless couples on the transient crests of cold waves. Was that a child's cry behind the wafting mist? The river breathes heavily. It is cold . . . so cold. On the wall the

28

huge screen flickers. Can you tell me what it says? He wants to know! Have you never learned to read the language of Fate? Along the riverbank the horses canter. A rider draped in black burqa *beckons with a jerk of her head. Do I know you? The voice has a nasal twang. She has read my mind. I have always known you. She holds out a hand mirror. I know where your daughter is. You must run ahead of me. Hold the mirror in front of your right shoulder. Like this. The river begins to run with me. There are sounds of ankle bells and the rhythm of dancing feet, somewhere ahead where the river cries. I smell the brine as the wind buckles against my face. She is still there, though falling behind. How far? The mirror no longer speaks. I move it in front of me. Nadine's drowning face pleads for help.*

Some time, in dawn's fading darkness, I found myself on the floor. Squirming. Afraid. My mouth dry and open in a voiceless scream. A throbbing pain where my head hit the floor.

We had a late night yesterday. It was a noisy family dinner garnished with anecdotes and old stories. We recounted incidents which made us laugh freely. We gossiped about the old men of Shopnoganj. I reported their latest concoctions.

'At least they are entertaining. You can never accuse them of not living up to the village's name,' Hashim said drily. 'The place of dreams should be populated with dreamers and raconteurs.'

Even Abba opened up with some of the tales he had heard in his days. I noticed he avoided mentioning anything to do with his grandfather. It was a happy evening terminated by a brief interlude of tension created by my unsuppressed curiosity.

Hashim is on his own and comes over for dinner every night. Farhana and the children are visiting her parents in Lahore. He does not know how long they intend to stay in Pakistan. The lack of warmth in his voice and Nafisa's warning nudge under the table cautioned me against further inquiry.

Shabnam was different. I had a right to know. Their reticence angered me. She was killed in a car accident fourteen years ago. She was driving at a high speed on a wet road. The car swerved and hit a tree.

'Her fiancé? What happened to him?' I asked innocently.

Nafisa looked apprehensively at Abba. He pushed back his chair and left the table.

'We are talking about my sister!' I persisted heatedly.

'You finally realised that, did you?' Deftly Nafisa put me on the defensive. 'That hasn't altered in all these years despite your silent absence. How often did you write asking about her? About us?'

She knew how to choke me into an embarrassed silence. It hurt to know that my own family was suspicious of me, unwilling to tell me more about the circumstances surrounding Shabnam's accident. But after the accumulated years of my appalling indifference, how could I presume a greater degree of trust?

It is quiet out here on my private balcony.

I was up early, brooding over the crowded collage of fragmented images. They were meaningless, yet strangely disturbing in their vivid intensity.

Bleary-eyed, I watch the vigorous morning forcing its way through a muslin veil to encroach on my cocooned sanctuary. The landscape begins to extend beyond the spacious backyard and reveal itself with a greater clarity. December is an unobtrusive ambassador of goodwill to Bangladesh. It bears gifts of mild, sun-soaked days and cool, clear nights to compensate for the wanton destruction of the monsoonal rains. The balminess of the year's farewell dims the nightmare of the raging, clawing monster which besieges the land with random strikes of unmitigated fury. The balcony overlooks a creek running past the gradual slope of a garden wreathed in circular beds of cannas, petunias and marigolds. A *mali* is already at work, scything the wet grass with a curved blade.

The suburb of Banani is a bastion of a lifestyle uncommon in the subcontinent. It is carefully hidden away from the damning marks of abject poverty that plagues the country. I have always thought of the creek as an unofficial dividing line between the privileged few and the millions out there. Somewhere. Out of sight. Beyond conscience.

There is a dreary homogeneity about the houses here. They look pretentious and uniformly vulgar. During the years I have been away, tropical fruit trees, exotic shrubs and vines have camouflaged the lack of architectural imagination manifested with a sustained monotony in the grotesquely large homes. Rich is big. That is the unstated suburban motto. Most of the houses are not entirely visible from the streets. One can catch glimpses of walls and verandahs. Windows and doors peep through *purdahs* of leaves and branches. Riotous mixtures of red and white, pink, purple and yellow spill over the boundary walls. In some ways nature is kind to Bangladesh. It is like a bad-tempered step-parent showering moments of guilt-ridden generosity on a maltreated child.

I choose to ignore the English dailies slipped under my door. I am weary of reading about militant students and food shortages, pompous ministerial statements and news on overseas aids to the country. The ominous political rumblings on the streets are never featured, even as inconspicuous news items. Voluntary censorship is the media's contribution to the fragile semblance of democracy here.

I opt for the unread newspaper I bought at Tullamarine over a week ago. I scan the front page. The woes of a once carefree, larrikin nation are reflected in the sombre headlines. More bad news on the balance of payments and unemployment. Procrastinating politicians with 'know-all' attitudes and glib statements. A photograph of a worm-like queue of interviewees at the rear entrance of a newly opened restaurant. Next to it, the woes of luxury car dealers. The polite concern over the growing level of Japanese investment continues. They have moved south. A more conservative newspaper would have reported it differently. A screaming headline honing in on long-held prejudices.

I cannot help feeling sad for the generous country I stepped into as a confused young man. Perhaps its generosity toward itself has been its greatest point of vulnerability. An unfamiliar spirit of meanness has begun to shadow the vision of a carelessly spendthrift nation. A Hobbesian instinct for survival has surfaced. Australia, as I once knew it, was too good to be true. It was a huge dream full of sharply defined rainbows and realisable wishes for those who cared to pursue them. The transition to an imperfect reality is painfully difficult.

I turn to the feature article inside. The warning is tinged with indignant hysteria. Our living standards will be overtaken by several neighbouring countries. It is the sort of speculation which causes communal consternation. What will they say behind the exclusive doors in Collins Street?

What? Singapore? South Korea? Asian countries? Surely not! What a preposterous idea! There is a rectifiable flaw somewhere in the evolutionary pattern. That is not how it was meant to be. It shall right itself. Let us march on with the all-conquering spirit of Europe. We carry the world's treasures of culture with us. How can we possibly allow them to catch up with us? Tradition! Tradition! Back to the basics. Loyalty to the crown. Honesty. Hard work. Christian morality. Let us not forget the pioneering spirit and those who built this nation. The digger's courage and the spirit of Gallipoli. We must revive this great country of ours! Meanwhile, gentlemen, we must keep foreigners out of the club. Shall we drink to it?

Bankers, businessmen, politicians, historians and army men. Tired voices stuck in a groove. Tremulous and unconvincing. Myopic, faded heroes playing sentimental favourites of the good old days when everything moral and righteous were with God, monarch and country.

History is slow and unfeelingly neutral in dispensing justice. It follows an unpredictable path of random selection in its choice of a few centuries of circumstantial favouritism. It tolerates abuse and misuse of its favours, making room for the tumorous growth of the fallacy of cultural superiority. It waits patiently until the pestilence of arrogance reaches an epidemic proportion. Then it strikes with a virulence which becomes an enigma to posterity.

It is not in our power to guide history. If it were, civilisations would never decay. It is history, as a subtle, living force, which taps in on our weaknesses and erodes cultures in a manner which is beyond the grasp of the generation it is humbling.

Were it possible to be an alert, double-century man, a little more than 150 years from now! Would I hear the same theme in a different language?

I shall probably be left alone for another half an hour until Nadine tires of her presents. I was half-awake when her elbows and legs bumped into me. A suffocating hug and sloppy kisses dragged me out of bed.

It was worth lugging the presents all the way from Singapore. She is a happy girl today. We enjoyed shopping on Orchard Road and in Little India. It was a day without the constraints of daily rituals. We ate when we were hungry and rested when we felt like it. There were no rules between equals. For several hours she was a carefree little girl without the surliness which has blighted our relationship since Michelle left for Italy.

Fortunately the myth about the North Pole and Rudolph and company was gently disassembled a few years ago. Otherwise I would have faced the daunting task of explaining his cheerful rotundity's entrance through an iron-grilled window.

We have already had a minor misunderstanding about the way Christmas is to be celebrated this year.

There won't be any turkey or pudding. Please don't make a fuss.

Not fair! Why not?

Because Christmas is not celebrated by most people over there.

Why not?

They are not Christians.

What are they?

Muslims.

Like you?

Well, sort of. They are more strict about religion.

But you enjoy Christmas! You stuff yourself with turkey and pudding!

Excuse me!

Sorry.

It's a bit different for me.

Why is it different? You are one of them.

One of whom?

Muslims.

Yes, in a way. It's a bit hard to explain.

Dad?

Yes?

Am I a Christian?

Er . . . not exactly. Mum is.

What's it like to be a Christian?

Don't know, mate. Never been one.

Are Christians much different from Muslims?

In some ways they are.

Dad?

What?

I want to be a Christian. Can I?

When you are old enough, you can choose to be what you like. Why do you want to be a Christian?

That's what the kids are at school. I want to be like them.

The necessity of opening the presents in the privacy of her room excited Nadine. She is thrilled with the idea of sharing a secret with me. We are coconspirators in a venture which has far greater ramifications than she can possibly envisage. So far no one has asked me about her religious education. I am almost certain that there is a complacent assumption about Nadine's upbringing as a Sunni Muslim. As yet I have been unable to formulate a suitably ambiguous explanation to ward off any prolonged period of curious inquiry.

My thoughts are diverted by a young girl dipping a pitcher in the creek. From this distance it is difficult to guess her age. Ten, perhaps twelve, and already burdened with the responsibilities of an adult world. I wave to her. She turns her face and draws the *aachol* of her red sari across her face. With the full pitcher under her arm, she hurries away.

That was thoughtless of me. She could be married or, at least, engaged. I think of Nadine in the next room, pressing buttons and zapping the invaders from outer space.

There is a loud, impatient knock on the door.

I have never been comfortable about Khuda Buksh performing the chores of a servant. He has been a friend since I was a child. I try to take the breakfast tray from him. I am curtly rebuked and told to follow him to the balcony.

Despite my request for toast and tea, the tray is loaded with a cooked breakfast. *Puris* and spiced omelette. Potato *bhaji. Jelabis.* There is tea in a silver pot that does not gleam the way it once did. The lacquer on the handle is beginning to peel. The white napkin is frayed at the edges. The tines of the fork are slightly bent.

Sticking out from under the saucer is a note from Abba.

Khuda Buksh has the status of a revered family elder in our house. He is over seventy. That is only an approximation. As far as I can remember, he has been consistently evasive about his age. When we were at school, Hashim and I managed to annoy him by exaggerating his years. *Fifty-five? Sixty? Sixty-five?*

Under unceasing pressure he would mumble, 'Past thirty'.

A couple of days ago I asked him again.

'Past thirty,' he replied, unable to comprehend the reason for my laughter.

He is a short, frail man with stooping shoulders and bony hands. His craggy face is a bird's-eye view of a randomly furrowed land. It would be a sad face if the eyes did not sparkle with a mischievous energy which belies his age. The hircine beard lends a touch of gravity without obviating the impression of a fun-loving rascal prone to childish pranks given the slightest opportunity.

Khuda Buksh was a village orphan adopted by the family as a playmate for my father. I have fond childhood memories of him. He was there whenever we wanted him for a game of cricket or soccer, stoically prepared to take the blame for broken windows and trampled flowerbeds. He took us fishing at strategic times of the day when he was needed in the house. An invincible air of superiority clung to him as he ordered the other servants around the house as though he were their imperial employer. He was fully aware of his special privileges and he abused them like a petty dictator without a modicum of guilt. The immunity he enjoyed, when my grandfather was alive, was a matter of considerable annoyance to Ma. He reacted to her scoldings in a manner that an overfed rhinoceros might respond to a stone thrown by a child. He yawned in an uncouth fashion, by opening his mouth as widely as he could, and then slowly ambled out of sight.

And what a captivating storyteller he was! The exploits of Ameer, Hamza, Hatim Tai and Sinbad were crafted into suspenseful episodes of unending adventures. In turn we told him about Jesse James, Billy the Kid and Wild Bill Hicock. Khuda Buksh had no inkling about the wild west or the six-shooters we claimed were superior to the *talwars* of the

Middle-Eastern warriors. In our world of heroic action, shaped into basic dramas of right and wrong by the brothers of the Holy Cross and reinforced by the Sunday morning westerns, the cowboy reigned as the supreme architect of the greatest nation on earth. Khuda Buksh listened politely with the amused composure of an adult who knew children tend to exaggerate.

He was a fanatical Muslim. In entranced astonishment we listened to his passionate accounts of Hindu atrocities committed during partition. In his narratives Muslims were the innocent victims of savage infidels. In his neat, compartmental view of good and evil, even the insect world was divided by religious antagonism. He spent hours convincing us that the harmless black ants were the special creatures of Allah. The vicious red ones, that bit people, were the disciples of *Iblis*. In his crippled perception of the world, there was no space for Jews, Christians or even Buddhists. There were only Muslims and Hindus locked in a kind of Manichaean struggle for the ultimate mastery of the universe. The advent of Imam Mehdi, he assured us, would break the deadlock with a decisive victory for the followers of the true faith.

It felt good to know I was born on the right side, destined to enjoy the pleasures of *Behaesht*. Despite the prejudices of my formative years, I occasionally felt sorry for the Hindus doomed in the flames of *Dozak*. It seemed unfair that, without exception, they should struggle through their corporeal existence without the slightest prospect of immortal bliss.

Spurred on by Khuda Buksh's religious zeal and keen to do our bit in the holy struggle, one afternoon Hashim and I dressed ourselves as cowboys and went out on a *jihad* to tilt the balance in favour of Islam. It did not strike us at the time that cowboys belonged to another religion and would not have been necessarily interested in fighting for the Glory of Allah. We went to a nearby field and fired imaginary bullets from our six-shooters made from empty packets of Capstan cigarettes. We made as much noise as we possibly could to soften up the enemy. Then we poured kerosene, stolen from the kitchen, on red ant hills and set them alight. The cowboy image, we reluctantly agreed, did not suit the occasion. The ant hills resembled burning wagons. We transformed ourselves into members of that inferior race, the Red Indians, and hooted and danced as the fire crackled with burning ants. The grand Islamic victory was a step closer.

Later Hashim must have felt equally guilty. We avoided each other for several days. I was so overcome by remorse that I even fronted up to Brother Leo at school the next day to ask if I could go to confession. The chaplain's unbounded joy and his lengthy exposition on the Catholic way to salvation confused me enough to decide against a visit to the cleansing box. My life continued in a miserable state of dark guilt. I lived with the burden of the burning ants for a very long time. Never again did the prospect of a holy war enthuse me into any form of violent action.

Khuda Buksh is curious about Nadine. He is desperately keen to know more about my personal life. He is fascinated by Nadine's grey eyes and her lighter complexion. I suspect he has been instructed not to pester me with too many questions. Nadine took an instant dislike to him the day we arrived. In his laborious pidgin English, Khuda Buksh tried to explain why young girls should never bare their arms and legs. Nadine had complained about the humidity and, at my suggestion, changed into shorts and T-shirt. I overheard Khuda Buksh use the word *shame* several times. He must have conveyed his disapproval effectively enough. Nadine's angry yell surprised us both. He had no idea what she meant. Helplessly I glared at her. Her rudeness appalled me and yet I was sympathetic to her bewilderment about a cultural expectation completely foreign to her. Her look of distressed anger accentuated her confusion and tempered my initial impulse to punish her. Khuda Buksh wanted to know what she meant.

It was just as well that I couldn't think of an accurate Bangali translation for *Get stuffed!*

The note from Abba does nothing to cheer me up. So far I have been left alone to contemplate the past and tussle with an uncertain future. Now I am compelled to confront a most unpleasant aspect of the present.

11.00 am sharp. Your mother has managed to make an appointment for you and Nadine.

I have dreaded this meeting. Whenever Ma mentioned it, my lack of enthusiasm has been patently obvious. I do not wish to offend her if I can help it. To have said *No* would have been cruelly impertinent. She would have burst into tears, sulked for the day and complained about my stubbornness to her friends and relatives who, Nafisa tells me with great glee, are critical of my behaviour toward them, especially my abruptness in rejecting their preposterous suggestions about Nadine's excellent matrimonial prospects.

I push the tray to one side of the cane table. My impending encounter with *Maulana* Azad is an unappetising thought. Ma's faith in him is unshakeable. I must admit I am curious about the old charlatan. I have an old score to settle with him. I want to face him with utter contempt, listen to him with a smug smile etched on my face and say *Bullshit!* to whatever he has to say. Of course that will not happen. I shall probably treat the whole thing as a taxing exercise in self-discipline and restrain myself. Nadine will not be accompanying us. That is certain. I am not willing to expose her to the traumas of religious superstition. As it is, she has faced enough problems with her grandparents in Australia because of my scepticism about Catholicism.

Downstairs I declare my intention. Abba comes to my assistance. His calm rationality shields me from Ma's agitation. There is no point in dragging Nadine to such a crowded place, he argues. The beggars at the gate will upset her. Ma glowers at him in speechless anger. She feels betrayed.

Smoothly Abba switches to his hobby farm in Savar. He suggests a visit to the mango orchard I have never seen. I fire a barrage of petty questions at him. Nafisa joins in, and we manage to keep Ma out of the conversation.

11.00 am sharp. I savour the minutes left before we embark on this excruciating ordeal of primitive faith.

From the air-conditioned comfort of the car, I view the third world with the critical eyes of an intolerant alien. For God's sake! I was born here, I have to remind myself. That does not help the readjustment process. The circumstances of birth are an accident, a quirk of fate. I am not plagued by guilt or torturous self-recriminations about my reactions to what I see. I fidget irritably. The tinted glass is an imperfect filter. If anything, it exaggerates the gloominess. Everything appears to be dilapidated. Old. Dirty. I am relieved I do not live here any more.

I make a concentrated attempt to relax my back muscles. My legs are aching. I have been sitting rigidly with clenched teeth. We have had several near misses. On each occasion I shut my eyes and braced myself for a collision. The blaring horn is like a knife's edge scraping an unhealed wound. I plead with the chauffeur to slow down. He is bemused by my discomfort. Neither he nor Ma look worried. They do not crouch in their seats as I do when the brakes screech.

Ma has been talking incessantly since we left the house. She is harping about responsibility and the need to respect those who are spiritually enlightened. I sense her disquiet about the way I might conduct myself in the presence of His Holiness. I allay her fears by nodding my agreement with her. I strain to play the expected role of an obedient son.

An uneasy coalition of incongruities—that is perhaps an excessively kind way of describing Eskaton. It juxtaposes the rich and the poor, the old and the new, the derelict and the ostentatious. The suburb is a conglomeration of extreme diversities. Surprisingly such discrepancies create very little tension among the inhabitants. It could have something to do with the acceptance of one's place in life determined by the Almighty in His infinite wisdom. Who is man to dispute His Will? *We created man to try him with afflictions.* I recall the Koranic words I struggled to understand as a young boy. It was drummed into me from an early age that submission was the defining quality of Islam. I have never reconciled myself to the notion of arbitrary suffering as a trial of faith. It must have been some form of genetic aberration which made me rebel against the acceptance of suffering and pain despite the assurances of a sublime meaning behind it all. That has not changed. I see as little dignity and purpose in the punitive harshness of life around me as I did when I was a practising Muslim.

Narrow dirt lanes branch off the main road and end abruptly like the amputated limbs of undernourished war children. The thoroughfare palpitates with the discordant jangle of blaring horns, bells, smoke-belching vehicles and brittle tempers. Trucks, buses, cars, cycle rickshaws, bicycles, hand-pushed carts, scooter taxis, pedestrians and animals mingle and move without the aid of lights or any awareness of traffic rules. Human safety is seemingly determined by a predestined quota of luck. If the speeding vehicles claim a few lives, well . . . that's the way it is . . . there are millions more to carry on the Sisyphean struggle. In this crazy, cart-wheeling world of man-made chaos, an individual life is a quantitative burden rather than a qualitative gift. One more or less does not alter the intensity of the swirling nightmare.

To my immense relief we are forced to slow down to a crawl. A harassed and weary-looking policeman stands in the centre of an intersection. He is surrounded by a protective circle of tin drums and performs like a clumsy novice at a dancing lesson. There is an ill-coordinated movement of arms and legs. A shrill whistle sounds in quick succession. The human and animal populations ignore him. Life continues to flow with a spontaneous rhythm uninterrupted by the restraining influence of electronic colour changes in a repetitive sequence of RED, AMBER, GREEN . . . RED, AMBER, GREEN . . . There are no STOP and GIVE WAY signs, flashing lights or zebra crossings. A blind reliance on instinct guides lives through the teeming snarl.

The disparity between the large, *pucca* houses and the tin and bamboo shacks underlines the glaring inequalities of a third-world nation. As it happens, Bangladesh is just about the poorest country in the world. It is a fact I have never been able to confront without a humiliating feeling of shame. Deep inside me there are doubts I shall never express openly because they threaten my most fundamental values. Are Bangalis, in some ways, naturally deficient? Do these deplorable conditions reflect a racial limitation which condemns us to perpetual abjection? As a race, are we destined to survive a technologically aggressive twenty-first century? I have made an effort to develop a mechanism of escaping the onslaught of such misgivings by reminding myself that I have adopted another country. These are not my problems. I shouldn't take them personally. The ploy does not succeed. I cannot remove the weight of this perturbation, this feeling of frustrated sorrow and pain as if I were somehow on the outside of myself, watching my own slow death.

Alongside the residential houses, there are ramshackle tea-stalls for rickshaw *wallahs*, labourers, domestic servants, professional beggars and their minions, sweepers and peasants who flock to the city in desperate search for work. The Chinese restaurants are still there. Only the names have changed. Or have they? I cannot really say with any certainty. I wonder if their discreet backrooms continue to offer more than the gastronomical delights of the Orient. We pass a bazaar, small general stores, tailors' shops and a barber's shop prominently featuring a bizarre handwritten message:

RAZORS AND SCISSORS FOR HIRE. I am amazed by the number of private schools which have sprung up like toadstools on a rainy day. Billboards, fixed like giant television screens on top of boundary walls, proudly proclaim the professional excellence of overseas trained teachers and the outstanding successes of the 'A' Level Examinations. OUR BUSINESS IS EXCLUSIVELY ACADEMIC, boasts one sign. That may explain the lack of a playground and the distinctly spartan and cramped conditions in the small old house. Interspersed among these landmarks are makeshift hardware shops, a second-hand bookshop with darkened windows and a crowded garage where Abdul, the chauffeur, informs me, all vehicles can be expertly dissembled and a few can be temporarily fixed. I comment on the lack of activity in the garage. Business is at its peak between midnight and dawn, I am told.

Eskaton's fame rests with its most venerated citizen—*Maulana* Khawja Rahmatullah Azad, holiest of the holy, reputedly touched by a divine spark and commonly acknowledged to be endowed with a gift of prophecy. *Huzoor, Baba, Pir* to his followers. *Purya* to those of us who believe he is a humbug. Befitting his puissant status, the *Maulana* lives in a triple-storeyed mansion surrounded by an unscalable brick wall which is topped with pieces of broken glass and rusty barbed wire. The rich revere him and the poor are awed by him. Rarely a day passes without a steady stream of wealthy visitors filing in through the massive cast-iron gates to seek his advice. With the utmost respect, they urge him to predict their futures. They hound him for amulets to cure embarrassing diseases, straighten wayward husbands, lose weight, win fortunes, restore potency, obtain quick divorces, evict tenants, ruin business rivals and charm away faded mistresses. They come from remote corners of the country with faith in instant miracles. Needless to say, the devotees are more than generous in displaying their tangible appreciation of the *Maulana's* hot-line to Allah.

As we approach the house, the memory of a dismal, rainy morning reinforces my bilious hostility toward this self-appointed communicator with Allah.

I was nearly thirteen. My mid-year school results made Abba silently angry and sent Ma into a fit of pyrogenic rage. For several hours she sat on a prayer mat and petitioned the Almighty for justice. What was her offence to deserve this sort of an insult? Why had she been cursed with a profligate son? Judging by her increasing vocal squeak, I assumed there were no answers from the sanctified precincts of Heaven. She turned on me with a fresh outburst of tearful hysteria. How dare I shame the family by failing so many examinations? What would our relatives say? How would her friends react after they heard about my disgraceful performance? Why couldn't I follow Hashim's example?

The problem was monumental and beyond human resolu-tion. Ma busied herself on the phone. I stole away to my room.

The next morning I was taken to see *Maulana* Azad. He listened attentively to Ma's animated account of my misdemeanours. She finished in a flood of tears. He looked at me with sheer contempt in his beady eyes. His thunderous voice made me cringe with fear. My destiny in the eternal flames was outlined in gory detail.

'You will burn forever!' He shouted. 'Forever! Do you understand? Forever!'

There was only so much of me that could burn, I consoled myself. It couldn't possibly take that long. To my formative young mind, struggling to come to terms with the notion of *forever*, the punishment was excruciatingly painful and grossly out of proportion with the crime of failing my examinations and making my parents unhappy.

It was the work of the Evil One, His Holiness concluded. *Shoitan* was hovering over me, waiting to capture my soul.

The Devil would have to be exorcised immediately, otherwise I would be beyond redemption. I was given a verbal blast on filial obligations. Did I not know that Heaven was under my mother's feet? (Even in my dazed state of utter confusion, that appeared to be improbable. I silently vowed to verify it later.) Did I pray? Did I read the holy Koran? I nodded vigorously as I clutched the arms of my chair. Did I wear a *tabeez*? I looked at Ma. She shook her head reluctantly. I did the same, petrified by the thought that I had missed out on something vital to my wellbeing. For several agonising minutes he whispered in Ma's ears. Whatever he said composed her. Abruptly he straightened up and limped out of the room.

Soon he returned, followed by a solemn-faced servant carrying a *tabeez* on a silver platter. Had I known the *tabeez* was merely a folded bit of paper scribbled over with Koranic verses and wrapped in a piece of black cloth sewn at the edges with a string attached on two sides, I might have accepted it more readily. I felt like a condemned prisoner being led to the gallows. The string held the terror of a noose as it was slipped over my head. It became a penitential millstone for several years and a constant reminder that failure of any kind was not permissible in our family. We were the Chaudharies—rich, clever, industrious. Infallible. Without human weaknesses.

I slaved for the rest of the year, not because I craved success but to avoid a return visit to the *Maulana* if my results did not improve. I left nothing to chance. I memorised everything I had to and regurgitated selectively in the final examinations. My marks improved beyond my parents' expectations.

Abba beamed proudly and patted me on the head. I became the proud owner of a new cricket bat made in England. Sussex willow. The best there was.

'The miracle of Allah!' Ma pronounced after reading my reports. '*Huzoor* be blessed! He is a living saint.'

The next day the car was loaded with sweetmeats and

flowers. My pleas of illness were unheeded. Back we went to thank His Graciousness.

We are led to a large rectangular room. The absence of furniture makes the room uncomfortably impersonal. It is probably meant to unsettle those who intend to keep the *Maulana* beyond the allotted time. The centre of the waxed mosaic floor is covered with a vinaceous Shiraz carpet intricately patterned with blue and white floral designs. Satin-covered bolsters indicate the seating areas. I lower myself gingerly on the carpet. Immediately I feel the pain of strained ligaments.

The whitewashed walls are decorated with expensively framed photographs of the *Maulana*, mostly with politicians who have enjoyed some eminence in a turbulent past. I struggle to my feet for a closer look. He is the constant in the political variable of Pakistan and Bangladesh. A young *Maulana* is shaking hands with Iskander Mirza. There are several enlargements of photographs featuring him with Ayub Khan. He looks grim and uncomfortable with an aloof Bhutto. With Yahya Khan he is smiling, as though he were the general's moral superior. There are photographs with Mujib, Bahshani and Ziaur Rahman. The *Maulana's* overseas connections are impressive. Smiling, sebaceous features of dignitaries from Saudi Arabia, Iran, Egypt, Turkey, Libya and Morocco are frozen reminders of the Enlightened Holiness' international standing. Then there is the *Maulana* on his own and with each of his five sons. There is a striking picture of the proud hunter with his eyes closed, standing over a dead tiger, with a gun in his hands. I assume, that for reasons of gender, his wife and daughters have been denied a place among the images of distinguished personalities imprisoned in the rectangular frames for posterity to admire.

Out of boredom I begin to count the frames. Ninety-nine. I count them again. Exactly ninety-nine. Interesting. Is it coincidence or does the man possess a bigger ego than I imagined? I deny him the benefit of doubt. Inwardly I chuckle at the irony of such outrageous blasphemy committed by a religious man. But then he probably does not realise it.

In a hushed whisper Ma tells me how fortunate we are to get an appointment. 'He is such a busy man,' she says. 'But so obliging. So nice.'

I look at her with mixed feelings of inadequacy and shame. I find it impossible to respond warmly to her presence. I try to conjure up some of the emotions of a caring son. There ought to be an affinity between us, a bond which is unharmed by the corrosion of time and distance. I am troubled by my lack of tenderness for this portly, grey-haired woman sitting on the carpet, fervently seeking a divine solution to my personal problems. I try again. Nothing. I might as well attempt to draw water from a dry well. I scrape the depths of my being without striking even a faint chord of feeling.

You have become callous. Selfish. Emotionally stagnant. Did you ever stop to think of your family here? Did you ever consider Ma? We all know she can be difficult. But she is still a mother. Your mother. She is generous with her love. She is easily hurt. You didn't even inform her you were getting married. Sure, you wrote to us later. That was considerate of you. Were you afraid we might come to your wedding and embarrass you? Aarey baba, we are not that unthoughtful. It is sad the way you have distanced yourself from people who should matter to you. You have always been so cautious about loving! Why do you treat love as an investable capital? If it doesn't pay handsome dividends, you want to withdraw your assets and go elsewhere. Why?

Nafisa had already diagnosed and dissected me mercilessly. My ponytailed little sister is no longer the gullible child who adored me and believed everything I said. There are sharp, cutting edges about her perceptions of people. I detect a bitter hostility she uses to ward off people if they show an interest in her. She has said very little to me about herself.

The accusation of being selfish is beginning to worry me.

47

I hate the word with its multiplicity of meanings. It has a reptilian quality about it. It has the feel of a slimy creature living in the shadows of life, heartless and wholly preoccupied by its own mechanical existence.

You do not know how to love. That was what Michelle said when we launched into the inevitable screaming bout after our restrained exchange in the café. *You never express your affections without appearing to be embarrassed. What is it with you? A severe emotional congestion? Does love mean anything personal to you? Is it simply a four-letter word with vague philosophical meanings to titillate you intellectually? Do you ever feel it? Does it ever come alive? Does it ever escape from the pages of books to become a living part of you?*

She goaded me into a state of ranting fury. I was vehemently aggressive in my denial which arose from a self-righteous certitude that I was being unjustifiably maligned. Now I am seriously beginning to have doubts about myself.

I walk across to where Ma is sitting. Impulsively I reach out and stroke her shoulders. She is startled by my unexpected show of affection. Her wrinkled, round face breaks into a smile of assurance. It tells me she has no difficulty in bridging the chasm of the intervening years. It is an encouragement for me to try and meet her somewhere, even on my terms. I falter and retreat. I withdraw my hand. My eyes feast on the floral web on the carpet.

The door to our right swings open. I recognise the limp. Only now it is more pronounced than before. Ma scrambles to her feet. With a deliberate slowness I cross my arms across my chest and stare at him. I hope he is insulted.

With a rare twinkle in his eyes, Abba once told me about the damaged legs.

During his college days in Calcutta, *Maulana* Azad was conscripted into the role of the ghost in a students' production of *Hamlet*. To the consternation of the cast, the eccentric, young director had insisted on lending more weight to the supernatural in Shakespeare. At rehearsals the clumsy spirit kept losing his balance on the turret whenever he appeared before the unusually tanned Danish prince with the slightly askew flaxen hairpiece. On the opening night, in front of a capacity audience, the young Azad slipped and fell backwards during a ghostly speech. As he vanished from the castle top, his ghoulish howl and excremental words were greeted with enthusiastic applause by the less learned members of the audience. They marvelled at the young actor's voice projection which captured the hair-raising ordeals of hell. Those who were familiar with the play were puzzled by the textual deviation. Disbelief was very reluctantly suspended. Poor Hamlet was left stranded on his knees until the ad-libbing ingenuity of the quick-thinking Marcellus and Horatio saved the performance from disaster and the college principal from disgrace. When the ghost made its next appearance, the voice had changed and the apparition was distinctly thinner. The drama critic for the college magazine wrote rather unkindly about a new dimension in ghostly realism. It was his contention that the infernal flames had melted away all the corporeal fat and left a trim and mobile figure to glide fluidly around the precincts of Elsinore.

I am startled by his appearance. A pair of owlish dark glasses gives him a sleazy touch. It is like looking at King Faroukh during his years in exile. *Maulana* Azad is a huge, urceolate man with a belly which juts out in front of him like a balloon on the verge of busting. It quivers like a terrified animal trapped under a cover as he rolls toward us on unsteady feet. The size of his head is grotesquely small in proportion to his massive torso. Perched on top of the head is a faded, black fez. The face is ridged and puffed. Layers of adipose tissue lie beneath the crinkled skin. The snub nose is like a polished stone nestling in a cushion of soft leather. The fish mouth is a mere slit. His lips are caked with dried betel-leaf juice. He is wearing a Rajshahi silk *kurta* and a blue *lungi*. The overpowering smell of *attar* nauseates me.

'*Aas Salaam a lai kum!*' He greets Ma.

She steps back in awed deference. She bows and touches her forehead with the fingers of her right hand. '*Aadaab Huzoor!*'

I am expected to bend down and touch his feet. They are encased in expensive leather sandals. The best that can be bought at *Bata*. I offer him a limp handshake and the coldest of smiles.

'Ah, the foreign way.' The slit widens. '*Mashallah*! How well you look, my boy! Your daughter?'

'Not well, *Huzoor!*' Ma answers on my behalf. 'She was so looking forward to meeting you.'

We are invited to sit down. I prefer to move to the large window overlooking a paved courtyard edged with rose beds and sheltered by an ivy-covered pergola.

From a brown paper bag Ma produces a carton of cigarettes and offers it to him! So! This was the reason for the frantic request which made me carry the cigarettes all the way from Melbourne.

'*Huzoor*, a small gift for you.' Discreetly she places a small white envelope on top of the carton.

Flared nostrils sniff the air suspiciously. He senses no danger. Esurient hands snake out like deep sea tentacles and snare the tendentious offerings. In a quick, smooth motion the envelope disappears into the side pocket of the *kurta*.

'*Dhonobad! Dhonobad!*' He responds with pleasure. 'The doctors tell me not to smoke. Rascals! They would deprive me of one of the few pleasures a man in my position can allow himself.' He raises his hands toward the ceiling. 'My life is entirely in His hands. Even without smoking I shall have to go when my time comes.'

The trite expression of Islamic fatalism draws words of comfort from Ma. By the Grace of Allah, may he live to be a hundred. The prayers of millions will not be unheeded. He is the light of hope for the unfortunate. A source of inspiration for the spiritually weak.

Maulana Azad looks impatiently at his Rolex watch. The hint is too obvious to miss. Ma launches into a long-winded exposition about my life in a foreign land. A melodrama of epical proportions about love, marriage and cruel betrayal unfolds.

I am blameless. *She* is the culprit. *She* is the one who trapped me into marriage and then heartlessly initiated the break-up. It is all *her* fault. I have been victimised by a witch. An evil creature. A wicked, wicked woman! May Allah bring her endless misery!

I cringe and turn away from Ma's outrageous distortions and simplistic moral stance. Fortunately I have not mentioned Colin. That would have lowered Michelle to the status of an unscrupulous whore.

Ma's story-line is worthy of a Bombay film studio. The effectiveness of her rendition is enhanced by sighs and extravagant gestures of lamentation. She wrings her hands and clasps her head. How can any mother ignore the suffering of her son? What could *Huzoor* do to bring me peace? Were there special prayers he could recommend? Could he bless me with a *tabeez*? Was there anything she could do?

Ma has said too much for me to contradict her in front of *Purya*. I should have intervened earlier. I should have had the courage to say that heaving all the blame on Michelle was a grossly inaccurate summation of my marital difficulties. Cause and effect are rarely one-sided in a broken relationship. I must accept a significant proportion of the blame.

I am not interested in what the *Maulana* has to say.

Outside a young boy is weeding the rose beds. The glare of the late morning sun is hurtful in its brilliant intensity.

I wish I could see Theo—have a few beers with him and carry on about the pathetic state of our lives. There is an aching compulsion to talk freely. I miss his caustic humour and his observations on human folly.

The flow of holy bullshit has not abated. Ma listens attentively like an overawed child.

I begin to reminisce about the September weekend in Apollo Bay.

THREE

As I think about it, I am cautiously convinced that the mutual striving to fulfil common aspirations is the basis of an enduring relationship. It is not so much the physical absence of Michelle that has made me lonely. Rather, loneliness in its most painful manifestation began in the act of extricating myself from unsustainable dreams.

I feel the desolation of abandonment in the barrenness of a dreary reality. An enervating present wraps itself around my consciousness of time. A robotic routine drags me through a seemingly endless series of limp, repetitive days. I live in the apprehension of vacant tomorrows.

I crowd myself with pettiness in a bid to keep myself occupied. I behave as an extrovert and pretend to cope with my altered status. I pretend I am not hurting.

You'll be right. Keep busy. Things will turn for the better. Be positive about the future. You have a lot to look forward to. The unsolicited advice keeps rolling in.

I immerse myself in work, return to the sparsely furnished flat as late as possible and crawl into bed, only to lie awake with my mind suspended in a deep void. I am afraid to think. I am not even game enough to seek refuge in a fresh batch of dreams. The pain has gradually subsided into a bearable ache. I am beginning to move cautiously among the jagged greyness which permeates my world.

I am not presumptuous enough to suggest that my experience is the definitive condition of every estranged couple. In fact, I have avoided a detailed assessment of what went wrong. I had no desire to confront myself with the accusations hurled at me; that is, until today. I have been forced into a reflective mode since we left Geelong. I didn't have much choice, did I? I mean, what else can you do on a long car trip when you've been pretending to be asleep?

Despite the efficiency of the heater, I am cold. I feel as if a slow paralysis is creeping up my legs. I dare not move. The slightest hint of awakening might set Theo off again. I've had more than an earful on what I should be doing to celebrate my freedom.

My neck is hurting. I cannot keep this up any longer.

From the height of the Great Ocean Road, snaking its way from Lorne to Apollo Bay, the sea is like a restless chameleon changing colours around the bends. Now turquoise. Then battleship grey . . . onyx green. A roaring, thrashing creature with white-tipped scales, hurling itself against the rocks with a maniacal fury.

A desperate need for company has overcome my aversion for the sea. Even in the heat of Victoria's shrinking summers, I find the beaches uncomfortably cold for a swim. Flies, sand, wind, glare, the burning sensation in the sun, the shivering in the shade . . . nothing is ever right. I am, what you might say, a beach wimp.

Hunched over the steering wheel of his battered Holden, Theo is at his garrulous best, full of cynical wisdom. Authoritative and irritatingly smug. A verbose school master, bursting with experience, eloquently expounding his views about the pitfalls of relationships and legalising emotional involvements to a dazed pupil.

There is no defence against his rampant words.

'The natural inclination for foolishness is a somewhat belated discovery,' he announced with supreme assurance. 'It isn't until you begin to creak and show all the unflattering symptoms of middle age that you convince yourself of the severe drawbacks of unripe males. Bloody waste of time, their obsession with the flesh! Leads to all sorts of trouble. That's partially jealousy, of course. God, it's hard not to rage and feel sorry for yourself and hate all the young, unwrinkled hunks of the world! But once you have self-discipline and call time out to turn to your real self, you're right. Comes as a bit of a shock to the system to realise there's another being inside you, no longer muffled by a bloated ego. It's a terrific finding. You learn to engage it in revealing dialogues. Not an easy process but worth the effort. Make it work for you! It defines the perimeters of living and teaches you to move within those limits. The trouble with young fellas is they assume the centre of world control is below the navel. Admittedly it is a great energiser, but it is also the source of incredible folly. To think that a few centimetres of erectile tissue can cause such dev-astation! Amazing, isn't it? What flawed creatures we are! Such talent for inflicting pain on ourselves!'

He pauses to pop a jube in his mouth. It's been nearly four weeks since his last cigarette. None of his previous efforts lasted beyond a fortnight. I can see how proud he is of his newly acquired self-control.

I draw his attention to the unruly sea. He isn't interested in what lies below. I brace myself for more experiential wisdom.

'Now I'll die of diabetes . . . where was I? Take me, for example. A model case study. Two marriages. Two divorces. Four kids. A neat buggery of my life. Maintenance payouts, complaints about not giving enough, letters from solicitors about children's rights, ex-wives' rights, everyone's rights except mine. Fights over access, educational expenses, swim-ming lessons, tennis coaching, music lessons, holidays . . . one long, lingering trail of financial disaster! All because I fell in love! *Fell*! Hell! The irony of it all! It didn't strike me until last year. This other bit asked me: "Theo, what happens when you fall?" You hurt yourself. Right? Simple question, simple answer. Even a child knows that. Then why the fuck didn't such basic logic rescue me when I was twenty-five? Or thirty-one? Huh? Why? What was it that made me believe I could fall, *fall* mind you, into a state of sublimity? Plato had his winged horses and chariot going up. Up! Up! Toward the ethereal unknown. That makes some sense. My ancestors made a lot of sense. But then along came self-sacrifice on two bits of timber and nails to complicate matters. A universal cliché was born. Suffer for the sake of others. Fall! Come and experience the crash. Shit, I've done some stupid things in my life! Here, have a jube . . . '

Ignore his bulk and Theo is a very handsome man. Women are fascinated by his dark, brooding eyes. They are pools of smouldering madness, never dull, primitive in their passionate intensity. Once I flippantly attributed them to his Dionysian heritage, a description he frequently uses to excuse his intemperance. His black hair, flecked with grey, is thick and curly like clustered tendrils of tropical vine. The nose is classically straight, its sharp definition slightly dulled by the excessive flesh on his cheeks. Theo looks his age except when he laughs. It is a full-throated laughter of hedonistic irresponsibility I sometimes envy.

Theo is a fascinating facet of the multicultural complexity of Australia. I think of him as an evolutionary accomplishment in the changing countenance of the land. His grandfather, with a young family, migrated from the island of Hydra and worked in a greengrocer's shop in Sydney. The shop owner, a widower who had lost both his sons in the Great War, appreciated the efforts of the hard-working Greek. The old man was a fair but tight-fisted Scotsman prone to early morning bouts with a bottle of whisky. The shop was badly in need of repair. Business was sluggish. With the help of his sons, George and Peter, Theo's grandfather renovated the shop and revived the business. The Scotsman remembered them in his will and the Katiz greengrocers prospered.

Theo honks furiously as he races around a ute. 'Bloody women drivers!'

A long-haired young man, I inform Theo. I crane my neck to catch a glimpse of a snarl and a middle finger held aloft in defiant contempt.

I am not entirely prepared to accept Theo's views. I protest mildly. How can he make such sweeping generalisations? Oversimplify such complex issues? Relationships must work for some people. They had to. What was life without its emotional coordinates? I cannot resist. I remember the lines.

Flower o' the broom
Take away love, and our earth is a tomb.

Nothing like vigorous nineteenth-century poetic optimism to confound a modern sceptic. It has the desired effect. Theo snorts like a distressed bull. Momentarily he takes his eyes off the road to look at me in stark disbelief. His eyes narrow and his lips curl.

'Christ!' he utters dismally. 'Holy Christ!'

The car leaps forward. We listen to the groan of the engine for the rest of the way.

I almost begin to enjoy myself.

Unlike Claire, there were no words of consolation from Theo. He sounded as if he had known my fate all along.

Claire was full of compassionate understanding. She invited me for tea. Her anxiety reminded me of the day she came to pick me up from the airport. She was solicitous and protective in her concern about my exposure to an unfamiliar culture.

'Hello!' She had thrust out her hand. 'I am Claire O'Hearn, the student housing officer. I hope you had a pleasant flight.' The calmness in her voice was comforting. There was a composure about this silver-haired woman that invited trust. I felt

I could talk to her freely if I needed help. A rare friendship developed.

I was delighted when she retired and chose to leave Melbourne to move into the house she had inherited from her aunt. The winter dampness was not good for her arthritis, but she loved the house and the view of the lake it offered.

Theo came to visit me a few days after I had moved into the flat. He explained why he felt obliged not to placate me with illusions about my innocence in the break-up. 'That would be dishonest,' he said, after announcing that we were going to the pub where he was shouting me for the entire evening. 'It's no use applying a bandaid to an infected wound, is it? There has to be further treatment. You will also have to be the doctor.'

The conversation at the pub was fairly heated. I resented his blunt assertion that I had to share the blame.

'Strip yourself of any notion of complete innocence.' He sternly wagged an index finger at me. 'You probably contributed to the fiasco as much as she did. Find your mistakes. Acknowledge them. Overcome your pride and come to terms with yourself.'

I quickly gulped the beer and asked for an orange juice. 'Don't pontificate so much, Theo. Just buy the drinks.'

He looked apologetic. 'A hundred bucks an hour advice, eh? Theo, the philosopher and psychiatrist. The expert with the experience of two divorces. I was talking rubbish! It isn't that easy, is it? I should know better. Sorry mate!'

It wasn't rubbish. I didn't say so. I had a vague feeling that some form of introspection was necessary to expiate the bitterness which had taken hold of me and showed no sign of abating. But how was I to go about locating this self? I assumed Theo was referring to that elusive part of my being which harboured the components of my personality. Perhaps I ought to behave like the disgruntled, sensitive type and make a concerted effort to explore the inner labyrinths in an effort to expunge the flaws. Grow a beard and go bush. Listen to the wind. Write poetry. Make an enlightening discovery, like they do in the search for meaning in books and movies. Catalyse a radical change in my present condition and return to live as a tranquil sage for the rest of my life. Equilibrium. Understanding. Spiritual rhythm. Somehow, it is all so sublime and achievable in art and fiction.

Not knowing where to begin has plunged me into the depths of helplessness. I am aware of a pressing necessity to negate the sense of inadequacy which has replaced my self-esteem. I am convinced that whatever this self is, it is now inextricably entwined with loneliness, fear and self-pity. My perceptions of my altered circumstances remain blurred. Changing directions is proving to be more difficult than I had anticipated. Had I been younger, I might have accepted it as a challenge. But not now, not at my age. Even in my most optimistic moments, confusion and doubt cannot be euphemised as a challenge.

Theo has booked us into one of the new motels perched on top of a hill. From our unit the sea looks awesome—a snarling, hungry predator, unleashing a satanic power of destruction.

We enjoy a cup of coffee before Theo decides to unload the car, brushing aside my offer to help. I unlock the sliding door and step outside into the monastic harshness of the leftover winter. The tired sun retreats behind thin long bands of cloud. Their colour changes as though invisible hands were manipulating a set of lights behind them. Saffron veins the sombre grey. They become livid strips of wounded flesh. A knife appears to have gashed the celestial belly. The sea and the sky begin to harmonise in a pall of gloom. Darkness will be overwhelmingly sudden. A deft assassin will snuff the ragged remains of the day with nimble hands.

I am glad Theo persuaded me to come.

'Leave the bloody problems behind, will you?' He

implored. 'Lock them up in the flat for the weekend. Unclutter your mind. Rug up and walk on the beach. Feel the space. Explore the frontiers of a new horizon. There's a lot more to do than feel sorry for yourself. Reflect on your suffering. There's some wisdom in it.'

I could relate to the suffering. As for wisdom . . . it was nowhere in sight. 'I am no Job,' I said. 'I don't know if I have his fortitude or his insight. I am no wiser now than I was a few weeks ago.'

'The suffering has to be prolonged and intense. Like mine,' he said cheekily.

Great. Another three marriages? Somehow I found it difficult to envisage myself as a tragic protagonist, spouting words of wisdom to aggrieved women and their solicitors.

Dusk creeps up on the fading afternoon and pounces on it with a feline agility. The transitory sky ripens briefly into a shade of bruised purple. The evening promises to be clear and capacious. An expanding shroud breeding disquiet and anguish.

Back inside, the drone of austere voices relaxes me.

Deus in nomine tuo salvum me fac:
et in virtute tua judica me. Deus exaudi orationem meam:
auribus percipe verba oris mei . . .

Theo doesn't approve of Gregorian chants. He mutters about the crippling effects of Catholic schooling on my identity.

He decides we are hungry. 'Scrambled eggs?'

I don't particularly care.

Theo has a habit of spending great lengths of time in the kitchen with predictably paltry results.

I pretend I am alone. The crowded flotilla of remembrances is like a freshly acquired wound. Raw and warm. Tender and runny. Each straggling memory is a sharp point of torment. In silent desperation I even think of planting God in the sky in the hope of a spectacular miracle.

I think of the weekends that used to be. A Saturday awakening with Nadine's cold nose and hard elbows urging me out of bed. The comforting awareness of Michelle sleeping next to me. The leisurely indulgence of croissants and percolated coffee. The litter of newspapers. Arguments over the Friday evening dishes in a sink full of greasy, cold water and the grocery items left off the shopping list. The pile of socks which never made the distance to the laundry basket. Nagging Nadine to tidy her room. Interrogations and impotent threats over the half-eaten sandwiches under her bed and in the compost pile. That feeling of irritable dissatisfaction that yet another weekend was being wasted on domestic trivia. Now I miss the secure boredom of the familiar routine.

A cork pops. There is no choice of drinks tonight. Theo is convinced I have something to celebrate. I hear the clatter of plates. Dame Kiri begins to purr.

Night continues to glide by with a regal aloofness, indifferent to my bewildered anguish, unaware of my groping desire to regain an imperfect past. Its presence burdens me with an increasing solitude. I long to reach out and strangle time. Prevent the birth of tomorrow. Cling to the jagged ruins of what remains.

I discipline myself to look ahead.

I have decided to visit my family. That is a modified version, a more realistic rephrasing of my initial sentiment to go *home* during the summer holidays. I have written a long, rambling letter to my sister, explaining the circumstances in a circumventive way. It took me nearly a week and several wastepaper baskets of crumpled up paper to phrase the euphemisms intended to lessen the shock. Eighteen years is a very long time; long enough to realise that for a migrant the word *home* is fraught with ambiguities. Eighteen years. Close to half my life; and I haven't been back. In the letter I made it a point to emphasise the fact that I am not divorced.

Nafisa will understand. So will Hashim when she tells him. I doubt if I can say the same about my parents, especially Ma.

I have brought shame on the family. Again. Abba will react with a stoical grimness and distance himself from Ma's histrionics. I wonder if she is still in the habit of fainting at specifically chosen moments. She will probably spend penitential hours on a prayer mat, apologising to Allah for having raised a profligate son. She will turn to Hashim for comfort.

My older brother epitomises Ma's ideal of a son. Hashim, the doctor, was educated in England. He has methodically acquired all the conventional symbols of success. Money. Cars. A flat in London. Antique furniture. A house in Banani. The model son goes dutifully to the mosque on Fridays and drinks Scotch and soda in the evenings. Hashim obeyed Ma's wishes and returned home, but with a Pakistani wife. It was forgiven as a minor aberration from his normal habit of seeking Ma's permission before he makes any important decision affecting his personal life. His wife, after all, was a Muslim. Hashim also happens to be the father of Ma's two grandsons. He has saved the family from extinction. He is the one who has ensured that the Chaudhary lineage will continue to prosper.

I am taking Nadine with me. Michelle agreed reluctantly. I suspect it was a concession to indicate her fair-mindedness. I offered to move out of the house with very few demands. I had no desire to remove Nadine from the familiarity of her home environment and traumatise her any further. We have already wrecked her emotional security. Besides, my plans are convenient for Michelle's own arrangements for going overseas.

Theo returns with a tray. The eggs are watery, but the bread is crisp and smells of fresh parsley with a bare hint of garlic. Near the open fireplace we eat silently and sip champagne as if it were a triumphant occasion. We find our voices again over mugs of black coffee heavily laced with cheap brandy.

We swap stories about our travel experiences. To transport

ourselves to distant oases of contentment is a form of pure escapism. It is indicative of the simmering dissatisfaction with the torn realities of our lives. We journey along a common route. In Athens we ignore the pollution and spend dreamy evenings in the Plaka. I initiate a trip to Delphi to pay homage among the ruins to my idea of a god. Theo manages to find us a hiding place in Mycenae. We spend a wondrous night under the blazing stars, half-expecting to hear Clytemnestra's shriek of fulfilment in her moment of awful glory. We sail to the remote islands, too primitive for the hoards of German and American tourists. In Hydra Theo pauses long enough to argue with his aging aunt who wants him to marry a local girl. We drift across the Aegean to marvel at Schliemann's discovery. We recreate the famous battle and mourn the death of Achilles. Bergama . . . Selcuk . . . Knidos. More champagne and we move far across to the city for aesthetic aristocrats. Theo shares my love of Florence. We are at peace here. It is a city of artistic harmony. Florence is a delicate creation. Fragile. Vulnerable. My idea of hell is a terrorist bomb exploding near the Baptistery. We marvel at what the Medicis left behind, wander through the Uffizi Gallery, admire the Bargello Museum and finally arrive at the Galleria dell' Accademia to gape at the monumental stroke of divinity. This is the only place where I have flirted at length with the idea of a benign, omnipotent god. I doubt if human hands alone can create such perfection.

Theo understands my passion for David. In moments of outrageous daydreaming, I have mobilised Michelangelo's masterpiece and whisked it away to another land where it stands white and resplendent in the fiery pink and silvery-gray light of an Agra dawn in front of the Taj. A discourse between Michelangelo and Shahjahan. That's what heaven should be all about.

We get carried away.

Feverishly we think about a trip. Resign. Sell up. Stuff the entanglements, the solicitors, the fights and the payments. One-way plane tickets and backpacks. No itineraries. No plans. Let the future languish here in Australia.

The sustenance of such imaginative stamina is beyond us. We surrender to the encumbrance of age and circumstances. We are too old for such risks. There are responsibilities. The kids are too young. We would run out of money. It would be impossible to find jobs after we return.

The dreams disappear into the night. We run out of excuses. The champagne has given me a headache. We slump in our chairs, glumly aware of the richness of a distant world we dare not pursue.

The fire flickers in a dance of death. The embers glow defiantly, radiating a drowsy warmth.

The silence returns.

The early morning light struggles to liberate the sky from its woolly greyness. The paleness of the curved surface is dabbed with the tentative touches of an indeterminate painter. The russet horizon suddenly flames into fibrous strands of orange and vermilion. The slaty covering is peeled away, leaving a new sky of soft innocent blue.

The sea has receded, leaving behind the debris of its nocturnal revelry. Pieces of wood, shells and the odd bottle. A solitary seagull lies beside a rock pool, its neck broken by the impact of a fierce wave. The beach could be mistaken for an abandoned battleground of a titanic struggle against any army of slaughtered Gorgons. Each mass of seaweed resembles the top of Medusa's severed head left to rot on the wet sand.

I have been walking for nearly an hour.

The cloudless morning offers precious respite from the bleak tyranny of icicled fingers. It is still very cold. Already the sun is weak, like a spent old man, passionless and without a vibrant warmth. Reluctantly it begins to climb into prominence, uncertain of its control over a seemingly docile day.

An early morning jogger has stamped the sand with his ascetic fervour. The impressions of a pair of runners are evenly spaced. I trace a random pattern between the imprints by furrowing the sand with the pointed end of a damp stick. A bearded man, in shorts and windcheater, smiles and raises his right hand in a friendly greeting. Before I can respond, he rushes past me. I feel self-conscious about my appearance. I must be an ungainly sight—shirt, windcheater, woollen jumper and a duffle coat. Scarf and a golf cap.

A huge labrador ambles up to me. I am worthy of a few sniffles and a nearby piddle.

My back feels stiff, and I could do with another cup of tea. The fresh air hasn't revived me or had any of those invigorating effects morning walks are supposed to induce. For all that, I think I am in a better shape than the snoring Zorba I left behind under a pile of blankets.

My brief moment of early morning enthusiasm has dissipated. I am feeling despondent at the enormous complexity of my bleak situation. I have reviewed the past weeks as a necessary precursor to a process of rationalisation to lift me out of the abysmal depths of depression and give some redemptive direction to my life. But the more I probe and think, the greater is my dismay at the fragile intricacy of the torn web which hangs around me. Among its loose strands I can perceive the hurt we have inflicted on Nadine. In her moments of introspective moodiness, she has sought some justification for the misery she is forced to endure as her world has disintegrated around her.

Briefly Nadine lowered her protective indifference over a Chinese take-away last weekend. 'Dad, have I done something to make you and Mum unhappy?'

I shook my head in an emphatic denial. The mere suggestion of any wrongdoing on her part was enough to upset me into a wordless misery of guilt. The chaos in her life had compelled her to turn inward to seek a cause where none

existed. Within her perceptions, she was seeking to understand the reasons for the changes in her life by apportioning
some blame to herself.

I stumbled through a laborious assurance that none of it
was her fault. Had I not held a condescendingly paternal view
that she was too young to understand the reasons for a failed
relationship, I might have articulated myself more expansively. I suppose I was also protecting my mauled pride. I
lacked the courage to explain that I was no longer a compatible partner for Michelle. I was afraid that in some way the
admission would make Nadine harshly judgemental about
my inadequacies as a husband and, perhaps, even as a father.
There was an apprehension about triggering a rejection mechanism in her and cutting myself off from her affection. It was
nothing less than a myopic selfishness which contrived to
ensure her emotional dependence on me. I had used my own
child to bolster my self-esteem.

Now I find it impossible to react to Michelle with any
degree of consistent hostility. The intensity of a scorching
anger was ephemeral. Her troubled face keeps bobbing up in
front of me. It is a face with many expressions of doubt and
anguish, none of which can cope adequately with the barbed
pity she has received. Over the years I have admired
Michelle's ability to thwart the insidious prejudices which
have attacked our marriage. Knowing her strength and the
resoluteness of her convictions, I cannot believe she was worn
down to a state of meek surrender.

I can hear the smug voices. *Their* voices. They echo all
around me. They were right all the time, weren't they? Keith
and Sarah. Martin and Judy. Lisa. Michael. Bev and Peter.
Those other aunts and uncles. Cousins. Names I don't care to
recall.

*It's a shame it happened. But we tried to tell you, love. It couldn't
work. He is . . . he is different. It doesn't matter how long he's been*

here or how educated he is. He doesn't think like we do. Our ways are different.

Michelle chose an unexpected moment to tell me. If she were counting on surprise to prevent any unseemly display of irrational outburst and sting me into a state of numb helplessness, then the planning and the execution, including my unsuspecting collaboration in giving her the opportunity, were flawless.

It was an early morning drive to Melbourne. One of those impulsive shopping trips I grumbled about but usually enjoyed. Plastic card therapy on Chapel Street for two over-worked teachers. Michelle insisted on leaving Nadine in Camberwell with Keith and Sarah. We drove to the Jam Factory in persistent rain.

It was the kind of tempestuous Melbourne day which makes the remotest town in the Northern Territory a tempting proposition. The wind howled and tore through the streets, driving the grab and run Saturday morning shoppers to the nearest shelters where their winter countenances of grim for-bearance were distorted into wordless expressions of frustrated abuse. Wrapped in layers of dreary grey, the morn-ing snivelled and sobbed like a professional mourner at a funeral.

Michelle wasn't in a very communicative mood. She had brought her own umbrella, a sure sign that I was out of favour. Mentally I ticked off the Friday evening chores. I had unstacked the dishwasher, cleaned the budgie's cage, tidied my side of the walk-in wardrobe, paid the paper bill . . .

She walked ahead of me, stopping to stare into shop win-dows, mindlessly eyeing clothes she would never consider for her wardrobe. Second-term fatigue and its resultant surliness, I concluded confidently and braced myself for an unpleasant walk and a cheerless drive back home.

I was coping rather well with the situation, I thought. All I had to do was to keep my cool and say as little as possible.

Look contrite, I advised myself. That was the only way to defuse her. Later she would tell me what I hadn't done. Over a brandy and dry I would point out the disproportionate absurdity of her puerile behaviour because of my negligence to attend to some insignificant household matter.

I amused myself with the fanciful notion that Michelle was colluding with the weather in what amounted to an aggregation of unremitting provocation intended to draw from me a thoughtless verbal barrage, exposing my latent chauvinism and my natural disinclination to help with the domestic routine of Friday evenings.

I mustn't fall for it, I resolved. I mustn't.

I continued to walk slowly, stopping well before she did. The wind numbed my face and my hands were painful as they clutched the umbrella which threatened to drag me across the road and dump me into one of the shops eagerly awaiting a customer.

The eleven o'clock need for caffeine struck with its usual timeliness. I suggested a cappuccino.

The café was trendy. Slate tiles. Glass-topped tables and chrome-framed chairs. Brick walls and cedar ceiling. The latest jungle noises blaring from the massive speakers fixed to the walls. Recess lighting and expensively framed prints. I recognised a Dali and a Kandinsky. It was crowded and noisy. Michelle insisted on waiting for a corner table near one of the full-length windows.

I looked around impatiently, resenting the wastage of precious weekend hours. It was the sort of place to make Keith and his return-to-the-past friends fidget uncomfortably at the diverse features of ethnicity, although there would be some relief about the owner being an Italian rather than a Vietnamese.

I felt comfortable among the olive complexions and dark hair, animated conversations and varied accents.

Two slightly built young women, in black leather skirts and

matching jackets, vacated the table Michelle wanted. Her frosty stare paralysed a waiting young couple into indecisiveness. She moved swiftly to seat herself with the haughtiness of an imperial figure asserting an unquestionable right.

A waitress, smartly dressed in a white shirt and black slacks, took the order. The cappuccinos arrived promptly. I changed my mind and asked for a slice of chocolate torte.

Michelle lit a cigarette. I thought I saw her hands shake slightly. I leaned back defiantly after pushing the ashtray to her side of the table. It was her fifth cigarette for the morning. Normally that was her quota for the entire day. She looked haggard and dispirited. Over the years the summer sun had not been kind to her skin. But the sparkle of rebellious honesty in her blue eyes retained their daring vigour.

She rested her left elbow on the table and cupped her chin in her hand.

The waitress came back with a sliver of cake, a generous dollop of cream and a wan smile.

There were no preliminaries or preparations. No hints. No lead-ins. I couldn't detect any uncertainty or contrition in Michelle's voice.

My dumbfounded silence was probably the reaction she had anticipated. Under the deluge of accusations I couldn't even struggle to put up a flimsy defence. The clarity of my awareness was confined to the rich texture of the cake. The measured movement of the spoon between the plate and my mouth was an orderly facade behind which I was able to hide my confusion and shock. Her words swarmed around my ears like attacking soldiers intending to ram home the advantage of a surprise attack. I continued to eat slowly, scooping up the crumbs from the edge of the plate.

There was little left in our relationship. Surely I must have realised it as well?

The conviction in her tone made me wince and look away.

She made me feel as if I were guilty of unpardonable matrimonial neglect.

Across the road a woman under a blue umbrella was admonishing her two young children.

I didn't listen. Few common interests . . . blunted sensitivity . . . I wasn't interested in spending time together . . . I took everything for granted.

A silver-grey BMW screeched to a halt. A polite beep of the horn. An old man, in a faded black overcoat and an ancient felt hat, stood in the middle of the road and gesticulated wildly at the calm, impeccably groomed woman.

The domestic drama across the road became even more complicated with the emergence of Dad with a set of golf clubs from inside a sports store. I was fascinated by his yellow socks. I would never dare wear such a colour.

I was merely there . . . a presence in a fog . . . couldn't be reached . . . too sure of myself . . . of her . . . patronising in a clumsy effort to be tolerant . . . lack of willingness to compromise.

The girl began to weep. The boy had his bottom smacked. The embarrassment of such an open display of anger was too much for the father. He turned and marched off, followed by the agitated mother dragging the kids with her.

I had become stubborn . . . smug and set in my ways . . . more ockerish in my behaviour . . . showed little interest in her as a person. We were tired of each other.

Also a bit of sexual boredom, perhaps? I ventured to suggest. Even well-bred Catholics, like herself, couldn't deny their polygamous instinct.

Michelle stabbed the cigarette in the ashtray and clutched her head in exasperation. We drew meaningful stares from the nearby tables.

She lowered her voice to a fierce whisper. How could I be so bloody casual? This was precisely what she meant. I treated everything as a prized joke.

I wasn't being intentionally flippant, I retorted. I was merely striving to match her veracity. The sarcasm was also unintentional, although it managed to flush Colin out into the open.

Colin!

Dear Whoever-up-there on your burnished throne! Of all the men, why did it have to be Colin? The dear old chap with the fake accent and a perpetual pining for jolly old England where he spent several years with his parents when he was a teenager. Colin, her childhood friend and much admired by Keith as a true Australian. The rich, balding accountant with the white shirts, pinstriped suits and the silk Italian ties. The golfer and the wine buff. Colin—pretentious, arrogant and in search of his royal ancestry. Divorced and on the prowl. Colin, who thinks of Australia as the emblem of civilisation in a region of unenlightenment. Colin, the mild-mannered bigot.

My face must have reflected the disquiet I felt.

Michelle reacted indignantly. No! It wasn't like that at all! Talk of jumping to conclusions! She didn't even think of him as a male, not in the way I was insinuating. He was . . .

An old friend?

A very old friend and nothing more.

I wasn't insinuating anything, I argued. She was the one jumping to conclusions about what I was thinking. I wasn't about to admit she had read my thoughts correctly.

Michelle felt obliged to give me a hasty explanation. She had spoken to Colin about going away during the Christmas holidays. Somewhere out of Australia. She needed a change of place. She needed time to think and sort out the jumbled mess she was in.

Colin was kind enough to offer help. He was a part owner of a villa in Tuscany. Would she consider braving a northern winter near a quiet Italian village?

He'd be there, of course.

She looked at me searchingly, not out of any great concern

for the way I felt but in the hope that I might spare attacking her vulnerable conscience. I was sorely tempted. Her professed agnosticism was constantly in conflict with an obsolete but deeply ingrained Vatican morality. I had always suspected she reluctantly believed in venial and mortal sin. The distinction was more a matter of convenience than conviction. Perhaps it gave her more room to manoeuvre in the shadowy world of Catholic guilt.

She answered the question I had no intention of asking.

No, she wasn't sleeping with him. She had never been unfaithful to me in our married life.

What a quaint word—*unfaithful*. A laudable sacrifice. *Father, I am not guilty of one of the big ones.*

Was it difficult? I even managed a grim smile.

My lack of apparent hostility disconcerted Michelle. Another example, she later told me, of my indifference.

It wasn't as though I didn't feel angry or distressed. On the contrary, my anger was so intense that it bottled me up into a state of seething silence. I even contemplated a dramatic build-up to a grand exit. Smash my cup against a wall. Kick the table and knock over my chair. A forgettable parting line about treachery and deceit. I imagined all sorts of ways of attracting attention and making an ass of myself.

I paid the bill and walked out.

On the way back to the Harringtons, I told Michelle I would move out of the house. It was the only way to salvage my pride. There was a subdued agreement to protect Nadine from any bitterness arising from our differences. I proposed a discussion about the division of household items. There was no hurry, she said. I could take whatever I wished. She was in no mood to be petty. Her vague generosity came as a sobering reminder of the stress she was under. I almost felt sorry for her.

I forgot her Catholicism and assumed she wanted a divorce. I thought I heard her gasp. Could we avoid making definitive decisions for the next few months? She skirted around the idea of a divorce as if the thought had never entered her mind. In my own state of turmoil I didn't push the issue. We found it easier to accept the uncertainty of a separation rather than come to terms with the finality of an irreparable break-up.

She had decided to stay the night with her parents and catch a train back the next day.

Would I tell Nadine?

Definitely not. It was her doing. Well, all right; provided we were both present.

Tomorrow evening?

Yes. The sooner the better.

I hear a shrill whistle behind me. Before I can turn, Theo is beside me. I get a friendly punch on the arm and an unflattering comment about my appearance. He looks terrible too. Tousled hair and bags under his eyes. A grey and white stubble on his chin and cheeks.

We could start a new trend among divorced, middle-aged men. Call it *The Frayed Look Crash Course Program*. Begin modestly and then branch out nationally. Go international. Export package deals and help the economy. Guarantee success in personal negligence. How to make yourself unattractive and remain free.

'Race you!' Theo shouts and dashes away.

We manage about fifty metres. Age loses ungraciously.

We sit panting on the soft sand and plan a day in the Otways to be followed by a crayfish dinner.

FOUR

I have blatantly ignored Ma's pointed invitation to sit next to my widowed cousin, Alya. I am wary of her ingratiating friendliness. The chair beside the rubber plant suits me perfectly. Discreetly I nudge the chair with my left foot. A few centimetres to the left and I can retreat behind the glossy green leaves.

I remember Alya as a sullen, fair-complexioned girl, epitomising the Bangali ideal of beauty. A round face and full lips, which had been trained to pout, conspired with smouldering dark eyes to ensnare aspiring young civil servants and whittle them down to a state of starry-eyed adoration. She knew she was attractive. She was flattered often enough about her looks. The absurdly Petrarchan compliments lavished on her had swelled her vanity into the cold arrogance of a beauty queen. Only her intellectual puerility prevented her from being an accomplished bitch.

I now see a plump, faded woman anxious to talk to me. She is on the hunt, Hashim warned me, armed with the fortune she inherited from her husband's shipping business. Her interest is in overseas commodities. The price is irrelevant.

'How long have you been divorced?' Alya asked coyly.

'Long enough to forget about her!' Ma snaps.

'I am only separated.' I curse myself for sounding so limp.

'Khurshida, did I tell you about the latest marriage proposal for Alya?' My aunt looks at me out of the corner of her eyes.

Ma swallows and shakes her head.

'He is a chartered accountant. Comes from a very good family. *Besh* upper class. You must meet him soon.' Raffat Talukdar turns to me. 'But now we must know all about you, *Choto Babu.*'

I fidget in the corner and struggle to answer the questions flung at me. I am mercilessly pinned under the gaze of inquisitorial eyes.

I think they can detect my boredom. My mind is on the other side of the city, in old Dhaka, searching among the maze of dark, smelly lanes. I was apprehensive about the phone call. He sounded unenthusiastic. He was unpacking after returning from one of the offshore islands hit by the recent cyclone. His reticence was not entirely unexpected. I felt like screaming at him. Anything to jolt his memory.

You expect a little more warmth from your friends, even after all these years!

And what if he came up with an appropriate rejoinder? *Friends? You?*

I picture the meeting. His face. His words. The reminiscings. What I wouldn't surrender to claw my way back through time and find myself in the university cafeteria again!

The voices slash through my imaginings.

'Are Australians racist?'

'Are Muslims hated there?'

'Is it easy to find well-paid jobs?'

'How much does a house cost?'

'What sort of a car do you drive?'

'How do people manage without servants?'

'Is it difficult to migrate to Australia?'

Age has not diminished Raffat Talukdar's domineering spirit. The other women—Husna Haider, Salma Aziz, Kishwar Zaman, Ma and Alya—interject occasionally, but it is my aunt who leads the charge. She is a vacuous flibbertigibbet with an unrestricted imagination and a viperous tongue for malicious gossip.

The interrogation continues unabated. My replies inflame their curiosity.

'Most Anglo-Saxon Australians don't know enough about Islam.'

'No, I don't own my house.'

'My car is not air-conditioned.'

'I don't really know about the immigration situation.'

'No, you cannot buy twenty-two carat gold jewellery there.'

'I believe there are sizeable Bangali communities in Melbourne and Sydney. I do not belong to any association.'

I disrupt the flow by inquiring about Moin Mamma. He was asleep when I called in yesterday. I remember my uncle as a tubby, acerbic man in his mid fifties, a successful civil engineer with an impressive record of rapid promotions under the military government of Pakistan. Moin Mamma was in the habit of describing himself as a liberal Muslim. Islam, he boasted, was a wonderfully resilient religion. He prayed regularly, fasted during the holy month, fed the beggars during *Shab-e-Barath* and read the Koran every morning. As if to test his hypothesis, he had no qualms about bending the tenets of Islam to comply with his addiction. He was hooked on German beer which was readily available on the black market. He spent his evenings in the sanctuary of his study with maps, drawings, set-squares and cans of beer stocked in the drawers of his filing cabinets. Islam lost its optimum degree of flexibility during *Ramazan* when his conscience forced him to take a break from his favourite pastime. He suffered headaches and was prone to fits of depression and bad temper. My aunt unsympathetically attributed these common withdrawal symptoms to the rigours of fasting.

Moin Mamma has been confined to a wheelchair after suffering a stroke a few years ago. He is cantankerous and tight-fisted with his money. He hates visitors. Ma does not appreciate the criticism, but she refrains from voicing even a token disapproval of her sister-in-law's unfeeling remarks. My aunt refuses to discard her peculiar notions about the functional role of a married man. A husband's love is what he earns for his wife and children. It is incumbent on him to prove a chivalrous devotion to his wife by silently absorbing her verbal abuse, learning to be an expert in dodging flying cutlery and keys and, at all times, being obedient to the whims of the domestic commandant.

Communication between the Talukdars revolves around money matters, with my aunt determined to squeeze as much as she can for household expenses, including her personal shopping extravagances, and Moin Mamma pleading unsuccessfully for her to consider the financial limitations of a pensioner. A perpetual state of mutual animosity has been the norm in their marriage. Years ago there were whispered rumours among Ma's friends that her brother's rapidly declining efficiency in somatic matters, requiring a somewhat vigorous form of recumbent athleticism, had led to separate bedrooms for the Talukdars without, in any way, lessening their connubial tensions.

I am steered back to the subject of migration.

I make discouraging remarks about the possibilities for doctors, lawyers and dentists. 'It is easier to get in if you are a Tandoori chef.'

'A cook?' Alya giggles as if she were responding to a joke.

The older women look at me in grim admonishment as if to say I have a poor sense of humour.

We are interrupted by Khuda Buksh as he wheels in a rattling tea-trolley. I refuse the snacks and accept a cup of tea. It is only half-past ten and yet they gorge themselves on *samosas, nimki* and *shondesh* as though they were starving. The tea is from our garden in Sylhet. I praise the brew, adding that the tea available in Australia is definitely inferior—weak and without a rich aroma. That pleases everyone.

Hafiz, the young servant, appears with a superbly hand-crafted silver *paan-daan*. Most of Hafiz's working hours are taken up with the elaborate preparations for the formality of the following morning. For several hours each day the *paan-daan* and its component pieces are meticulously cleaned and polished until they gleam as if they were radiating a life sustaining energy vital to the survival of Ma's coterie of friends.

The *paan-daan* is an elliptical-shaped box with a hinged lid fitted with a collapsible handle. It is delicately overlaid with floral designs, a testimony to the craftsmanship of an anonymous nineteenth-century Dhakaiya silversmith slaving at his highly skilled trade to flatter the vanity of the *Nawab* of Dhaka. In a moment of drunken generosity, the *Nawab* had presented it to my great-grandfather as a gesture of friendship.

Inside the *paan-daan* a silver tray holds the heart-shaped betel leaves kept moist with a cover of damp cloth. The hollow chamber under the tray is crowded with small, round containers brimming with the ingredients of an exotic *paan*. There are two varieties of cardamom seeds coated with scented silver foil, finely chopped sweet and plain betel nuts, cloves, aniseeds, fennel and lime.

As if she were performing an elaborate *jadoo* to guarantee a continued insight into the bedroom gossip of the most prestigious families in the neighbourhood, Ma makes each *paan* with a ritualistic seriousness. Like a skilled artisan, her fingers work deftly with a tiny silver spatula to spread a thin coating of lime on each leaf. Pinches of condiments are placed in the centre of the leaves. Each leaf is folded in the shape of a triangle and held in place by piercing it with a clove.

My refusal to have a *paan* draws a mild reprimand from Mrs Haider. It is only to be expected that local customs have become alien to me. I am goaded into a compromise by her gentle smile. I reach out for some cardamom seeds and betel nuts.

Mrs Aziz is curious about Queensland. She is particularly interested in the city of Brisbank.

'Brisbane,' I correct her, and give her a sketchy account based on my solitary holiday in Queensland a few years back.

Mrs Aziz is immediately besieged with questions. Why does she want to know about Queensland? Does she know someone there? Is she planning to visit Australia?

Mrs Aziz enjoys the attention. Coyly she examines her fingernails. 'There is nothing certain, but there is an excellent chance that Younus will be offered a job there with a firm of chartered accountants.'

This is devastating news for Mrs Haider, Mrs Zaman and my aunt. Their highly qualified sons and daughters are seeking jobs overseas. Ma looks composed. Alya is indifferent to the fortunes of Younus. He is married with three children. She catches my eye and favours me with her best smile. My attention quickly falls on a caterpillar crawling up a leaf of the rubber plant.

The interested trio is visibly distraught. They gulp like desperate *talapias* who suddenly find themselves out of water. They masticate furiously. The veins in their temples swell noticeably under the strain. They are outraged at the natural injustice of such an opportunity coming Younus' way.

The mashed leaves and nuts fail to stimulate a suitable response. Ma is alert to their angered frustration and calls for a spittoon which is immediately put to use. Jets of thin, carmine fluid find the mark with unerring accuracy.

Ma congratulates Mrs Aziz. She can afford to be calm and charitable. She can boast of at least one son who lives overseas.

'When is Younus leaving?'

'It is too early to say. He sent his application only yesterday.'

'Oh!'

'Ah! He doesn't have a job then!'

'Oh! There is no certainty!'

The relief is audible. They lean back on their sofas and stuff their mouths with more *paan*. They manducate with a renewed vigour. Younus is no better off than their own children. The commonality of their disappointment ensures Mrs Aziz's survival.

Ma calls for a fresh pot of tea.

I make a move to leave. I need to give myself plenty of time to find Iftiqar's flat. I only have a rough idea of the layout of the old part of the city.

'Raffat!' Ma snaps with a sudden urgency. She jerks her head in my direction.

Mammi puffs her chest and smiles broadly as if she is about to usher in some good news. '*Choto Babu*, a few more minutes of your time. There is some important family business to be discussed. There is nothing to hide! We are among close friends. It is about Nadine.'

Mammi's syrupy tone makes me wary. 'What about her?' I ask suspiciously.

I realise I have become excessively protective toward Nadine. Her surliness and supercilious manners have given way to shy diffidence suggestive of a growing state of confusion. She is having difficulty in working out the behavioural codes of her relationships with the family members. Inflexible notions of decorum and respect for elders have imposed severe restrictions on her casual manners. The cultural barriers are too formidable for her to overcome in such a short time. I feel guilty she has not been adequately prepared for this trip. But even with hindsight I doubt if I could have done any better.

I am barely beginning to understand the tact and patience necessary to unravel the complexity of a child's world and find a willing acceptance in it. The discovery of the startling sophistication of ideas behind the deceptive simplicity of her language has made me listen to her very carefully. I no longer feel as if her perceptions of change in our family situation are unworthy of serious attention. I am having to make a diligent effort to be honest with Nadine. Learning not to hide from her is a new experience. I am relieved that she knows I am vulnerable. She accepts my shortcomings—the fact I can make mistakes and that I am not the ultimate repository of all knowledge. Her father has lost the mystique of invincibility and become more human in her eyes. I have come down to a level where she can understand some of my frustrations and anxieties. My status as a nebulous figure of authority has disappeared. I am proud that she values my presence and the time we spend together. We talk as two people who have reached the conclusion that an acknowledgement of human fallibility is a crucial first step in the development of a relationship. There is now a bond of mutual trust which is precious to both of us. I have started to relate to her as a person, as a distinct entity, and not as my genetic clone who has inherited my perceptions and values. I accept her intellectual independence and her right to formulate opinions and make judgements incongruent to mine, without being wrong.

' . . . as is our custom. We have to recognise her social identity by formally bestowing on her the name you have chosen. It is not an Islamic name but we have to accept it.'

'The *aqeeqa* ceremony!' Ma chimes as if my aunt's Bangla is too sophisticated for my understanding.

In astonishment I listen to the details of the arrangements made without consulting me. I digest the information and mull over its implications.

My memory flits back to a July Sunday in Melbourne.

It was wet and miserable. Scattered leaves dotted a deserted suburban street hiding its houses behind the weeping limbs of gracefully aging trees.

This was no ordinary Sunday lunch. Sarah had taken out the best from her cupboards. Starched white tablecloth and matching serviettes. Her best china and crystal goblets. Silver cutlery gleamed in the wavering light of the crackling fire. In the next room *La Traviata* added a sobering touch of pathos to the winter's gloom.

'Thank you Lord for what we are about to receive . . . '

My stomach growled impatiently.

Keith's voice never varied. He always said Grace with an awed reverence as if the food were a direct offering from Heaven.

This was the month for pumpkin soup sprinkled with cinnamon and garnished with parsley. Hot white rolls and soft butter. To follow—roast lamb and mint sauce, roast potatoes, boiled carrots and beans. Pavlova and coffee.

Sunday lunch with the Harringtons was an event I accepted without dissent. At least it brought us to Melbourne once a month and released us from the stranglehold of provincial bovinity. This particular Sunday was a very special occasion. There was an additional family member asleep in a bassinet behind Michelle's chair.

The pleasantries ended half-way through the soup. Keith turned to me and spoke with a polite firmness. There was no help from Michelle. Her eyes were focused on her soup bowl.

Even in a state of shocked indignation, Keith's voice was subdued. The Harringtons prided themselves on their self-control. Emotions were carefully monitored and rarely allowed unrestricted expression. Michelle was an embarrassing exception.

'I am not sure I understand. What do you mean you don't want her to be baptised?'

'Exactly what I said. I don't see the point in it.'

'She is a Catholic. It's an essential part of our religion.'

'I wasn't aware she was born with a religious tag around her wrist.'

A shroud of desolate silence descended over the table.

Michelle was up quickly to remove the bowls. Keith pushed back his chair and moved to a side table to carve the meat. There was a surgical precision about the way he used a knife. The vegetables were passed around. Knives and forks scraped the plates in a collective apology for the lack of conversation. Sarah turned her head toward the fire and coughed. She looked nervously at Keith. His face was flushed and I noticed his tight hold on the knife and fork.

Lisa excused herself and went to the lounge to change the record. She turned up the volume. I had serious misgivings whether the liveliness of Strauss would alleviate the tension which had developed with such unexpected suddenness.

There was a stunted murmur of compliment from Tom. 'This meat is beautifully tender.'

Sarah's mouth twitched into a smile. 'Thank you.'

'More wine?'

'Yes please.'

'Oops! Excuse me!' Michelle's knife slipped on her plate and a piece of potato flew past my right arm and landed on the carpet.

'You have to understand we are a very tradition-oriented family. Rituals are important to us. They are essential land-marks of our faith.'

I felt the pressure of Michelle's foot on my ankle. Her look pleaded for restraint.

Sarah offered Tom and Keith a second helping of meat and potatoes. Her disapproval of my intransigence was evident. Her mouth tightened into a puckered slit and her eyebrows were raised into ridges of silent anger.

I had to help myself to some more meat and vegetables.

'What do you have against baptism?' Keith was determined to corner me. He persisted despite my peace-making effort of uncorking another bottle and pouring him some more claret.

Tom continued to cut his meat with the utmost care. I

sympathised with his embarrassment. Thomas O'Linn was the local parish priest and a long-time friend of Keith's.

'What is your objection to baptism?' Keith repeated patiently.

'None at all. It's of no significance to me. But I do object to your assumption that it is an affirmation of my daughter's identity. How did you determine she is a Christian and not a Muslim?'

'I thought you didn't care about your religion.'

'I am not particularly taken up with your brand of Christianity either.'

'Is there anything you believe in? Anything at all?'

'I believe in Nadine's right not to be imprisoned to a faith. I insist on her right to have a freedom to choose when she is capable of making a rational decision. She should know about religion. About Catholicism, if you like. I'll grant you that.'

Keith stopped eating. The knife and fork clattered on his plate. 'Religion is not about rationality. It is about a sense of purpose in life. There is a commonality of unshakable belief among Catholics which gives us strength and a clarity of vision about ourselves. It is all about sharing and participation in the richest communal tradition in the world.'

'It is also about illusions. I won't have yours preserved at my daughter's expense. You want her to be baptised because you believe in it. It affirms your faith.'

The pavlova arrived, beautifully decorated with fruits, cream and a drizzle of grated chocolate. Michelle grabbed the salver. I received more than a generous serving of dessert.

'That looks brilliant!' Tom patted his stomach ruefully. 'I shouldn't really, you know. I was telling Pat the other day about Sarah's pavlovas. He'll be angling for an invitation soon!'

Poor Tom. His clumsy attempt to steer the terse exchange toward a banal level of light-heartedness was thwarted by an impatient grunt from Keith.

Sarah leaned over and whispered a concerned inquiry about the young Father Patrick, new to the parish after a stint in Mildura.

'Every child is born into a tradition.' There was fierce conviction in Keith's voice.

Across the table, our eyes clashed again. 'Nadine will be among a slowly growing minority which will learn how to combine traditions. It won't be easy.'

'No.' Keith shook his head as if the idea were repulsive to him. 'No. That will only confuse her. She must grow up with a clear understanding of who she is and where she belongs. If she lives here, it is only right that she be brought up in the mainstream of Australian life. There is no advantage in being a fringe dweller.'

'Like myself?' I felt my pulse quicken. Like most first-generation migrants I was sensitive about the uncertainty of my place in the community.

'This is a Christian society. Even you cannot deny that. My grand-daughter must not be deprived of a place here.' Keith leaned forward aggressively and gulped a mouthful of wine. His face was flushed and his jaws clenched like a rusty vice. All the stress of a rigid self-control were mapped on his face.

'By the time she is an adult, the narrowness of life within a single tradition may become a handicap.'

'She must have security! Don't you understand that?' He slapped the table with his right hand. A red stain splotched the tablecloth.

'Keith! Please.'

'Sorry.' He dabbed the spot with his serviette.

Lisa looked at me murderously before announcing she had an assignment to complete.

To say that Keith and I don't always get along would be a masterly understatement. That is not to say we quarrel frequently or do not communicate. We are usually civil toward each other, especially in the presence of Sarah and Michelle, but there are occasions when we play a silly and nasty verbal game intended to assert a cultural superiority. The aim is to belittle the other with an exaggerated air of condescending politeness meant to push the adversary into a demonstrable state of pyrogenic rage. There are faint echoes of an ancient feud in our jostles. We use words instead of swords, sarcasm instead of force. I think I know which sides we would have chosen in the battles between Richard and Saladin.

I represent most things Keith believes are going wrong with Australia. He really works to annoy me by claiming to be stunned by the revelation that I was not among those who had smuggled across in a boat and surreptitiously made my way to Melbourne to begin a cosy life at the expense of the honest, tax-paying Aussie battler. I have my moments. He is often lost for words when I draw his attention to the Vietnam disaster or the inconsistency between his stated beliefs in the doctrines of a church which espouses compassion, equality and justice, and his bias against Asians.

What makes me unacceptable to Keith, even dangerous, is not my colour or my background. It is my refusal to uphold what he considers to be the immutable virtues of every decent Australian—a blind devotion to the monarchy, an active support for the policies of the RSL, a life-long membership of the Liberal Party and an undying belief that Australia should continue to draw all its spiritual and cultural sustenance from Europe, even in the distant future.

Although Keith's dislike for the Japanese is particularly intense, at least he compliments them inadvertently by identifying the people by their specific nationality. As for the rest of us, from the dark, unknown regions of the north, we are lumped together as Asians, recognisable by our absence of Christian principles which outweighs any discernible differences in ethnic characteristics. We are devious, unscrupulous, greedy and godless. Our unstated philosophy—copulate and populate. We are a bunch of untrustworthy ratbags extending our sinister shadows to blight the country he claims to be God's gift to Christians.

What irks me is the calm certainty with which Keith expounds his extreme views against a changing world moving rapidly beyond his understanding and exposing him to the foreignness of secularism. Keith experiences no doubt about his myopic vision of Australia. A serene certainty guides his view of its social structure which is essentially medieval in origin. The stratified layers of modern barons, knights, ladies and serfs are determined by background, wealth, religion and colour.

To my surprise I was spared the predictable diatribe against the Asian influence. My stand against baptising Nadine had shocked Keith into a state of verbal constipation. My anger dissipated quickly, giving way to a state of euphoria, as if I had won a tactical battle. It made me feel victorious in a shallow, mean sort of way.

Tom stepped in with his booming voice and, aided by Michelle, shepherded us away from further ugliness. Judging by the gusto with which he attacked the pavlova, he was the only one whose appetite was undiminished by the hostilities around the table.

I like the old priest. His range of interests sets him apart from some of the more parochial members of his tribe. Tom has an astounding knowledge of modern theatre. I share his enthusiasm for Bach. He enjoys cooking and never refuses a drop of good red. He is a keen astronomer and was a cricketer of some merit in his younger days. Unfortunately, his intellectual vigour is a danger to the establishment. He is an independent thinker, unafraid to articulate his opinion that the church, in its present state, is not an effective spiritual model. Frequently I have talked to him about Kingdom values. He agrees that the precept of equality is difficult to implement, given the structure of the church. Its application is easier to preach to a wider community outside the direct influence of the church. Tom's questioning mind is his greatest shortcoming. It disadvantages him from attaining the higher ranks of clerical hierarchy.

For a very long time I was prejudiced against Tom for no other reason than he was a priest. I am not proud of my hostility toward him after we were introduced. Eventually we became friends after my distrust thawed under the warmth of his uncomplicated personality.

Ever since my school days I have been resentful of religious men. Catholic brothers and fiery *mullahs* turned my early years of adolescence into a state of prolonged misery tainted with confusion, pain, guilt and rebellious anger. It would be unfair to blame my parents for sending me to a Catholic school. How were they to know how tortured a child's life can be? They were keen for Hashim and me to have the best possible academic education available in the country.

Of all the harm colonisation has inflicted on the subcontinent, none has been more damaging than the cultural havoc wrought by that hallowed and sacrosanct institution, the English medium school. It is a remarkable mechanism which has survived the insular fury of nationalism and continued to flourish. It uses impressionable children from affluent families as raw material to be shaped and moulded into arrogant stereotypes before spouting them out as aliens in their indigenous environments.

Had my parents realised the harm being done by the contradictory claims of Christianity and Islam, I doubt if my brother and I would have been so cruelly exposed to the mental torments we endured. The devil lurked in the safest of places and confronted us in every conceivable shape of Gothic grotesqueness. We were consistently lectured on sin and forced to imagine its painful consequences.

Caught between Catechism and Koranic lessons, I was like

a young Everyman in a variation of a morality play. Instead of the good and bad angels fighting for my soul, the principal antagonists were the Brothers of the Holy Cross and the Peshawari *mullah* whose job was to indoctrinate us at home after school had ended for the day.

At school the sterling figures of male celibacy ('They have wind tunnels between their legs,' Iftiqar had once confided to me) were committed to the propagation of a fundamentalist brand of Christianity and the destruction of communist ideals behind an imposing facade of academic excellence. Unabashedly the good American brothers extolled the virtues of the Yankee way of life bought by the mighty greenback and sustained by those exclusive American qualities of honesty, generosity, patriotism and an unswerving belief in *Ghaad*, that great benefactor and designer of the stars and stripes, known for his immense love for his favourite citizens.

Enthused and inspired by the men in white, we exercised our molars on Wrigley's gum, wore checked shirts and jeans, listened to Elvis, Ricky Nelson, Buddy Holly, Fabian and the other faceless multitudes of rock 'n' roll croakers with snappy fingers, rubbery knees, toothy smiles and greasy hair. We played softball and basketball, thought cricket was okay and openly scorned soccer as the poor man's game. Collectively we bought packets of Camel and Lucky Strike since it was beneath our lofty status to smoke anything made locally. We revelled in American colloquialisms and hung around the Dhaka Club swimming pool, drinking coke and munching crisps.

For our imaginative sustenance we rummaged in the vast junkyard of cheap American paperbacks. Mike Hammer was the most admired tough guy in the business of exterminating the bungling commies. The softies went for Perry Mason and the colourless Della. The handful of deviants who were interested in Hemingway and Steinbeck were branded as spineless homos.

Hollywood was a rich pasture where we nourished our arrogant assumptions of superiority. Sunday mornings were spent watching westerns in Gulistan and Naaz cinemas. Those were the good ol' days when the clean-cut cowboy shot all those wicked and barbaric Red Indians without recriminations or guilt-laden soliloquies, and rounded off the hour and a half of celluloid predictability by riding into the sunset with the blonde who had little to say and plenty to hide under her dress.

At high noon on Mondays, the Bangla medium government schools, further down the road, became the target of spirited attacks with ropes, toy pistols and an arsenal of gutter language. It was a swift, surprise attack which amounted to a lot of noise and verbal abuse. The stunned natives were annihilated, and the English medium cavalry returned in time for the afternoon lessons after their overwhelming victory.

We prostituted ourselves willingly to the glamour of a culture we did not fully understand. We enjoyed being snobs and openly rejected non-English-speaking Bangalis as our intellectual inferiors.

Although Iftiqar was my best friend, he hovered on the periphery of our group of insufferable upstarts. Our guarded acceptance of Iftiqar rested on a grudging admiration of his academic excellence, though, in other ways, he was a bit of a goofball who could neither dance the cha-cha-cha nor the twist. He had no knowledge of Mickey Spillane and indulged in the odd habit of reading Dickens and the Bangla novels of Saratchandra Chattopadhay and Madhusudan Datta. Instead of listening to the English programs on the commercial service of Radio Ceylon and familiarising himself with the top nine on the Binaca Hit Parade, Ifti wasted his time with *Nazrul Geethi* and *Robindro Shongeet*. He even refused to go swimming with us at the Dhaka Club pool and leer at the American girls we wanted as our girlfriends.

'They are all dark where it counts,' he would mutter, unimpressed with the prospect of a white girlfriend.

Religion was altogether a different proposition. Despite the sustained endeavours to brainwash us into accepting *the true ways of our Lord, Jesus Christ*, the brothers made no headway. At home Islam struggled to make us submissive to the Will of Allah. Rejection, the natural camouflage for adolescent confusion, led to outright insubordination.

At school we were confronted with a pretentiously titled subject called moral science which operated on the premise that students were cretinous creatures incapable of independent thinking. The text consisted of 365 questions and answers about God, His designs for universal redemption and the dangers of succumbing to the seductive illusions of the Devil. After the first half of the book had exhausted the commonplace descriptions of the ordeals to be suffered in the eternal flames, there was a section on the Grace of God and the infinite bliss for those sinners who repented (recalcitrant young infidels were not specifically mentioned) and recognised the merits of the true faith. The answers to all the questions had to be memorised for an examination once a term.

At one critical point of extreme frustration (not a single student had expressed the slightest interest in borrowing a highly recommended book entitled *Coming Close to Christ*), Brother Paul, the moral science teacher from the state of Georgia, had a vision of a burning cross impaled on the peak of a snow-hooded mountain. Rumour had it that when Brother Paul sought the headmaster's advice on the meaning of this unusual phenomenon, Brother Martin paled visibly and interpreted it as a warning of Lucifer's power to create chaos by promoting hatred between Christians and Muslims. What was the good brother from the Deep South planning to do about it? With true missionary dedication, the zealous Brother Paul vowed to undertake the mammoth task of proving that

God was Love for those who had the Devil sowing the seeds of hatred in them.

Brother Paul disappeared quite suddenly. He was busy with important matters beneficial to the students, we were informed at assembly one morning. Brother Leo would be the new Moral Science teacher.

At morning recess, that day, we formed a spying committee to sniff out the truth. Hashim and Iftiqar volunteered to spend their lunch hours prowling around the brothers' residence in the hope of locating Brother Paul's room. Their simple plan was to peep through his window in a seditious attempt to unravel the mystery of his absence.

The reports we received behind the toilet block were muddled and needed clarification with the aid of the most imaginative minds in the school. Brother Paul had been sighted, working slavishly in his room, sweating profusely and writing sporadically, eating chocolates and drinking from various bottles. Occasionally he was seen to grapple with invisible beings who, we concluded, were evil spirits blocking his flow of ideas and frustrating his efforts on our behalf. He was heard to roar like a wounded tiger (it sounded more like a frightened kitten, judging by the imitative noises Hashim made) to ward off the Devil and his henchmen who appeared to be gaining ascendancy, presumably aided and abetted by the biological quirks of Brother Paul's extraordinary cranial density.

Brother Paul's tenacity must have prevailed in the end. After nearly a month, he reappeared with several printed sheets of paper with seven itemised arguments vindicating the power of Divine Love to bring about a lasting global peace. Brother Martin was so overwhelmed by the tonal sincerity of the Pauline arguments that the document became obligatory reading in class after we had recited the Lord's Prayer. The Moral Science examination was extended by

another half an hour to accommodate questions on the trea-
tise.

As a class we responded by failing the final examination.
Angry parents questioned the competence of a teacher with
a failure rate of one hundred percent. Soon afterwards, Brother
Paul was stricken by a mysterious illness which had to be
treated in the United States. His thesis disappeared with him.
Back we went to the Moral Science text with the 365 questions
and answers.

For Hashim and me, there was little relief at home either.
Each day, after returning from school, we found a dreaded,
malodorous *mullah* awaiting us with the Koran and a waxed
cane. In the thick afternoon heat, overbearingly perfumed
with the sweet sticky smell of ripe jackfruits, the *mullah* leaned
on a bolster and dozed. We sat on a straw mat in the shade
of the back verandah. The first part of the lesson was a
mechanical reading from the Koran. We swayed backwards
and forwards and read aloud in a shrill, sing-song voice.

'*Ah ouz zoh billah eh minash shoitan er rajim . . . Bismillah er
Rahman er Raheem . . .*' we droned without even a basic
understanding of Arabic. To relieve the tedium, Hashim and
I made faces at each other and communicated in an
improvised form of sign language.

Intermittently the *mullah* was awakened by buzzing flies
landing on his sweaty face. He felt obliged to prove his
alertness by smacking us on the shoulders as though we were
responsible for disturbing his nap. The reading was followed
by a stern lecture on the Islamic way of life and the necessity
to avoid the Devil's temptations. The Pathan used the cane
liberally to emphasise his belief in the evil lurking in young
boys and the need to purge *Iblis* from our souls.

'The body and soul must be clean!' The voice warned in
Urdu before the cane descended on our shoulders. 'Clean!'

It was our habitual response to make a great show of pain.
Faces distorted, we whimpered in agony.

'The mind must be pure! Pure! Understand? Hah?'

Our vigorous nods satisfied him.

'What is the greatest religion on earth?'

'Islam!' We cried in unison.

The power of the cane was vindicated. His smile indicated he had extracted the desired answer. His tongue darted out of his mouth like a startled lizard. He licked the corners of his mouth with immense satisfaction. The tongue left a streak of saliva on his moustache. His clawed fingers combed his beard in a slow brooding manner. The ultimate question was yet to come.

'Who is the greatest person in history?' It was a confident whisper of hope.

Our bemused looks and winks made him sit up erectly.

'Who is the greatest person who has ever lived?'

'Jesus Christ!' We shouted triumphantly.

His fingers released the cane. There was a gasp of horror. '*Chup*! Ignorant peasants! *Ullu! Ghadey ka baccha!*'

'George Washington!'

'*Ya Khuda!*' Repeatedly he slapped his forehead with the palm of his right hand. 'Forgive the failure of this humble sinner!' The aggression drained out of him as he buried his face in his hands and mumbled a prayer of repentance.

Our answers were prearranged. They ranged from Buddha to Gandhi, Mozart to Paul Anka; virtually anyone except the Prophet. Without mercy, we hastened the termination of the lesson by farting or making rude noises.

With a weary, 'We shall try again tomorrow,' the *mullah* departed with the aggrieved air of a Samaritan who had failed miserably to reform hardened criminals.

He often complained bitterly to Abba and threatened to resign. But he never did. The pious man of Allah was paid thrice the sum of money he received in the other houses in the neighbourhood. It was enough to revive his optimism and

bring him back the next day to confront the young followers
of the Wicked Spirit.

' . . . family and close friends only. A small gathering of about
150 people. We propose a modest dinner to keep the cost
down to about 90 000 takas. Maybe a little more.'

There are murmurs of approval.

'Very reasonable by today's standards!' Ma assures me.

I calculate feverishly. About thirty takas to a dollar . . .
90 000 takas . . . $3000! It's a sum of money I have rarely
managed to muster for anything, let alone a party.

My silence is misinterpreted as acquiescence.

'I have asked Mateen to send us the cows and the goats
from the village.' Ma has a beatific look on her face. 'Your
father wrote to Morich Mia and managed to persuade him to
come out of retirement and cook the dinner. Allah! What a
time Hashim had in finding him! The old man was recently
divorced. Again!' She stifles a giggle. 'He needs the money.'

Mammi is shrewd enough to read my thoughts. She hastens
to placate me. 'The invitations have been printed and sent
out. We thought of arranging everything without troubling
you. You have enough to worry about. We knew you wouldn't
mind.'

'I . . . I don't know what to say. I would have preferred
about twenty or thirty people.'

'Impossible!' Ma explodes indignantly. '*Choto Babu*, how
can you even think of being so miserly? We have to think of
our *izzat*. The cost is not important.'

'Think of the family's reputation!' Mammi pleads with me.
'It will be an absolute scandal if we did not celebrate such an
important occasion in a proper way. What will people say?'

'Anyone who is well-known in Dhaka will laugh at us. *Che,
che. Key shorom!*'

I bristle with resentment. I have no control over my life. I am constantly making adjustments to accommodate others. Theo's words sound a note of ominous warning.

One of the secrets of avoiding middle-age cramps is to surrender yourself to life. Let it control you. Don't fight it! Get rid of the foolish desire to tame it. Don't try to swim against the current simply because you fancy yourself to be a good swimmer. Float. Go with the tide.

Somehow this comforting advice on how to conduct myself, as I rapidly approach the middle stage of my life, overlooks its most despicable necessity—money. I would be quite happy to let go—slide, glide, go with the flow, forgive life and embrace it without reservations, entertain a thousand people . . . whatever, as long as I can be certain of staying afloat. I must tell Theo about the odds in favour of drowning.

'I cannot afford that sort of expense!' I splutter in protest.

Ma is embarrassed by the pointed looks and the raised eyebrows. She dismisses my serious concern with a careless wave of her hand. 'We can talk about that later. I must ask Nadine if she would like to wear a sari with some of the jewellery I have set aside for her marriage.'

I am excluded from the tinsel discussion about *jamdani* and *banarsi* saris, Mysori and Banglori silk, French chiffon, emeralds, diamonds, rubies and twenty-two carat gold. Moloch is glorified, the trivial sanctified. The tempo of the excited babble increases until it resembles a menagerie full of animals on heat.

I raise my voice. 'Will the animals be slaughtered in the backyard?' I have to repeat myself before I can penetrate their rainbow-coloured world draped in jewellery and expensive clothes.

'Naturally!'

'*Choto Babu!*' Ma frowns. 'You have forgotten everything about our customs.'

'Nadine is not to see or know anything about the animals.'

'*Eish! Shorbonash! Choto Babu*, you are being stubborn!'

'Unreasonable!'

'You cannot change our ways! It is a custom our family has always followed!'

'Nadine has to touch the animals before they are blessed and sacrificed. She can do it the day before, if that pleases you.'

The nightmare of *Eid-ul-Azha*, nearly thirty-eight years ago, is grafted in my mind. It remains untarnished despite my sporadic attempts to purge the memory of the dreaded incident. Now it springs on me like a clawing, hungry panther.

I stand on the steps of the backyard verandah, apprehensively curious, clutching the *ayah's* sari. I am hiding behind her back, peeking around her right buttock. A few yards away the servants tackle the cow with a rope and bring her down. The cold glint of the butcher's knife frightens me. As he begins the sawing motion, there is a desperate struggle for life. The animal bellows in pain and anger. The servants lose control. The *ayah* pushes me aside and runs inside the house. I am too scared to move. I feel cold. The animal is snorting and weaving its way in my direction, its half-severed head dangling from side to side. There are thick jets of crimson arching in the air. I want to touch the pretty coloured spots on the dusty ground. There is a pounding inside my head. My vision blurs. I cannot stop shaking. I hear the shouts. I am aware of frantic movements near the steps. It falters and paws the earth. Mustering its dying strength, it makes a final charge toward me. That is Ma screaming. The servants grab the hind legs. There is a sickening thud on the bottom step. The butcher straddles the animal again. There is a dying gasp of surrender. Now there are noises somewhere inside me. My face feels moist and warm. Darkness nibbles at me from every corner.

'Nadine will not go anywhere near those animals. She won't see them or touch them.' I stride purposefully toward the door. The conviction in my voice does not surprise me. I have never felt more certain about anything in my life.

Behind me I can feel the frigid silence of disapproval.

FIVE

How easy it is to wear the gilded masks of gods when we are twenty! The world is willing to bow low in servile compliance to our wishes. Swirling galaxies stop at whispered commands. There is a pilgrim's faith in those huge, quivering dreams. We chart the course of self-fulfilment with a compelling conviction that the universe is ours to control.

Where do you want to study law?

Harvard. Maybe Oxford.

It's not easy to get into those places.

I'll get in. I have to. I want to be a qualified prime minister. I have to be sure of what I am doing. And you?

Don't know. The family business, maybe. Hashim isn't very interested. He lives for the day when he can have his own surgery.

You are not too certain of your future, are you?

Oh, I am in a way. Are you?

Of course! I remember it all.

How can you remember the future?

Easy. Don't you recall the White Queen? 'It's a poor sort of memory that only works backwards.' 'What sort of things do you remember best?' Alice asks. 'Oh things that happened the week after next,' comes the reply. As for me, I remember things twenty years from now.

The swearing-in ceremony?
I want you to be there.
I'll be there.
I mean it.
I'll be there.

Sense impressions are unreliable indicators of my perceptions of reality. This is not a nightmare, I remind myself. I am here, alive and awake. I twitch my nostrils and continue to look around me.

Were it not for the rotting timber poles strung together with sagging overhead wires resembling shackled prisoners in a malnourished chain gang, this could have been a credible science fiction setting for the adventures of a time-traveller trapped in a street of a medieval town.

I have a vague idea of my whereabouts. Knowing the language is no great advantage, although I have slowly regained my fluency in Bangla. No longer do I have to think in English, panic and then attempt to verbalise a poor translation. I have stopped several times to ask for directions. Even when I was a child, obliged to accompany Ma on her fortnightly visit to her ailing brother in the faded splendour of a once palatial house, Wari was a sprawling suburb of sinewy lanes choked with a conglomeration of two-storeyed buildings.

I do not remember any of the decaying landmarks. The houses look dangerously fragile. They have known a safer, vertical past. They appear to lean on each other like sad, aging lovers seeking the dwindling warmth of a dying passion. Like peeling blisters revealing raw flesh, large chunks of plaster have fallen off the walls. The bricks are exposed to the parasitic embrace of tropical fungi. The vermicelli-thin lane is fringed with open, overflowing gutters clogged with a black viscous filth spilling over to harden into moulds resembling scabs on diseased skin.

The nauseous stench compels me to reach for a handker-chief. Every conceivable state of decomposition assaults the nostrils with a heady pungency. I feel filthy as though I have been immersed in the warmth of a reeking cesspool. There is nothing fresh or wholesome about life here. No trees or grass. Children play mechanically, without laughter. The people I pass bear the burden of a murky life on drooping shoulders, their grimly chiselled faces reflecting an enforced preoccupation with suffering. Shrivelled crows sit on windowsills. Greasy rats scurry between piles of festering rubbish. I can barely see a patch of the sky. Its azure brightness appears artificial among the gloom around me as if a child's hand had clumsily painted it over a dark landscape.

My capacity to be shocked has upset me. Here is further damning evidence of my realigned perspectives. My reactions are those of someone who has never been exposed to such degradation. A part of me feels like a superior being, grateful that I do not have to live among such squalor. My stomach churns with revulsion. I am ashamed, sick, helpless and agitated. The warm bitterness of vomit burns the back of my throat. I lean over the drain with eyes closed. I feel the spasmatic movement of my throat muscles. I retch and cough. The nausea subsides. I rest against a post and fumble for the last remaining cube of barley sugar in my pocket. I crumple the red and white wrapper and throw it in the drain. An invisible life bubbles to the surface and sucks the paper into its evil depth.

Here I can readily believe in the deformities of a physical hell springing from the caverns of a dark, tortuous mind. There is no compensatory dignity anywhere. Life is a raw, unhealed wound, painfully ugly. It is as base as the gutter rats that scourge the streets and the houses; base as the feral coolies who carry crushing loads on their heads and shoulders and walk all day on bare feet. It is the forlorn cry of the wretched homeless belched out into the open by an uncaring and overstuffed city. Life is as demeaning as the depravity which transforms children from toddler innocence to glassy-eyed perversion. This poisoned patient ought to have died by now. But despite the gravity of its condition, I can feel the throbbing pulse of humanity unwilling to surrender a natural gift. It defies prognosis, baffles logic and flouts time. There is an awkward rhythm of joyless tenacity which humbles me into an obeisant respect for human resilience.

The clatter of wheels makes me jump to one side. A push-cart brushes past me, leaving a black mark on the left leg of my jeans. I accept it as a mark of condemnation. It is impossible to avoid being touched by life here. Resistance to its seedy overtures is futile. It hounds, grabs and weakens before it draws you into its folds. It is like an insect that stings its prey into submission before devouring it. You are nagged and stung until you willingly suffer the pain of ignorance and the meanness of your petty concerns.

A woman appears in a doorway to dump a pail of garbage near a flight of broken steps. She stops to stare at me with a childish curiosity as if I don't quite fit into the scheme of things here. Self-consciously I pocket the handkerchief and move on.

I am being followed by a group of bedraggled, solemn-eyed children carrying dented aluminium bowls of varying sizes. I have given them all the loose change in my pocket. I can smell their nearness. They tug the back of my T-shirt. Rudely I have to tell them to leave me alone. They stare at me defiantly, with the derisive suspicion of time-worn cynics. I am from another world, not to be trusted. A little boy keeps tapping my backpack. His tenacity wears me down. I unzip the pack and show him the towel and the water bottle. He grabs the bottle from me and holds it up in the air. He looks at it from different angles. He shakes it violently and holds it up again. The five others form a circle around him and excitedly await, it seems, the liquid's transmutation into an elixir of wealth. They see froth and plenty of bubbles. The bottle is tossed back to me. They stare at me as though I had betrayed them. I am subjected to a string of obscenities casting aspersions on the legitimacy of my birth. They are fluent in abuse. I look at them helplessly. I find it impossible to be angry with such young and deprived children. In unison they expectorate. Globs of mucus-tainted saliva fizzle and shrink near my feet. I am not wanted. It is not an unfamiliar situation. I have seen those eyes before; much older but brimming with mistrust and the same sort of fearful contempt.

Buy a ticket and win a car!
Help the old diggers!
Hey Fred! Here comes another one!
Bloody country's crawling with 'em.
You Indian?
Nah! Japanese mother, Turkish father.
Fred, look at the bloke's name! Woggy Wobbler!
Woggy . . . Smart-arsed little bugger!

I turn a corner. Ahead of me is a small grocery store. I should be able to get some assistance there. A scrawny, fly-ridden dog stops pawing a pile of rubbish and growls weakly at me. My doctor's warning about rabies puts new life into my lethargic steps. The dog buries its snout in the garbage and continues to feed.

I am beginning to doubt the wisdom of walking these lanes. I declined the use of a car. The chauffeur and the *darwan* looked perplexed as I stood outside the gate and waited for a rickshaw. I am immensely relieved that Nadine decided not to come with me. Nafisa's offer to take her to the arts and craft shop to buy a jute doll was an allurement beyond resistance.

I pass a tubewell where several women wait patiently to fill their pitchers. Naked children play around them, splashing in the puddles. Oblivious to the domestic needs, a man sits cross-legged under the spout, his eyes closed, as a small boy pumps the squeaky handle for his lordship's ablution.

My growing apprehension is like a knife's edge caressing my belly. How much does he know? Does it really matter? It was far too long ago. You cannot burn in anger forever. My mouth feels parched and I can hear the breathing of a long-distance runner. My mind is a murky seabed where the ruins of the past lie in scattered heaps. A scintilla of nostalgia probes feebly among them. Briny ghosts dance nimbly around the remnants. They beckon me.

I am already one of you. Can't you see?

Her sharply defined shadow looms between us as a stabbing memory of my selfish impetuosity. The coiled past jumps to life like a striking cobra when I think of Shabana. I can recall every detail of that fateful afternoon on the river. Every feeling, every sensation. The guilt and self-recriminations. They are alive, imprisoned inside me like criminals clamouring for release.

You were wrong, Ifti. Wrong. I can recall everything. Feel everything. I don't need a young man's imagination.

I drift toward the vaporous shores of the university cafeteria. I see the unravaged faces without the shadowy traces of mortality. Ebony eyes flash with the energy of restless curiosity. I am among the babble of young adults seeking instant solutions where none exist.

Life was about observations and neat conclusions. About doing and changing. Discoveries and meanings. Serious bullshitting. It was a time when we paid no attention to the curling edges of our burning dreams. We disputed everything—fought over politics; disagreed about purpose and meaning; quarrelled about religion; argued about sex and worried about its transient pleasure. We envied Iftiqar and cursed his luck with his retinue of admiring females. He could speak with a monarchal authority. He knew. With his experience he had to know.

His voice echoes crisply as if I have just heard him speak before tunnelling my way to the present from the tin-roofed room with the dirty floor and the spartan wooden chairs and tables.

The argument began after a unanimous decision to miss a lecture on deductive logic. Despite our reverence for Aristotle, an analysis of *Prior Analytics* held little appeal before several cups of morning tea. We preferred to listen to Iftiqar boasting about his latest conquest. With a typical undergraduate enthusiasm for vulgarity, we pressed him for graphic details.

'Describe it?' He looked at us incredulously. 'How can you describe? It dies as it fulfils. It's like looking at a withered flower. You can envisage its peak of bloom, recall the vitality of its colour. But the fragrance! The fragrance eludes you. Its essence is beyond remembrance. Memory cannot revive the thrill of sensuality. It is impossible to recapture the sensations of those burning ripples of pleasure which pulsate in the limbs as if there were writhing snakes inside you. Memory can give shape to an experience; recall a face, a place, an object, a conversation. Stir emotions. But it can never bring back that fleeting ecstasy, that unique moment when you are trapped between a raging fire and a mountainous slab of ice. That instant when you feel your senses trilling. That moment when the mind releases itself from its earthly anchorage and levitates, oh so briefly! That explosion into an awareness of the self torn between the bliss and the pain. Then that vague twilight sadness as you become conscious of the calm within you and the dullness of your surroundings. How can you describe all that with any measure of accuracy? There is very little proximity between the recollection and the actual experience. That is what gives reality the anxiety of uncertainty.'

Extravagant words from a treasure-laden mind. His life, we

often said enviously, spreads before him like a lavish feast. He can do anything. Be anyone. Have whatever he chooses.

But we were wrong, weren't we Ifti? The future blew up on us with a punitive violence as if fate had finally run out of patience with our arrogance and decided to hand out a severe sentence for ignoring the fragility of the human condition.

I have often debated whether I treated myself with undue leniency. The excuses have been plausible enough in the comforting obscurity of another continent. Unhappiness sometimes creates a harsh moral climate, be it only for a short period. There is a tendency to survey the past for blemishes which may, in the natural scale of retributive justice, account for one's current predicament. Guilt becomes a natural ally for primitive superstition to spin an imagined web of ill-fortune waiting to trap the offender for past misdeeds. Publicly we may boldly denounce such misgivings as utter nonsense, but within our own minds the disquiet lingers. Perhaps that is the reason I am seeking some form of atonement, even though a part of me remains unrepentant. I know of no certain way of redressing a situation I did not deliberately plan.

Reason dictates that there is no logical connection between my inexpedient circumstances and those few unguarded hours with Shabana. Until recently I regarded it to be of paltry significance; one of those memorable but inconsequential interludes to be attributed to a common weakness in a young man's character. I have argued that a sense of decency, fair-mindedness and loyalty to my best friend should have made me more responsible and compelled me to assert enough restraint to avert the encounter. But isn't that looking at a slice of the past from a frosty and inflexible perspective of middle age? At the time there was some regret, guilt and self-chastisement, but I did not feel like a cheat.

She was special. He had made that quite clear. I was to keep in touch with her and help her while he was away with the *Mukhti Bahinis*, fighting the Pakistani army. She reached out to me in her loneliness. We often met for lunch. We took enormous risks by taking day trips into the countryside where the war raged after dusk.

It was Shabana who suggested the boat ride. I have never believed there was anything sinister in her motive. She wished to escape the reminder of a chaotic city gripped by fear, rumour and panic. It led to one of those spontaneously reckless moments of youthful passion one lives to regret, and yet without which life would be an endless blur of unbroken grey, utterly predictable and without a trace of honesty to one's instincts.

I stop at the shop to ask for more directions. The bare-bodied shopkeeper sits cross-legged behind bulging sacks of rice, lentil, tumeric, flour, onions, sugar, ginger and garlic. Behind him there are rows of shelves with an assortment of glass jars and canisters of mustard oil, *ghee*, pickles, biscuits and sweets. I am surprised to find such a well-stocked shop amid such poverty. There is not a customer in sight.

He points with a hand-fan and mumbles, 'About two miles.'

Here a mile can mean anything up to five kilometres. A ten *taka* note does wonders for his descriptive precision. It is only about half a kilometre straight ahead followed by a right turn. The money mobilises him. He squeezes out of the shop. I refuse his offer of a cup of tea and a cigarette.

He sidles up to me. '*Charas, Shaheb? Ganja?*' He whispers, his shifty eyes alert for lurking strangers. 'First-class quality.'

It was a mistake to bribe him. I have exposed myself to be an assailable foreigner, super rich by his standards. I detect the glint of greed in his eyes. He hitches up the front of his *lungi* and walks beside me.

'Girls, *Shaheb?*' He grins lecherously, exposing a set of honey-coloured teeth. 'Fresh from the village. Young and unspoilt. Special rates for you, *Shaheb*. Only seven hundred *takas* for the night in *Shaheb*'s hotel. No extra money for delivery. Hello, *Shaheb!* Five hundred for you. What is your offer? *Ay je Bhai! Shonen! Shaheb!* No need to be angry. I am a reasonable man. Four hundred. Last offer!'

I am furious with myself for behaving like a bumbling foreigner unfamiliar with the local customs. I was gullible enough to be cheated by a rickshaw *wallah* and offloaded unceremoniously before reaching Wari. I have lost the cunning for bargaining. I was no match for his skills. After a feeble negotiation, I succumbed to a highly inflated fare. I was stung into a state of surrender after seeing his reed-thin body, his torn singlet and his bare feet. How could I listen to the tale of his wretched struggle without being ashamed of the comparatively trivial concerns which continue to fluster me? In the end he dropped me off near a dug-up lane nowhere near Wari. With consummate ease he managed to extract a *baksheesh* as well. My reward was a toothless smile and an oracular prediction of a place in Heaven. The ways of the world have caught up with ethereal living. I should be on a short list for deluxe accommodation, judging by the money I paid. It may be of some comfort in my old age to know that I had the foresight to invest in a celestial cubicle to rest my weary soul.

The number 21 has been scrawled with charcoal on the low brick wall. The house looks liveable from the outside. It has been whitewashed recently. The window frames look new. Near the front entrance a fruitless guava tree stands like a sentry, tired and droopy after an uneventful night's vigil.

The dingy corridor smells strongly of urine. The walls are unevenly splotched with expectorated *paan* juice forming irregular patterns as if a painter had shaken a wet brush in a barren moment of artistic exasperation. There are no name plates or numbers. I knock on a door facing the steep and narrow stairs. A frazzled woman, with wet hair and a crying baby in one arm, flings the door open. I step back a couple of paces. I assume the bellicose man glaring over her shoulder is her husband.

Iftiqar? Iftiqar who? She has never heard of a Mr Fazal. Upstairs maybe. She slams the door shut. The bolt clicks with a savage finality.

Indecision makes me linger at the bottom of the stairs. My enthusiasm deserts me. What shall I say to him? How do I greet him? Should I be reserved and settle for the formality of a handshake? Would Bangla be more appropriate than English?

A vendor's high-pitched voice draws my attention, the way it used to just before morning recess at school. I hurry back to the doorless entrance. The caged wooden trolley with the glass compartments is a replica of Mastan's cart of savouries. My mouth waters at the memory of the delights which awaited us at the break. *Amsat*, chillied cucumbers, hot nuts, spiced rice bubbles, pickled berries, guavas, *chaat* and *phuchka* with a filling of chick peas and tamarind water. The one-eyed Mastan was never rattled as we milled around him with coins in our hands. He was a striking figure with a black patch over his left eye and a matching coloured Jinnah cap perched at a precariously tilted angle on his head. We never found out much about him. He avoided our questions about his eye patch. He never told us where he lived or who prepared all the food he sold us. With a deadpan expression he gave us enough information about the old part of Dhaka to fuel our gossip. We speculated about his true identity. He was a smuggler, a spy for the brothers, a notorious gangster at night, a professional gambler wanted by the police, a man with a voracious sexual appetite and a dong like a blunt *talwar* rampaging through the *bustees* crowded with deprived females.

Gingerly I begin to climb the steps. I think of the excitement of uncertainty we experienced during our last few weeks together.

The ascent toward our dreams, our fellow Bangalis, is difficult. There are sacrifices we have to make for our new country, the land Guru Dev described for us . . .

How well I remember that rich, hypnotic voice!

In the dark and chilly corridors of Bengal's history, Sheik Mujib was a brief respite, an ephemeral flash of light, a flickering glow of warmth. He kindled hope in a battered race. Above everything else, he deprogrammed our servile acceptance of the military yoke and made us believe in our ability to be free. His vision of an idyllic Bangladesh belonged to the pristine realm of a mythical past. He was an amateur fisherman determined to challenge the sea. Sheer courage and a stubborn faith in his own ability made him steer the overcrowded boat into the rough waters where the monstrous waves awaited us with a ferocity no one had anticipated.

7 March 1971. Close to the day of reckoning.

We pay no attention to the heavily armed soldiers patrolling the streets. More than one hundred thousand Bangalis wait patiently in the Ramna racecourse. The young and the militant are pathetically defiant. They carry rocks, sharpened bamboo sticks and knives.

We squeeze into a space near the raised wooden platform. There is a roar of victory when he finally appears. We see him in the light of a shimmering white haze, like an angel of redemption.

The messiah stands under a red and white awning, soaking up the adulation of a desperate people. He smirks with grim satisfaction. His arsenal of willing Bangalis is stocked to full capacity. The young are willing to die for him. No one has told them about the infinitely dark magnitude of death. They covet posthumous glory. They wish to be *Shaheeds*. There are patriotic songs and slogans. Handclaps and cheers. Thunderous voices. Passions simmer in vats of thick anger. He waits patiently until we flagellate ourselves into a state of self-sacrificing carelessness. Slowly his hands rise in the air. The Rasputin eyes flash with authority. The rumbling ceases.

'*Bhai Shob!*'

'This is how an ancient god would have addressed his tribes,' Iftiqar whispers sarcastically. He is tense and uneasy about the impending confrontation. He is not a wholehearted supporter of the Awami League. He has been uncharacteristically cautious. He has a contingency plan. He has borrowed money from me. I have been given Shabana's address and phone number. He has assumed that my lack of involvement in the students' political skirmishes will enable me to stay behind in Dhaka, should the situation deteriorate.

The crowd is transfixed into a state of worshipful silence. *Bongobhandu* pauses again to look around him. The timing is perfect. 'My beloved countrymen!'

There is a volcanic eruption of euphoria. The earth reverberates with the noise of stomping feet and triumphant voices. '*Aamar desh, tomar desh, Bangladesh! Bangladesh! Joi Bangla! Joi Bangla!*'

The rest of the fiery oration is, as usual, faultless.

Eighteen days later the world turned upside down. Futures altered. Dreams vaporised. I did not see Iftiqar again. He disappeared into the darkness of an evil night which opened its belly to allow the Pakistani soldiers to tumble into the streets to unleash Yahya's demonic wrath.

25 March. Midnight—the hour when evil revealed its contorted visage of hatred. Dhaka had closed its eyes like a weary Duncan, unaware of the stealthy footsteps of treachery. Pye-dogs and stray cats watched the *jawans* spreading themselves like the microbes of a deadly disease, their presence undetected until the malignancy was beyond remedy.

The spring night lit up like a carnival celebration. Like errant arrows, tracer bullets jagged across the inert dome of darkness. The dull noise of automatic weapons sounded harmless. Fireworks to mark the conclusion of a political settlement, many thought as they rushed out to be killed.

The subcontinent was being reshaped again. It was destined not to live in peace. It gripped life too intensely, with a primitive passion, to allow a serene existence. India was a soul in perpetual torment, burning in the flames of its own vitality, consuming itself and others with a voracity which flabbergasted its conquerors and ultimately defeated them. The British had hacked Pakistan from its flanks. And now this . . .

There is a sharp click of a latch.

Even without the beard the face would have been difficult to recognise. Unknown hands have inserted a hypodermic needle and siphoned the sparkle from him. His face is a shrunken blank canvas from which the iridescence has been washed away. It is like a fertile green land struck by drought and transformed into a death valley landscaped with skeletons. They have all disappeared—the alert eyes, the poetry and music, the passions, the desire to outrun life itself. Everything that made him such a vibrant personality has gone, swept away by the purling river of time into the murky oceanic depths of the past.

The roar of an avalanche begins to recede from my ears. A layered fog rolls in. It is around me. It creeps inside me. The derelict mansion overlooking the infinitude of my dreams is reduced to a shrunken pile of rubble near my feet. The impossible hope I have kept alive and brought with me shrivels quickly and dies without a sound. There is a hollow being carved inside me.

The past seems like an impeccable lie.

The meagrely furnished room is dismally dirty. It is lacerated with the negligence of a careless bachelor's life. An unnatural light filters through the dust-streaked window and tinctures the damp patches on the walls. There is something ominous about the light. Something sad and lingering. It is the colour of withering mortality, of silence and finiteness. It is a room for storing mutilated dreams.

A dust storm appears to have swept through the room. Between two makeshift bookshelves of buckled timber and chipped bricks, there is a large rectangular table. One of its missing legs has been replaced by a stack of bricks. It is the nerve centre of the room. It is like a crowded bazaar in the middle of a thinly populated village. My eyes sweep over the mess. There is a sheaf of unopened letters stacked against the wall. Four unripe guavas and bottles of spices surround a telephone partially hidden under a phone book and a folded newspaper. There are tea bags, stationery items, a manual typewriter, cigarette packets, a pair of scissors, boxes of matches and burnt-out matchsticks, coins, razor blades, toothbrushes and a tube of toothpaste, a bar of soap touching a mouldy loaf a bread, a dirty towel reeking of overuse, cooking pots and cutlery. I spy a camp stove, a tin of kerosene, bottles of water and a kettle under the table.

On either side of a small bed, there are rusty tin trunks crammed with books. I think of them as rotting treasure chests in a pirate's cave. Some of the books have fallen on the floor. I am familiar with a few of the titles. *The Myth of the Magus. The White Goddess. Travels in the Moghul Empire. Towards Universal Man.* There are a few old university standards—*The Oresteian Trilogy, The Birth of Tragedy*, an Arden edition of *The Winter's Tale, The Romantic Imagination.*

He motions me toward the only chair in the room. It is an oversized armchair covered in faded green brocade. With a sweep of a hand he clears a space for himself on the unmade bed. A pile of unwashed clothes slide to the floor.

One of the bookshelves is within touching distance. I am secretly delighted with the illustrious company he keeps. There's Borges, Cela and Marquez. Llosa and Namora. Fuentes. Mahfouz. Other names are beyond me. Luis Arturo

Ramos, Ariel Dorfman, Vincenzo Consolo. Leonardo Sciascia. Consolo and Busi. It is strange to find their works in such shabby surroundings. I associate them with roomy studies and proper shelves, subdued lighting and leather recliners, fireplaces and chamber music. They would give soul to Keith's study.

We begin a sluggish and uncomfortable journey through convoluted streets echoing with hidden voices and muffled footfalls behind us. Intuitively we reach a tacit understanding about not looking over our shoulders too frequently.

He is curious about Australia. 'I've heard good things about the country.'

I fumble for words.

'You don't sound very enthusiastic.'

I had not intended to allow a detectable note of pessimism to enter my voice. It is difficult to be positive about the Australia of the 1990s. Had he asked me fifteen years ago, I would have given him an unequivocal answer. It was a rich country in more ways that Iftiqar could have imagined. Australia used to remind me of a naive, uninhibited youth born into affluence, intelligent yet thoughtless about an opulent lifestyle, unintentionally arrogant, yet to discover the pains of growing up. It was a simple country in terms of its hedonistic priorities and its earth-bound pride in its diggers' courage, in the unifying spirit of *fair go* and the prized bonds of mateship, certain about its virtues in a good-natured but blinkered and unquestioning way. Australia now stands tottering on the brink of adulthood, enmeshed in the process of finding its soul and learning about the traumas of maturity. It is beginning to think for itself and grappling with the self-destructive nature of greed. It is trapped in a cultural flux, reluctant to shed a nostalgic ancestral image in favour of an evolving mixture whose shape and ethos cannot be predicted. Australians are learning about the commonality of the human flaws it shares with the rest of humanity. We are learning all there is to learn about imperfection. The country is slowly teaching itself the difficult task of being humble.

Iftiqar tells me about his job as a journalist and the voluntary work with a relief agency. He spends most of his holidays on the devastated coastal islands in the Bay of Bengal.

I ask him about the recent cyclone.

There is a faraway note in his voice as if he is narrating an experience he struggles to believe. He looks at me with soft, kind eyes as though I am a child incapable of comprehending what he is about to tell me.

'It was almost as if some invisible hand had stripped the world to its bare essentials. There was the schizophrenic sea showing us its gentle face, sounding its innocence. There was hardly any wind. The bleached sand did not stir. There was little else around us. This was how the planet could have been in its infancy. The twentieth-century mind was useless here. This was no place for logic or technology. Language was mesmerised by the awesome dimensions of space gaping at us like a toothless idiot. We were like a travelling circus of fools. There we were with tents, blankets, food, medicine, doctors, nurses, builders and all kinds of equipment—the sorts of things you need in a major catastrophe. The only problem was there was no trace of a village. No one to attend to, no corpses to bury. I walked on the beach with a Swedish doctor. The sun was fierce. The earth, sea and sky were locked in a conspiracy of burning silence. We stopped several times to listen. Nothing. Not even a vulture's triumphant cry. "*This is a very strange land*," the Swede whispered. I could see his confidence in a neat Lutheran scheme of life and the universe was badly shaken. He stepped into the sea and scooped up a handful of water to wash his face. "*Even God loses his voice here.*" It was like standing on the edge of a distant star, looking into a deeper darkness, trying to make some sense of the universe and one's place in it. There was a feeling of utter desolation. I felt small and incomplete. The mind became a mechanism which refused to work. After we had walked several kilometres, we came upon some high ground. We walked inland. The roots of a few naked trees barely clung to the earth. Several dead cows straddled the top branches, their teats dangling like Chinese chimes without any sound. It was the calmest place I have ever known. Entire villages, with their populations, had settled quietly under the sea.'

My stunned silence draws a soft laugh from him. 'Unbelievable, isn't it? There are no limits to the frontiers of human calamity. Even the most monumental personal problems become insignificant after I come back from one of those islands. Nothing seems to matter except an awareness of inadequacy. I grieve about existence.' Wearily he lights the stove. 'Tea?'

Without thinking I say, 'No, thank you.'

'Oh, the water is safe,' he assures me in a caustic tone of voice. 'I boiled it twice this morning, especially for you. Of course, it may still upset your delicate foreigner's constitution.'

Iftiqar knows he has made me uncomfortable. I tell him about my struggle to become an inconspicuous part of the mainstream life here. He looks amused.

The poverty has shocked me to an unexpected extent, I confess. I am not idealistic enough to dignify its manifestations of suffering I have confronted. My family has been the other disappointment. What upsets me most is my inability to slip back into a tradition I assumed was an integral part of me.

'Tradition is such a common word, isn't it?' Iftiqar muses aloud, kneeling on the floor to fill the kettle. 'Yet when you think about it, the concept is not easy to understand. It can impute stagnation and exclude change. It may suggest fear and insecurity. The desire to cling to a past may be an admission of an inability to change, or it could indicate a wish to escape unhappiness by reverting to a world we once knew.

It is so easy to evoke the past as a stable routine of familiar practices and call it tradition.'

'It's more than that. Tradition has to do with a sense of belonging,' I say stiffly. I am unimpressed with his comments. He has encapsulated my crisis. 'There is a lingering foreignness about Australia that I find disturbing. I don't have anything to hang on to with conviction, nothing I can really call my own. I don't feel passionately for anything that happens there.'

'As a first-generation migrant you probably sacrificed the right to belong.' He turns to face me. 'What made you leave? Was it the continuing violence? Was that it?'

I nod uncertainly. 'It was at the time.'

'So you went looking for a morally better world. I won't ask if you found it. That would be a silly question.'

'I did what I thought was right at the time.'

'Sometimes conscience leads us to questionable decisions. Look at me. The way I am, the way I live. It shocked you when you walked in. No! It's all right. There's no need to hide your disgust. I might have done a lot better if I had chosen to ignore the plight of the Biharis.'

'Why?'

'I paid a hefty price for speaking up. I came back to Dhaka nearly two months after the Pakistanis surrendered. You had already left. One evening I saw some thugs beating up an old Bihari. I managed to chase them away. I saw several ugly incidents, including one where a man was stabbed to death in front of an approving mob. His crime was that he spoke Urdu. Nothing more. There is nothing worse than spiteful victors. The hysteria for revenge made us a very unforgiving people. I complained to the government and to the army chiefs. I made a public fuss about the treatment of the Biharis.'

'And? Did anything happen?'

'I became unemployable. No one wanted to know me. I became a hate-figure, a supporter of the *mauras*. A despicable traitor. I had to go into hiding. It was a time for patriotic opportunism. There were some in the *Mukhti Bahini* with plenty of money and a leisurely life in Calcutta. During the war they disappeared. They turned up in Dhaka for the victory celebrations with heroic tales and loud voices to demonstrate their fanatical patriotism. They demanded the death penalty for collaborators and repatriation for the Biharis. There were ample rewards for the zealots.'

'How did you manage?'

'I scraped a living by tutoring. I couldn't even go near the university. I soon realised I had no chance of completing my honours. Nafisa and Zafar helped me. I owe your sister a great debt. She assisted me financially without ever touching my ego. With time the witch-hunt exhausted itself. The headhunters had their fill. The grimness of Bangladesh sobered everyone. After a couple of years Zafar offered me a job with *The Voice*. Even now there are people who think I am a traitor.'

'Why didn't you ever try to leave the country?'

'Because I didn't want to. You probably think I was a fool, but I doubt if I could live anywhere else. This is me. I am not resilient enough to take on another identity. I would feel as if I had betrayed myself. It is a shortcoming I occasionally regret.'

My attention wanders back to the shelves. I am fascinated by the diversity of the titles. *Krishna and Orpheus, The Literature of Fidelity, Is this Theosophy?, Extreme Situations, The Art of Mugul India, Two Faces of Time, The Dream and the Underworld* . . .

'These books . . . it's quite a collection. Most of them wouldn't be available here.'

He looks at them proudly. 'They are my family. Through them I know I am alive. They have given unselfishly without ever demanding anything in return.' He picks up a book and caresses its cover. 'They are all I need. They enable me to leave this wretched space and live in worlds where I can dream and feel. My evenings are spent in great luxury.'

I fidget irritably. I have to goad myself to venture into his personal life. 'You never married?'

He pretends not to have heard me. 'Are you sure you won't have a cup of tea?'

'I think I might,' I say bravely. 'Without milk and sugar.'

I detect a faint, discerning smile. 'You must tell me more about your life in Australia.' He busies himself with cups, tea bags and hot water.

The world changes to an éclat of shifting shades and variable moods, flushed and breathless, gasping in summer's tightening embrace. Beads of perspiration, like melting pearls, caress me with the lightness of a butterfly's wings. I taste their saltiness on the tip of my tongue.

The boat rocks gently.

I lift my head to see where we are. Beyond the narrow bamboo arch is summer's glorious display of madness. The wavering horizon is smudged with broad, careless strokes of ripe orange and shimmering gold streaked with angry vermilion.

A sensory definition of our location becomes meaningless in the openness of the susurrating river. I feel careless and light-hearted. Let it take us where it will.

I have a yearning for the winged companions of my childhood afternoons under the forbidden jackfruit trees where the spirits play. There is a premonition of a painful loss, as if something precious is about to slip out of my grasp.

Her presence continues to disturb. It has weakened me to a state of muteless wandering. Wilting modesty smears the lines of propriety.

We fear the insecurity of curfewed nights. The darting shadows. Gunfire and explosions. The dreaded knock on the door. We shiver in the chill of uncertainty.

'When will it end?' she whispers.

I draw her close to avoid an answer.

I become a child without bearings in a densely foliaged land. There is a struggle to understand the sporadic intimations of incomplete knowledge.

There are sensations beyond experience.

Voices beyond memory.

'We should be heading back.'

'Soon.'

'How soon?'

'Whenever soon.'

Affectation dies by degrees. Coyness flees. Beyond burning reason we behold a mad country crowded with sinuous intentions. For now she is everything. Everything.

> And I will make thee beds of roses
> And a thousand fragrant posies,
> A cap of flowers, and a kirtle
> Embroidered all with leaves of myrtle . . .

How often I have heard him say the words! Does he remember them in a watery ditch, his fingers gripping the coldness of death?

Her eyes laugh wildly.

How soft and flushed the skin she wears!

Leap over the wall of guilt, the river urges. Leap over it!

Frigid angels tumble from the trembling sky. Musical serpents devour them. His voice serenades us.

> A belt of straw and ivy buds,
> With coral clasps and amber studs:
> And if these pleasures may thee move,
> Come live with me and be my love.

There is a shrine to be sought in summer's deep grove with the tip of a leaping flame. How frail and fresh the blessing glazed with the dew of heavenly youth! I have to steal this moment of silent creation and remove it from the torturous grip of unfeeling time.

We are taut, entwined wires charged with a power to glimpse the world as it should be. We become impressions of overlapping prints on wet sand. We touch forever in an instant of abandon.

Later, we mumble the promises of ingenuous lovers. We are too drowsy to watch the horizon's transition to a crepuscular grey, like a thin band of eye-shadow on a sleepy lid.

Under the bruises of the twilight sky, there is a forlorn journey home. Resolutions die quickly. I am left with the burden of a sad wisdom.

The memory. Oh, the memory!

'. . . a winter city. That is perhaps an apt description. Do you remember the geography assignment on gold? We picked Ballarat. Never imagined I'd live there one day. It's a city of pubs, schools and howling winds, conservative and politely curious about the rest of the world. There is a medieval dankness about the place in the long winter months. In some ways Ballarat is a very Christian city. It encourages propriety, self-restraint and tolerance. Perhaps that has something to do with its stoical acceptance of anything foreign, as long as it is not too outrageous. Culturally it is an active city. There are several theatrical companies which tirelessly churn out their yearly share of musicals and comedies. Never anything too serious or intellectually demanding. We are too provincial for that. Then there is an art gallery patronised by the grey-suited and pearl-strung members of the establishment with time to practice their modulated voices and stylised gestures of proper upbringing over long lunches. It is a community I do not threaten. I feel safe in the streets, knowing that at any given time I normally form a minority of one. Suburban life is comfortable and conducive to cerebral inertia. I live in a lovely area, shaded with wattle and gum trees, quiet and unpretentious. Like a good Australian I have been seduced by the common dream of a brick-veneer house on a quarter of an acre of land. The neighbours, unlike the free-roaming koalas, are politely amiable from a distance. There's Tom and Bev. Nick and Penny. Gavin's been recently divorced. Brian and Jane. The others are a composite of hands and faces. We wave to each other and occasionally discuss the state of the backyard vegie . . . er, vegetable . . . patch, the fickleness of Ballarat's weather and the rising cost of living when we meet at the local supermarket or the petrol station. On weekends we reinforce the cult of community uniformity by starting up our lawnmowers within minutes of each other. On Sundays you can almost swear the neighbourhood is a discordant industrial forest alive with the noise of manicuring machines. I am a school teacher. I have no idea why I chose to teach. I sort of walked into it. I now feel as though I have undertaken an extended exercise in masochism, a desperately contrasting alternative to the unbearable privileges of a *zamindar*. I wanted to erase the past and assume a more humane identity. I wanted to prove to myself that I could make it on my own. The desire to preserve my independence keeps me going. I don't owe gratitudes or favours to anyone. I can resist family pressures without remorse or guilt. But what a price I have to pay! Teaching has become a painful interlude between two holidays. There is little to recommend it. It is stressful and unrewarding. The idea of gentle scholars dedicated to the intellectual advancement of motivated students has been destroyed by the frightful realities of a pseudo-academic jungle where we are simultaneously the predators and the victims. We hunt for power and authority . . . ah, the current euphemism is *responsibility*. We draw on our cunning and reserves of strength to drive ourselves to the top. By the time we are there, no energy is left to do anything clever or innovative. The guts has gone out of learning. The curious young mind is a rarity. The young have to be entertained. The

accent is on enjoyment. Kids want to cram a life-time's pleasure into their adolescence. Alcohol, sex, drugs—whatever
turns them on and detracts them from thinking about a shaky
future. As parents we don't often contribute to their security.
It is one of the tragedies of the West that we thrust responsibilities on the young before they are ready. We want them out
of our homes when they are eighteen, and unconsciously we
create such impossible conditions that they are only too glad
to leave. When I first arrived in Australia, I thought it was an
ideal sanctuary, prosperous and inexperienced in suffering. I
knew nothing about the Aborigines then. It appeared to be a
humane society, a just society—generous and friendly. I suppose if you get to know anything well enough you discover
its flaws. It was my mistake to think that Australia was nearly
perfect. It was an ill-judged conclusion. Behind its ornate
facade of wealth lay the weaknesses of any human society. I
soon discovered a broad streak of narcissism in its extroverted
personality. But more recently it has become a very frustrated
youth unable to see a clear reflection of itself to reaffirm its
self-love. I don't know if my criticism is an outpouring of
disillusionment or whether it is an uncharitable comment on
a tired society rapidly running out of creative energy and
searching for someone to blame. We look with envy at Singapore. South Korea makes us apprehensive. We are eager to
spend more on the armed forces because of Indonesia's proximity. Japan scares us witless. We play down their success
with prejudices. We console ourselves by exaggerating their
mechanical existence, their lack of leisure and their suicide
rate. We don't wish to be like them. We would rather continue
to wallow in the established pleasures of our lives—the pub,
the beach, the footy and the barbie. We'll be right, we mutter
to ourselves, even though the tone has been unconvincing of
late. But don't let my views give you a distorted impression.
Australia's problems diminish into insignificance when I com-
pare them with what I have seen here. Greed probably makes

me very critical. I don't want to do with less. It is still a very liveable country. You can develop an indescribable communion with the emptiness of the continent. There are times when I go into the outback and swear to become a hermit. There's space out there for the expansion of one's vision, for self-renewal. Its vast empty centre is like the microcosmic eye of the universe—mysterious and full of wonder. You feel as if there is something in the emptiness which I am not yet ready to see. What else can I tell you? My personal life is in shambles. You probably know I married an Australian girl. It didn't work out. We separated a few months ago. I have a daughter, Nadine. That's about it, my life in the intervening years. Not very exciting. Not exactly the way I had planned things.'

His face softens. There is a sheen of curiosity in his eyes. 'Your daughter?'

'She is with me. Nafisa took her shopping.'

'I would have enjoyed meeting her.'

'You can!' I pounce on the opportunity. 'Her *aqeeqa* is next week. I would like you to come.'

'No.' He purses his lips and shakes his head. 'No. I would be out of place. Everyone you knew—we knew—will be there. It will be an occasion for successful people—the top public servants, army personnel, barristers, surgeons, executives, businessmen. I don't belong there. It's no longer my world.'

He remains firm despite my attempts to convince him.

'By the way, did you ever see Shabana after the war?' The toneless question sounds innocuous enough. I concentrate on the heavily creased spine of a paperback edition of *Ulysses*. It must be the same copy I presented him on his twentieth birthday. I remember the words I inscribed inside. *Love is of the beautiful.* It was a year we were heavily under the influence of Socratic wisdom.

His eyes narrow. He looks at me closely. 'Once. After that I never saw her again. She married a diplomat.' Something in my face makes him smile. He waves his hands in a careless manner. 'There's no use chasing shadows from the past. It's best to leave them where they are. A daughter . . . I can imagine you as a contented father. That is my greatest regret. I have no one to love. I spent too much time being bitter. You know the Pakistanis killed my family—my parents, my sisters. They were very thorough in avenging my escape. When the war ended, I came back to a block of land. An army tank had demolished our house. I became so scared of relationships that I isolated my feelings and imprisoned them somewhere inside me. They died of neglect. I couldn't bear the pain of loss again.'

The afternoon light begins to steal away like a voyeur who has seen enough. Mutable shadows begin to announce the approaching evening. I have that empty sensation which reminds me of a visit to a graveyard. I have spent time with my memories. I feel sad and lost. The senses dull. I feel obliged not to leave too hastily. But now that it is time to go, there is a feeling of immense relief.

He follows me to the door.

'I would like to see you again.'

'Come to the office and meet Zafar. He'd enjoy seeing you. Come with your daughter and have some lunch with us. Will you find your way back?'

'I have been lost before.'

The door shuts behind me.

I know we are not friends any more.

SIX

The shrubs rustle and then subside into an innocent silence. I must have frightened the animal away. Like a skinned snake, part of an intestine lies under a banana tree. The odour of offal is a powerful reminder of the innate passion for ritualistic killing.

'Bismillah eh Rahman er Rahim . . . ', the imam would have chanted, his mind on the plentiful bounty of food and money, as the cold edge of sharpened steel descended on the quivering throat.

Where the ground begins to slope toward the creek, a mixture of sand and sawdust has been dumped to cover the traces of the early morning slaughter. It was a job carelessly done. I can see russet stains on tufts of grass. Columns of red ants crawl in opposite directions with the mechanical precision of battle troops on the march. Khuda Buksh's militant Hindus continue to conduct their nefarious campaign against Allah's favourites. I prod a spot where they burrowed into the ground. The moist earth gives way. The front of my runner is slathered in reddish sawdust and sand. I feel conspiratorial, as though I have participated in a forbidden pagan ritual. I wipe the runner with a withered banana leaf. The stains spread to the sides of my shoe.

From where I stand, the dome of the red and white marquee looks like a huge helium balloon. This is where the commoners will dine—those relatives and acquaintances who are a numerical necessity to the evening's success. They will be the marginal guests, neither wealthy nor too influential, undeserving of our personal attention inside the house. A few more names have been added to the guest list, Ma informed me yesterday.

In the distance there is a dull sound of an axe thudding against wood. Wispy trails of smoke curl upwards into the crystalline morning like strips of muslin drifting in a breeze. The fires will soon be blazing.

9.26 am.

I have to meet Morich Mia to express my gratitude in anticipation of a dinner only an *Ustad Baorchi* can prepare. Morich Mia is the great-grandson of the legendary Dhakaiya cook, Mezaj Mia, who catered for the gastronomical greed of many a *nawab* and hastened their departure for the pastoral joys of *Behaesht*.

It must have taken some coaxing to bring Morich Mia out of retirement. It wasn't at all easy, Hashim boasted, to find the dwarf with four splenic wives, a gaggle of aging and aggrieved mistresses and a brood of vengeful children, legitimate and otherwise, on his heels for a slice of the fortune he amassed as Dhaka's foremost chef. In his old age, Morich Mia has reputedly turned into a rabid misogynist, sick of women and their greedy demands, their insistence on fidelity and their lack of understanding about his polygamous needs. I am told that because of his lack of trust in females, he has reluctantly turned to male company for solace and relaxation.

Servants were sent out to comb the old areas of Dhaka. After several days of effort, they found him at a *qawali*, stuporous on *thari*, among a group of noisy boys. Hashim himself undertook the unpleasant trip to the foul-smelling interior of Chor Bazaar to flatter and bribe the old man into cooking one final meal to celebrate an auspicious event for the family he and his forefathers had served with such distinction.

We are apprehensive about the dinner. Morich Mia's temper is remembered and dreaded by all the families who have been able to afford his service. There is a well-founded rumour that his favourite pastime is to coin nasty invectives which he unleashes on unsuspecting guests and servants if anything displeases him. He is in the habit of standing on a stool or a ladder to expectorate his curses into the copper pots before walking away from half-cooked meals if he suspects that the *ghee* is adulterated or the saffron is not genuine.

I thought it was prudent not to see him yesterday. He was not happy with some of the arrangements. We heard him yelling at his helpers all evening. Early this morning, even before the butcher and the *imam* arrived, Hashim's car was sent to fetch Morich Mia. Among his helpers are four chubby young boys, specially brought from Shopnoganj, to look after his personal needs. They have been taught to make *paan* and cups of scalding sweet tea flavoured with cinnamon. A camp cot has been placed under a *neem* tree for his hourly petrissage. The boys are under strict instructions to keep their hands warm and not to question, contradict or cross the great man. All his needs are to be fulfilled. I sounded a note of cautionary concern, but Ma was in no mood to listen. All his needs! She reiterated innocently. If Morich Mia scolded them, it was to be considered a privilege. If he did not allow them time off for lunch, they were to go hungry without complaining. Under no circumstances was he to be upset.

Behind the marquee, a khaki awning shelters the food. The formidable task of peeling, cutting and grinding mounds of ginger, garlic and onions has been entrusted to three of Morich Mia's assistants. They arrived yesterday afternoon and worked through the night.

The best possible ingredients are at Morich Mia's disposal. Specially made *ghee* was ordered from Brahmanbaria. Milk arrived in stainless steel containers from our dairy farm in Savar. Saffron has been flown in from strife-torn Srinagar. Hashim's friends in the Iranian embassy were gracious enough to supply us with sultanas, pistachio nuts and almonds. Several sacks of basmati rice have been purchased from a shady merchant in Nawabpur. Ma herself has undertaken the tedious job of making the yoghurt.

The menu has provoked arguments and tantrums. My contribution was negligible, although I can claim responsibility for surprising everyone into a momentary state of speechlessness. My opinion was sought more out of politeness than necessity. My thoughtless suggestion about some vegetable dishes stopped the quarrel and drew frozen looks of disbelief. I backtracked rapidly after the belated realisation that the quantity and variety of meat would determine the success of such a feast. Any sign of vegetable, barring niggardly mixtures of lettuce, tomatoes and cucumbers floating in lemon juice, was bound to be misconstrued as a cost-saving exercise, sparking rumours about the decline of the Chaudharies. That would never do. Reputation before health. *Izzat* before nutrition. Ma's will prevailed.

The menu looks superb. *Shirmal* is a rare treat these days. It is to be served with a mixture of *shami kebabs* and *bhoti kebabs*. They are to be followed by mutton *biryani, kata masala* and *murgh mussalam,* all to be washed down with *borhani.* For dessert there is to be a choice between *shahi tukra* and *zafrani firni.* It is not the sort of food to be found in the Indian restaurants of Melbourne where little beside the coloured spectacle of the Tandoori creates much of a stir, even among the self-educated epicureans of Indian cuisine.

It is Ma's expressed desire that the house comes alive and breathes like a Persian garden. Yesterday the *mali* was summoned and threatened with instant dismissal if he failed to permeate the rooms with a heavenly fragrance.

'I want sweet smelling flowers in every corner of the

house,' Ma demanded. 'Pretty flowers. Lots of colour.' The *mali* bowed obsequiously and retreated toward the kitchen.

'No excuses!' Ma followed him doggedly. 'Get them!'

Abba was harangued into using his connections. The national airline obliged by flying in three baskets of flowers from Calcutta.

Through the haze of my morning's drowsiness, the house appeared to be a double-storeyed florist's shop. In every available space there were vases, bottles, buckets and canisters crammed with roses, cannas, zephyranthes, carnations, geraniums and marigolds. I hoped Nafisa would exercise some aesthetic judgement with a pair of scissors and discreetly remove the bulk of the Persian garden during one of Ma's inspections of the backyard.

Nadine was half-asleep when I bundled her into the car with a hurried explanation about the *dhobi ghat* and the freshness of the countryside in the morning. It was carefully prearranged. In the back seat there was a picnic basket with a thermos, some fruits and a strictly rationed supply of dry biscuits and cheese.

'The butcher is here. We are waiting for the *imam*,' Khuda Buksh whispered dutifully as I stepped into the car.

Fortunately Nadine was too drowsy to hear him.

It does not take long to drive past Rupganj and enter the rice-growing area. Nadine is more interested in the Kraft cheddar than in the bright tropical greenness of the paddy fields. We stop near a small pond.

Huge water lilies, like bone-white soup bowls on verdant tablemats, crowd the water's surface. Just above the eastern horizon the sun is a radiant young magician with spindly fingers glazing the fields with a hue of golden yellow. Green filaments of grain ripple sensuously in the slight breeze. I think of a young woman responding to the warm lips of a tender lover. There is a youthful harmony here. I do not feel as if I belong to the morning. I am a being apart. I do not have a sense of renewal. I look at Nadine. She is now alert to the rapidly changing morning. She draws my attention to the wild ducks gliding in the pond.

Somewhere, up ahead, the river runs quietly. I can smell its tangy presence. It is a meandering tributary of the Meghna, where we hired boats for picnics on the other side of the river. We decide to walk the distance.

The dew on the grass is like masses of tangled cobwebs. Nadine slides the soles of her runners on the grass as she walks. I put my arm around her shoulders, unafraid of rejection. She is no longer embarrassed by my open display of affection. She draws closer and rubs her nose on my chest. I feel warm. Possessive. Proud. I did something right. That would have drawn a reprimand from Michelle. *We did something right. She is our child.*

Not today, Michelle. Not at this moment. Yes, all right. I am being selfish again.

Nadine continues to be fascinated by the intricate orange patterns on the palms and fingers of her hands. She holds them up in the morning light as if to confirm they have not disappeared. I am punched on the arm for laughing. I have never known her to be so absorbed by anything as when she closely watched Nafisa carving out the delicate floral shapes from the moist wad of mashed henna leaves covering her hands. After Nafisa had finished, Nadine sat with outstretched palms for nearly two hours, refusing to heed my advice to relax her rigidly held body. When it was time to remove the dry paste and rub her hands with mustard oil, the look of sheer amazement on her face made me laugh.

She clasps my hand as if she suddenly needs me. 'Khuda Buksh read my fortune yesterday. He said the lines on my hand were clear.'

'What else did he say?'

'He said I would soon be like a happy princess.' She giggles as if the idea amuses her.

'Did he? That's clever of him. I wonder what he meant.'

'Dad?' The grip tightens.

'Yes pet?'

'Are you happy?'

'I am happy to be here with you. Are you?'

'What?'

'Are you happy?'

'I dunno. I wish Mum was here.'

'I don't think she'd approve of your hands.'

'Why not? They look cool! Dad?'

'Yes?'

'When will we see Mum again?'

'You'll see her soon.'

'Will you?'

'Probably. We have to sort out a few things.'

'Will I see you on weekends?'

'Yes.'

'Every weekend?'

'As many as possible.'

'Can't you and Mum make up? Sort of pretend you had a fight and then became friends again?'

'It isn't quite as simple as that.'

She draws her hand away. 'You once said only little kids fight and don't get along.'

'In lots of ways adults are like kids.'

'How?'

'Well, they often want to have things their own way. Sometimes they don't think of others.'

The *dhobi ghat* is a revelation to Nadine. The sight of wet clothes being mercilessly whacked on a wooden platform, wrung by hand and then spread out on the grass to dry, amazes her. She is full of questions and shrewd in deductive thinking.

'Why are only men washing the clothes?'
'What are those funny looking trousers called?'
'Why are their legs showing?'
'Why don't you wear *dhotis*?'
'Why do the *dhobis* dress differently?'
'How are Hindu men different?'
'What does circumcised mean?'
'Are all Muslims circumcised?'

Before she can ask the inevitable question, I encourage her to run down to the riverbank for a closer look at the imperturbable, bare-bodied men in their *funny looking trousers*.

To my left the river widens. The western horizon is layered with ragged strips of mushroom-coloured clouds. Above it is the bright presence of an unbroken blankness. My creaking imagination tries to splatter it with afternoon colours, decorate the taut canvas with faces I have known, scribble on it the lyrics of yesterday's songs. But all I manage is the faint etching of a pallid face, creasing and crumbling. The breeze is her breath scattering the cold ashes of our lives beyond the reaches of memory.

I stand outside myself and look at the sad, tired stranger. He watches the boat plough slowly through the muddy water. The breeze blows strains of the scratchy songs and teases his loneliness. The washed curvature of the pristine sky mocks him with its hollowness. *Let go*, he says to himself. *Let go*. And he feels for all that is left among the pain of the present.

I have been standing at the front door for over an hour—shaking hands, bending down to touch wrinkled feet, smiling and murmuring words of welcome to people I do not know. Next to me Ma verbalises magnanimous greetings like a good-humoured empress at a royal gathering. She has a sharp eye and an unfailing memory for the colourfully wrapped gifts. Twenty-two carat gold jewellery from relatives and close friends. Anything even slightly inferior for her grand-daughter and they face her undying wrath and certain ostracism. Unknown to the guests the presents are being catalogued by my aunt in a spare bedroom.

They have come from every corner of the city—the fat and the ulcerous, the rich and the fashionably grotesque, the proud and the powerful. To be invited by the Chaudharies! It is mandatory for any self-respecting *bhodrolok* and his *begum* to grace the occasion and behave like privileged members of Dhaka's elite.

I do not envy Hashim. He is sweating profusely as he scurries between the front door and the study. It is his responsibility to lead the guests into the study where Abba awaits their sycophantic salutation.

The aroma of rosewater and saffron wafts through the door. Morich Mia elbows his way in. His scowl looks ominous. He is wearing a two-piece suit, spotted with grease marks, which clings to him with a fatigued limpness intimating at least a decade's rough handling and innumerable encounters with the dry-cleaners. An olive-green tie and a matching woollen scarf stand out in startling contrast to the faded brown suit and the pink shirt with rebellious collar points curving upwards like a cow's horns. The comical effect is topped off by a greasy, perforated straw hat which serves as a cylindrical trellis for wispy white tendrils seeking to escape through the small round holes.

We dare not laugh.

The aquiline nose quivers. He looks up at us defiantly. 'Dinner is served!' He announces as if he were a prison warden who will tolerate no dissent from the inmates.

'But it is only eight o'clock!' Ma protests. 'Everyone isn't here yet!'

I lay a restraining hand on her arm.

'Dinner is served, *Begum Shaheb,*' Morich Mia repeats slowly, intimidating Ma with a fierce stare. 'I have taken what

I need. *Khuda Hafiz! Choto Babu* will be generous with some *baksheesh* if the food is to his liking.'

I nod obediently and accompany him to Hashim's car which is being loaded with pots and pans. The night hums pleasantly. The noise I left behind is dreadful. There are people in every corner of the house like excited flies crawling over a dead animal. This momentary reprieve is an immense relief. The smell of jasmine hangs heavily in the air. Morich Mia grunts an acknowledgement as I hand him an envelope. He orders the chauffeur to drive away. I loiter outside until Khuda Buksh comes looking for me.

With some trepidation I make my way to the dining room. All pretensions of civilised behaviour have disappeared. The guests elbow, shoulder and shove their way to the row of tables against the wall. Like hyenas feasting on carrion flesh, they drool and gnash their teeth as they lean over the family's finest china to pile their plates with bread, rice and meat.

Hashim looks across the room at me and shrugs his shoulders.

Muscles tense. Limbs press against sagging flesh. There are empty smiles and terse apologies. Bangles clink and jangle. There is an air of anxiety about the way the food is wolfed down. For a few short hours most of them have escaped the choking dreariness of their wealth-infested lives to play bit parts in the Chaudhary production of razzle-dazzle glamour. The nouveau riche are awed by our *zamindari* background. It gives us class that money cannot buy. There is an aching compulsion to enjoy themselves by overindulging. The carpe diem theme is enacted with a feverish intensity. The desire to encapsulate a large hunk of pleasure into a minute fragment of time drives them into an avaricious display of appetites. Munch, crunch, tear, gulp. Big mouths, small mouths, ugly mouths and shapely mouths triturate interminably to contribute to the distension of flabby bellies. It is hard work. They sweat and grunt like labouring beasts. Under the cover of a vapid chatter, they shall burp, snort and fart their way into a state of moronic lassitude.

I have seen enough. This unabashed display of greed is enough to make me leave the room. I have a fleeting vision of the multitudes of despairing faces wallowing in abject poverty—homeless children, with the chronic pain of hunger in their bellies, those with ravaged bodies and minds trapped to endure the unremitting miseries of mortality. I try not to think of the woes of this accursed land and those of us who have perpetuated its destitution. I cannot escape the shame of our circumstances and this unpardonable exhibition of selfish greed.

I feel a hand on my back. 'This is a feast like the old days!' Mateen smiles contentedly. 'Why aren't you eating?'

'I am not hungry.'

'You are not well?'

'Mateen, we are all ill in this room. Enjoy yourself.'

Aachha! A foreigner who can afford the decorative luxury of a social conscience! I hear their sneering voices. *Wasn't migrating an act of greed? Who are you to come back and preach to us?*

Not everyone, I discover, is mired in gluttony. The L-shaped lounge is less crowded. The women here are much younger and more elegantly dressed. Slim figures, draped in silk and *banarsis*, glide across the room. They are at ease with the surreptitious lechery in men's eyes stalking their movements. The colours breathe a rich life into the room. Turquoise. Maroon. Red and white. Green. Purple. Brocade borders and golden paisleys. Diamond and emerald earrings. Delicate bangles and expensive watches. The necklaces are ostentatiously heavy. Shapely ringed fingers curl around tumblers of lemonade and coke.

The men are more conservatively dressed. There is a depressing uniformity of grey suits, white shirts and flowery ties—affectations of their brushes with the West.

This is the younger generation, outside my experience.

There is an air of self-confidence in the room, an assuredness which speaks of a prosperity that is not deemed to be a hard-won privilege but an inherent right.

I am more than a little self-conscious about my open-neck shirt and ill-fitting trousers. I linger inside the door. I need not worry. No one notices me. I feel the thrill of a familiar invisibility. It gives me the power to drift through the room, to listen and observe without resorting to the stealth of an intruder.

The centre of the room is deserted, as if no one is particularly keen to be seen under the light of the ornate chandelier. Directly under it is a walnut-stained coffee table with a bowl of chrysanthemums and a sandalwood cigarette box. The sofas and the side tables have been pushed against the walls.

In dim corners, whispering men, partially hidden by lampshades and potted plants, have their hopes kindled by throaty laughter and stifled giggles. It is that age when so much of life is consumed by carnal advances under the cover of emotional commitment.

Men with twitchy hands and sweaty faces breathe eternal love and fidelity. Most of the women look amused. I imagine they experience no difficulty in unravelling the insincerity behind the earnest tones of flattery. Some will wish to be pursued for an evening's entertainment. As for the men . . . I fear the evening will nosedive into miserable failures for most.

The lustful vagary of progenitive instinct reveals itself quite differently in this part of the world. I have grown accustomed to a culture more openly expressive of its sexuality and one which has not felt the need to develop as many trite symbols and coy gestures to signal amorous intentions. Here it is a cunning game of interpretation and guesswork. It requires alertness and animal patience I no longer command.

It was not that long ago when the Hindi movie factories in Bombay were packaging love scenes where the obvious

movement toward oscular foreplay was immediately trans-
muted into one of nature's tranquil moments, in a lush garden
under a cloudless sky, with one hectic bee commuting
between two swaying flowers in a fan-blown breeze. Adding
an audible dimension to this standard piece of visual symbolism were screeching violins and twittering birds encouraging
the nectareous impregnation.

What can I expect to see if I stay around? A raised eyebrow?
An index finger held coyly between the teeth? An oblique
glance and a sly wink? Perhaps a jerk of the head. Subtle
directional movements of the hands? The restraint and caution
will be admirable. Will the messages be accurately unscram-
bled? Will it be a patch of grass under a tree? The back seat
of a parked car? A friend's nearby flat? A quick getaway.
Fumbling, eager hands. The orgasmic peaks of brief encounters chaperoned by a series of primordial sounds on a scale
ranging from disappointed groans to deliciously ecstatic
moans. Back before the next shift of dinner?

A servant holds up a silver tray in front of me. Fizz and
exploding bubbles in half-full tumblers. I shake my head and
move further into the room. Around the dividing brick wall,
a group of men are locked in an animated conversation. I
recognise most of them from my university days—Munir,
Haroon, Shafiq, Naseem, Taufiq, Khorram. They aspired to be
civil servants. They were intelligent, ambitious and dedicated
in their pursuit of bureaucratic prestige. Judging by their
officious manners, they have all made it to the top.

The greetings are muted, the handshakes limp.

'*Key Khobor? Kemun accho*?'

'How's life in kangaroo land?'

'All these years! And this is your first visit!'

'Didn't you miss your family and friends?'

'*Aarey baba*, why Australia of all places? My brother lasted
six weeks in Perth. The place is full of South Africans with

their imported prejudices. How do you put up with the racism and the misconceptions against Muslims?'

That's a bit rich coming from Taufiq. It was common knowledge that he was instrumental in whipping up a frenzied mood of patriotism after the war with Pakistan. Under the catchcry, *Bangladesh for Bangalis*, he and his group of nationalists terrorised the Biharis. Taufiq was too cunning to have a direct involvement in the torture and killing of those suspected of collaborating with the Pakistanis. I find it almost inconceivable that this portly, harmless looking man could have harboured such intense hatred.

I am looked up and down. My clothes must be a telltale sign of a struggling migrant in a hostile land. A can of beer is thrust into my hands in recognition, it appears, of my failure in my adopted country. Sympathy creeps into their voices. The questions are polite; the remarks—perfunctory and fatuous.

They return to their troubled world of political wrangling. Their lack of trust in the army makes them cynical. They glance nervously at the uniformed men on the other side of the room. There is concern about rumours of an imminent coup d'état.

'It annoys me no end the way we pretend to play this game of having a democratically elected government,' Haroon complains.

'It's no game!' Naseem says impatiently. 'We meekly accept the fact that the army runs the country.' He lights a cigarette and inhales deeply. 'There's nothing to be done about it.'

'How can we function efficiently in such chaos?' Haroon demands loudly. 'The minister calls me in the morning. I stall him. The cantonment rings me in the afternoon and I have to leave a message that I am at a meeting. How long can this continue? Who do you listen to?'

'*Aarey yar*, you are an old hand. Stop worrying!' Taufiq pats him on the back. 'A good civil servant never worries because he is his own boss. Pretend to serve and continue to rule.'

'Have you forgotten the code of behaviour for third-world civil servants?' Shafiq asks. 'Work for your own survival. Be loyal to yourself and treacherous to everyone else. Ear against the wall. Read everything, discreetly vary your handwriting and signature, always pay for your lunch, say nothing to the wife about work, use the mistress' address, drink tea when you feel like speaking up, carry a dictionary of ambiguous phrases and pretend not to know anything. Argue with your minister, if you must, but never with the khakis. The minister can make your life difficult. You may have to take his wife shopping and resist her advances. But what's that compared to residentship in an unmarked grave? That's indefinite. If you are lucky, someone may dig up your smashed skull one day.'

'You never take anything seriously,' Haroon grunts. 'Is that how you manage to survive so well?'

'He's right, whether you like it or not,' chimes Khorram. His reedy voice has not changed from the days when he led protest marches against the university administration whenever he was inadequately prepared for an examination. 'Cross the fat cats of the cantonment and you shall be lucky to find a place among murderers and thieves in Central Jail. Oh, they'll release you after a few weeks because of the overcrowded conditions. But then, poof! You will not return home one day. Cantonment *jaddu*, *baba!* Potent stuff! The government will pretend not to know a thing. There will be an inconclusive inquiry. Case closed. Justice done.'

They look glumly at each other. The Bohemian crystal decanter and the papier mâché cigarette box are passed around. I speculate on the number of bottles of Scotch Hashim managed to smuggle into the house.

Go easy, I feel like saying. I am the one paying for the stuff.

'How I would love to get out of this godforsaken country!'

Haroon declares in exasperation. 'I should have been an army officer. I could have arranged a coup d'état designed to fail. The president of the year wouldn't have the guts to treat me harshly. Mustn't upset the other officers! *Na, na*. That's not done. Solution? I'd be bundled out of the country as an ambassador to make an ass of myself. But at least it would get me out of here.'

'*Bah! Bah!* What a novel idea!' Naseem applauds ironically. 'You should publish the formula and sell it in the cantonment.'

There are embarrassed titters as if their innermost secrets have been revealed.

'What you say has happened, though I am not so sure if the coups were intentionally bungled.' Khorram winks at me as though I should make a sensible contribution to the discussion. 'Look at some of the diplomats who have been appointed over the last few years. Amin, Latif, Mazhar, Rahim, Zahoor . . . army strong men known for their political ambition. The trouble is these fellows have no idea about protocol. They come in for briefing and sit in a daze, probably stunned by the discovery that they will actually have to use speech instead of guns to communicate. They are a disaster with journalists. There is no understanding of the basic principle that a diplomat must make a journalist feel important without saying anything worthwhile. Diplomats of most third-world countries present themselves more credibly than we do. We are the imbeciles in a world full of cunning beggars.'

'But they are all like that!' Munir moans. 'It's not just the khaki brigade which behaves as if they are members of a degenerate subculture. Do you remember the former minister for food and agriculture? Halaluddin Alam? Well, some time before the last cabinet reshuffle he decided to address the Press Club about the bumper crops we were expecting last year. Mind you, this was after the unusually heavy monsoonal rains had water-logged half the country. The journalists were reluctant to have him. I had to beg them and bribe them with vague promises of trips abroad. Seraj was called in and given twenty-four hours to write a speech and have it approved. He did a terrific job. He made it sound as if we were to become entirely self-sufficient in food within a couple of years. He inserted all the 'ifs' and 'buts' in the right places. But the speech didn't please Halaluddin. It wasn't long enough, he insisted. It had to be more patriotic. He decided to rewrite the whole thing himself. Well, on the day he droned on about all sorts of things and how rapidly we were progressing under the dynamic leadership of the prime minister. It was the kind of *chamcha giri* ministers stoop to when they feel threatened. This went on for nearly fifteen minutes. Then he began to speak about poultry farming somewhere near Narsindi. He must have skipped a page because the next thing we heard was . . . '

Munir pauses to imitate the fidgety mannerisms.

' " . . . eggs . . . ah, eggs can be seen growing abundantly on trees in every village. But since there are no facilities for organised picking, most of them drop off and lie rotting under the trees." There was some embarrassed laughter. Halaluddin paused, unable to understand the reason for the disturbance. Very caringly he asked if we wanted a break for a few minutes. That's when everyone collapsed into hysterical laughter. He stared at the text of his speech and then at the scattered audience with a blank look on his face. When the noise died down, he moved on to the prawn industry, leaving the smashed eggs under the trees.'

Munir chuckles at the recollection. There are wide, self-satisfied grins on all the faces. They bask in the glory of their undisputed intellectual superiority over their masters. From their hive of conviction flows a warmth of togetherness. They are kindred spirits. Internal wrangling and professional jealousies are forgotten. Like any normal family they have their problems. The decanter is passed around again with an apostolic sense of brotherhood. Generously they pour for each other.

I am not worth even a fleeting glance. The reality of my presence is as insubstantial as a transient shadow destined to disappear without a trace of its unwelcome presence. It is a blunt way of letting me know that I do not deserve to be in their company. Hashim invited them. They are his friends. Their loyalty to Hashim has brought them here. In their eyes I am a traitor to the Bangali cause, an opportunist who turned away from his country in its time of patriotic need.

A blind rage possesses me. There is an overwhelming urge to explode all over them with expletives to crack their self-righteous insularity and force them to understand that I need not apologise for what I did and what I am.

Do you know what it means to be a migrant? A lost soul forever adrift in search of a tarnished dream? You live in a perpetual state of conflict, torn between what was and what should have been. There is a consciousness of a permanent loss. You get sick of wearing masks to hide your confused aloneness. You can never call anything your own. But out of this deprivation emerges an understanding of humanity unstifled by genetic barriers. No, I wouldn't have it any other way. I have had my prejudices trimmed to manageable proportions. You realise that behind the trappings of cultural differences human strengths and failures are global constants. That is a very precious knowledge. A Bangali can be just as indifferent, mean, egotistical, loving, creative, heroic, generous, humane, cruel and greedy as an Australian. It makes you appreciate the homogenous blueprint of human life. It is this impossible mixture which binds humanity, and I am a part of it. No better or worse than anyone, but an equal. An equal because I know I am a composite of all those contradictory characteristics which are far stronger than any racial or religious differences. And that is worth celebrating. Difficult for you understand, isn't it? You, who allow yourselves to be blinded by your pride in a singularly blinkered tradition which fertilises the grounds of bigotry.

I am weary of exploring the barren coldness of rejection. It is the helpless despair of being stranded on an iceberg, talking to a world empty of understanding. I have learned that pariahs are unsettling for any community. They bring with them too many strange ideas. They upset the communal rhythm of ignorance. They need to be kept out.

A magnificent Rajastani silk painting captures my attention. It must have been hung up this morning. No one notices my nonchalant movement toward the wall. The empty beer can feels awkward in my hand. It is not an unfamiliar feeling.

Of all the days to be stopped by an aggressive weekend cop on the prowl! With honking cars lined up behind my bomb, an idiotic smile and a shrug of the shoulders followed by 'Me no speak Engleesh,' worked on Elizabeth Street. On the free-way there is no urgency. He is overweight, sweaty and looks irritable. I wait for him to tap on the glass before I roll down the window.

He sticks his head in. The white hairs in his nostrils need to be trimmed. In thick clusters they have escaped the moist darkness to curl upwards in the open. They are like the formative tusks of a young boar. His breath is laboured and smelly.

'Put you blokes in the driver's seat and you are a bloody danger!' He sneers. 'You darkies are all the same, aren't you?'

'No we are not,' I reply tonelessly. 'There's mahogany, walnut, teak, ebony. The variety is great.'

He stares at me with watery eyes. The rudiment of a conditioned mind slowly absorbs the fact that I have spoken in English. A red flush of anger spreads across his face. The bulldog jowls wobble. I have offended him by contradicting a sacred belief. I prepare to duck for cover under the dash-board.

'You cheeky . . . Licence! Let's see your licence!'

I am in trouble here. I go through the routine of contrition. No eye contact. Let him feel powerful.

'Sorry, mate! I am running a bit late . . . You know how it is . . . Won't happen again . . . Thanks!'

Licence back in the wallet. A final warning. A submissive nod of the head. He even returns my wave.

Pedigree prick.

The slow drive to Melbourne ensures a late arrival. The cacophony of backyard chatter can be heard from the street. Smoke rises from behind the tiled roof. Part of a libation to the god of indulgence.

Except for Michelle and her parents, I won't know anyone. I was reluctant about coming, but I couldn't really say no. Michelle and I are at that stage of our relationship when it is mandatory to meet family and friends.

I fumble with the latch on the freshly painted gate. What shall I say? I am up with the cricket and the tennis. I am in conservative territory. That rules out politics. Cars do not interest me. Discuss the stock market? Auctions and house prices? Renovations? Antiques? Furniture restoration? Beach houses? I could manage to look interested, perhaps nod in the right places and make a few ambiguous remarks. I have memorised the recipes for pork *vindaloo* and beef *korma*. I could talk about the Taj Mahal or Kashmir. I promised Michelle not to say anything about the *Kama Sutra*.

The brick paved path between the fence and the side of the house leads to a shrubbed arbour. I stop among the red bottle-brushes and brace myself for the bland smiles and wary, inquisitive eyes—the guarded expressions of polite welcome reserved for ethnic strangers. Through the gaps in the inter-locked branches, I can see the drinks table. I'll grab a beer first. That will establish my familiarity with the priorities of the backyard bash.

They stand in small groups, drink in hand, enjoying the facetious banter of camaraderie. I am greeted by the crackling noise of burning fat and the sizzle of sausages, chops and steaks.

Before I can get a drink, Michelle pounces on me with a friendly admonishment. I apologise for being late. She introduces me to her older brother, Martin.

Martin is the really bright one in the family—articulate, witty and successful. The visible signs of prosperity are all over him—a white silk shirt, a heavy gold chain around a sunburnt neck, imported jeans and hand-crafted Italian leather boots. He is tall, with small rounded shoulders and a sizeable pot belly. He has Michelle's eyes and short, curly brown hair.

He looks at me with a smirk on his face. There is a delayed handshake after the obligatory, 'Pleased to meet you.'

His wife, Judy, is pale and blonde. She has a toff English accent. She says, 'How do you do?' in a perfunctory manner and continues to sip champagne.

'Do you go back to India often?' Martin sounds immeasurably bored. His eyes search the yard behind me for compatible company.

'No, but then I am not an Indian.'

'Huh?' He snaps to attention, his eyes narrowing suspiciously. 'What do you mean? Michelle said you were from the subcontinent.'

'I am.' It is my turn to smirk. I relish his discomfort. Martin is the type of person who believes himself to be knowledgeable about most things.

'Pakistani?'

'No, no. I am a Bangali.'

'A Bangali?' He asks curiously.

'Yes.' I deliberately refrain from volunteering any further information.

'He's from Bangladesh,' Judy informs him. 'We lived near a Bangali doctor in London. In fact there were quite a few people like you living in Putney.' She holds the stem of the flute between her thumb and index finger and gently swirls the champagne around. 'Too many for my liking.' The coup de grâce is accompanied with an Arctic smile.

'Just like there were too many Britishers in India not so long ago.' I smile back at her without managing the severity of her frostiness. 'We have more subtle ways of colonising countries.'

Martin throws back his head and laughs raucously, savouring his wife's displeasure. He looks at me with a grudging respect in his eyes. 'Bangladesh? Weren't some people killed there some time ago?'

'There was a war.'

'That's it! I read about it at the time!' Suddenly his voice is friendly. I am offered a beer.

Michelle drags me away. I must be sociable and meet the others. Circulate. Mingle. 'Behave yourself!' She whispers a warning. 'You are supposed to be nice and straight, without a wacky sense of humour.'

I am led by the hand and expected to develop instant friendships. The faces are indistinguishable.

'Hello John!'

'Pleased to meet you, Mary.'

'How you doin'?'

'Hi Susan!'

'Gidday, Tony!'

'How are you Mark?'

The brief conversations are marked by trite pleasantries about beach holidays, fishing, my culinary skills in making curries, life in provincial Ballarat. A few are intrigued that I have never been back to the subcontinent, even for a brief visit. I have no explanation. It simply hasn't happened.

They have a prototype image of me as an Indian. It is laundered and made acceptable in their own minds. Everything, from language to food, religion and accent, has been moulded into a composition to fit a uniform view about an Indian. And I am one of them.

Is it worth the effort? I ask myself as I set about breaking the cast. There is a stubborn streak inside me. This sort of ignorance cannot be left alone. Hound it! Punch a hole through it. Go on . . .

'No, no. I am not an Indian. I was born in Pakistan. I am a Bangali.' That complicates the issue even further and convinces them that I am being flippant about my background.

'Indians are such gentle people,' chirps Aunty Louise.

'Are they? I wouldn't know. I am not an Indian. I am from Bangladesh.'

'Bangladesh? Bangladesh . . . That's where you have the floods!'

'There was a war, wasn't there?'

'Do you speak Indian at home?'

'There is no such language,' I explain patiently. 'I speak Bangla.'

'Pardon me, but are you a Hindu?'

'No. I was born into a Muslim family.'

'Do you go to church?'

'No.'

'Do you believe in Christ?'

'Only to the extent that it is probable such a person existed.'

'Help yourself!' Someone calls.

I am the first to grab a plate.

Under a pear tree, Michelle and I sit on a rug with sausages and steaks, bread and salad.

'That wasn't too painful.'

Her tone of assertive confidence irks me.

'No.' I agree meekly. 'Not too bad.'

Michelle is aware of the poor impression I have made. Instead of making them feel safe and superior with the blandness of a mythical oriental passivity and an inscrutable smile, I have scowled, refuted, contradicted and corrected.

'What did you think of Martin?'

'There are more things in heaven and earth, Horatio,
Than are dreamt of in your philosophy.'

'Yes, all right! But he has a bitch of a wife.'

'She's honest. I must have evoked a nostalgic longing for the days of the Raj. At least I know where I stand with her. I doubt if we'll be invited to their house too often.'

'It's worth going with you just for the sake of being struck off her dinner party list,' Michelle teases. 'What about the others?'

'I don't know. It's hard to say. I had a feeling they were cautiously disapproving of me. Perhaps I should have been less forthright.'

'They are more worried about you being a non-Catholic than your outspokenness.'

'I am a *non*, am I? Jews, Hindus, Muslims—we are all *nons*. Outside the human race?'

Michelle stabs the meat with her steak knife. 'You are in one of your I-want-to-whip-the-world-today moods. Why?'

'Because I am fed up with being treated as an oddity, a stray from the forbidding darkness of the world up there. I'm tired of misconceptions and assumptions, of being an object of curiosity!'

'What did you expect?' Her voice is coldly discomforting. 'We are a conservative, white Catholic family. We go to mass on Sunday and pray for equality and universal brotherhood. As soon as the final Amen has been said and we have crossed ourselves, we unlock our prejudices and set them free. *Are you sure you want to marry a black man, dear? I hope you know what you are doing.* Christ! They can't even get your colour right! That is my family. I cannot do much about them. But tell me, how would your family react if they met me? Wouldn't they be curious? Wouldn't they be offended if I went around correcting them so bluntly? You are overreacting to people who have reservations about you. I warned you, didn't

I? Are you going to combat ignorance with anger? See you in a few minutes with the dessert.' She snatches her plate and goblet and flounces off toward the pavlova.

Much as I hate to admit it, she is right. My family would have met her with a festering potpourri of prejudices. A white woman, a Christian and a consumer of pork, would have been treated as a catastrophe destined to ruin my life.

I feel chastened and a trifle ridiculous sitting here by myself, holding a can of beer, surrounded by decaying pears. The high-pitched sound of a slightly inebriated conversation makes me feel the sadness of isolation. They are oblivious of my presence. I can listen and watch with impunity. I have melted into the shadows of a fear they vaguely perceive and vigorously suppress.

I have discovered the powers of invisibility.

I did not hear her coming up behind me.

'Shahjahan in durbar. That is a good reproduction of Bichitr's painting in *Shah-jahan-nama*. It's in the royal library in Windsor Castle. You must be Iqbal. I am Nadira Hussein. I used to work with Hashim in London. I hope I didn't disturb you. You . . . ' She hesitates. Her face is dimpled with a smile. 'You were somewhere else.'

She thrusts out her hand in a business-like manner. Her slender fingers grip mine with a confident firmness.

'Ah . . . yes . . . I was far away.' I stumble over my words. 'I was recalling the antics of a younger man and feeling foolish.'

I have reacted to her in a most primitive manner. A cluster of suggestive images swirl in my mind. She is exquisite. Delectable. Delicious. I think of her as though she were no more than an exotic fruit I desire because of its rarity and freshness. It is a nakedly physical response to an instinctive force that bursts into life after a prolonged period of dormancy. I am helpless under its power. It is so blatantly sexual that I fear it may manifest itself in a lecherous look on my face.

Theo's words ring in my ears. I recall laughing at the ease with which he annoyed Michelle. She was earnestly arguing how impulse had to be controlled by rationality to achieve order in life.

'Crap!' He roared, his face flushed and his speech slightly slurred. 'You women are full of bullshit! You always want to control and civilise instinct. I reckon old Moses buggered it up on the old mountain. Fair enough he should be told his crowd down below had to behave. The rabble needed laws. But then he should have asked for something more. "Now God," he should have said, "teach me a way of controlling their sexual instinct and I promise to make the laws work." That would have stitched up the Big Fella good and proper. It would have taken more than seven days to find an answer to that one!'

My embarrassment makes me take a step backward. She exudes an overpowering sexuality which has an anaesthetising effect on my in-built sense of propriety. The clearly defined contours of her breasts run riot on my imagination. I take a quick look at her hands. There are rings on the third finger of each hand; not that they mean anything here. Her composure is upsetting. What is she thinking? Does she know what is on my mind? Can she hear me breathing? I hide in my sparse knowledge of Moghul art. She talks about tone, texture and colour with the felicity of an articulate art connoisseur. I nod timidly, appendaging her comments with ambiguous remarks in an implausible note of authority.

Nadira is not beautiful in an idyllic, photogenic way. Her face lacks the beguiling innocence which attracts Bangali men. She will not be popular among the men in circulation tonight. The potential mothers-in-law and the matchmakers will ignore her. Too dark and thin. Unusually tall for a woman.

Snub-nosed. The smooth, flawless skin will create some uncertainty about her age. I am struck by the unusual strength in her face. She carries herself with a mildly disdainful poise that defiantly proclaims her independence and threatens to expose the fallacy of male omnipotence.

In some aspects her life parallels mine. She lived overseas for nearly sixteen years. She studied medicine in England, worked in London and married a Welsh surgeon. She divorced him after seven years of childless marriage (she smiles as an "Oh", fraught with possibilities, escapes my lips), changed her job and then decided England could never be her permanent home.

I am curious about her reason for coming back.

'I am not the stuff migrants are made of,' she tells me in fluent Bangla. 'I am not resilient enough. I am not good at sustaining my illusions on hope. I prefer to live with the despair of reality. I wasn't a political refugee. There were no family ties to keep me there. I could not justify my life in a foreign country by claiming its future benefits for my children. I was forced to question my motives. Was it money that was keeping me there? Professional advancement? A better living? I had to remind myself of the Hippocratic oath. Were there any altruistic reasons for choosing medicine as a career, or was I motivated by money and prestige? Some of the answers were not too comforting. The turmoil of my personal life added to the confusion. When Hashim proposed a partnership in a clinic back here, I grabbed the opportunity. Coming back was like a second migration. My perspectives had to be readjusted. It wasn't easy to go through the whole process of acclimatisation. The attitudes of men were enough to make me think I may have made a mistake. Marriage offers were quickly converted to less permanent propositions once they realised I was divorced. But do you know the most important feeling? My dignity was restored. I was once again a part of an ethnic majority. That was vital for my self-confidence. No abuses or snide remarks about my colour or my dress, no fear of racist attacks, no blame for Britain's difficulties. There were many disadvantages about coming home. Many. But the compensating factor was the comfort of belonging. There was nothing artificial about it. I no longer had to call the past my home. Everything around me spoke intimately. It was all a part of me. It was a great feeling to be in love with life again, to embrace it without the fear of rejection.'

I am envious and spellbound by her joyous conviction. She listens intently to my misgivings about a land I can never claim to be my own. I sometimes feel as if I am permanently perched on top of a high wall. There are people down below on either side, oblivious of each other's presence. It is not in my power to come down. All I can do is look at them and laugh occasionally. It is not a malicious laughter. It rings with the empty sadness of recognition. I see so much more than they can. The world seems to open up just a little more each day to expose the magnitude of its imperfections. I am merely a tormented viewer. If only they knew how much they had in common! I am not any smarter than those down there; only more dissatisfied.

We are interrupted by Nadine. She bounds in, excitedly waving a pair of gold and pearl earrings—a gift from Nafisa. She blushes when I compliment her on her sophisticated appearance. With her hair brushed back and tied in a bun, she looks much older than her age. She is wearing a blue silk sari with a gold border. She moves with a feline grace which jolts me into a shocked awareness of her femininity. I dread the stage when I shall begin to feel the loss of her childhood. That must surely be some time away. Is my apprehension a symptom of a possessive parent?

I brush aside my thoughts and listen to her breathless chatter. She tells me about the jewellery she has received. I rejoice in her happiness. There is such an overabundance of pride in my parental love that I feel like drawing everyone's attention to her.

'This is Dr Hussein. My daughter, Nadine.'

Immediately Nadine's eyes narrow shrewishly, and a wary woman replaces the ecstatic child.

'Dr Hussein is Uncle Hashim's friend,' I explain hastily.

'Hello Nadine! You are a beautiful young lady!' The rich caramelised voice flatters soothingly. 'Will you show me your presents?'

The resentment melts and Nadine's aggression fades behind a shy smile. 'I'll get Grandma to show you! They are upstairs.'

'See you in a few minutes?' Nadira smiles warmly and completes the conquest.

Nadine nods and skips away happily.

There is something coldly clinical about the way Nadine has been manipulated into a state of amiable cooperation. I must concede that it was spontaneous, but achieved with a precision which makes me think of a brilliantly efficient general commanding a military operation without knowing the enemy's strength.

Nadira turns to me. Will I have dinner with her?

She derails my thoughts. This is all too sudden.

The time lapse is awkward. Her smile almost disappears.

I manage a poker-faced reply. I cannot remember ever being asked out by a woman before. This is looking very promising. There is a rejuvenated heart somewhere, beating like a tom-tom. I must not blow it! I mustn't! Keep calm. Don't fidget. Take deep breaths. Whoa boy! Keep still. Easy does it. Easy now . . .

Yes, eight o'clock Thursday night is fine. I graciously accept the offer of a pick-up in a chauffeured car.

I make an excuse to leave the room. I have to be by myself to savour the infinitude of possibilities. I am like a secretive child, unwilling to share my joy with others. I don't want to think of practicalities. Bugger it! I won't be logical. I don't care about consequences. Why shouldn't I be impulsive? There Theo, that's positive thinking! Thursday looms large like a shiny myriad of sculptured phrases and snatches of adolescent daydreams. But have I read her correctly? Was she merely trying to be friendly? She must know that most men find it impossible to be friends with attractive women without fancying their chances with them.

How typically male and chauvinistic! How very narrow-minded and ugly! Michelle would have erupted if she could read my mind. Now why did I have to bring Michelle into it? I don't care about her. Why should I? Nadira's eyes . . . Did I misunderstand them? She was flirting, wasn't she? Encouraging advances without expecting or offering even a vague hint of serious commitment. Can it happen so suddenly? It does in the movies. Damn! Have I got it all wrong? What shall I wear? I don't even have a decent aftershave. There's no chance of getting rid of that curvature on my belly. I inhale deeply and suck in my stomach. There is a painful twinge of unused muscles. No, no chance at all. Is there enough time to have a pair of trousers altered? A haircut perhaps?

I leave the uncertainties behind. A youthful recklessness seizes me. I hurtle past the known frontiers of caution and dance with my imagination among undiscovered stars.

It is pleasantly cool outside. Night wraps itself loosely around me and allows my dreams to play in its expansive darkness. My imaginings subdue an indefinable guilt and proliferate into fragments of unfettered desire.

Near the gate I hear angry voices. With outspread hands the *darwan* is arguing with a couple of beggars. The cast-iron gate is padlocked. No leftovers tonight, he tries to convince them. There is only enough food for the guests. A sceptical female voice continues to harass him. He is relieved to see me. He points to a girl, holding a wailing baby on her hip, demanding to be fed. The feeble lights silhouette alien shapes behind her, enacting a mime of ominous hostility. They are a motley collection of disease-ridden, mutilated, impoverished outcasts destined to live as peripheral shadows in a land that glibly preaches social justice to its prosperous parasites who flock to the mosques for their daily fix of religious piety.

Her name is Yasmin. She stinks of sweat and urine. She earned a good living before the baby came along. I can sense her defiant pride and a will to survive, hardened by the onslaught of unremitting adversities. The baby has almost certainly made her unacceptable to the pimps in the city. I tell her to wait.

Under the awning the copper pots are still warm. A sleepy servant reluctantly removes the lids. There is enough food to feed at least fifty more guests. Nothing can be taken, he informs me diffidently. He has his instructions from Ma.

It is not frequently that I lose complete control of my temper. It is an ugly experience. It is not the poor fellow's fault.

Startled servants scurry into the night with trays of food.

The *darwan* looks jittery as he fumbles with the lock.

The servants are reluctant to go into the street.

'For you,' I say to Yasmin. 'Enjoy it.'

There is a whoop of jubilation as the shadows materialise into clawing hands swooping down on the food. In the mêlée a tray overturns. The street becomes a dining plate. Women and children dive in. The graunch of eager jaws sound like an unseen monster feeding itself in a horror film.

Behind me there is an audible sound of unrestrained laughter. Through an open window I can see them like richly dressed puppets on a stage bathed in a soft golden light.

Yasmin has not moved. 'One day we shall eat with *Shaheb* at his table.' She looks at me with undisguised hatred.

The night is no longer friendly. I move away slowly, resisting the urge to run back inside.

SEVEN

The study table was a gift from my grandfather on my thirteenth birthday. That was the year he drowned in the river.

A feeble arc of light illuminates the scarred wooden surface. A diversity of expressions highlights the moods of a youth grappling with the instability of a formative personality. There are carved drawings and terse phrases echoing the sorrows of unrequited love. Angry expletives and lines of maudlin rhyming couplets. A couple of clichés. Snatches of advice to myself. Bawdy limericks with the obviously unmentionable words left out.

The name FARIDA is engraved at the top of the table. I remember shedding tears of frustration as I painstakingly coloured it in with black ink. Where was she now? The haughty Punjabi girl, who scorned my clumsy advances, was my first infatuation. It was a singularly one-sided affair of idolisation, confused sexuality and tormented passion. The men in her family were all in the army. She is probably a contented wife of an army officer; a fat, cheerful mother of a brood of children living in a posh suburb of Lahore. I wonder if she ever thinks of the gangly 'Bangaal', the 'naapak half-Hindu' who wrote her such awful poems. Does age ever make her regret the virulence of her adolescent scorn?

Until today I ignored the inscriptions with an indifference

with which one disowns unsophisticated and bumbling relatives. But now, as I scrutinise them, they speak to me with a tender eloquence. I bask in their memories. Time has eradicated the pain. I can smile at the agony of the raw emotions which consumed me. It is a lengthy reunion.

It is very late. I flick the switch and the room floods with the darkness of midnight. I feel a surge of loneliness as if I am in an empty train compartment after waving goodbye to friendly faces on the platform.

In the solitude of night the voice of my mind speaks in many tones. Accusatory. Anxious. Reflective. Vexatious. I listen to the murmuring disquietudes of my ongoing troubles. Another explosion in an already fragmented world has once again made me retreat into the gloomy shelter of my inner self to brood on the wilting landscape of my life. To orchestrate myself toward a sustained period of uneventful predictability is seemingly beyond my control. It is not as if I am presumptuous enough to nurture even the slightest notion of manipulating destiny. Even in my reckless moments I am not egotistical enough to think I can have an influence over life or death, pain or happiness. But is it asking too much to be left alone? What, I ask repeatedly, have I done to be pursued so doggedly by misfortune? I find it difficult to pacify myself with the thought that if I do not provoke life, the run of ill luck must pass.

A state of prolonged contentment is a rarity, even unfashionable, nowadays. I suspect many of us harbour the idea that it betokens a lack of intellectual vigour; a condition of near blankness is indicative of an uncreative spirit. I am at a point where a state of soul-destroying, mentally crippling boredom is appealing. I long to reach a point of stasis where nothing really happens to me. I do not wish to remember the past or contemplate the future. My life is like a mischievous child I cannot control. If only I could glide backwards over a smooth surface of time and reach another beginning without the remembrance of what has been!

The house is quiet at last. I managed to convince everyone to go to bed.

'I am quite capable of staying up until morning,' I said with cheerful confidence. 'I will be fine. I'll call if she wakes up and needs help.'

So far the night has been without threats. I have implicit trust in Hashim's professional judgement, but despite his assurances I decided to spend the rest of the night in Nadine's room. I slept soundly for a couple of hours in the afternoon. My weariness is not due to a lack of rest. It is a mental condition of fatigued dullness. The uncertainty of a crisis has a way of stretching the hours with an agonising slowness until you feel that eternity is no longer an incomprehensible concept because you are actually experiencing the essence of its timelessness. It is the burden of a guilt-ridden responsibility that has exhausted me.

I am comforted by Nadine's gentle, even breathing. It has the same peaceful effect on me as the sound of a calm sea under a moonlit sky. For the second night in succession she has slept without being troubled by the retching, vomiting and diarrhoea which have reduced her to an emaciated mass of skin and bones. I am unable to rid myself of the impression of being in a hospital. Even near the open window the room smells nauseatingly of antiseptic. The room is cluttered with drip stands, bottles and packets of medicine, bowls, piles of fresh towels and clean sheets.

I am content to pass the night in the sterile calmness of the room, comforted by the near certainty that this most precious gift of life is intact. I knew it was very serious a few days ago when Hashim cancelled all his appointments to be with Nadine. The entire family hovered around her bed as if she was the focal point in their lives. Little was said. The strength of their silent presence gave me the fortitude I badly needed to steer myself with composure until the worst was over. Nafisa was no less than I expected—optimistic and calmly practical. Hashim was professionally consoling, even though his wrinkled brow betrayed his concern. But it was Ma who surprised me. I have never thought of her as a very down-to-earth person. Yet at a time when I feared that Nadine's illness would trigger an outburst of erratic behaviour, Ma conducted herself and her household with a commonsense efficiency I have never experienced before. Even Khuda Buksh made himself available on the first day of Nadine's illness instead of drifting away to the corner shop for his hourly smoke and gossip with the servants of the neighbourhood. Later that night, without telling us, he rolled out a straw mat and slept outside Nadine's room.

Not since those fateful December days in 1971 have I felt this sort of magnetic unity among us. I am tempted to believe that we tacitly agreed to pool our energies and direct them at Nadine as a form of family therapy. We have almost willed her to recover.

Each day Abba sits beside her bed, on my grandfather's old rocking chair, with a folded newspaper on his lap. He says very little. For hours he looks at her with sad, wistful eyes as if he were regretting some part he may have played in activating her illness. He looks haggard and dispirited. Yesterday I spoke to him about missing his afternoon nap. There was nothing to be done except wait for the antibiotics to take effect. It was not at all necessary for him to sit there without a break.

'We don't want you to be ill,' I said as gently as I could. 'Why are you doing this?'

He did not reply. Instead, he gripped my arm in both his hands. For him it was a rare gesture of extreme emotion. I patted his unsteady hands. His hold tightened. I felt as if we were united by an invisible bond capable of visceral transmission across generations of our family's history. There was a strengthening of my collective identity. I was a Chaudhary, capable of overcoming the most serious of adversities. The uniqueness of individuality was insignificant.

Abba waited until he had asserted control over himself. Any further display of weakness was unthinkable for the head of the family. There was only a slight tremor in his voice. 'Because she is family. She is one of us. When she hurts, all of us feel the pain.'

I did not have the heart to say she will never really be one of us. In some ways I am destined to become a stranger to my daughter. She is likely to carry my name into adulthood. But it will be a name without an instinctive grasp of the pride of the Chaudharies. It would be unfair to demand that understanding from her. I can affect her perceptions of her self and her world. I can even sharpen her sensibilities. But I cannot program the way she feels. I am not empowered to alter the cultural pulse of her life that is tuned to a different rhythm. She simply does not belong here.

I, who have to tear myself between the emotional claims of irreconcilable worlds, am determined to help her establish her cultural roots where she was born. That I should reach such a definitive conclusion about my daughter contradicts my resolution to allow her to evolve without parental interference. All I can say is I have been more conscious of an awkward problem which is irresolvable even in its conceptual stage. I am using it as an excuse to justify my overprotective concerns about her. Nadine is not old enough to grasp its complexity or its long-term implications. The tensions of being a child from a mixed marriage have not yet been apparent in any serious crisis. It is my sporadic fits of anxiety, to shelter her from experiencing ridicule and the pains of non-acceptance, that make me apprehensive about the exacting and sometimes cruel demands of cultural dualism. Will she be strong enough to withstand its ordeals and harvest its bountiful riches? Or will she be cowed into a rejection of her

Bangali heritage? Will she be happier if the genetic strains of the subcontinent were starved into silence?

I have toyed with the prospect of staying here and joining the family business. It is hardly the perfect solution since it ignores the more practical considerations which ultimately must have a bearing on my future. I am tempted by the likelihood of an indolent life without the worries of mortgage, debts, bills and trickles of painstaking savings. Once they are conjured up, fantasies develop at an unbelievable speed. They transcend the limits of reality and elude the snarls of commitment to create unfettered worlds in the privacy of one's mind.

I am envious of Hashim's decisiveness. He has no regrets about coming back. It was the right thing, the only sensible thing to do, he keeps telling me, as if I should obediently follow the trail of an older brother who knows. In my presence, Ma has made it a point to praise his sense of family duty. Even without the *burden of a foreign wife*, it could not have been an easy decision.

Last week I stifled a retort that it was the foreignness of her son rather than that of his estranged wife she was unable to accept. In Ma's parochial world, Farhana should have had a worse standing than Michelle. Hashim's wife is a Punjabi. One of those who butchered us. Had Ma forgotten the bitter memories of war? The atrocities of the Pakistani soldiers? The callous indifference of Punjabi civilians fed on propaganda and lies? Was her hostility toward Michelle's foreignness based on colour rather than religious differences?

I lacked the guts to verbalise my perception of her racial intolerance. I retreated behind the safety of a cowardly silence. My inability to stand up against her was a savage indictment of my own double standards I condemn in others. Had Keith made a similar remark, I would have jumped into an argument without hesitation. I would have derived a malicious pleasure in exposing him to his own untenable prejudices. I can make Keith uncomfortable. I can make him tussle feebly against his upbringing, against his education (he attended one of those joyless and snobbish Melbourne private schools which desperately treats itself as hybrid of the British public school system, aping its customs, bigotry and its condescending view of the rest of the world) and against his South Yarra upbringing which has ossified his conservatism. I can make him think about the contradiction between his inherent belief in Anglo-Saxon superiority and the kingdom values he rigorously defends. At least I force him to reach within himself to examine his beliefs even if it leads to no perceptible change. I doubt if I could have the same influence on Ma. Deeply entrenched as she is in the rightness of her world, she is incapable of raising herself to a level of objective thinking from where she can recognise, let alone confront, her prejudices. What irks me even more is my unwillingness to try, lest I am confronted with the irrefutable evidence of her racism.

Hashim has set me thinking. I am convinced there has been some feverish plotting behind my back. The bait was timely dangled. The convoluted declaration of his intention to divorce Farhana saddened rather than shocked me. Nafisa had said enough for me to conclude all was not well with his marriage. But I had misjudged the seriousness of his marital difficulties.

Hashim sat on the edge of my bed and spoke earnestly. His meticulous arrangements made me feel incompetent but perhaps a little more human. Farhana has agreed to a proposed settlement—a house in Lahore and a sizeable sum of money in an Isle of Man bank account. He is to pay for the children's educational expenses in England. As if to nullify even a hint of wrongdoing on his behalf, Hashim repeatedly emphasised his selflessness in the generosity of the deal. Financially he would be very tight for some time. The cost of setting up the clinic had been exorbitant. He had to sell some land in Savar and borrow money from the bank. Abba was pressuring him to spend more time looking after our handicraft industry. It was impossible for him to squeeze any more time for the business.

I felt the trap as soon as his hand clasped my shoulder. There was a pregnant pause. His eyes softened and a helpless look preceded a passionate plea. Would I consider helping out, say for a couple of years? There was no need to concern myself about Nadine. She could attend boarding school in England with her cousins. He had it all worked out—the school, the term dates, vacations and air fares. The family would bear the expenses. He had Abba's approval.

The scepticism on my face must have been fairly obvious.

'Look, we need to help each other. Right now we are like lame ducks in separate ponds. Things are not too good. We must come together. Abba has left it to us to work it out. He wants you to come back. We all do. The family needs to be reunited. We've had our overseas flings. It's time for you to come home.'

'And ease your load. You want a share in the profit without doing the work. That's a very generous definition of help. You know how to look after yourself, don't you?'

I did not wish to prolong the discussion. As long as he understood that I was not gullible enough to think that his motives were unguided by self-interest, I was prepared to think about the offer without making a quick decision. At that moment I was too preoccupied with Nadira and the dinner, which was only a few hours away, to give it any thought.

Hashim has not changed much over the years. He is a cautious man. A survivor. If he were caught between the Devil and a stretch of water, he would always head for the sea where, he would make certain, a pick-up boat would be waiting for him. Hashim and I think very differently. The patriarch in me is not quite as strong. He did not mention Michelle or her right to have a say in Nadine's future. Although a divorce is a distinct possibility, it will not alter the balance of mutual decision-making about Nadine. I cannot deny Michelle's level-headedness as a mother. She deserves the right to be consulted. I know we both have strong reservations about boarding schools. Even if we agreed to send Nadine to England, how would we coordinate the necessary strands of our relationships from the distance of three continents?

I said nothing further. Hashim is not pushy. He inches his way forward like a worm, slowly but methodically. There was an element of uncertainty in my reticence. For him that was enough encouragement. He was bound to recognise it as a weakness to be probed and exploited with arguments and tangible allurements. It would be a genuine effort to straighten out my life and, at the same time, benefit him. It was to be a conveniently symbiotic arrangement designed to replace the mess I had made of my life. To prevent me from inflicting further harm on myself was an act of brotherly love. That would be Hashim's point of view.

As the purple dusk gathered over Banani, I became anxious for him to leave. 'Can we talk it over some other time?'

'Of course! Think it over.'

I did not quite understand the reason for his gleeful smile. He sounded supremely confident as if he knew more about my future than I did. Perhaps he felt like an overenthusiastic salesperson who sensed he had clinched a lucrative deal even before a commitment had been made.

The evening was to be a beginning . . . a renewal . . . a blossoming . . . ah, the permutation of possibilities in those imaginative mega jumps! I was led by the promises of half-formulated images curled coyly around a reawakened desire. Naturally I made allowance for all that could go wrong—the hesitations, the doubts and the major lines of resistance. It could even develop into a long-drawn and crafty game. All the better. Nothing that the patience of maturity and gentle persistence could not win.

Well, it turned out to be a pile-up of unexpected disasters.

In my single-minded pursuit of what can only be described as a lonely man's far-fetched fantasy, I managed to discover the fragility of my interpretative power. I, who prided myself on reading people's minds and motives, had mixed up the signals with the felicity of a born bungler. A common male trait when it comes to dealing with females, I know. But it did not make me feel any better afterwards. It might have been simple enough to hide behind an innocent exterior to beguile someone else. But a cover-up from myself! Impossible. Failure made me feel cheap, coarse, humiliated and foolish. It left me searching for a mechanism to camouflage the sudden volatility of middle-aged sexuality and the guilty embarrassment of its unfulfilment.

The evening had been carefully structured. That much is evident when I view it in retrospect. I was not the only one with insidious intentions.

I run my fingers across my chin. It feels soft and smooth without a trace of the white stiff stubble which makes me peer into the mirror and prod my face despondently in the mornings. I have overdone the aftershave. *Drakkar Noir*. One of the better ones. Outrageously pricey on the black market.

An entire morning was taken up before I found it in a shop where the imported stuff was stored behind the counters. Customers with foreign passports received immediate attention. Only American dollars were acceptable. No traveller's cheques. Cash and no receipts.

I was an expatriate Bangali. Was a compromise possible? Thirty-five dollars in cash and the rest in traveller's cheques.

'Please wait.' The young assistant spoke to the senior assistant who whispered to the manager. The manager came over and introduced himself. He asked to see my passport. He scrutinised my photograph and examined the visa. I was only interested in buying some aftershave lotion, I reminded him.

The manager motioned the senior assistant in the direction of the door behind the cash register.

An obsequious proprietor entered, bowing and smiling. He pumped my hand up and down as if it were the handle of a tubewell. 'Australian? Australia! Fine country! I wish to go there myself.' He made a great fuss about wrapping the aftershave in white tissue paper. 'Sir, I would be much obliged if you kindly gave me your address in Australia. We Bangalis must help each other!'

Reluctantly I scrawled my name and address on a scrap of paper with the fervent hope that my handwriting was illegible.

'Thank you, sir! No, no money. Please! Consider it to be a gift!' My firm refusal drew a broad smile and a gesture of surrender. 'Whatever you wish. But allow me the honour of offering you a drink. Lemonade? Tea? Please! The room at the back is most comfortable.'

I have enslaved myself to the abject Australian mentality that anything French must be sophisticated and seductive. I roll down the window and let the cool air brush my face. That should take the edge off the smell and leave behind a tantalising whiff. Just right for subdued lighting and . . . I don't know her taste in music. Schubert. A little Mozart, perhaps?

The dozen red roses are fresh. Khuda Buksh emerged from the shadows of the garage to hand them to me with a sly toothless grin, as the car was about to pull out into the street. His fingers wrapped greedily around the money I held out to him. He winked in a most objectionable manner. His entire face twisted grotesquely as the right eyelid closed in a message of sleazy approval.

I am uncomfortable and self-conscious in the tie and jacket. It is like being back at work, screeching at kids and parroting the rules of proper conduct.

I must remember not to overeat. Let her talk. Be an alert

and interested listener. Ask the right questions. No disagreements. Nothing too demonstrative. Keep the voice low and warm. I sound all the warnings I can remember.

A sparsely illuminated night hums past. A nervous apprehension unwinds inside me like an awakening snake.

Flat 2. Fifth floor. I check the idle elevator. It looks new and well-maintained. Under the wall-phone there are clear instructions in case of an emergency. I withdraw my finger before it can press the button marked 5. I decide to use the staircase.

It is hard work. By the time I get there, I can hear myself panting. My knees are ready to collapse and my calf muscles are tender. I pause in the foyer. An elderly couple eye me suspiciously as they wait for the elevator. They saw me enter through the door marked STAIRS—EMERGENCY ONLY. The woman frowns at my sheepish smile. Impatiently the man jabs the button even though the lights on the overhead panel indicate the elevator is on its way up.

Flat 2 is on my right. I knock on the varnished door before I see the buzzer. I feel awkward holding the flowers. I resist the urge to straighten my tie knot. I transfer the flowers to my left hand and try the buzzer. There is no urgency in the heavy footsteps. I cradle the flowers in my forearm. I think I look more relaxed that way.

There are two sharp clicks. My best smile is in place.

It cannot be. It must be a horrendous mistake. The wrong day? A professional presence?

The grin reflects no surprise. It is friendly enough with a faint trace of smugness. I would have no hesitation about scraping it off with sandpaper.

'Hello once again! You didn't think you'd see me so soon, huh? Come in, come in!' Hashim notices the flowers. The grin disappears.

I cannot tell whether the frown is one of confusion or disapproval.

'Here!' I ram the roses against his chest.

'You didn't have to!' He grimaces and shakes his head in disbelief. 'Thank you! You have changed!' He puts his arm around my shoulders and we go inside.

I could cry in disgust and anger at myself. I think of what it has taken to get me here. Not since that day across the river have I really wanted to hit Hashim. Now I want to smash his face and obliterate that look of contentment. Everything about him irritates me—his scruffy jeans, faded T-shirt, thongs and, above all, his air of familiarity with the flat. I bitterly resent the inescapable conclusion that he is not here as a visitor. He is at home.

There was a story my grandfather repeatedly told us about Lobi Mia, the ambitious young *zamindar* with an obsessive desire to present his future wife, a lady renowned for her beauty, with land extending as far as she could walk in a day. His acquisitive passion for land led him to a relentless campaign of deceit against the landowners around him. Ultimately my great-grandfather's threat to whip him out of the area chastened Lobi Mia enough to keep him away from Shopnoganj and prey on the less resolute neighbours on the other side of the river. With money and patience, Lobi (or Greedy as we dubbed him because his name translated into English made him sound more villainous) persuaded enough *zamindars* to sell their land and claim the unofficial title of the richest man in the district. With no more land to buy, his thoughts turned to marriage. It was with some regret he realised the years had stolen away. He had aged, and his fiancée was now an old woman.

The morning after the wedding, Lobi Mia stood proudly with his wife on the verandah of their house. With a sweep of his hands he offered her all he had accumulated over the years. 'Whatever land you can cover in a day's walk is yours.'

She looked at the endless expanse of paddy fields stretching as far as she could see. Without speaking, she led her husband by his hand to the back of the house. With his walking stick she marked a small, rectangular plot of land. 'There! This is what I claim,' she said. 'This is all I need. The rest is useless.'

Dada broke off at that point and beckoned us with his index finger. When we were close enough, he whispered, 'Never waste time with the unimportant things in life.'

Our bewildered reaction made him chuckle. 'You will understand one day after you have made the same mistake.'

With the recollection I can taste the bitter truth in the tale. *Never waste time with the unimportant things in life.* He was right. He knew about human weaknesses. How am I to know what is unimportant unless the trivial is pursued and its worthlessness discovered? Experiential learning is the toughest form of education. It is an ongoing course without the satisfaction of completion. A high level of failure is assured for the slow learners like myself.

The rest of the evening crawls by quietly. I sit opposite them during dinner. My presence does not inhibit their expression of mutual affection. They hold hands and laugh at their own private jokes.

Teenage stuff, I think scornfully. Symptoms of starved affections. Even then I cannot deny the jealousy that rises in me like a poisonous fume. I join the conversation whenever I can, but most of the time I feel out of place and resentful of Hashim.

Nadira is a superb cook and a charming hostess. Her poise and graciousness absolve her of any misdemeanour in misleading me. I direct my silent wrath at my brother. We listen to Vilayat Khan and Ali Akbar Khan. Later in the evening, when she excuses herself to tidy up in the kitchen, Hashim brings out a bottle of vintage port and we settle down for the evening's main purpose.

I have been fed and softened up. He comes directly to the point. Was I prepared to do them a favour?

Yes, if I could. I commend him on the choice of port and

proceed to tell him about the quality wines produced in Australia.

He leads me back to the predicament he is in. For the first time in the evening I relax. Hashim's caged tension amuses me. I have to listen to a detailed exposition of how his relationship with Nadira began. Pure chance, of course.

'Of course,' I echo and upset him for some unknown reason. I assure him that there is no need to flagellate himself with moral justifications as long as he exercises his parental responsibility. These things happen despite the best of intensions. Love (I try to sound noble), even at our age, does not seek excuses. It does not care for conventions or rules of conduct. It has a way of bursting out from the cage of self-discipline to show us what volatile creatures we are.

Hashim leans forward and looks me in the eyes.

I wink and blow him a brotherly kiss. 'I am all yours to command.'

His whisper is barely audible. Would I be prepared to tell Ma about his changed circumstances? About Nadira?

'What about her?' I ask innocently.

'You know what I mean! About us.'

I know what he means. Only kidding. I am prepared to try. Were they thinking of marriage?

'All the time! We want to be married as soon as my divorce comes through.'

I suggest it may help to set a tentative wedding date. I was not game enough to tell Ma that her oldest and best was in a de facto relationship without any serious matrimonial intention. Hashim mutters something under his breath when I raise the possibility of a visit to the *Maulana* for a prayer session and a *tabeez* to protect him from further temptation.

As long as there is some assurance for Ma to begin working on a guest list, I think I can handle her initial outrage and the inevitable lecture on the infectious immorality we have caught in the West.

Hashim becomes thoughtful. He is like a general who has prepared the battle strategies with great deliberation, only to find the opposing army in a state of abject surrender. He looks dissatisfied as he refills the glasses. My willingness to cooperate so readily is most uncharacteristic. He decides to press on.

Had I given any further thought to our afternoon's discussion?

'None at all.'

Hashim does not like the abrupt firmness of my reply. He leans forward again. His body language is off-putting. All it does is make me aware of the disproportionate distribution of his body fat.

Isn't it time for me to sort out my life? Leaving the country was a grand gesture of a romantic idealist. At the time it was an admirable token of protest. My moral revulsion for the indiscriminate slaughter was understandable. But that was years ago. Why did I insist on gashing myself on the rusty remembrances of another life? Memory was a matter of convenience.

'The past shouldn't distort your vision of the future. All of us cannot be held responsible for what happened. War is full of excesses. It is not your responsibility to feel the guilt of a once vengeful nation when you were personally not involved. You have been away too long. It's about time you realised that this is home.'

I promise to think it over. I am not stalling for time. I mean it. It is an alternative I must seriously consider.

Nadira comes back to sit next to Hashim. There is a homely ambience about her flat I find very relaxing. There is an all-pervasive tranquillity in their lives. I am struck by Nadira's calmness and its settling effect on Hashim. I remark on the smoothness of her transition to a different rhythm of life.

'I get the impression you are very settled, as if you regret nothing,' I say enviously.

She strokes the back of Hashim's head. 'To regret would be to go back and rummage among the junk I have discarded. I am learning to live with a new set of priorities. I am committed to them. Life can be such a creative act if you make the effort. I no longer treat living as if it is a treacherous enemy. It is subtle and full of obtuse meanings. I intend to devote my life to their discovery and understanding.'

Talking to Nadira gives me confidence. It makes me think that perhaps the terms of life are renegotiable. Maybe life was not meant to be a linear, one-way motion. There may be opportunities for U-turns and diversions, for slowing down, for pausing to search for a previously missed niche in the haste to keep going.

When I tried to ring Melbourne I was in a ponderous frame of mind. I had been thinking about my conversation with Hashim. I was adrift in a maze of possibilities. The enlarged doubts of the unhappy forties and all those tangential connections, which were seemingly unimportant once, now clung to me and cautioned against any rash undertaking.

I did not think I could stand another day of Nadine's whining. It began with a reasonable request. She wanted to talk to Michelle. Within moments there were tears and outpourings of a recuperating child missing her mother. I felt helpless under the onslaught. I was reasonably conditioned not to react immediately to the whims of a distraught daughter. However, I had to admit I had never consciously taken steps to develop a workable mechanism to actually counteract her occasional tantrums. I justified them as a part of the growing process. Hormonal changes. She would grow out of them. I would have been angry if anyone had suggested I was among those guilty of parental laziness.

I want Mum!

I want to go home!

Why can't you call her now?

Now, Dad!
I don't care! I want to talk to her now!
God! I hate you!
I don't want to see you again!

The acrimonious barrage was flung at me in a growing crescendo of shrieking noises until Hashim intervened and managed to calm her with the promise of a special treat in Shopnoganj where Dad and Uncle Hashim were born.

I explained I had to ring Melbourne first. Michelle had given me her Tuscany address without a phone number. She had mentioned there was a phone in the villa. Trapped in her self-pity, Nadine refused to understand why the entire world could not synchronise itself to suit her whims. The time difference was of no consequence to her. Knowing Keith's obsession with his hours of sleep, I was not prepared to wake him in the middle of the night unless it was unavoidable. I promised to call early in the morning.

It is a forlorn sensation to be making a cup of tea for myself. It is easy to adapt oneself to the luxury of servants. I bumble around the kitchen for a kettle.

It must be past nine o'clock in Melbourne. In his cotton dressing-gown Keith has finished breakfast—cereal with fresh strawberries and Kiwi fruit, white bread, thickly spread with butter and marmalade. Weak tea.

A nasal-toned operator is reluctant to tell me when I might get the call.

'It's an emergency!'

'Aren't they all?' She responds indifferently.

I check again, after twenty minutes. She tells me to be patient. It is another half an hour before the phone rings.

I hear a snatch of the soprano genius of Emma Kirkby before she is remote controlled into an indistinct background voice. Even from this distance she sounded ethereal.

Keith's measured voice says, 'Hello?'

He is in his study with those splendid walnut-stained wall-to-wall shelves and the leather armchairs. On the Edwardian side table next to the door, the crystal vase is crammed with white carnations from the garden. Behind the phone is the smiling jade Buddha I bought for him in Bangkok. I can imagine him stroking the curvature of its smooth belly, his mind tuned to the eleven o'clock mass.

'Keith?'

There is a crackling noise.

'Keith?'

'Yes! Who's calling?'

'Iqbal.'

'Who? Can you speak up please?'

'Iqbal!'

'Oh! Yes. What can I do for you!' His free hand drops to his side. His shoulders straighten. He stands erect, his lips pressed together in a thin tight line of forbearance. From the cedar-lined wall Her Majesty smiles at him.

I dispense with the formality of a greeting. 'Do you have Michelle's phone number? She said there was a phone in the villa.'

The pause insinuates a rapid scrutiny of my motives. 'Is Nadine all right?'

'She has been ill for the last few days. Nothing very serious. A little diarrhoea and vomiting. She wants to speak to her mother.'

His voice loses its Sunday morning God's-in-Heaven-radiating-His-Grace-on-Catholics complacency. 'She is not in any danger, is she?'

'None at all.' I am emphatic in my denial. 'She is well on her way to recovery. Another couple of days and . . . '

'Thank God! I suppose one has to expect these illnesses in your country. Hold on for a sec.'

I do not know the time difference between Bangladesh and Italy. I shall wait until Nadine is awake before I try to call

Michelle. I can hear Khuda Buksh pottering around in the kitchen, coughing occasionally. He has probably lit the first of his many *biris* for the day. He is forbidden to smoke in the kitchen. The morning smoke is one of his regular triumphs over Ma. Sunrise is another half an hour away. I might go for a walk and think of what I have to say to Michelle. What if whatshisname answers the phone? Dammit! Why am I so fucking jealous of him? It should have passed by now. Why do I let him make me feel as if I am a eunuch? I better grab a pencil. I'm still holding on.

'Hello?'

I am as certain of the voice as I am of being alive. Yet I refuse to believe it. I feel a hot rush of perverse triumph. My stomach growls. I feel giddy and weightless as if I have drunk too much champagne too quickly. I want to goad her. Hurt her. Make fun of her. I am helpless to subdue the meanness that rears in me like a gigantic tidal wave, crushing everything in its way. Just as suddenly it subsides and withdraws, leaving me as empty as a deserted stretch of sandy beach.

'Hello?'

'Michelle?'

'Iqbal, how is she?'

'Fine! Just fine! She'll be out of bed today. I didn't think you'd be back so soon.'

'I'd rather not go into that now. I have written to you.'

'I didn't mean to pry. Sorry.'

'Hello?'

'I said I didn't mean to pry!'

'Has a doctor seen her?'

'Of course a doctor has treated her! That's a bloody stupid question!'

'Was the doctor properly qualified?'

'This one was trained and experienced in England. You know, where they know everything and never make mistakes. He happens to be my brother.'

'I'm sorry. I wasn't trying to be rude.'

'I am sure you weren't. It comes naturally when your family talks about the third world. What happened to your friend?'

'Who?'

'Collie.'

'God! You can be a callous bastard! The name is Colin, okay? Now, may I speak to Nadine?'

'It's early morning here. She's still asleep.'

'I want to talk to her.' When Michelle is angry she lowers her voice in order to control herself. It rasps and rustles like a snake slithering on dry leaves.

'Well, make the effort and call back in a couple of hours.'

'I will!' she says firmly and cuts me off.

Nadine springs to her feet when I tell her about the impending call. The colour rushes back to her cheeks and her voice is shrill with excitement. She checks her watch every few minutes and prances around the house, telling everyone how much she has to say to her mother.

The house is unusually quiet. Nafisa left for the university immediately after breakfast. Abba has gathered all the morning newspapers and retired to the study. Ma passed me grimly on her way to the kitchen. The servants, I suspect, are in for a rough morning.

I wander back upstairs, unable to ignore the spectre of Michelle's invisible presence which has cast a gloom over the house. I resent the strength of her influence on Nadine. I have done all I can to be a caring parent. I thought we had managed to open all our lines of communication. I know she loves me. Yet I cannot help feeling inferior to Michelle. I cannot flatter myself to think that Nadine would have responded in the same manner had I been in Michelle's position. I have always thought that squabbling over children is a ridiculous exercise in power-play. It should not occur between sensible adults.

Even then, as I tenaciously cling to that belief, I instinctively parallel my situation with someone who has begun to savour the benefits of hard labour, only to be overtaken by an unexpectedly catastrophic reversal.

Nadine is all compliance. She has showered and shampooed her hair. Quite amazingly the bathroom floor is dry. No wet towels or dirty clothes. She does not even make a fuss about taking her capsules. The bed has been neatly made and there are no books on the floor. I receive an impulsive hug and a kiss on both cheeks.

We go to my room for a game of Scrabble. She keeps looking at the phone on the bedside table as we go through the motions of a serious contest.

She screams and lunges for the phone when it rings. She grabs the receiver and yells, 'Mum!'

I get up to leave the room.

Her shoulders droop dejectedly and she mumbles 'Yes' several times before handing me the receiver.

It is Hashim calling to tell me he will be dropping by later in the morning to see Nadine.

When Michelle finally calls, Nadine makes no move to pick up the phone.

'I think that might be yours. Go on!' I urge her. 'Pick it up.'

Almost shyly she does. There is a cautious, 'Hello?' Then an exuberant, 'Mum? Is that really you?'

I pause to watch the transformation in her face. As I close the door, I hear her sobbing. 'Mum, I miss you! I want to come home!'

Ma is near the kitchen. I can hear her questioning Khuda Buksh about a neighbour's complaint. The old fellow was seen behind a tree, watching a young servant girl bathing in the creek.

I am hesitant about going down, even though I feel like getting as far away from my bedroom as I possibly can.

I linger undecidedly in the middle of the staircase as if I have suddenly realised I have nowhere to go.

I allow myself to feel lonely again.

EIGHT

N ot like this. It was never like this.' Abba shakes his head ruefully. 'There were no fewer than twelve of us for *Jumma's namaz*. Twenty-five, sometimes more, for *Eid*.'

He taps the driveway with his walking stick. I had a new one made from the best available cane—hand-carved and varnished to the colour of burnished gold.

Abba's pride is undiminished. He shrugs off my helping hand and stumbles into the car with an uncoordinated movement of withered limbs.

I slide in beside him from the other side.

'Isn't there anyone else?' He sticks his head out of the window and sees Ma standing at the front door. He ignores her wave and slumps into the warm leather seat. 'We were a strong family,' he mumbles sullenly. 'Able-bodied men and boys. Brothers, cousins, uncles, nephews, fathers and sons. But look at us now! An ailing old man and his two sons. The rest are either dead or scattered around the world. There is no sense of family responsibility any more.'

I cannot tell whether his last remark was intentionally directed at me.

There is a dreamy look in his faded eyes. They are soft and watery, without the hard glint we once feared and respected.

His brothers unkindly called him Cobra Eyes behind his back. He could speak his mind without uttering a word.

I am sad to see him like this—confused and dejected, forced to live among the shadowy ruins of his dynastic dreams, tortured by the memories of his days of patriarchal glory.

They were good times before the war with Pakistan. We lived in a state of unthinking opulence, frigidly secure in the stability of the family's inflexible traditions which never made us think beyond our chronically wasteful needs. It was a foolishly dangerous mixture of self-gratification and lazy igno-rance which was not disturbed until the Pakistani soldiers embarked on their genocidal rampage on that hot and crazy March midnight and turned the world upside down.

How well I have preserved my childhood memories of the fun and pain generated at the family gatherings during *Eid-ul-Azha*! Relatives arrived from different corners of the subcontinent—Karachi, Lahore, Calcutta, Chittagong and Sylhet. Extra cooks and servants moved in. Mattresses, pillows and starched sheets were to be found everywhere in the house. The crowded dining room became the nerve centre of our lives. We ate and drank with an undisciplined energy. There were excited chatter and animated conversations. Bark-ing dogs and frightened cats. Tearful children. The lingering aromas of spices and curries, frying *samosas* and *nimkis*. The bathrooms smelled of Dettol and tincture iodine. Meatsafes, crammed with *chomchoms* and *roshomaalie* were happily incor-porated as booties in the noisy games of banks and robbers. We were at that age when sweets were far more seductive than rupees.

Above everything else, I remember the laughter. The house seemed to ring with the sound of passionate, soulful laughter as if the family had discovered the elixir of ultimate happi-ness.

There was something peculiarly satisfying about the grow-ing disorder which rapidly displaced Ma's rigid household routines. It was one of our rare opportunities to triumph over the tyranny of set times for meals, play, bath and bed. As if the perpetuation of domestic chaos was the ultimate vindication of our vitality and the indomitable Chaudhary spirit, Hashim and I worked stealthily to hasten the deteriorating situation. Knowing Ma's fetish for cleanliness and well-behaved children, we exhorted unsuspecting cousins to eat and drink on the run, criticise the food, play ball games inside the house and exercise their rights of freedom which included screaming, fighting, teasing each other, bumping into helpless servants, stripping the guava trees and pelting passers-by on the street with ripe fruits.

There was one particular activity which drove the adults into a frenzy of speechless anger, compelling them to abandon the principles of seasonal goodwill and resort to corporal punishment. Just before lunch we gathered on the landing, halfway up the stairs. Usually there were ten of us old enough to launch into such daring action—Hashim, Nafisa, Shabnam, Shomu, Dilu, Moin, Rani, Bacchu, Heera and me. At the sound of Hashim's whistle, we streamed down the stairs, imitating what I would now liken to a banshee's wail. The object of the game was to run into an unsuspecting servant carrying food into the dining room, and knock him against a piece of furniture before running off to tell Ma about the accident. It was a malicious little exercise of vindictive children hell-bent on mischief.

'Never again! This is the last time!' Ma vowed every year after the guests had departed and she went from room to room surveying the damage. Fortunately she never really meant to carry out her threat. Her generosity and desire for family unity overcame her angry resolution and dictated handwritten letters of invitation which were sent several months before *Eid-ul-Azha*.

The vagaries of the lunar calendar added that tantalising touch of uncertainty to prevent the excitement from waning.

On the twenty-ninth day of the holy month the entire family assembled on the terrace, well before dusk, to scan the fading sky for a glimpse of the silvery sliver. The idea was to spot the moon before the siren from the local mosque confirmed its appearance. Unknown to my parents, bets were placed on the possibility of an extra day of waiting. Playful arguments were fuelled by Chonchol Chacha's facetious remarks about Muslims celebrating *Eid* on the moon one day and having to change, what he thought, was the unscientific system of the Islamic calendar.

In the excitement of inane conversations and sky watching, it was easy for Nafisa and me to slip downstairs to farewell the cows and the goats in the backyard. They were inconsolable moments of sadness for us. We grieved for the helpless animals. It did not seem right that an auspiciously happy occasion should revolve around an act of such inexplicable brutality. In our own clumsy way we consoled the animals by rolling small bales of hay from the garage to the trees where they were tied.

I was plunged into the throes of unsurpassable terror. I imagined the collective curses of the animals would eventually take effect, and that one day I would be dumped on my back and held down by the servants to feel the edge of a butcher's knife sawing my throat. This was a period of my life when death vividly presented itself as a barren land of unending darkness. I associated death with a prolonged and intense pain which continued to torture me as I was floating my way to wherever I was destined to go. It was all up there somewhere, I was told. I would understand when I grew up. Although the idea of a soul was pounded into me from a very early age, I never drew a convincing distinction between my physical being and this unseen and unfelt part of me which was supposedly indestructible.

We were with the animals when the wailing sirens prompted the celebratory explosion of firecrackers in the neighbourhood. The deafening noise made me cling to one of the animals and weep unashamedly at the monumental cruelty which governed our enjoyment of *Eid* and my own inexcusable part in it. I felt like an accomplice to a heinous crime. In the darkness I sat among the animals with growing animosity toward the unfeeling adults and their peculiar customs.

Nafisa was there to comfort me. She held my head against her palpitating chest until I quietened down. Even though she was younger than me, she managed to cope with our accumulated pain with a serene dignity that has characterised everything she has done in her life. I resented my dependence on her. I was brought up with the implicit belief that women cried and men consoled them. The reversal of roles worried me. Was there something wrong with me? Why wasn't I like Hashim who eagerly awaited the butcher's arrival after we returned from the mosque? He was fascinated by the way the animals were skinned and their entrails removed. He had no hesitation about touching the warm organs, probing and prodding with an innate curiosity I was never able to understand. He was almost proud of the blood stains on his hands.

I had to be coaxed back inside the house by Khuda Buksh. I hated the sight of the happy, smiling faces. I turned away from the hugging and the kissing. I did not wish anyone *Eid Mubarak*. I watched Nafisa drift back into the mainstream of noisy merriment. I sulked in obscure corners until before dinner when Abba went through a laboriously stylised ritual of presenting us each with a set of new clothes.

We gathered in his study. Usually a man of few words, Abba kept us waiting as he made his annual speech about cohesion and blood ties and the need to come together more often to renew family commitments.

'We are Chaudharies. Not for a second should we forget our wonderful identity. It is a privilege! A privilege with responsibilities which are an essential part of this great and proud family . . . ' And on he went, gathering momentum like a runaway cart down a sloping road.

We heard the same sentiments every year. Trite phrases, spoken in a barely audible monotone, endeavoured to glorify us into some sort of noble creatures living out our utopian ideals of self-sacrifice and altruism in our pursuit to help the people of Shopnoganj. Of course we needed wealth to succeed. He sounded as though the villagers were our excuse for making money. I guess he was aware of the greed and the lust for power and what they were slowly doing to us. Abba was a man of principles, torn between his fierce family loyalties and his uncompromising sense of fair play. He needed his illusions to give his working life a moral purpose.

'Dinner's on the table and I don't have all night to serve people!' Ma's curt and business-like reminder rescued him from the embarrassment of a limp conclusion to a speech which became increasingly maudlin. As if he realised he had stepped out of character into a foreign world of expressed emotions, Abba quickly withdrew into his impenetrable shell of aloofness. He avoided our eyes and busily handed out the labelled boxes wrapped in coloured paper.

We pretended to be surprised. Each member of the family went up to Abba to touch his feet and receive a box.

My spirits lifted at the sight of the white *Panjabi* with gold buttons and goffered sleeves, matching wide-bottomed trousers, a cotton prayer cap and a pair of leather sandals from Bata. The only yearly variation was the accompanying toy each child received. I banished the waiting animals into a dark, enclosed corner of my mind and suppressed the guilt until the following year.

I became part of the family again.

A restless night of whispered conversations and fits of dozing led to a dawn awakening for the adults and servants. After sunrise the children were awakened. I had to be dragged into the bathroom for the obligatory shower and *wazu*. The males ate first. A breakfast of *parathas*, eggs and vermicelli set the tone for the brisk walk to the mosque for the special morning prayers.

We must have been quite a sight. With swaggering steps, we stepped out in close formation, the male servants carrying the prayer rugs at a respectful distance behind us. The women stood on the front verandah and waved us off. People on the streets acknowledged our presence.

'*Eid Mubarak*!' They greeted us. '*Eid Mubarak*!'

'Chaudhary *Shaheb*, how well your family looks!'

'*Mashallah*! What a blessed family!'

'*Aadab*, Chaudhary *Shaheb*! *Eid Mubarak*!'

It was a feeling of immense strength to walk among the men and receive the undisguised adulation of the neighbours. It made me feel invincible and quite superior to those who greeted us. We were Allah's chosen people, thoroughly deserving of the respect shown to us.

No, it was never like this. I know what Abba means.

Unnoticed the car crawls out of the gate. The street is deserted, except for a group of boys quarrelling over a game of marbles on the nature strip.

We are now a shrunken family without a youthful gloss. Unlike Dhanmandi, Banani teems with the young nouveau riche engrossed in compiling their fortunes and buying the expensive symbols of prestige to give their moneyed status the respectability they crave. I think Hashim is hurting with the same feeling of loss as I am. He stares broodily out of the front window.

We are three silent strangers imprisoned in our private memories of the way we were.

Abba's wobbly chin drops on his chest. His eyes close but his hands firmly clutch the knob of the walking stick.

'Baitul Mukarram,' Hashim instructs the chauffeur.

Abdul steps gently on the accelerator.

We are too early for Friday's prayer. Abba runs into some friends who are anxious for free medical advice from Hashim. I drift away from them, unconvinced of my purpose in coming here. It was Ma who organised us and Hashim who requested me not to upset her.

This is to be a prayer of thanksgiving for Nadine's recovery.

'Allah willed it!' Ma asserted. 'We must be grateful for His generosity.'

'Modern medicine may have had a part,' I suggested quietly without looking at Hashim.

He edged close to me. 'Keep trying and you will get another appointment with the *Maulana*,' he hissed between clenched teeth.

Ma ignored my claim and turned to Abba with instructions for a donation to the orphanage. An *imam* has been commissioned with the reading of the Koran every morning. *Maulana* Azad has been consulted. On his advice one hundred beggars have been fed. All that remains to be done is thank Allah personally in Arabic and Bangla.

It is warm and muggy. The tropic's brief flirtation with the cool season is over. The midday sun resembles the coagulated yoke of an overfried egg—a faded yellow, streaked with white and surrounded by thick, albuminous clouds.

From the top step of Baitul Mukarram, Bongobhondu Avenue is like the fossilised backbone of a giant, prehistoric monster. It curves slightly as it heads toward the old part of the city. A narrow strip of raised earth, cemented on the sides and profusely populated with wild grass and weeds in different stages of unrestrained growth, runs along the centre of the thoroughfare. Like impaled crucifixes, thin wooden posts support neon lights branching over either side of the busy road.

The mosque itself stands at the end of a wretched stretch of cemented wasteland, its massive dome rising like the bald head of a helpless giant, whose neck is imprisoned in concrete, to enshrine a landmark of striking ugliness.

To my right the market has grown far beyond my recollection of a few sparsely stocked shops. The intervening years have transformed it into an overcrowded oriental bazaar likely to be encountered in a Spielberg adventure. Hawkers, barbers, tricksters, shoeshine boys, hardened housewives with hands tightly gripping their bags and wary eyes on their children, scalpers, fruit sellers, clothes merchants, fortune-tellers, snake charmers, fakirs and animals form kaleidoscopic patterns of life's infinite idiosyncracies which fascinate my timidly ordered mind attuned to one of suburbia's most deadening pursuits.

My senses respond joyously to the acrid smells, the palpitating sounds and the swirl of colours. I have grown accustomed to the sanitised predictability of the supermarket and the soul-numbing trolley pushing under neon lights on alternate Thursday evenings. My mind, inactivated by the softly piped middle-of-the-road music switches to the automatic mode as I weave the trolley between shelves of tins, bottles and packets. It takes me exactly forty-seven minutes between grabbing a trolley and the fatigued check-out person's toneless, unvarying 'How are you today?' This includes the stop at the deli for Hungarian white salami, kabana, Virginian ham and slices of chicken loaf.

This is unbelievably different. No restraints. No clearly defined patterns of movement. Everything appears to be on the move. Fact and fiction collide, separate and then collide again. Anything seems possible. Any minute I expect the white adventurer with the American accent to race through the market, knocking over stalls and onlookers, in a daring attempt to escape the evil clutches of the grubby little oriental villains.

Across the market, in the open square, crowds have congregated near the massive twin gates leading to the stadium.

A seedy throng of several hundred men, waving crudely made signs, moves closer to the steps of the mosque.

'Infidels! Barbarians!' An incensed voice bellows behind me. 'What shameless daring to hold protest meetings in front of Allah's house!'

The indignant man, I assume from his officious bearing, is one of the mosque's caretakers. He strokes his long, untrimmed beard with the fingers of both hands.

'Don't you support a just cause of the beggars' union?' I draw his attention to a large banner entreating the city's beggars to unite against police atrocities.

The slightly built *mullah* is distressed into uttering a short prayer for the imperilled souls of the misguided militants who have organised themselves without any outward sign of trepidation for disturbing the peace near Allah's sacred domain.

There is a roar of approval from a smaller group further away.

'*Bhai!* Over there!' The *mullah* touches me lightly on the arm. 'That's the servants' union. Further on, the street cleaners. The bank clerks are on the other side with the factory workers next to them. I ask you, is this the place for such meetings? *Bhai,*' he pleads as if I am empowered to disperse the gatherings at my pleasure. 'What has happened to the respect we should have for our glorious religion? These are the signs that the end of the world is near. Who could have dreamed of such unforgivable behaviour from beggars and servants in the old days. *Yah* Allah!' He sighs. '*Maaf kohrow!* Spare us your wrath. Forgive these ignorant sinners!'

This is becoming extremely interesting. I move down the steps.

The beggars are listening with rapt attention to a remarkably well-fed speaker elaborating on the Islamic imperatives of equality and justice, with lengthy quotes from the Koran. He raises his voice and demands free housing. There is rapturous applause. He insists on a free meal a day to be provided by the government. They clap and whistle. Encouraged by the support, he smiles at them. 'Police must stop bothering us!' He shakes a defiant index finger. 'Seeking alms should be encouraged by the government as a means of self-employment! Do you agree?' They whoop and hoot and go wild.

Their noise level threatens the rival groups. The equally portly leader of the servants' union reciprocates by producing a megaphone from a hessian sack, turning up the volume and reigning supreme.

Near the stadium gates three police vans pull up. Armed and helmeted policemen begin to appear in ones and twos.

Over the public loudspeaker there is an announcement that the congregational prayer will commence in half an hour.

Absorbed by the likelihood of a confrontation between the police and the union, I am unaware of the close attention I have been receiving from a gang of beggars. They have formed a tight circle around me.

No need to call for help, I tell myself. Don't panic.

A man swathed in pieces of torn clothes reaches out with a bandaged hand and jabs me in the ribs. His face is covered with a dirty scarf, as though he were a guerilla fighter unwilling to reveal his facial features. There is a faint, lingering smell of decaying flesh.

'Do you think your demands are reasonable?' I ask him awkwardly, managing to keep a tremor out of my voice.

There is no reply. They press closer. Several hands reach out to stroke the crisp whiteness of my *Panjabi*.

Through the jagged oblong slits in the scarf, two dark orbs gaze at me without expression. A long-drawn whine, like the noise of a chainsaw slicing through timber, makes me step back into a wall of bony limbs. I smell sweaty, unwashed bodies.

'Don't go *Shaheb*.' It is almost a polite request.

My hands are grabbed and pinned behind my back.

Enough pressure is exerted to convey the seriousness of their intention.

I cannot see a policeman within calling distance.

I can hear a roar near the market.

I try to follow the movement of their hands. I wonder who has the knife. Never before have I been this close to a serious injury. The palms of my hands are clammy, and I can feel the perspiration on my face.

Suddenly I have a fierce desire to see Nadine. We are inseparable—walking to school, climbing in the Grampians, catching yabbies in the dam, arguing over popcorn at the movies, strolling along Sturt Street and comparing our diminishing ice-cream cones. I have a fleeting vision of her on a lonely hill. Head bowed, she is weeping. In her hands she holds a bunch of droopy flowers.

My mind works furiously on survival. I let my body become limp so that there is not even a faint sign of resentful resistance. Grimy hands dive into my side pockets. A handkerchief flutters to the ground. A hand is inserted again to grope among the hayfever tablets and a bunch of keys. In my other pocket I carry a small bottle of eye drops and a leather wallet I bought recently in a handicraft shop.

'I don't have much money!' Despite my resolution, my voice now trembles with fear.

They count seventy-five takas. The wallet is flung to the ground and then picked up again.

I am pushed forward roughly to the middle of the circle.

'I don't have any more!'

Someone spits on me. I feel an uncomfortable wetness on the thin cotton sleeve of my left arm. I dare not make a move to wipe it. Other hands grab me.

Like giant spiders, there are fingers crawling all over me. They linger near the groin. The probing intensifies as my body tenses involuntarily. My grimace of pain evokes a harsh sadistic laugh.

I hear the *azan*. '*Allah O Akbar!*'

'No money belt!' The man sounds disappointed.

'There's not much we can show you for seventy-five takas, *Shaheb!*'

'We are honest men. We don't want you to feel cheated.'

'Here, have a look at Amjad!' A bare-bodied beggar, his torso covered with lumpy sores, pounces on the frail, helpless man who looks like a walking mummy. The scarf is torn from Amjad's face.

The face is brought close to mine.

I forget my humiliation and fear. I stare in horrified disbelief. Between the nostrils and a crescent of a chin, a yawning hole gapes at me. The inside of the exposed mouth is dotted with suppurative wounds. The ulcers ooze with a thick, gooey pus flecked with blood. The grey flesh, behind what appears to be an obscenely oversized tongue, quivers as Amjad wheezes. It is like staring into the bubbling crater of an active volcano.

The stench chokes my nostrils. I feel my stomach heave.

Amjad whimpers a feeble protest and raises the remains of a stumpy hand to hide his shame.

They laugh, not at the leper, but at my nakedness. I am made to feel incomplete. Ignorant. Petty. I stand there without the trappings of my civilised world to protect me from the rawness of a dark knowledge too terrible to confront.

The bare-bodied man places a gentle hand on Amjad's head. 'Is that reasonable, *Shaheb*? Is there anything reasonable in our lives? Is there anything worthwhile in his life? Look at him! He has no home, no money. He even finds it difficult to beg for food. People don't go near him. He has few friends, even among his own kind. He doesn't have a face? Not even that! How deprived can a man be? Tell me, *Shaheb*, how much can a man do without?'

They let me go.

Unsteadily I run up the steps. I hide behind a pillar and

cover my face with tremulous hands. I know people are staring at me.

The nightmare bursts through the darkness and taunts me mercilessly with its silent presence. I see every detail of his ruined face. I feel alternate waves of revulsion and compassion in the pit of my stomach. A fit of shaking seizes me. I long for a hot shower with plenty of soap to lather away the uncleanliness of my ignorance which has seeped through the pores of my skin and dirtied me inside.

I stumble to the water trough where people are washing themselves in preparation for prayer. The slap of water feels cool against my burning skin. I wash my hands and face repeatedly. I run a wet hand around the back of my neck.

I drag myself back to the top of the steps. The meeting is over. There is a scuffle between the beggars and police. There are shouts of encouragement from several directions. The threat of serious physical violence subsides as truckloads of policemen arrive. The servants and the sweepers join the beggars. There is a vociferous argument about the right to hold meetings near the mosque. The bank clerks have not moved. They stand with an aloof disdain near the farthest gate.

'Where did you go? We have to find a place inside.' Hashim has been looking for me with a couple of prayer rugs rolled under his armpit.

We enter the main prayer hall and find a spot at the back, in front of a pillar.

'Abba?' I ask, hoping we do not have to sit together.

'Somewhere in the front with some friends. We can stay here.' He spreads the rugs on the freshly wiped floor.

My knee joints creak noisily as I sit down. Tentatively I cross my legs in a compromised lotus posture. Stretched tendons send out painful warnings. I uncross my legs, squirm sideways and lean against the pillar.

'Is there a leper's hospital in the city?' I whisper.

'Why?' Hashim looks startled. 'There isn't one anywhere near here. Why do you want to know?'

'I ran into a leper near the steps. He was with a group of beggars.'

'So what?'

'What do you mean, "So what?" Can something be done about him? Can he be taken to a hospital?'

'Testing! Testing! One, two, three . . . testing . . . ' One of the mosque attendants checks the loudspeaker system.

Hashim has turned around sharply to face me. There is a look of incredulity on his face. 'Don't be silly. I know you are not in touch with the way things work here. I had similar problems when I came back. Of course, you have been away far longer than I. But surely you haven't forgotten how it was before you left? You are not naive enough to believe that things have changed. Are you? There are hundreds of lepers wandering around the city. What's the point of taking one to the hospital? Who will pay for him?'

'I think that is an appalling attitude!'

'Look, don't make the mistake of imposing your adopted values here. They don't work. It sounds harsh, but in a poor country compassion must firstly be directed toward oneself. Ignore that rule and you will be ruined.'

'You don't have to be rich to be compassionate to others!' I protest indignantly. I cannot believe Hashim can be so callous.

'Compassion . . . charity. They are expensive items on the moral shelf. It's a question of affording them. If you had twenty loaves of bread, it would be easy to give one to a hungry neighbour. But if you only had a couple of slices, would you give one away just as willingly? Here you have to discipline yourself and obey the rules of self-survival. Practice charity when you can. But don't let it get out of control. Otherwise you will begin to feel the pain of an incurably crooked and unjust world.'

The *imam*, leading the prayer, is a white-bearded old man. 'My brothers! Welcome to the House of Allah on this the most auspicious day of the week. You are all welcome—the rich, the poor, the healthy and the not-so-well. We are equal members of the same family. In the Name of Allah, the Compassionate, the Merciful, the Benevolent . . . ' He begins to preach about the principle of *zakat*. 'Give to the poor so he may survive. Give to the orphan so he may find some comfort. Give generously so you may live with your conscience.'

'I don't know what I am supposed to be doing here.' I whisper out of the side of the mouth.

Hashim ignores me and continues to listen.

There was a shocked silence of disbelief when I confessed I had forgotten how to pray.

'Forgotten how to pray? How is that possible?' Ma snorted. 'How can anyone forget how to pray?'

Abba looked at me thoughtfully. 'It's a habit implanted in a Muslim from an early age. It can never be lost.'

'I have forgotten,' I repeated nonchalantly. 'I have forgotten the *surahs*.'

'Don't you pray in Australia? There must be mosques there.'

'I know of one about two hours' drive from where I live.'

'Do you pray in English?' Ma was shocked at the prospect of praying in the Christian language.

'How often do you go to the mosque?'

'I have been there four times.'

'Four times a year?'

'Four times in the years I have been there.'

'You must be going for prayers during *Eid-ul-Azha* and *Eid-ul-Fitr* each year?'

'Usually *Eid* is on a working day for me,' I replied nonchalantly.

I did not think it was necessary to tell them my reasons

for stopping the biannual trips to Preston. It had nothing to do with my belief or lack of it. I could have easily maintained a cultural habit without an attempted renewal of the spiritual commitment I had abandoned even before going to Australia. It had to do with a lack of communal empathy; a sense of non-belonging. I was like an untrustworthy distant cousin the family preferred not to know.

My first visit to the mosque in Preston was a forgettable experience. It began badly with an unpleasant encounter on the footpath. A red-haired man, who had deliberately pushed a *burqa*-clad woman against a fence and was taunting her with racist abuse, did not see me coming up behind him. I am convinced my language startled him into a speedy getaway. In his scheme of life, dark-skinned foreigners were probably meant to subject themselves passively to verbal insults and physical abuse in return for the privilege of living in his country. They were not supposed to retaliate and yell, 'Fuck off, you diseased convict dick!' at the tall, white residents of the land. He will never know how scared I was of his size and how I loathed myself for stooping to his level of obscenity.

The mosque was crowded. The men were disconcertingly different in speech and mannerisms to what I had expected. Lebanese, Syrians, Palestinians, Egyptians, Iranians . . . who knew? . . . formed a middle-eastern fraternity to which I could not be admitted. They spoke Arabic. I introduced myself to them in English.

'From Bangladesh!' They exclaimed meaningfully and turned to the Pakistanis who were taking a hostile interest in me. 'He's from Bangladesh.'

I soon discovered the Arabs were unsympathetic toward Bangladesh. They had swallowed the fabricated tale of religious betrayal and treachery against Islam. The Bangalis had been in cahoots with the Hindus. An Islamic state had been dismembered and weakened.

I spent a lonely, uncomfortable hour in the mosque. It

transformed my vague awareness of the irreconcilable diversities within the Islamic world into a living experience. I had nothing in common with those people other than a tenuous link with a medieval desert tradition.

'I feel like a hypocrite sitting here. I don't buy any of this!' I did not mean to put it so bluntly, but I am becoming agitated by the *imam*'s repetitive and hollow words about the economic strategies formulated in Heaven and bungled by sinful mortals blinded by greed to the inequalities and suffering we continue to tolerate in the community.

So what's new?

Hashim has stopped listening. He scowls at my fidgetiness. 'Are you still claiming to be an atheist?'

'The word is *zetetic*.'

'What?'

'Zetetic—spelled Z-E-T-E-T-I-C.'

'What does it mean?'

'A sceptical inquirer.'

'Sounds like a dressed-up word for an agnostic.'

'It's quite different.'

'This undergraduate stance of anti-religion you maintain is so childish. So fake!' Hashim looks around anxiously to see if anyone is listening to him. 'There was a time when we all questioned religion and walked around with frayed copies of *Thus Spake Zarathustra*. I am not saying what we did was useless. We opened our minds and became receptive to strange ideas. But there was a lack of awareness, a loss of respect for the unravelled complexities of the universe. We didn't need to cling to anything then. The very lack of a spiritual structure gave life a rebellious purpose. Unless we ridiculed, disbelieved, tore down ideologies, we weren't intellectuals.' He pauses to see if I am listening. He speaks ponderously, like a sagacious older brother determined to dissuade me from perpetuating my foolish ideas. 'It was all very well when we had youth to support our vain notions of independent thinking. It's a little silly to live those illusions now. No one has complete spiritual independence. The soul needs support. Religion is the backbone of our spiritual dimension. As a vine grows and matures, it needs a sturdy trellis. Otherwise it will collapse on itself. So it is with people as we grow older. How can you turn away from the strength of belief? From rituals which enrich our lives?'

This is a Hashim I do not know. I prefer to stay clear from the strength of his religious fervour. I am curious about the changes in him. Why has he become so conservative? Does he really believe in what he is saying? Is this his way of ensuring communal acceptance which he craved in vain during his years in England?

Several people have turned to look at us with disapproval.

It would be prudent to terminate this whispered argument. My stubbornness will not allow me to quit.

'I cannot see how I can claim to be a Muslim.'

Hashim looks at me indignantly. 'It's the other way around. The religion claims you. You were privileged to be born a Muslim. The matter ends there.'

'It doesn't end there! That is putting a seal of finality on a simplistic and unconvincing argument. I have the fundamental right to choose what I am and what I believe in.'

'No you haven't. That is where *you* are being simplistic. Belief is integral to you. Islam is your identity. Your culture. Your entire being. It defines you as a man. You cannot escape from your religion any more than you can run away from your shadow. You cannot elude yourself. Belief is what you were and what you are now. It . . . it is your life.'

' . . . and to conclude, my brothers, may I remind us all that we are responsible to each other as Muslims—beggars, servants, princes, ministers. It does not matter who you are. We share a common faith. That is our greatest strength. Those who are fortunate, be charitable without being proud. Give without arrogance. Give as an equal. As a man to his fellow man. The principle of *zakat* is the measure of our worth. It is a unique feature on Islam's human face which is radiant with the light of unquestioning belief. Now let us pray.'

A murmur of approval ripples through the congregation.

As we scramble to our feet, I think of Amjad and the man with the sores.

Not even a face. *How deprived can a man be?*

An impossible question. Its implications are awesome. Its awkwardness could only arise from the raw depths of an untrained mind; from a natural cynic who is unable to draw on the resources of formal learning to frame a problem whose cutting edges cannot be dulled because he lacks the rational faculty of an educated thinker. It defies religion for an answer.

What would Hashim have said if I had told him about the incident?

Why didn't you inform the police?

How would the *imam* respond to Amjad's problem?

My friends, the question cannot be considered because the answer is not in the Koran.

Hashim would probably think of me as Amjad's metaphysical half. A man with a deformed soul, suffering from the hideous spiritual disease of scepticism. I am deprived because of my refusal to give life the power of belief.

'Allah O Akbar . . . Ah ouz zoh billah eh minash shoitan er rajim . . . Bismillah er rahman er Raheem . . . '

I am forced to renew an old acquaintanceship with a deity I have not sought for a very long time. Oh, I have been conscious of his myths and their pervasive influence—in church, in a cemetery, in birth and death. Occasionally in moments of deep, personal crises.

Mechanically I raise my hands to my ears, let them drop to my sides, clasp them across the belly. I bend down when the others do, straighten up and then sit down with my back straight and my legs tucked under me. It is sheer agony. My knees feel the softness of the rug as my forehead touches a part of the floor. There is something touchingly vulnerable about the posture. This act of homage is so utterly submissive. It is an acknowledgement of Allah's omnipotence and a calm acceptance of man's lack of control over his destiny.

For me it is a mechanical mime. Most of me stands apart and views the ritual with patient indifference.

How similar to the dragged-out time I spend in the back pew of the school chapel! At least I know the people there. I marvel at the students who play the roles of pious solemnity to perfection, especially the ones who delight in the harassment of the Chinese and the Thais by kicking their lockers and whispering abuses in unsupervised corners and corridors.

'Bloody slants!'

'Why don't you go home, gook?'

'Fuck off, chinks!'

Nothing physical. The violence is in the words. Enough to instil fear and make them know they are unwanted.

Resplendent in their blazers, with their ties knotted and their shirts tucked in, the boys sit quietly under the watchful gaze of their haggard-faced tutors, pretending to listen attentively to the words of Christian wisdom which has little bearing on their prejudice-haunted lives. They sing hymns, take communion, mumble prayers and then go outside to succumb willingly to their ignorance and hatred of the funny little people who are invading their land.

Draped in my academic gown and looking like a daytime disciple of Dracula, I pass the time by admiring the ceiling, the stained-glass windows and thinking about participating in a Holy War to end all wars.

We often listen to sermons on peace. There are anti-war sentiments (even though we loved Bush and assumed all Arabs to be our enemies) and dreamy organ music. We wish for universal brotherhood and global harmony. We pray for peace. Then comes the jarring contradiction no one minds. It is a popular request, we are glibly told.

On our feet. Prayer books open.

Joyous voices sing blithely.

Onward, Christian soldiers,
Marching as to war
With the cross of Jesus
Going on before . . .

I have found it impossible to reconcile the demonstrated desire for peace with the full-throated call to move forward into battle. I asked the chaplain about the apparent contradiction.

Father Alex is an intelligent man. Compassionate and scholarly. I admire his understanding of adolescent problems and his phlegmatic acceptance of the lack of religious enthusiasm among teenagers. He smiled benignly, as if he understood the point I was making. I was invited to his office for a chat.

'The beauty of Christianity,' he declared with a self-righteous assurance, 'is its subtlety. Very few of its rituals and dogmas can be taken literally. Perhaps that is difficult for a Muslim to understand? I don't mean to be patronising. I hope you understand that. I am not laying the ground for an unfavourable comparison. It's just that our two religions are so very different. The image of the soldier going to battle is not an encouragement for a Christian to be militant. It is not a reason to take up arms and fight. It is a symbol of commitment, a crusade against evil that is vivified by the image of going to war.'

I expressed misgivings about a sweeping view of evil. What was evil? Did Satan's legions comprise the Arabs, the Jews, Hindus, Parsees, atheists . . . those who did not adhere to the tenets of Christianity?

'Oh no!' He assured me, fingering a wooden cross on his table. I had it all wrong. The implied definition of evil wasn't directed against specific groups of people. It had a more general, a more universal application directed toward man-made situations. Poverty was evil. Crime was evil. Racism was evil. I was misinterpreting the hymn, taking it too literally.

Did impressionable young people understand what he was saying? I had in mind the indiscriminatory attacks on Arabs during the Gulf War. I recounted some of the outrageous comments I had heard even as we continued to pray for peace and sing with voices that reverberated with virtuous zeal.

Well, he conceded, perhaps some didn't.

I expressed the view that the hymn was unnecessarily provocative and smacked of un-Christian militancy.

Alex looked mildly offended. He rubbed the cross as though he were seeking divine assistance against a dogged and literal-minded Muslim who could not see the meaning behind the meaning. He swung his swivel-chair until he faced a bookshelf near a window to his right. His fingers moved along the creased spines of the paperbacks. He checked the titles again, this time more slowly. He grunted with annoyance and lifted himself reluctantly from his chair. He walked in slow motion to a shelf further along the wall.

'Here it is!' He exclaimed with relief. He handed me a book on the importance of allegory in Christianity. 'That may help. There's a section on prayer and hymns. Maybe we could talk further after you have read it.'

I read the book but did not go back.

Even now as we bend, straighten and move our hands in a mesmerised unison, I question the sustaining powers of Christianity and Islam. How much running fuel is left in them?

Behind Christianity lies a vast, dense forest of allegories and symbolism protecting the New Testament. Its interior hums with the mysteries of life and living created behind the screen of time. In the past no one dared approach it. That has changed. There is an unbridled eagerness to hack a way through centuries of nurtured foliage to get to the centre. We live in a world which seeks to solve religious mysteries instead of being awed by them. Curiosity without fear is uncreative. It makes nothing of the shadows of the mind and the heart. It shatters myths instead of enriching them. It unravels instead of adding new dimensions to the unknown.

Alas Islam! Poor, unprotected creature with nowhere to hide. It stands defiantly, grounded on the stark plain of absolutism. Allah's words are enshrined in eternal glory. Immutable. Timeless. Beyond the manipulative capriciousness of cerebral progress. Islam is an old-fashioned hero, standing its ground and waving its sword menacingly at the forces of curiosity creeping closer toward it. There is a tragic grandeur about its inability to hide among the mazes of allegories and symbols.

My forehead touches the floor again. I can hear Hashim's mutterings.

Sometimes I have these moments of absurd imaginings when I envisage myself as a United Nations referee appointed to supervise a battle between Christians and Muslims. It is an honest confrontation. There are no political or moral pretensions. It is an open display of bigotry, prejudice and ignorance in a conflict for global supremacy. There is one all-important rule. Instead of weapons, the hostility is to be conducted verbally with propaganda, hymns, sermons, *surahs, fatuas* and prayers.

There are important issues at stake. Who has more power? Who can be more persuasive? Who can frighten more? Those without fervent belief in their cause may not participate. Rational thinking is forbidden. Compromises are not allowed. Inflammatory placards and banners are compulsory.

I am perched on a high platform in front of a large department store in a deserted mall. The building must not be attacked. It is sacred to both Christians and Muslims.

In my right hand I hold a silver crescent. In my left there

is a wooden cross. A four-star Israeli general stands beside me. I tell him to blow the whistle.

There is a mad rush from opposite directions. Mitres fall, crosses are raised and medals jangle. Bishops, priests, nuns, members of various clubs and the National Front run forward. Suited members of the RSL are arguing among themselves. The Vietnam veterans insist on leading them. They cannot decide on a representative banner. A solitary member of the breakaway Ku Klux Klan Party of Philanthropists has to skirt around them.

The whistle blows again. Back to the starting positions. They must all sort out their problems before the battle commences.

The general cries out in a foreign language. It is Hebrew, he tells me with great pride. Reluctantly he repeats the message in English. 'Five minutes! You have five minutes!'

A bishop calls for order among the RSL members. After a rowdy meeting there is a show of hands. The banner proclaiming the semi-divine status of the royal family is reluctantly abandoned in favour of a smiling picture of the Bishop of Johannesburg. A large contingent of World War II veterans pull out.

The other side is equally disorganised. The Iranians will lead the Muslims. The *mullahs* are a formidable sight. They are the bearded warriors in skull caps and emblemed T-shirts declaring they are ALLAH'S ASSASSINS. Behind them are the Syrians, Jordanians, Libyans, the Saudis and the Pakistanis. The Iraqis have been banned from participating. They cannot be trusted to stick to the rules. It is a fragmented group, suspicious and alert to the possibility of sectarian treachery. The clash of words is deafening.

A large stone lands on the Christian side. The general claps gleefully as I award a penalty point to the Christians.

The Iranians get the blame. The Sunnis launch a successful

takeover bid for the leadership. The Ahmadiyyas, the Agha Khanis and the Whahabies have pushed the Shias to the back.

The general blows on his whistle.

We hear the Muslim voices. *'Know that we send down to the unbelievers devils who incite them to evil. Those who say: "The Lord of Mercy has begotten a son," preach a monstrous falsehood, at which the very heavens might crack, the earth break asunder and the mountains crumble to dust. That they should ascribe a son to the Merciful, when it does not become Him to beget one!'*

The Christians respond with organ music.

There is an immediate protest. 'No music!' The Muslims cry. 'Foul! The infidels are cheating!'

Penalty point against the Christians. 'Words!' I cry. 'Words!' The voices are sombre.

Onward Christian soldiers,
Marching as to war
With the Cross of Jesus
Going on before
Christ the Royal Master
Leads against the foe;
Forward into battle,
See, His banners go!

The Muslims rush forward, urged on by the Libyans. *'Allah loves those who fight for His cause in ranks as firm as a mighty edifice.'*

At the sign of triumph
Satan's legions flee
On then, Christian soldiers,
On to victory . . .

There is a shooting pain in my ribs. Hashim is glaring at me.

'What?'

'What are you doing?' He demands between gritted teeth

as we go down on our knees again. He is trembling with anger.

'What?' I say to the floor.

Heads down, we can barely see each other's face out of the corners of our eyes.

'Have you gone mad? Is there no limit to your disrespect?'

I do not know what he means.

'This is a mosque, in case you have forgotten! This is not the place to sing *Onward Christian Soldiers*! Are you trying to get yourself lynched?'

'What! I didn't!' I look around apprehensively. There are people giving me strange looks. 'Sorry!' I say sheepishly.

We are asked to raise our hands in a humble supplication.

I close my eyes and concentrate. I am loud enough for everyone around me. 'Allah be praised for saving my child . . . It was Your Mercy . . . Your Grace . . . Your Benevolence . . . Allah grant her a long and happy life . . . '

Suddenly there is a vision.

A gigantic red and white capsule looms in front of me like a spaceship. Nadine appears in front of it, smiling and full of life.

A miracle.

I open my eyes.

'*Aameen!*' The congregation drones.

'*Aameen!*' I sigh with relief.

The end, at last.

NINE

From the solitary window of Nafisa's third-floor office, I have a sweeping view of the halls of residence and the drab grey buildings which house the university teaching staff in subsidised flats. Across the road is the Vice-Chancellor's residence, a lovely double-storeyed house with a sprawling garden, built before partition to ease the white *shaheb's* discomfort in an unfriendly land.

My eyes flit across the unkempt expanse of the open ground below me. Its desolation is a pitiful contrast to the tumultuous days of Bengal's defiant glory. A stray cow grazes on the turf once crowded with protesting students waving placards, distributing leaflets, holding up banners and reiterating Sheik Mujib's call for resistance and civil disobedience. Even the crusty conservatives of the administrative staff discarded their mantle of snobbish aloofness and joined the meetings under the banyan tree.

The tree was the rallying point of our nationalistic aspirations. Its shade nurtured the dreams of a desperate people. It was a shelter where years of victimisation and accumulated frustration vented themselves in fiery speeches peppered with hyperboles, impotent threats and the emotive language of martyrdom.

The Pakistani army thought no more of the students than as an amusing nuisance. We were young and volatile, full of revolutionary zeal, capable of inciting the uneducated masses to a display of uncharacteristic courage. There was some danger in that, but nothing that could not be snuffed out if necessary. We were known to be a cowardly race tuned to servility. The army had no doubt we could be kept in that state of obsequious acceptance.

History has treated Bengal with supreme disdain.

Supposedly there is much wisdom in ancient Sanskrit texts. Bengal is warily mentioned as a backward, hostile land of ignorance. The plight of King Adisura is an illustrative point. It is, indeed, lamentable that the good king was unable to find a knowledgeable priest in Bengal to perform the rites of an intricate Vedic sacrifice. *Ram! Ram!* What could be a more damning proof of this barbaric land?

For centuries the Senas and the Palas ruled without asserting a complete monarchal authority over these treacherous and deceitful people. For mutinous generals in the Moghul army, Bengal was reserved as the dreaded place of banishment to reflect on their misdeeds before they succumbed to the curse of the anopheline mosquito. By the time the Moghuls arrived, Islam had already made significant inroads into Bengal with its customary martial fervour. The *talwar* glinted menacingly. Bribing, threatening, maiming and converting, the latest of the desert enterprises exceeded the impassioned righteousness of its older rival which perceived more promise across the Atlantic and headed that way. An inferior task force was left to tackle the savagery of the east and campaign for the peaceful virtues of the cross, to say nothing of the beneficial virtues of greed.

The Christians, following St Thomas the Apostle, arrived with the aroma of spices in their nostrils and the promise of eternal bliss in their words.

May the Peace of Christ be with you!
(Accept it you heathen wretches, or else!)

Dominus illuminatio mea!

(He better become your light too, darkies!)

Bangalis were initiated into the strange ways of foreign religions. Islam prevailed. But the doubt remained. Could these *Garsals* ever attain the purity of the true believers? Unlikely . . . highly unlikely, given their past. They had to be viewed with suspicion and monitored carefully.

Centuries later, that was the prevalent attitude in the bazaars of Lahore and Karachi when the general played his elaborate hoax of calling a general election. Shock! Horror! Things went dreadfully wrong. The election was won by a political party known for its favourable views on relationships with the arch enemy. West Pakistan was stunned.

It was common knowledge that the swamp dwellers in the East were of base Dravadian stock. Lousy fish eaters. No wonder they were physically and intellectually inferior. Rice bloated them and made them lazy. They observed despicable Hindu customs. Their major poet was a Brahmin. How could they be given charge of the country?

The controlled contempt with which our old masters, the *Beelathis*, treated us, rubbed off on the *bahadurs* of Baluchistan, Sind and Punjab. The attempted cultural assimilation and economic subjugation of East Pakistan were valid expressions of genetic superiority of the people from the west.

Why should there be changes after twenty-three years of comparative prosperity? How dare the *Bangoos* complain of maltreatment? Ungrateful wretches! Had they not been saved from the Hindus? And what was all this clamouring about recognising Bangla as a national language? Had not Jinnah himself settled the issue? Didn't the father of the nation declare that Urdu, and only Urdu, was to be the language of Pakistan? Who was this troublemaker, Sheik . . . whatever his name was . . . claiming equality and seeking political power? What was the army doing? The generals ought to imprison the charlatan and shoot a few thousand of the miserable bastards to show the west's intention to continue ruling the Islamic Republic of Pakistan.

Such was the complacent arrogance three thousand kilometres to the west as East Pakistan simmered and rumbled.

It was inevitable that the wrath of the Pakistani warlords should target the university. To the dismay of General Butcher of Baluchistan, who also happened to be the Chief Martial Law Administrator of East Pakistan, the worst miscreants had escaped the army intelligence network and found their way across the border into the hospitable bosom of Mother Saint Indra. Others went into hiding in remote border villages.

However, there remained one enemy of significant danger. It was stubbornly entrenched in its place of origin, instigating rebellion by its mere presence.

The butcher was outraged. It was an unbearable insult to his reputation.

'*Kyah himmat!*' He shrieked and rolled about on the floor of his office. His hushed attendants retreated. Throughout that night there were fearful noises of gunfire and breaking furniture.

The best of the army doctors were flown in from Karachi. They checked his blood pressure, determined the cause of his ire and sedated him. They took it upon themselves to summon his trusted officers and formulated a strategy for an extraordinary mission.

On a sultry spring morning, truckloads of *jawans* prepared to launch an attack on the campus. (Later it was rumoured that for several years there raged a vehement debate among the university scholars about the likelihood of Cervantes' spirit gracing the occasion.)

The efficiently drilled soldiers surrounded the humanities campus and crouched outside the iron-grilled fence. Walkie-talkies crepitated with brief messages. The bellicose *jawans* waited impatiently. The primacy of the operation had been hammered into them in the cantonment.

Pedestrians panicked. Taxis and motor scooters ignored their yells and hand-waving. Rickshaws rushed past them. Within minutes all vehicles had disappeared from the road. The pedestrians dived for shelter behind the shrubs and trees in front of the Vice-Chancellor's residence.

Teeth chattered and prayers were murmured. Some, to their shame, discovered their lack of control over their waste-disposal mechanisms.

Overhead, eagles and crows whorled in anticipation.

A heroic confrontation was imminent. It was made all the more suspenseful by a seemingly clever and well-hidden gang of militant Bangali students ready to burst into the open and confront the soldiers.

The reluctant spectators waited uneasily under the unbearable burden of heightening tension.

The authoritative voice of the commanding officer cracked the silence.

The terrified onlookers raised their hands to Allah. Some vowed to double their donations to the orphanages. Others rashly swore to legalise their alliances with their mistresses and marry again. The more affluent committed themselves to the rigours of *Haj* the following year.

They crouched and waited with their hands over their ears. There was no noise of guns firing or grenades exploding. Wild, incoherent shouting accompanied the charge. A brave handful ventured to bob their heads over the shrubs. To their amazement they saw axes and hacksaws glinting in the sunlight. Soldiers, hundreds of them, from all sides scaled the fences and ran full tilt toward the banyan tree.

The enemy stood firm in tragic isolation.

There was a flurry of hacking and sawing. Manful grunts and loud groans were heard. The resulting discrepancy between the effort and the outcome was a severe blow to martial pride.

The tree stood tall and defiant.

An infuriated Baluchi soldier butted the truck with his forehead. He became the first notable casualty to be carried away.

The onlookers threw themselves to the ground as automatic rifles opened fire. They need not have worried. The targets were the inquisitive crows who had the effrontery to perch on the branches for a closer view of the hubbub. Several hundred rounds of ammunition were spent.

The commanding officer was heard to cry, 'Halt! Stop fire!' He blew a whistle. 'Retreat!' There was genuine alarm in his voice.

The soldiers withdrew to a huddled meeting in a corner of the ground.

Under the tree lay one stiff old crow, riddled with bullets.

The meeting lasted several minutes. The enemy was formidable. Reinforcement was necessary. A large truck lumbered up the road and dumped thirty bulkier soldiers (presumably capable of louder grunts which, unfortunately for the story-tellers, were never verified) carrying bigger axes and saws.

Within minutes the valiant enemy, which had proven to be a champion of passive resistance, succumbed to brute strength. The serrated edges of the monstrous saws toppled the tree. Oh what a fall there was! The earth heaved. The birds cried and circled the air. The hidden civilians wept decorously like sophisticated theatre-goers watching the heart-wrenching demise of a tragic protagonist. A bulldozer crashed through the fence and uprooted the massive stump. The cathartic effect on the privileged audience was so overpowering that, with the emotional purgation, their promises to the Almighty were also expunged.

The *jawans* were ecstatic. The heathens had been thwarted. Animism was successfully truncated. Tears of joy streamed down their cheeks. They dropped their weapons, faced the west and sank to their knees in thankful praise of Allah. Islam was victorious! Allah was great! They prayed and sang about Karbala. The commanding officer was lifted into the air, like the captain of a winning soccer team, and carried to his jeep. The fallen tree was sawn into cartable proportions and taken to the cantonment kitchen.

By mid afternoon the performance was over and the props removed. The bare and dusty stage was a sobering reminder to all mortals of the transitory nature of anything that stands firmly erect.

As one might expect, there are many versions of the heinous attack on the banyan tree. It depends on who you talk to. There are some incredibly clear memories and potent imaginations. The fall of the *bhat gaach* has been indelibly mythologised in the oral tradition which continues to grow and flourish with a primordial vigour.

'Back by half-past eleven,' Nafisa said before she breezed out to lecture on the Umayyad caliphate of Cordoba.

That gives me more than enough time to caress a few memories, dodge some ghosts and reflect on the sharp bends of a pernicious fate. I had such a rotten day yesterday that I feel a soulful need of Nafisa's gentle-humoured sanity to lift me out of the life-is-a-dry-fuck mode I am bogged in.

I coped reasonably well with Mateen's self-pitying petulance and Abba's fragmented ramblings of a man drowning in the pool of his stagnant dreams. Hashim continued to annoy me with his phone calls, urging me to talk to Ma about his divorce. But the business at the post office over the letter was another matter—a ridiculous display of exploding frustration which left a messy residue of contrition and embarrassment. I derive no satisfaction in blaming Michelle for throwing me into a turmoil of rage, confusion, triumph, relief, uncertainty and, much against my inclination, some hope. Damn her and her unquiveringly eloquent voice of honesty! Why couldn't she have lied . . . left a few gaps for my illusions to spread a protective shield over a fragile ego? Why couldn't she have sounded vaguely sorry and tentative instead of reaching across and twisting my entrails, forcing me to listen even as I hated her?

The torn, crumpled envelope and the missing stamps sanctioned my offensive behaviour as I slipped into the miscast role of the indignant foreigner with a superior moral sense, sanctimoniously desiring to teach the natives all about the ways of an honest world unblemished by such petty corruption.

Strewth! That's not the way we do things under the Southern Cross, mate!

We resorted to inimical glares over the dusty counter. My protests and threatening accusations were blunted with a defiant silence. The feisty little man was in charge. I was in *his* post office. He would speak when he thought it was necessary.

I must have been quite a sight, banging the palms of my hands on the laminexed surface and shaking the envelope as if I were fanning the air. I was outraged and unforgiving about the blatant assault on my privacy. The flap of the envelope had been savagely ripped open and then messily stuck in places with mashed rice. The stamps had been more carefully removed.

At home they thought I was quite mad to make a fuss. Nafisa could not understand why I was not prepared to attribute the abuse of my private mail to the vagaries of the third world and forget about it.

I responded to her advice by storming into the post office to make an ass of myself.

It was hot and stuffy in the airless room. The queue behind me quickly extended into the street. There were murmurs of mutinous support for me. I gathered that the problem was not an isolated incident, and I was not a random victim.

He relented with an asperity intended to let me know that precious time was being wasted. *'Aarey baba*, what can I do about it? You received the letter? Only the envelope was torn? Three stamps were missing? The letter itself was intact? What is the problem then?'

Bluntly I made the point that it was unacceptable for any part of the letter to be torn in that manner. For all I knew someone could have read it. That was not on. I insisted on making a formal complaint.

He looked disgustedly at me over the rim of his cheap plastic frame encasing thick glass lenses which exaggerated the impression of a sour owl in a state of perpetual dissatisfaction with the world.

'You have to go to the GPO and see the Post-Master General. I can do nothing here.' He sneezed and made a show of blowing his nose in a stiff, mucus-stained handkerchief. 'You must fill in a form and make an appointment.' A white plastic comb appeared in his hand. Methodically he flattened the oily, dandruffed hair on his scalp. Haughtily he adjusted the spectacles on the bridge of his nose, as if they were the redoubtable symbol of his officiousness.

I asked for a complaint form. To my surprise he gave me one immediately.

'My signature is necessary,' he said superciliously.

He left me in no doubt that I was entirely in his control.

He went back to a cup of tea on his table behind the counter. The temperature of the tea preoccupied him. With the back of his index finger he tested the heat of the cup around the rim. He poured some tea into the saucer. He slurped it noisily and then grimaced as if his tongue had been scalded. With pursed lips he fanned the tea with his breath, like a wind stirring a torpid stretch of water. The tip of his tongue ventured out, like a tentative lizard reluctant to leave its hiding place, and brushed his lips. From a drawer he took out a jar of white sugar. As if to compensate for a critical element missing from his life, he lit a cigarette. He inhaled slowly and closed his eyes. The facial muscles relaxed. A seraphic glow suffused his face as a thin stream of smoke trickled out of the catarrhine nostrils.

I filled in the form with a growing sense of futility. I wanted to capitulate and walk out of the post office. Only a stubborn pride kept me going.

He scrutinised the form, ignoring the biro I offered him for his signature. He rubbed his unshaven chin and massaged his scalp with the aggrieved air of a man being forced to take a monumental decision unlikely to favour him. He looked at me dubiously, with a touch of pity in his eyes.

'That is very light,' he announced.

'Pardon?'

He balanced the paper on his outstretched palm and moved it up and down as if the form were on a delicate balance. 'It needs some weight to hold it in place. If there is nothing on it, it may blow away and get lost.'

'Excuse me?' I inquired irritably. 'What weight?'

A look of contempt twisted his face into a predatory snarl. With a studied deliberation, intended to bully me into submission, he leaned heavily on the counter. He bared a set of rotting teeth and enfeebled me with an overpowering blast of halitosis. Insidiously he repeated the advice.

I must have appeared utterly lost.

An old man, wearing a black *lungi* and a white shirt, came up to me. 'You are from abroad?' he asked.

I nodded eagerly as though my foreignness were a valid reason for my bewilderment.

'Are you a Bangali?'

'Yes,' I replied self-consciously. I was afflicted with a guilt-ridden impression that somehow I had betrayed my race.

'*Bhai*, put some money on that form or we shall be standing here for hours.' He spoke with a gentle patience I found immensely annoying.

I wasn't cerebrally retarded, I informed him testily. I knew what was expected and I was not willing to comply. I tore the form into tiny pieces and flung it across the counter.

Sympathetic eyes followed me to the door. Someone laughed softly behind me. It was not a derisive laughter meant to mock my undignified exit. Rather, it seemed to betoken an understanding of the immutable corruption entrenched within us and my childish refusal to accept one of its lesser manifestations.

Outside I felt strangely at home among the dust, the noise and the flurry of movements. I was no longer a being apart from the disordered pattern of living. This unpredictable rhythm, with its wildly irregular beats, was also my pulse of life. It had taken time to find it, but it was there beating feebly. I was no longer imprisoned within my own resentments. There was an acceptance of irreconcilable facets of my polarised self. Perhaps I was meant to live as a fragmented being. The idea did not disturb me any more.

I inhaled deeply. The air smelled of exhaust fumes. I did not recoil in revulsion of the pollution. I did not walk away rapidly from the beggar girl who began to harangue me. The glare of the sun appeared to have peeled off the remnants of an imperfect filter from my window to the world. I even felt a twinge of remorse for those I knew. It could not be easy to accommodate people like me—bumbling agents of change who spread themselves across the globe and unwittingly seek to impose their hybrid perceptions on closeted cultures.

Nafisa is appreciative of the privacy of her room. I remark on how relaxed she looks here.

This is where she can shed her cast, she tells me. 'This is where I can recreate my life with many happy endings. Here, among the deceit of words, I feel like a swindler in the company of thieves.' She looks affectionately at the crowded bookshelves. 'I am surrounded by trusty acquaintances. They steal me away to a world where I do not have to dress up and receive male visitors and their mothers. I do not have to bore myself with polite conversations under Ma's supervision.'

I look at her with brotherly pride. Age has not diminished her youthful good looks. Her dark eyes dance impishly, alert and ready to challenge those ageless conventions of behaviour which are meant to upgrade female worthiness in an overcrowded marriage bazaar. Her hair is tied in a severe matronly bun. Her clothes never seem to vary. White saris with modestly coloured borders.

I reach across the table and clasp her hands. They are small and soft.

Her smile is reserved and distant.

I have missed her. Had I bothered, she could have been a very enriching influence on me. Fine tuned my emotions, given me more balance. I cannot help regretting the hiatus of the years I unthoughtfully tossed aside.

'Ma worries about you.'

A flicker of concern crosses her face. 'I know.' Her hands slip away. She leans back on her chair and looks at me warily. 'But she is more concerned about you and *Bhaiya*. I appreciate the problems both of you are creating. I have faded into insignificance. I like that. Have you told her about Nadira?' She laughs to see me surprised.

'What about Nadira?' I ask stiffly.

'Tohtah, don't treat me like the others do. Please.'

Tohtah. Parrot. No one has used that nickname since I was a child with an obsession for repeating what others said in an imitative tone of voice.

'Yes, I have.'

She arches her eyebrows. 'And?'

'She wasn't pleased about the divorce. She fears another

scandal. I have given her enough of a headache and I am only separated. I spent several hours talking to her. It felt strange to discover her as a person. She is quite different from the mother I know. She talked about you. She said you were stubborn.'

'Why am I stubborn?'

'You won't marry and have children.'

'Oh that! It's a little late for children.' She speaks definitively as though she has been confronted with overwhelming evidence of her procreational redundancy.

'Ma doesn't think of us as aging. Her children have been blessed with eternal youth. We are wayward kids being implored to exercise some responsibility.'

'Think of the family's reputation. Don't worry about yourself.'

'She has been hurt by all that has happened. I think she feels we ought to be able to arrange our lives so that they fit her notions of propriety. Do what is right. Make her proud. She wants accolades for having brought us up properly. She needs that sense of achievement. She talked more about you than anyone else. I'll be honest with you. She asked if I would be prepared to . . . How shall I put it? . . . If I could . . . '

'Be a marriage broker. Find out if there is someone I like?'

I am daunted and puzzled by her aggression. She is like a cornered animal—scared and bristly.

She frowns and looks vaguely at last year's calendar hanging from a peg on her door. 'All right, there is someone.'

I don't know for whose sake I am pleased. There is a glow of elation inside me. 'Why are you being so secretive about it? Don't get me wrong! It's a personal matter. I am not questioning that. But if it is serious enough, have you considered marriage?'

There is a misty sheen in her eyes. Shit. Have I gone too far? I seem to find the sensitive spots with unerring accuracy. 'I didn't mean to pry.'

'It's best if people didn't know.'

'Is he married? Is that the problem?'

She shakes her head slightly.

'Is he a Hindu?' The words tumble out with about as much subtlety as an army interrogator's on the verge of wrenching a confession from the lips of a tortured victim.

Her stare is a plea for understanding, a look that peels away the years to draw on the dependence we shared as confidants in our adolescence.

'Even you assume the person to be a "he".' Her words are a sandpapered whisper of pain and resignation.

My immediate reaction is to say, 'Pardon?' I need more time to digest what I have just heard. I wish to misunderstand what she has said. I want an acceptable interpretation of her words.

There is a dreadful din in my ears. It is the roar of a tropical waterfall cascading on huge boulders in a pleated drape of silver. Above the noise I can barely hear her voice.

Do you like girls?

What?

Do you like girls?

I suppose.

I don't like boys. I don't like being near them. Sometimes I think they want to touch me. I hate that. It makes me feel dirty.

Something in my face hardens her. 'Are you shocked? Disgusted with what I have said?'

I must not allow her to burrow into the convoluting folds of my thoughts. She is watching me, waiting for a reaction of condemnation which will place me on her scrapheap of hypocrites with their bright labels of *Right* and *Wrong* to be tagged on others as a vindication of their shrivelled morality.

I force a mumbled 'No' from somewhere within me.

She is now the hunter who has sensed a weakening prey. 'It's wrong, isn't it? What I am shouldn't be. Why don't you say so instead of looking at the floor? Tohtah, be honest with me!'

I am disappointed with myself. *Right* and *Wrong* can be such dreadfully crippling words. So often they tend to reduce the complexities of behaviour to the lowest levels of inaccurate simplicity. I try to use them sparingly, and then too in relation to myself when I am not prepared to go through the analytical process of cause and effect. I think I am fairly tolerant and reasonably broad-minded, legacies of my exposure to the diversities of the world. How then do I explain my initial reaction to what Nafisa said? How can I deny that the first images which sprang to my mind could be summed up by that commonest of condemnatory words? If I did not think anything was wrong, why the consternation and the shock?

I am dismayed by the revelation of my double standards. For God's sake it is my own sister! I do not love her any less for what she is. I have been unequivocal in my support of gay rights. Yet I cannot deny that nauseating revulsion which scythed through me like a sharp blade.

Was it wrong? Nafisa had asked. Of course it wasn't. What, then, made me shrink in my chair? Why the clenched fists and jaws? The impulse to leave the room?

The silence has spread like a winter fog, creating apprehension and exaggerating distances. I fear something between us may have died. I have treated her trust cruelly. I made her feel lonely, turned down her unstated request to share the weight she staggers under. For all that I am unable to go around the table and comfort her.

How much more is there to know about myself? The thought depresses me.

I revert to my original purpose for coming here. I am concerned and curious about the extent of the family's misfortunes. At home it is almost impossible to talk to Nafisa without interruption. The flow of visitors, curious about me, has not abated.

Nafisa knows much more than she let on yesterday. 'I am not supposed to know about these things,' she said with a wink. 'The financial worries of the family should be beyond my understanding. There is no place for me in the tough male world of business. I am expected to lament and wring my hands in anguish when I am told about our setbacks. Until then, I know nothing.'

I trust her incisive mind and her acumen to give me a clear profile of the crisis. Hashim has been vague and reticent. Abba said he would talk to me later. With some urgency I sought Nafisa. I also had in mind Ma's request to talk to her. It was Nafisa's idea to meet in her office.

The decision to sell the land in Shopnoganj intrigues and saddens me.

Hashim gave me the bare details of the transaction. 'An industrialist with considerable assets in the Middle-East has made an offer. It's too good to refuse. We have to pay off the debts,' he said with a pointed emphasis on our collective responsibility.

Nafisa resumes her usual calm as soon as I mention my brief exchange with Hashim. She is shrewd and unsentimental. 'The land should have been sold years ago. It's a crippling burden. Mateen *Bhai* wouldn't agree. He does very well living off the land, although he constantly complains about the hardships he endures for the family's sake. He shows a huge loss each year. Abba won't do anything about him.'

'Mateen's a bloody crook!'

'You have become so blunt about what you say.'

'Bloody oath!'

'What?'

'Bloody oath. It's an expression of affirmation. You don't sound as if you are sorry about losing the land.'

'Are you?'

'Yes! I didn't think I would be. The land may not be of

much use, but it's a part of me. I have a bank of memories stored there. Doesn't the past mean anything to you?'

'I teach about the past,' she says indifferently. 'But I don't languish in its withered embrace. My experiences of Shopnoganj aren't the same as yours. I couldn't go across the river to explore the other side Hashim gloatingly described during the long summer evenings on the verandah. You wouldn't take me across. Remember? I was only a girl. My memories of those holidays are mostly about sewing, being taught how to cook and endless hours of boredom. I have no affection for the land.'

I find it unbelievable that we are in such serious financial strife. The dormant vestiges of *zamindari* arrogance spring to life like a snarling, wounded animal prodded out of its dark lair. The peculiarly innate faith in our invincibility has been severely jolted. The last stronghold of my psychic security, the one I have never jeopardised, has been breached. The cold touch of mortal fallibility is a fearful sensation. It can't be! Something is dreadfully out of sorts. It must be a transitional phase, a structural ripple which will shake the foundation and then disappear, leaving us wiser but unharmed. Tradition cannot change so swiftly. It always lags behind the sudden quirks of history. We are the saviours, the magnanimous agents of rescue for those in trouble. We are the ones people turn to for help. I was brought up with the tacit assumption that altruism was an inherent family trait rather than a rare individual virtue. We helped the people of Shopnoganj because of our god-like ability to bestow favours on unfortunate mortals. It was a task we relished. We enjoyed the power of life and death over the villagers without ever feeling vulnerable or apprehensive about the forces which might control us. It was a notion as remote and absurd as asking if there was an omnipotent power above and beyond Allah Himself.

There is a touch of smug satisfaction in Nafisa as she launches into a chronology of neglect and mismanagement.

She is critical of Abba. His careless generosity toward a populace that knows the value of implicit obedience does not align itself with the pragmatic principles of accumulating wealth.

The people of Shopnoganj are astute enough to tap our weaknesses. They pretend to be helpless and exploit Abba by reminding him of his patriarchal obligations and the generosity of his predecessors. Once every three months they send a delegation of villagers to Dhaka for an audience with *Boro Abba*. The sick, the elderly, orphans and deserted wives arrive on a chartered bus. It is a regular *durbar*. The practice, Nafisa tells me, began after Hashim and I had left the country. Mateen initiated the move, and its immense popularity has not declined.

Depending on the weather, they meet in the backyard for several hours in the morning before feeding voraciously on *pilau*, mutton curry and sweet yoghurt. They know how to flatter an old man's vanity. They cry at his feet and soften him up with woeful tales of misfortune. Shopnoganj belongs to the Chaudharies, they remind him. He is the head of the entire community. He is like a benevolent father to all of them. Noisy children play around him as he listens patiently to their pleas.

I am alarmed to hear that he sits with wads of money, distributing takas as though they were scraps of worthless paper. The overdraft reminders from the bank have become less deferential in tone and more legalistic in content. Abba uses them to light his *hookah*. Visits from the bank manager have become a disturbingly frequent occurrence.

I am reminded of the plight of Bahadur Shah toward the end of Moghul rule. History has left him without achievements—a weak, snivelling old man who brought a sparkling period of Indian history to an inglorious end. I wonder how much of it was his doing? The profligacy of irresponsible ancestors ultimately descends on the sons. History thirsts for scapegoats to conclude its chapters neatly.

Nafisa is aware of Mateen's villainy. Each year he convinces Abba to make up the deficit. We have not made a profit from the harvests for over a decade. Abba pays for the renovation of the village mosque every year. It is an old structure, Mateen argues. It needs to be frequently repaired.

'Why hasn't Hashim done something about Mateen?' I ask.

'He made a feeble attempt to check the books. Abba stopped him. Mateen *Bhai* is family. He cannot be touched. Did you meet Mr Siddique yesterday?'

'His nephew. I'd seen him before, the day I was in Shopnoganj. He didn't recognise me.'

I was there only for a cup of tea, and as a token symbol of the family's solidarity, not that my presence in any way affected the ebullient nephew. My contribution to the conversation was minimal, being confined to a few replies to the standard questions of familiarisation. My sullenness did nothing to stop Mr Azam's dazzling words of flattery about the Chaudharies. The rings on his fingers sparkled with a seductive promise. He flaunted the number of cheque books he was obliged to carry with him all the time. He awed Hashim into a dumbfounded mood of acquiescence. Abba puffed dreamily on his *hookah*, quietly pleased with the praise heaped on him.

'No problem,' Mr Azam assured us and offered to write a cheque when Abba expressed a mild concern about the effects of such a drastic change on the villagers. 'No problems! We can keep them happy. Money is the perfect medicine for the ills of the heart and mind. What do you say Chaudhary *Shaheb*?' He named an impressive sum of money for compensating the villagers.

Mr Azam took no notice of our gloom or our terse economy of words. He was all compliance. There was no hurry, he said. Of course they would pay us the full amount in advance.

Chaudhary *Shaheb's* word was good enough for them. His uncle had a great respect for our family. We were famous for our honesty. The words dripped sweetly from the lips of a professional manipulator.

'Only after the villagers have been resettled, shall we remove the shacks and the huts,' he assured us.

'Resettled?'

'There was nothing said about removing anything.'

'Mr Azam was unperturbed. 'Please understand that the people cannot live there with all the construction work going on. There will be office buildings and houses for the workers on the village side of the river.'

Our accusatory stares had some effect. He took out a red silk handkerchief and mopped his brow. 'Bulldozers will have to level the ground for construction work to begin. Naturally, the mosque and the family graveyard will not be touched. We shall employ a full-time caretaker to look after the graveyard.'

'The entire village? Are you saying the entire village will be destroyed?'

'Impossible!'

'That can never be! It's our ancestral home!'

Mr Azam was confounded by our sentimentality. He looked at us kindly as if to say he understood why we were in financial difficulty. 'There won't be anyone there,' he said patiently. 'What is a place without people?'

'It is not our intention to have the village razed to the ground. That is unthinkable! What will happen to the people! Where will they go?'

'No problem! We can build you a new village a few kilometres away if that will satisfy you.'

'That's not the same! Mr Azam, you don't seem to understand what Shopnoganj means to us.'

'We shall build it exactly the way it is now—every hut and shack, every path. All the landmarks. It won't be near the river, but the water will be supplied from tubewells. Far more hygienic than what they now have.'

'It's not the same thing, Mr Azam. It's not the same.'

'But there will be an improvement in every way. What more can we do? I do not understand your objection. There is no practical reason behind it.'

'It is our spiritual ties with the village, Mr Azam,' Abba said slowly. 'The land is our umbilical cord. I do not expect you to understand. Our reasons are not at all practical.'

'Mr Chaudhary!' He turned to me as though I were sympathetic to him. 'We must be sensible. We are paying a huge sum of money for the land. The land, Mr Chaudhary! The land. Not the village! There has to be benefits for us. We cannot afford to be sentimental.' He whipped out the cheque books from the inside pocket of his jacket. 'Do we have an agreement?'

His weapon was too formidable. We surrendered without further protest.

'Did he say what they were doing with the land?' Nafisa asks with some concern.

'Building some sort of a refinery. I wasn't interested. It was sufficient to know that they would own the land. Our land! I can just imagine what it will be like—trees chopped down, concrete and steel everywhere, fumes belching from ugly chimneys.'

'Ultimately the villagers will be better off.'

'I doubt that.'

'Look, they will have some money. There will be jobs for them in the future. They will have some degree of control over their lives. It has to be done. The debts have to be paid. You live in a developed country. Don't you see the advantages? You surprise me. I thought you would be the one to push it through.'

'I might have, had I not lived in the West.'

Nafisa begins to lecture me on history and progress. I lose track of what she is saying.

I am not as adaptable as I thought myself to be. Age? Or is it just me? In the arcadian surroundings of the villa, I thought I could come to terms with myself, calm the turmoil inside me, understand the dissatisfaction which brought me here. It isn't quite as easy as I thought. More questions. More problems. I am now more of a stranger to myself than ever before. A few weeks have created a restlessness for the familiar. I cannot believe that I yearn for the imperfections which landscaped our lives. Little things, which became tedious and irritating, were also habitual, a part of what made me tick. Now there is this indistinct paleness of quiet days which merge together in a timeless vacuum where I float without purpose. I cannot even have a decent argument. Colin gives in easily. I am a temperamental sheila. What would I know? I have to be humoured. The pig . . .

I have lost count of the number of times I have read the letter—ten rambling pages in her neat, cursive handwriting—written over ten days. I know the words as if I had written them myself. They could be my memories, my questions, my uncertainties. I know the moods. I recognise the exasperating note of playfulness which can suddenly take over when she thinks she is revealing too much. A sombre reflectiveness pervades the letter. Michelle is not a person who wastes her talents on subtle implications. She writes about Colin without inhibitions, as if he were an obsolete robot. Poor fellow! (I relish my charitable condescension.) Imagine discovering that he cannot simply push a combination of keys and get an expected set of illuminated numbers. Michelle's unpredictability has upset him. I can almost empathise with him. Now that I know he has been effectively blunted, I have to admit that, in his situation, my expectations would have been the same.

The embarrassment of it! Didn't I find out! Stiff, just the same. Stiff! Serves the bastard right!

Today Colin sulked off to Florence. He won't be back for a couple of days. Thank goodness for the luxury of solitude! Mission thwarted, he doesn't know what to do with himself.

Reluctantly he took my advice to see the artworks in the city. He didn't ask me to go with him. I hope the galleries do something for him. He hates looking at paintings, he told me. They are meant to be hung in one's house to be envied by others.

He is terribly upset because he hasn't found a formula he can apply to me and get the 'right' answers. A confused, restless female, willing to share accommodation with a male in exotic Tuscany, can only mean one thing—and in a hurry too! What else was he supposed to think? I hear you say. I have known him for most of my life and neutralised him in my mind. That was a mistake. I must admit I once told him he wasn't bad looking. At the time I was on my fifth or sixth port and feeling a trifle generous with the world.

I didn't believe you when you said it is very difficult to be just friends with attractive members of the opposite sex. I remember the argument I had with you and Theo. I insisted on the attractions of a personality, and you kept saying that was a typical female way of avoiding a direct expression of sexual interest. Despite Colin's neanderthalic single-mindedness, I still don't think what you said was necessarily true. I shouldn't be writing so much about Colin, should I? I don't mean to sound like a conniving bitch trying to make you jealous. That's not the case, believe me. From this distance I feel I can speak to you openly without the retaliatory bite of your cynicism. I doubt if you realise how much it hurts sometimes.

Before he left, Colin said I had an Anglo-Saxon exterior with a Latin soul. That was his way of insulting me, even though I took it as a compliment. That confused him even more. He feels I have used him. I can't see how. I have insisted on paying rent and I buy the groceries. He chops the wood and I do the cooking. All I wanted was a change of place and some company. Colin happened to be there. He had different ideas about companionship, ideas he wished to implement as soon as we arrived. He wasn't boorish about it. But all the signs were there and getting stronger. After the second day I decided to have a chat.

I am at a villa near Viano. It is badly in need of repair. But it has that aura of decadent elegance we Australians love. Well, sometimes . . . I have just seen a rat run across the floor. There is a magnificent marble fireplace in front of me. There is a feeling of secure comfort to know I have more firewood inside than I shall need tonight. The evenings are very cold and quiet. Tonight I have the company of a bottle of chianti and a little Brahms. They might make the absence of Nadine a little more bearable. And dare I say, even to you, that I miss her more than I could have imagined. There is some sorting out to be done in the next few days . . .

Through the haze I hear Nafisa. 'You are not listening! In some ways you haven't changed at all!'

'Ah . . . sorry . . . just drifted away. There are quite a few things on my mind. You were saying?'

'Will it be all right if I took Nadine to the museum tomorrow?'

'Tomorrow? Not really. I have something planned for tomorrow.'

'Thursday?'

'I want to take her shopping. She doesn't know about it yet.'

'I see.'

'Another day perhaps.'

I know she is staring at me with a wan smile that says everything about me I would wish to deny.

TEN

'The future, hah? Do you think about it?' He pauses to drag on the *hookah*. It gurgles and responds to his vigorous sucking. 'You have wasted enough time. Have you decided what to do with the rest of your life?'

I resent Abba's overbearing attitude. Does he realise how old I am? How long I have managed without his support? I am not a capricious young man sponging on the family. My independence threatens his autocratic authority. He would prefer to see me under his control.

'You have had your years of flirtation with the west.' He looks at me with cold, vulturous eyes as if he disapproves of my excessive indulgence in a life of profligacy. 'You should be thinking of coming home.'

To what? Another beginning? I do not have the space to harbour a young man's delusions. Once I was reckless enough to propel myself into an unknown territory. There was never any trepidation about the consequences of a sudden change in direction. There was a deposit of dreams to replace the ones that were lost. The future, uncertain as it was, never threatened. I did not have the ability to look too far ahead or torment myself into a state of inertia with hypothetical problems. I left with the arrogant confidence of ignorance. That was the wondrous feature of being young—the awareness of being loaded with realisable potential without even a brief contemplation of what could not be achieved.

There was shock and outrage when I told them.

Australia? Don't be absurd!

Be sensible! If you must leave, go to England.

Or at least America.

Australia? The boy must be mad!

His crazy dreams will ruin him.

The fierce energy, fanning the curiosity of rebellious youth, obviated the family's cynicism and overrode the apprehension of venturing into an unchartered terrain. No Chaudhary had been to Australia. It was an opportunity to be different. There was more than a touch of stubborn individuality in my thinking. Unlike Hashim and some of my cousins, I was firm in my resolution not to head for the privileges of that remote island which was an obsessive ideal with the older Chaudharies. I wasted time by being angry with history. I despised the British for humbling us, using us and creating the political mess before they left.

'I never want anything from them,' I declared brashly, even as I secretly admired British culture and its institutions. They enslaved my imagination like a powerful drug. At school I had attempted to emulate the American way of life and failed miserably in a tragicomical sort of way. I did not wish to be like the Yanks, I decided later. In my dreams of insufferable snobbery, I revered all things British—the BBC, test match specials, their literature, the universities, even the pinstriped suit, the umbrella and *The Times*.

I listened with bemused incredulity and laughed cruelly behind their backs when my grandparents spoke wistfully about the Raj. I heard about the pomp and ceremony of Curzon's Great Durbar of 1903, the splendid tea parties and the *shikars*, polo at the gymkhana club and the efficiency of the governmental bureaucracy. They craved for the order and the imported discipline the British imposed on India when waves of political turbulence began to rock Pakistan. It was a serf's mentality, docilely accepting of a rank in the lower tiers of His Majesty's hierarchy. We were the natives meant to be ruled by a superior race. At least my grandparents reacted honestly to their conditioned servility.

My generation was guilty of the worst kind of hypocrisy. Publicly we were vociferous in our denouncement of British imperialism and its redundant offspring, the Commonwealth. At the same time there were those who hung around the British Council, filling in forms and appearing for interviews in the hope of a bursary or a scholarship—any form of financial assistance and a tertiary admission to enter the land of hope and glory they pretended to hate. The sun may have set on the empire, but the aura of dusk lingered long enough to create the illusions of a utopia for those of us born immediately after the territorial divisions of the subcontinent.

'Well?' He asks impatiently.

'I haven't made any decisions as yet,' I mumble weakly. It isn't entirely my choice. I shall have to wait and see.' Limp and gutless as it may sound, it is the truth. With the emerging alternatives, doubt has coiled around me like a binding rope. I am scared of making the wrong decisions, more for Nadine's sake than mine.

Michelle's letter has been a further complication. Why did she bother? Her uncertainties have compounded mine. I have read a thousand meanings into that letter. I have created hope around every sentence. I have found meanings to flatter myself.

'You cannot continue to ignore your responsibilities.'

'You have a duty to your daughter. Every child needs a mother. A family.'

I had temporarily forgotten Ma's presence in the corner chair.

'Nadine has a mother.' Abba contradicts her with the calmness of a lifetime's habit.

He draws the expected reaction. She explodes in exasperated fury. 'Stop finding fault with everything I say. You know
what I mean, Pyareh! I can always tell when you want me to
leave.' She sums up our moods and decides against further
tantrum. 'I have work to do.' With as much dignity as she
can muster, Ma huffs off to the kitchen.

Abba puffs contentedly on the *hookah*.

Years ago I would stand in front of him, wilting under his
stare, after I had been summoned to explain my misconducts.
Usually they involved the neighbours' complaints about
broken windows, stolen lychees and trampled flowerbeds.
Sometimes it was after Brother Martin had phoned for one of
his lengthy chats about my lack of academic progress and my
misdemeanours at school. Abba never raised his voice. There
was never any threat of violence. Such outrageous paternal
conduct was unthinkable in the dead calm of his study. It was
Ma's prerogative to chase me around the house, brandishing
a stick and spouting mild expletives to garnish the descriptions of my long-term residence in *Iblis'* fiery chamber. In the
study it was very different and far more threatening. In his
quiet, cold way Abba had the uncanny knack of deepening
my guilt. He simply stared at me, his eyes pinning me with
unstated accusations. My misdeeds expanded and magnified
themselves with a torturous slowness in my mind. Harsh,
accusing voices rang in my ears. When he sensed I was
vulnerable and contrite, Abba admonished me softly. He made
me feel as if I were standing naked among the clouds on the
edge of a high, cold peak. I often ended up by shivering
involuntarily before he had finished pronouncing the sentence
of banishment to my room for the rest of the day.

I fail miserably to whip up my reserves of defiance and
meet his eyes without the shadows of childhood fear. I am
buffeted by the tidal strengths of pity and guilt. His emaciated
body speaks to me of decay and death, of the ephemerality
of passions and achievements, of the echoing hollowness of

vanity and the madness of unopposed power. This man, my father, who created me in a singularly short-lived moment of self-gratification, is a fragile and suffering symbol of mortality. The skin on his hands and face hang loosely in unevenly defined ridges. It is like wet parchment left under a fierce sun. His face is etched with lines of disappointment, as if he has finally conceded the inevitability of a bleak ending after a treacherously long stretch of unmitigated glory.

The contract for the land sale is to be signed tomorrow morning. The lawyers will be here at ten. The money has been advanced, as promised. Abba has never been one for discussion and collective decision making. He has never faltered in his belief that whatever he did was right and beneficial for his family. To divulge information about his business dealings was demeaning to his authority and an aspersion on his judgement. 'I am answerable to no one, no one except Allah,' I have heard him say on the very rare occasion when someone has had the temerity to question him. I have had serious misgivings whether even the Almighty qualifies for a superior status, given the way Abba exercises his regal authority.

'There will be money, a fairly large sum, left over after the debts have been paid.' He leans forward with a glint of greed in his eyes. 'Part of it is yours,' he whispers feverishly. 'You cannot take the money out of the country. Government restrictions.' A note of triumph has crept into his voice. He reaches across with his left hand and taps the *hookah*.

Made of solid silver, the *hookah* is a visible reminder of our indulgent days when vulgar, aggressive industrialists were unknown, and there were no ill-consequences of our wasteful habits. Fitted to a three-legged wooden stand, it is a cylindrical-shaped contraption, intricately carved with scenes of an imperial hunt, with a flue topped with a funnel-shaped receptacle for the tobacco and embers. A small round hole in the middle is fitted with a long, flexible tube made of jute and copper threads. The end used for puffing is badly worn out.

The lower part of the *hookah* is a hollow chamber filled with rose-scented water to prevent it from overheating.

'It needs more charcoal. Shall I ask Khuda Buksh to fetch some?'

'Yes,' he says slyly. 'I am not allowed a second smoke in the morning. It will upset your mother.'

I make no move to call Khuda Buksh. Abba looks disappointed.

'You better listen to your doctors.'

He pretends not to have heard me. 'Do you like that double-storeyed house further down the street? Number 79.'

I know the one he means. It is a splendid house bought cheaply from a Bihari businessman. After struggling for years to re-establish himself in Bangladesh, he had reached the inescapable conclusion that his future was in Pakistan.

'The UNICEF people rent it now. The lease expires soon. You and Nadine could be very comfortable there.' He watches me closely. He is worried about my lack of enthusiasm. He flexes his fingers. They remind me of a trapped spider frantically moving its legs in a bid to escape. 'When I was a young man,' he reflects quietly, 'I did some silly things. Foolish acts of immaturity. Up to a point it is normal, even necessary, to be impulsive and behave in ways you later regret. Whatever you did in the past cannot be changed. But you refuse to admit your mistakes! You continue to be headstrong and irresponsible!' His hands shake as he grips the arms of his chair.

'What mistakes?' I snap furiously. I have never been rude to him before, but I cannot take this without a strong retaliation. 'If you think I made a mistake in leaving the country, then I disagree with you. Broadening my outlook was not a mistake. Experiencing cultural diversity and learning from it, discarding superstitions and removing ignorance . . . they were not mistakes. Marrying Michelle was not a mistake! How can anything that has brought me happiness and made me think be a mistake? Was Nadine a mistake?'

He snorts a disapproval as if I am being extraordinarily stupid. 'People of your generation seem to marry with the purpose of discovering their capacity for unhappiness.'

I stop short of hitting back with the unpleasant anecdotes from his married life. It isn't my marital problems which have offended him. He has accepted Hashim's impending divorce without acrimony.

'You are bitter about me because I married a white girl. A foreigner. A Christian. Someone who can never be a silent addition to your family. Isn't that it? I am used to that sort of thinking. Michelle gets the same kind of message from Keith, her father.'

'Do you call your father-in-law by his first name?'

'Yes.'

He is astonished by the revelation. 'That is impolite!'

'It is accepted in Australia.'

Abba cannot understand my reluctance to act resolutely and retrieve my honour by divorcing Michelle. I am seen to be dithering unnecessarily about ending a marriage which was never destined to last.

Our family view of marriage is a very functional one, cleansed of all the nonsensical notions of romance. By all means fall in love and have a fling before and during your married life. Needless to say, that unstated precept applies to males only. The only stringent requirement is discretion so that the family's honour and the sacredness of the institution are not publicly damaged. Marriage is a family obligation. A young Chaudhary male has a duty to ensure the continuation of the family. His worth is measured by his procreational prowess. Preferably, male offspring. If his wife bears him daughters, they have to be accepted with good grace in the best tradition of Chaudhary tolerance. The marriage of a male member of our family is a cause for considerable apprehension. The wife is a necessary intruder being grafted into the family. There is an element of risk in the choice of the girl. Will she conform? Is she fertile? Is she capable of conducting herself in a manner befitting our family reputation? Will she care about upholding our *izzat*? The desired girl, with a reputable family background, endowed with beauty, charm and subservience has never been easily found. An independent spirit is to be discouraged. A girl with the right temperament can be trained as a domestic caretaker of some merit, destined to wander through the house with a heavy bunch of keys, directing the servants, waiting on her husband and sons, and preparing her daughters for a fate identical to her own. Her happiness is her service to the family. A more expansive world awaits the man. His happiness is to be found elsewhere—in exercising power, accumulating wealth, travelling and having the odd affair to keep his hormones active. His domestic contentment is in the knowledge that he has fathered several children who are being looked after by a brood of servants and a wife.

'Were you ever happy with her?' I find his scepticism offensive. 'Really happy? Can you assure me you did not merely experience the joyous moments of certain attractions she may have had for you?'

Had I been less angry by his unthoughtful encroachment on my privacy, I might have been amused by his archaic phrasing. I am amazed by his assumption that I owe him a convincing explanation about the happiness I experienced in my married life. My resentment is kept under control by the realisation that he is making a laborious effort to reach out and understand me. Even in my present mood of stubborn reticence and anger, I feel a stirring of sympathy for him. His children have not given him the obedience be craved. Hashim and I chose our wives, and now we have shamed him. He has never understood or accepted Nafisa's fierce independence and her defiance of his wish to give up her academic career and marry.

I have never regretted the early years of my relationship with Michelle. How can he ever understand the obsessive emotional intensity we carried into our marriage?

Abba never saw my mother until their wedding evening. They were minor participants in a convenient arrangement which combined land and wealth to give more power to two rich *zamindari* families. Abba's stoical consciousness of family responsibility and the need for moderation would have controlled his young passion. A few sparks and then nothing. Duty. Temperance. Honour. He was brought up to believe that any open demonstration of love or desire was a profanity. Matrimony was a serious business, its purpose the legitimate extension of the family empire. Abba must have learned to live with the guilt of his fantasies, letting himself loose in those ecstatic imaginings which were beyond the tyrannical control of his religious upbringing.

For me the memories of a particular autumn in the countryside around Castlemaine and Maldon have not tarnished. It was a short season, gracious enough to time its disappearance perfectly. It left a melancholy awareness of unfulfilment, much in the same way as one feels inexplicably cheated when a beautiful face passes by before there is an opportunity to appreciate it at length and discover its inevitable flaws.

It took me a fortnight's accumulated courage to ask Michelle out for lunch.

I met her at a party—one of those house-warming affairs choked with cocky young social workers and enthusiastic first-year teachers bravely attempting to implement their newly acquired theories in the unpredictable environment of the classroom. We were comfortably pissed fairly early in the evening. We stood in little groups in the lounge and the dining area. Some squeezed into the tiny kitchen. Others found a place in the laundry. There were people sprawled on the carpet, wherever there was a space, like destitutes with no place to go. We were full of self-importance in our varied judgements of what should have happened to the governor-general and the prime minister who had connived with Her Majesty's representative with such Machiavellian cunning.

Swilled with beer and cask wine, we did our best to behave like cultural sophisticates. Before the drinks took hold of us and began their devilish tricks, there was some stimulating conversation about the arts, education and the plight of Aborigines and non-English-speaking migrants. In the 1970s the stockpile of sympathy for the underprivileged was high. No one at the party was unemployed, and there was no price to be paid for the gush of altruistic words.

By the time the April Friday had settled itself into a pleasantly cool night, the voices had lost their tertiary modulation. The accents were noticeably slurred. The footy fortunes of Carlton and Collingwood assumed a critical dimension and sparked off some ugly arguments. A repository of racist jokes about Italians, Greeks and the Aborigines surfaced and fuelled the party along toward an inebriated silliness. I contributed a few about Sikhs and Hindus and was immediately embraced as a rare foreigner, a damn good bloke able to take it all in the right spirit. We made pathetic efforts to be clever and witty and succeeded admirably in creating a zoological din.

The fact that I was an older first-year teacher may have had something to do with the Friday evening tiredness and boredom which I did not hide. Having exhausted my severely limited supply of tasteless jokes and fake laughter, I slunk away from a raucous bunch of football fanatics doing their utmost to prove that all members of the teaching fraternity were not necessarily civilised people. I stood leaning against a door, contemplating a discreet exit. I had been foolish enough to come with Theo. He had disappeared, undoubtedly pursuing works of art into the depths of night.

I had not noticed Michelle before she introduced herself.

I had no idea why I amused her so much. Years later she told me I was looking comically lost with my face all screwed up under a mop of uncut black hair.

She could barely suppress a giggle. 'Hello! You look bored.'

'Hello yourself!' I scowled. 'I have a limited endurance for ethnic jokes and footy talk.'

Then I had a good look at her. The boredom vanished instantly. How could I be bored with what was in front of me? My thoughts leaped from one possibility to the next in a spiralling series of plots that would have delighted the editors of Mills and Boon. Too much beer, I concluded glumly and cautioned myself. The apparition must soon disappear.

The ash blonde, shoulder-length hair framed a lightly freck-led, no-nonsense face which would have never made the front cover of a fashion magazine. It wasn't a soft, seductively submissive face. There was too much strength and indepen-dence in the crystalline blue eyes to delight a professional photographer. Yet I thought I saw the mischief of Puck lurking behind their calm seriousness.

We had little by way of common interests, I soon discov-ered. I hated jazz. She enjoyed Japanese food. I knew nothing about Indonesian art. My tolerance for Lawrence had dimin-ished. Camus made her uncomfortable. Yes, she had been to Greece. She was not impressed with the men there. France was the ultimate experience, she sighed. Carlton? Never! I barracked for Hawthorn.

It was a strange conversation. There was no coyness or caution, no euphemisms; only a disarming frankness about the way we were and an expression of what interested us.

I wasn't like the other Indians she had met. I corrected her about my nationality. She confessed her ignorance about Bangalis, although she had followed the events in the subcon-tinent with interest.

I couldn't resist. Why was I different?

I wasn't shy or excessively polite to the point of awkwardness. Was I a Hindu or a Muslim?

My reply surprised her. Her image of Muslims was essentially a distorted composite drawn from the Arab world.

Wasn't alcohol forbidden to Muslims?

Not for the relapsed ones. Did she have a boyfriend?

None of my business. Two in the past three years, if I had to know. They had not lasted very long.

Religious denomination?

I was a curious bugger. Catholic.

I tended to be wary of them.

Oh?

Past experiences with Catholic brothers. I had to tell her about my schooling.

All Catholics didn't share the cloistered, sanctimonious world of nuns and brothers.

Point taken.

Michelle said 'No' to lunch when I rang her. She had to be in Melbourne over the weekend. A close friend of hers was in hospital. She would call me. Okay?

A quick brush-off. Understandable, since I hardly knew her.

She called me a week later.

Our initial outing incarnated the early years of our relationship. I planned to take her to a local restaurant. The late autumn morning hung lazily from an azure canopy, quietly promising to mellow into a golden afternoon.

I changed my mind as we left her flat.

'Perfect day for a drive,' I said.

'Sure is.'

'We could easily find somewhere to eat in the country.'

'Uh-huh. That would be nice.'

There was a shared sense of enhanced freedom as we spent most of our free time in each other's company. We dared ourselves to live spontaneously. We planned nothing and managed to do most of the things we enjoyed. Time ceased to pressure us. We viewed the future as an extension of the present. If not today, then tomorrow or the day after. We created a life of alternatives and diversity. If we could not be together, we looked forward to the next time. No questions asked. No suspicion or strain. We overstepped the petty jealousies of a formative relationship and encouraged each other to maintain a private space to let our individuality grow. We managed not to tighten the strings of our commitment to a breaking point. We were being sensible, we thought, and felt smug about it.

We avoided discussing any long-term propositions. The vaguely perceived fear of the difficulties ahead made us cling to the stability of the present. We were selfish. The microcosm we had created was so self-containing that there was no room to consider anyone else. It was our creation. Others had no choice but to accept it. It was a naive belief we developed to protect ourselves from the unpleasantness of family disapproval. We continued to be irresponsibly happy. How did Yeats put it? Something about loving and being ignorant. It was nearly six months after I met Michelle that we had our first serious quarrel. It was also my first meeting with her parents.

I don't know how long he has been staring at me, waiting for a reply.

'My reason for coming to see you has nothing to do with my future plans. I came to see if you had found that painting of your grandfather.' I remind him of the request I made several days ago.

Abba has not asked why I wish to see the only known portrait of Ishtiaq Ahmed Chaudhary. I have known of its existence since I was a child. The agitation and the hushed whisper of its discovery, in an old trunk during a clean-up of the house in Shopnoganj, had left an indelible impression on me. The canvas was in poor condition, damp and torn on the sides. The colours had paled and the picture was faded. I have an uncertain memory of a thin, effeminate face dominated by large, dark eyes and cruel lips. It was Khuda Buksh who invited me to see the ragged piece of canvas as it lay stretched on the bare floor of the dining room, its corners pinned under the weight of broken bricks. At the time I thought Khuda Buksh must have done something dreadfully wrong, judging from Ma's angry reaction. Even Abba reprimanded him with the threat of a pay deduction. I was sent outside to play. I never saw the painting again. As far as I know, Abba took it.

Abba gets down on his knees, scavenging among a stack of old files and documents piled behind his chair. 'I don't remember where I keep things any more,' he grumbles, fossicking among the papers. 'It was here, somewhere. In the drawer!' He stands up and comes back to the desk. He checks the drawers, slamming each one with an increasing force.

'When did you last see it?'

'I don't know. Five years ago?'

'That long?'

'I don't know.' He looks disconsolately at me. 'My memory. It's gone. I don't remember much.'

I know how difficult it is for him to make an admission of his declining years. I am disconcerted by the despair in his voice.

'Leave it. It isn't important.'

My irresolute effort to calm him has the reverse effect. He goes behind the chair and scatters papers and files in a frenzied search to find the painting. A haze of dust reveals itself in the thin shaft of sunlight peeping through the partially parted curtains.

'Must find it,' he mutters to himself, his nose almost touching the floor. 'Must not lose it. Bad omen.'

I remain silent, determined not to encourage any superstitious forebodings despite my inability to laugh at my own flights into the sinister shadows of my mind.

The horseman is a more frequent visitor. It came back again last night. It is as if an ancient power has broken loose and taken refuge inside me. I have no means of understanding this force which steals me from my sleep to a dim atavistic world of inexplicable incidents. I am beginning to fear that somehow these nightmares will break lose from my psyche and harm me in some tangible manner.

Last night was more threatening than ever before.

I was waiting to cross the river. There was no war on the other side. I paid the fare but the boatman refused to take me across.

'Special passenger,' he kept insisting. 'Wait.'

The muffled sounds of destruction continued to explode behind me. The war was coming closer.

'How long do I wait?'

'Ssh! Listen.' He pointed to the river.

There was a faint flapping of wings. Herons rose out of the mist like the ghostly emissaries of an aeonic power and disappeared into the floating white pouches. The prow of a dinghy broke through the flimsy barrier.

'Is he the one? How far across?'

That voice. I had heard it before. A veil covered her face.

I did not hear his reply. The noise was much closer. I turned to gauge the distance. The house was still ablaze. Thick, sinuous columns of smoke rose upwards like giant pythons slithering away into the sky.

It happened then.

The seemingly impregnable barrier of a dark, unknown world was penetrated by an irresistible will resolved to weld the triadic dimensions of time into an unbroken chain of cause and effect. Generations flashed past in a barely unrecognisable blur, echoing a sustained howl of condemnation. As one, the horse and the rider leaped at me from the heart of the blaze. It was a terrible truth I had vaguely perceived and never fully acknowledged. My feet refused to move. I was incapacitated

into a perplexed stare. I saw Fate—uncaring, dogged, blinding
Fate—in the demonic eyes; eyes charged with a burning
revenge, holding me in its sight as it came at me.

I saw the rider's face. It was a swirling composite of faces.
Mateen and Chonchol *Chacha*. Dilu. Hashim and Abba. Me
. . . Then it changed again, becoming pale and gaunt with
eyes like glowing embers above a contemptuous snarl. An evil
face. Malicious. Cruel. Unrepentant.

The hooves smashed into my forehead. The waking pain
was the conscious burden of the unanswered questions.

Exhausted, Abba drags himself back to the chair. His breathing is irregular and heavy. I pour him a glass of water from
a jug on a side table.

He reaches out and clasps my forearm. 'These ought to be
peaceful days for me,' he gasps, tightening his grip. 'Haven't
I deserved them? Old age should be a time for expansive
speculation, to ponder beyond this demeaning life of selling,
paying debts, settling quarrels, talking to petty-minded bank
managers. I am not all here these days. I tend to wander past
the known horizons. Does that make any sense to you?' He
pauses for my reaction; for an outward sign of scepticism.

My nod assures him of the seriousness of my interest in
what he is saying.

'I should be free to map other courses, to grasp the awesome dimensions which confront me.' He looks at me sharply.

'I understand.'

'I think you do. You have always had the imagination to
reach beyond the obvious. I can never talk to your brother
about what is important to me now.' He reaches for the
half-empty glass. 'Each passing day the universe opens up a
little more to reveal its terrifying darkness. Cavernous spaces
gape hungrily at me. I am scared of being dragged into them.
Allah does not make it easy for me to find Him. I know he
is there somewhere beyond the deepest darkness.' He slumps

in his chair as though he is bereft of all his fighting strength. 'Toward the end of my life I have become dangerously demanding within myself. My belief in Allah is strong, but I now want a whiff of an afterlife. The barest proof that immortality is out there. Waiting. All I have to do is stop breathing and it is mine. I believe but I also listen. All I hear is the feeble echo of my heartbeat above an endless plain of timeless silence.'

I have never heard him speak with so much feeling. With so much uncertainty. He is a haunted man, troubled by an intelligence he has never directed to the greater questions of living, in case his beliefs faltered.

'There is nothing to motivate me,' he complains. 'Yet I suffer from this obsession of wanting to drag out my survival as long as I possibly can. Another year. Maybe longer. I don't want to let go. If I fell seriously ill, I shall say I want to die. But will I mean it? I don't think so. The greed for living is our most lasting flaw.'

Just as I think his despair will end our conversation, the bony frame stiffens with resolute pride. His tenacious hold on mortality rescues him. 'I have had nothing but problems all morning!' The snap returns to his voice. I prefer him this way. 'Mateen was here earlier. His only concern is the house in Shopnoganj. Will he lose it? Can I do something about it? Where is he to go? How will he survive? I offered him a job in our tea garden. He won't go because the labourers have a strong union there. Tears, temper, grovelling. The fellow will try anything.'

'What will happen to the house?'

'They may convert it into an office.'

Despite Mateen's myopic self-interest, I empathise with him. I have a growing sense of pained deprivation as if an integral part of me is being torn away. An office. How vulgar! Neon lights and wires. Rooms crowded with tables and chairs, typewriters, telephones and computers. Staff, ignorant of the invisible presence of our lives, invading the rooms. It is not possible to hide my displeasure.

He looks surprised. 'Are you upset about losing the house?'

'Yes!'

'It will be left intact. They won't do anything to it or build near the mosque.'

'The mosque doesn't concern me. So what if they build anything near it?'

'It should concern you. It is our family's special place of worship. I prayed there as a child. So did you and your brother. Hashim tells me you no longer follow our religion. Is that so?'

'Yes.' I think of an explanation but decide against vocalising it. I have no intention of sounding apologetic.

'You are still a Muslim. You were born as one.' The old authority returns to his voice. 'You do not have a choice. You may have moments of private doubt about religion. We all do. But you cannot shake off your heritage. A tradition of 1300 years has shaped you. 1300 years! How can you deny yourself its richness?'

I have never sought to deny my background. However, this sort of badgering never fails to incense me because it attempts to create guilt and extract a hypocritical submission to conformity. I am not about to be lured and trapped under this burden of 1300 years. It is too heavy a weight to fall under. I would never be able to get out in one piece with my independence intact.

I point out that I value the agony of free thinking and freedom of choice above the cosiness of belonging. I am a free floater. I take and adapt what suits me. I have been indelibly tainted with a diversity of experiences embracing a cross-current of customs and behaviour. I am a composite of lifestyles and rituals. I can never blindly follow. Yes, there are times when I feel very lonely. But I don't really have a choice. To entrench oneself in the groove of an established tradition

requires a certain amount of unconscious dedication to ignorance. As a child I was told to be broad-minded even as I was
being poisoned by inbred prejudices. It was traditional to
regard the Jews as our enemies even though I had never met
one. Hindus were to be hated and Christians tolerated with
suspicion. Tradition taught me that I was among the elite of
the world. Why? What proof is there that Allah is superior to
God? To Yahweh? To Bhagwan?

He listens closely, unconvinced of my point of view. 'It is
not about being better than someone else. It is about being
different and being proud about it. And your daughter? Will
you refuse her the right to have an identity?'

'Her most important identity is that of a human being. I
hope she never takes that for granted.'

'You are avoiding my question!'

'How can I give her the kind of identity you are talking
about? My claim on Nadine as a Muslim is no greater than
Michelle's as a Catholic.'

He is shocked and offended that I should concede Michelle
has any right over Nadine's upbringing.

'Does my grand-daughter receive religious instructions
about our religion?'

'No.'

'Do you read the Koran to her?'

'No.'

'Have you taught her how to pray?'

'No.'

'Have you talked to her about Islam?'

'I have talked to her about my background. About the way
I was brought up.'

'How can you let the child grow in such ignorance?' He
hisses venomously.

I have to steady myself. This confrontation was inevitable
at some stage. I could not have avoided it. I choked myself
into an inarticulate recalcitrance when Michelle's parents

brought up the subject of Nadine's baptism. That was a coordinated, two-pronged attack—Sarah's silent hostility, broken with sighs of growing impatience at my inability to understand the crisis, and Keith's aggressive attacks about my spiritual indifference and callous disrespect for their Catholic tradition. I had not developed an immunity to such criticism in those days.

Now I respond without anger. 'What you say is not true.'

'Not true?' He screeches. 'You have not even bothered to teach her the basic principles of Islam!'

'Nor of Christianity.'

'That is not a compensation! She must know about her religion!'

'Which is?'

'You are being impertinent! Don't forget! You are speaking to your father! Living in the West does not give you the right to be so brash and bold. Your brother has never spoken to me like this. Never! You have forgotten all your manners!'

Like a good son, I should not argue with him. I should have calmed him with promises I would have never fulfilled. That is how Hashim would have behaved.

'We have tried to bring her up to respect religions and different beliefs.'

'*We! We!* That is your weakness. Can't you do anything on your own? What are *you* teaching her?'

He pauses for another drink. I am mindful of his blood pressure.

'Can she recite any of the *surahs*?' He demands aggressively.

'No. But I am teaching her about the significance of rituals. About tolerance and kindness. I have told her about the importance of charity and the idea of equality. I encourage her to be kind and just. I keep telling her that a regular dialogue with her conscience is more important than mechanically mumbled prayers she cannot understand.'

'You are such a foolish idealist!' He sighs in exasperation. 'You always have been. All that will confuse her.'

'Will she be any less confused praying in Arabic? Would it be very practical for me to employ a tutor to come up from Melbourne and teach her Arabic?'

He shakes his head sadly. 'You are good at finding arguments to justify your negligence. Still, it may not be too late.' He looks at me meaningfully.

There is a knock on the door. '*Kahnna, Boro Shaheb!*'

'What?'

'That was Khuda Buksh calling you for lunch.'

Abba peers at his watch. 'I have to go. This is one of your mother's peculiar household customs I am obliged to follow. I can have a late dinner with everyone. But lunch? I have to eat early at the same time every day. She thinks a late lunch affects my digestion and makes me ill-tempered for the rest of the day.'

'The painting? May I look for it?'

He waves toward the shelves and hobbles out.

I try the bookshelves and the cupboards. There is nothing in the filing cabinets except for business files and old documents. I try the desk. The top four drawers are crammed with letters and postcards, paid bills and old cheque books. The bottom drawer is stuck. I can move it slightly. I can see a white towel spread over whatever is under it. Excitedly I exert more force. It does not budge. I slide it back and then jerk it out with an upward tilt. It slips out of the grooves on the sides and strikes me painfully on the thigh. I remove the towel with care.

I am greeted by the salubrious breasts of a coyly smiling brunette gracing the cover of last month's *Penthouse*. Under it are past copies of the magazine. A few editions of *Playboy*.

I return to the brunette. A creature fit to dwell in the gardens of *Bahaesht*. Superbly rounded. Dark, erect nipples. Moist lips, slightly parted. Shiny eyes *dancing with the devil's promise*. That was what the Peshawari *mullah* told us about the deadly powers of females and prompted Hashim and me to scour the neighbourhood in search of diabolical promises.

She is worth the obsession of dragging out one's survival for another year. A month. Even a day. Ah, the charms of our most lasting flaw.

ELEVEN

Nadine's must be the only happy face in this snarling traffic madness. The rickshaw ride has been another Spielbergian experience—exhilaratingly adventurous without losing the feeling of a dangerous reality.

My pleas for caution were ignored. Nadine's delighted shrieks of excitement exhorted the rickshaw *wallah* to fearless feats of giddy manoeuvring. We nearly hit a cow, almost injured several pedestrians and narrowly missed bounding off the side of a bus. Nadine thought it was great fun, an experience to boast about to a captivated audience at school.

The noise and the colours fascinate her. I shudder at her insistence that we do this again. 'This is unreal!' She declares with complete conviction.

I am quite content to be sitting patiently on the stationary rickshaw. It has not been able to move for several minutes. A harried policeman is waving his hands and blowing shrilly on his whistle in an increasingly futile show of authority. The problem of the blocked traffic is due to a broken water main and countless merry-making kids on the road. Motorists, truck drivers, cyclists and rickshaw *wallahs* have plenty to say. They honk, hoot, tinkle and shout. I am carefully selective about translating some of their remarks for Nadine.

Naked, squealing children shower under the fountain of

spouting water. They run back and forth across the road, adding to the confusion. A policeman slips in a puddle as he chases a group of boys for throwing stones at the plumbers.

There is a spontaneous cry of "Call the tanks! It's a job for the army!'

'Let the generals earn their money!' Someone shouts.

Curses and abuses castigate the police and the plumbers. Outrageous insults about their parents are greeted with malicious howls of laughter.

The driver of a white Mazda loses his patience and stupidly negotiates an impossible U-turn. The bumper bar of the car buckles the back wheels of a rickshaw. A heated disagreement about the damage and payment for the accident draws a ring of pedestrians around the vehicles. The sticky heat draws the worst out of everyone. The argument turns ugly. There is a torrent of mindless vilification, with the onlookers urging the rickshaw *wallah* to be firm in his demands. The windows and balconies on both sides of the road are crowded with bemused spectators deriving a warped pleasure from the behavioural ugliness of people under stress.

The driver of the car, a smartly dressed young man, is told to pay up. Two thuggish looking men step out threateningly from the throng. The driver relents and reaches reluctantly for his wallet.

A cheer goes up. 'Justice for the poor!'

The police pretend not to notice this blatant act of communal blackmail by chasing the children more vigorously.

I decide to walk the rest of the way. There is no point in bargaining. I pay the rickshaw *wallah* the agreed fare plus a *baksheesh*. We hop on the road with his words of blessing accompanying me.

We stop for a drink of coconut water from a roadside vendor.

'Is it nice?' Nadine asks dubiously.

'Find out for yourself.'

She is fascinated by the way he cleanly chops off the top of the hard green shell with a short-handled axe and punctures a hole for the straw.

'Drink it straight,' I say sharply.

'Why can't I use a straw?' She demands.

'Just do as you are told, please.' I am unwilling to give her my reason in front of the vendor. 'Drink it like this.' I place my mouth around the small opening and tilt the fruit. A trickle of tepid liquid dribbles down my chin.

'That's not very neat,' she comments in an undertone.

'Try!'

Tentatively she follows my instruction. The vendor offers words of encouragement.

'Yuk! It's gross!' She splutters. She grabs her throat. 'That's enough. Can I have something else?'

'You are not having a fizzy drink.'

She makes another reluctant effort. 'No more, thanks.'

The vendor is an astute salesman. From under his brightly painted wooden cart he takes out a familiar shaped bottle. 'Coca-cola?'

'Dad?'

'No!'

'I am thirsty!'

'He pulls another bottle and invites me to feel its icy coldness.

I give in wearily. At least I held firm against taking her for a hamburger yesterday. I simply could not reconcile myself to the blandness of the multinational hamburger, watched by hungry, scavenging kids hovering on the footpath in the dim hope of an abandoned take-away.

Everything attracts Nadine's attention. Energetically she skips between the street-side stalls, pausing frequently to examine the trinkets and practice her limited range of Bangla words.

I have to be patient. The experience is worth months of

classroom learning with the additional difference that her enjoyment is spontaneous and unbounded.

We approach a huge billboard on a tiny block of land. The coloured advertisement is striking. It proudly boasts of the superior hospitality of the national airline over the more established carriers of the world. A chic air hostess, in a green and gold sari, with a caramel complexion, spine-tingling eyes and a coy 'maybe . . . maybe not . . . try your luck fella' smile, holds a gleaming silver tray. Fruits, caviar, cheese, paté, smoked salmon and an assortment of savoury biscuits promise an alien luxury high in the sky to millions of desperate Bangalis scraping together a semblance of a ragged life. The label of a chilled, uncorked bottle is discreetly pressed against the contour of a shapely breast. Below the tray a message in Bangla, scribbled in charcoal, reads: WE ONLY WANT RICE.

In the shadow of the billboard an emaciated old woman squats on her haunches, breaking old bricks with a rusty hammer. Each brick is smashed with an emotionless precision. Other than the mechanical motion of her right hand, the woman looks as lifeless as the bricks she is battering into small pieces. Each measured blow is like a stroke of fate pounding her into a submissive continuation of her programmed function beyond which life promises nothing. Behind her, two boys, on all fours, sniff and paw a rotting pile of rubbish. Stray cows, with pink powder-puff wounds on their flanks, move about with a desultory slowness, chewing tufts of dry grass. Only the flies swarm around the garbage with a buzzing energy which defies the enervating power of the muggy heat.

'Can I give her some money?' Nadine whispers, visibly moved by the harshness of the woman's labour.

'Can you afford it?'

'I have twenty takas.'

'I thought you were saving to buy a set of glass bangles.'

I test her a little further. 'I am not giving you any more money this week.'

She screws her face and sticks out her tongue at me. 'I think I'll give it to her anyway.' She digs into the front pocket of her jeans and offers me two crumpled notes.

'You give them to her. Go on!'

Shyly Nadine moves in front of the old woman and offers her the money. '*Baksheesh*,' she murmurs. '*Baksheesh*.'

Startled, the woman looks up incomprehensibly. Slowly she breaks into a toothless grin. She drops the hammer and reaches out with an unsteady hand. She takes the notes and rubs them on her forehead. Her demeanour changes. The joy on her face makes us smile. Before I can move forward to assist her, she manages to struggle to her feet. She beams like a benevolent grandmother and returns one of the notes to Nadine.

'*Mishti kayno, baba! Allah aaro deh boh.*' She reaches out and places the palm of her right hand on Nadine's head.

Nadine turns to me. 'What's she saying, Dad?'

'She wants you to buy sweets for yourself. She says Allah will give more.'

It is an act of supreme willpower for Nadine to step forward. 'Thanks!' She forces herself to look at the old woman. 'Thank you!' Her voice is humble and full of gracious acceptance.

'*Dhonobad!*' I add. I am grateful to her. In a simple act of selflessness, she has taught Nadine what we have been attempting for the past few years with little success. For an only child, swamped with the temptations of consumerism, the concept of sharing is neither easily understood nor readily accepted.

The old woman raises her hand in a friendly farewell.

I feel as if we have been truly blessed.

We smile our goodbye and turn away.

A persistent lad, in his early teens, has gathered enough

courage to quicken his steps and move up to us. He has been watching us for some time. He is wearing a pair of shapeless, canary-yellow cotton trousers and a black T-shirt. His raised right hand holds a biro as if it were a magical wand. The strap of a leather satchel, grimy with sweat and dirt, is strung around his scrawny neck. It makes him lurch forward as he walks. Out of the corner of my eyes I can see his lips moving silently in a quick rehearsal of what he is about to say. He coughs and clears his throat.

No luck. I keep talking to Nadine.

'*Shaheb*!'

Nadine stops and turns.

'*Ay jey, Shaheb*!'

Nadine tugs my arm. 'Dad!'

Reluctantly I stop. He jumps in front of us.

'Only twenty-five takas each! First-class quality! Best buy in Dhaka, otherwise my name is not Ghulam Mohammad Kibria. Quality guaranteed! Made by the newest machines from Germany.' The hand lowers. His right eyelid shuts. The aim is unerring. The biro is sprayed with spittle. A frantic rub on the front of his T-shirt makes the shiny plastic worthy of renewed admiration.

Nadine looks horrified.

'All your important letters can be written for a year without a refill! Business letters, love letters, blackmail letters, protest letters, letters to your mistresses, friends and boss. Anything *Shaheb* desires. It is magic!'

'I don't want any!' I snap rudely, grabbing Nadine's hand.

We walk at a brisk pace.

He falls a few steps behind us. '*Boro Shaheb*! Any problems and you get your money back!'

I cannot resist the sarcasm. 'Who shall I write to? Let me guess. Ballpoint Anonymous, Fraudulent Products, Across the Buriganga Where Anything Goes, Zanjira?'

He marches ahead of us and then does a sharp about-turn.

A pained expression crinkles his face. He protests indignantly. 'I am trying to earn some money honestly. People like you prevent me from making a living. What right do you have to force me to beggary? Do you want me to become a thief? Pick your bulging pocket?'

I should fold my handkerchief properly before sticking it in my pocket. He strikes a note somewhere inside me. I like his guts and enterprise.

'How many pens do you have in that bag?' We move over to the edge of the footpath.

'Five hundred. Reduced price if you buy fifty.'

'Five!' I say firmly. 'I will buy five and pay you seventy-five takas. No bargaining!'

The mind calculates. The eyes, aged with the survival wisdom of a lifetime, narrow. The face scowls. He expectorates in the gutter. He looks at Nadine and manages a smile. Females are infinitely more pliable. I am a hopelessly hardened case. He counts the biros and reaches into his pocket for a rubber band. He tries to outstare me into a belatedly better deal.

'Here!' He thrusts the biros in my hands. 'I tie them with a rubber band only for those who buy a dozen or more and pay the right price.' He snatches the money from me. 'Wait!' He holds up the notes and examines them with care. 'They are not new,' he observes with disapproval.

'Do you sell those as well?' I manage to keep a straight face.

'*Nah, Shaheb*! But I make a few,' he boasts. His attention is diverted across the road. '*Memshaheb*! Wonderful gifts for family and friends! Guaranteed to last for years! No refills for two years! Made by the best machinery in America!'

We watch him run across the road to a woman in a parked car, buying fruits from a vendor.

Many, many dreams ago, a newly painted sign hung proudly outside a squat, box-shaped building. It radiated its naive intention of speaking on behalf of the people and delivering the truth, however unpalatable, to the educated thinkers in Bangladesh. The aftermath of a brutal martial victory is an intense period of moral anxiety. There is a massive search for an untainted national soul. There is a keen desire to begin anew, a spirit of generosity toward oneself, a renewal of faith in humanity, and a burning energy to create a new social order whose virtues are not merely remote ideals. The sanguine eagerness bubbles from a fallacious belief that a rejuvenated population has arisen from the rubble after stripping itself of its ignoble instincts and burying them alongside the hideous acts of savagery which are hastily explained away as deviational behaviour to be expected under difficult and abnormal circumstances. There develops a mood of smug self-satisfaction, as though the entire population has been injected with the vaccine of nobility to immunise itself against those dark impulses which surface so readily in ugly outbursts of war atrocities.

In its first few editorials, *The Voice* praised and congratulated the people of Bangladesh on their historic victory over the barbaric army of Pakistan. The paper vowed to reflect the new nation's lofty moral standards. There was to be no pandering to the government, no flattery of the rich and no excuses offered for any involvement of the army in civilian affairs. *Aak dhom!* Intentions made perfectly clear. The newspaper had nothing to fear if it had the support of the people to whom it pledged its exclusive allegiance. *The Voice* would echo the community's concerns and monitor the government's efficiency.

For the first couple of years its sales raked in the takas. There were praises and awards, commendations and pay rises for its journalists. But its provocative comments about the armed forces and its leftist sentiments did not pass unnoticed. They were duly registered in the cantonment. After Mujib's brief romance with the nation was brutally terminated, the military government (before it camouflaged itself behind a civilian visage) sniffed the danger, seethed in anger and made its plans. Outwardly it made a public show of appreciating a newspaper with such meritorious qualities.

That was many governments ago. The original sign, I am told, was stolen. Its replacement was badly defaced, the office ransacked and burnt by masked thugs and the staff threatened unless the newspaper stopped printing views harmful to the nation. Government press releases laid the blame on street hooligans intent on senseless violence and harassment of honest journalists. On television, an ashen-faced minister for home affairs bravely admitted that he should have acted sooner after consulting the minister for law and order. There was an impassioned appeal for apprehending the miscreants.

The police responded with telling effect. The vandalism stopped. The *goondas* were never caught. It was assumed that they were struck with remorse and became law-abiding citizens who opted to join the armed forces. A few weeks later the minister for home affairs suffered a serious heart attack as he was reading the morning newspaper. He died in an ambulance that had to stop some distance from the hospital to change a flat tyre. It was never established whether the fatal attack was precipitated by a feature article insinuating a widespread corruption among the ranks of the military government.

A few days late a mysterious fire damaged the building and forced the newspaper to cease publication for more than a month. There was another coup d'état. When publication resumed, the new government made it known to the media that it would not tolerate criticism from left-wing journalists inclined toward atheism.

The staff of *The Voice* deemed it prudent to remove the battered sign hanging over the front entrance. Several emergency exits were constructed by labourers brought from across the Buriganga River and sworn to secrecy. The remaining journalists on the staff chose to find accommodation in the old part of the city without phones or reliable addresses. The editorials became less controversial. Sales dropped. An army officer dropped by regularly for a cup of tea and a friendly chat. Life settled into a routine third world struggle.

The deafening clatter of the printing press greets us as we walk through the iron-grilled door after a perfunctory check by a disinterested *darwan*. The airless corridor, inadequately lit by a neon light, is like an underground tunnel. I knock on the door with the chipped nameplate informing us it is the editor's room. Just below the name plate an unknown hand has crudely painted in black the words MARTYR-IN-CHIEF.

I knock again before trying the rusty door handle. The room yawns vacantly at me. There is a thick coating of dust on the floor. Nails and thumbtacks are strewn around the room. An evil-looking noose, made from coir rope, hangs from a hook on the ceiling. Under the noose there is a clean space. There is a pair of shoes, a neat pile of books, a fountain pen and a pair of spectacles.

'Further down. First down on the right!' The *darwan* calls. 'That is the dummy room.'

'What's the dummy room?'

'The dummy room,' he smiles, unwilling to offer an explanation.

Zafar Mahmood, the indefatigable and battle-scarred editor of the ailing daily, is locked in an argument with Iftiqar. I am shocked to see how much he has aged.

'Memorabilia from the past!' He greets us with a friendly wave of a miniature national flag.

We embrace warmly. Iftiqar and I shake hands.

'This is my daughter, Nadine.' I push her gently in front of me.

'What a lovely girl! Must be her mother's genes,' Zafar

teases. 'Very pleased to meet you, Nadine. Your father and I are old friends. We went to university together.'

Iftiqar pats her on the head. 'Hello, Nadine. It's nice to see you.' He looks at me with an approving wink.

I feel the tension seeping out of me. Iftiqar is more relaxed here than he was in his flat.

Nadine is slightly taken aback by the warmth of their greetings. She keeps looking at me with uncertainty furrowing her brow.

'Well, do sit down.' Zafar wipes a couple of fragile-looking wooden chairs with a rag. 'Be careful! As you can see, the room is an obstacle course to slow down an unexpected raid and make a quick exit possible.' He points to a rear entrance. The army knows about that door, but they don't know about the other . . . Have a seat! It's at your own risk. If the chairs collapse and you hurt your back, don't sue. We've already been refused a meeting with the bank manager.'

'What's he on about?' Nadine whispers.

'Something wrong?' Zafar inquires.

'She's a little tired after walking in the heat,' I say casually.

The room is like a neglected godown. Cobwebs hang from the ceiling like fishing nets left to dry. The roughly hewn wooden shelves are mostly empty. Nearly everything has been laid out on the floor, creating the effect of a number of twisting passages leading to Zafar's table. He watches us closely as we follow a winding path between stacks of newspapers, books and journals stored in cardboard boxes and massive tea chests. We manage to avoid the heavy rolls of newsprint, packets of envelopes, folders, manual typewriters, bottles of glue and ink. I can smell kerosene. Broken tables and chairs have been stacked up near his table, giving the impression that all is in readiness for a fire, should it become a necessary strategic diversion.

'Quite a fortification, you must agree! I am thinking of buying some toy cannons to decorate these hilltops and make the room look like an authentic battlefield,' Zafar cackles with glee. 'What do you think, Nadine?'

She makes a face and declines to answer.

We laugh a trifle uneasily.

The walls are swamped with revolutionary posters. I recognise Che, Allende, Mandela, Arafat, Charun Mazumdar, a young Mao, Ortega. Unsmiling faces, frustrated by their inability to peek over the horizon of time and confirm their dreams of the future. In a corner an old teleprinter activates itself to rattle a few lines before relapsing into a fatigued whine. The windows have been boarded up and reinforced with nailed strips of wood. The only sign of extravagance is the blazing neon lights which expose the damp patches on the walls. A vintage ceiling fan creaks overhead and circulates enough stale air to keep the fat blowflies buzzing around the room.

'You have a choice of tea or South Indian coffee, with or without sugar. No milk,' Iftiqar offers. He turns to Nadine. 'Coca-cola or Seven-Up?'

Nadine avoids looking at me. 'Coke please.'

'The tea is excellent,' Zafar suggests. 'Nafisa keeps us supplied with the unsold stuff from your garden. Bless her heart! She is the kindest and the least pretentious of the Chaudharies. Present company excepted, of course. She is even generous enough to write a monthly column for us without bothering about the inconsistent payment. Now, there's a true journalist's soul for you!' He reaches under the table and presses a buzzer. 'There is no milk because the milkman will not deliver unless we pay what he says we owe him. We can be generous with the sugar since one of our proofreaders lives on the other side of the river. His father runs a sugar refinery. You may get bits of crushed gravel in your mouth. Ever had crunchy tea before? Exercises your teeth. There isn't a dentist nearby, so you must be careful.'

The consternation on Nadine's face makes Zafar laugh.

There is still that purity in his laughter, like the sound of a fresh-water stream, which used to remind me of a happy child who had never seriously known grief. I know that is not true in Zafar's case. Somehow he has consistently managed to sound as if life is more liveable than it often is.

'Nadine, my child,' he says affectionately. 'It is a mad world adults live in. Have you ever been on a roller coaster? Yes? Well, imagine one that keeps going down steeply all the time. That's the way life is for some of us. The excitement of it makes us slightly mad.' He presses the buzzer again. 'Bearer! Bearer! Is he on strike again? Didn't we pay him last month?'

'We paid him last month for the previous month,' Iftiqar answers laconically.

'No wonder he is so slow with everything!'

Nafisa has spoken to me warmly about Zafar. I can see what she meant by age having no effect on his personality. For years they have been close friends for reasons I have never fully appreciated until recently. He is a rare character. In my experience Zafar is the only person who has more friends than acquaintances. Whatever he says or does is born out of conviction, untainted by malice. That is why people extend a helping hand when he is in strife, which is fairly often judging by what Nafisa has said.

Zafar has one of those constitutions which cannot cope with fresh air, exercise or a selective diet. By his own admission, Nafisa tells me, he is an imposing piece of ruin with an aura of bygone magnificence. Strong tea, cigarettes, fatty food and alcohol have wrecked him. Nafisa was uncharacteristically callous in remarking that he should have died, if not years earlier, at least some months ago. He has barely survived several heart attacks. Zafar writes his epitaph once a month and then tears it up in disgust, once life has betrayed him into facing another monthly cycle of pain, pills and debts. He is a slow-moving, beefy man in his forties. He has a puffed-up face accentuated by fleshy lips and a round face, a possible model, I am tempted to think, for Plato's androgynous being.

A sullen, lethargic young man, with slim fingers and striking long eyelashes, ambles in.

'Naushad, my lovely boy! May we have three cups of *cha* and a bottle of Coca-cola? No dead cockroaches in the kettle this time.' Zafar sighs. 'He has such possibilities!'

'Use the paper cups,' Iftiqar calls as Naushad leaves the room. He offers Zafar a cigarette after I refuse one. 'You took care of the last proper cup we had.'

'Only a little accident!' Zafar protests.

'Throwing it at the postman? Lucky for us your aim is so lousy. Better a smashed light than the postmen's union members surrounding the building and demanding justice.'

Zafar senses Nadine's boredom. He offers to show her the printing press. I encourage her to go.

I don't waste any time. An unbreachable distance separates us. It couldn't become any worse.

'There is something you ought to know,' I begin awkwardly. 'It may be of little significance now, but it has been on my mind for a long time.'

'Confession time, is it? A bad habit from the school days. Did you ever try it?'

'Shit no! Did you?'

'Only once.'

I feign indignation. 'You never said anything to me about it!'

We spar like old times.

'I wanted to keep my newly acquired knowledge to myself. Within minutes of sitting in the mystical darkness of the magic box, I became an expert on the sin of masturbation. I didn't want to tell you where you were headed if you continued the filthy practice.'

'You selfish dong!'

'As always.'

We laugh and talk about the brothers who taught us. We remember them well. There is an affectionate amusement in our memories of their repeated failure to convert us to believe in the Gospel and to dissuade us from being seduced by the unspeakable abominations of communism.

Iftiqar sits on the edge of Zafar's table and dreamily blows smoke rings in the air. His playful tone changes. He looks despondent. 'I think I know what you are about to say. It's not really necessary. I know more than you think. A lot more.'

He is considerate enough not to look at me. I remain silent.

'After I came back from the war, Shabana came to see me. It was a strange meeting. It seemed as if we were casual acquaintances. The conversation was jerky. It stuttered and stopped and began again like a car with an old battery on a damp morning. She told me about you. Then she waited for me to get angry. It didn't happen. I expected some excuses. She gave me none.'

'You must have been angry!'

He shakes his head firmly. 'There was no anger left. The war had drained me of all feelings. I was surprised by her honesty. I didn't know she had so much courage. And you? How did you feel about it after you had escaped?'

I overlook the sarcasm. I had expected worse. 'I cannot say it was a mistake committed in a moment of rashness. I saw her all the time you were away. I wasn't sorry about it.'

'Were you in love with her?'

'As far as I understood love then, maybe. I wanted her. There was the additional thrill of taking her off you,' I blurt without restraint. 'It now sounds so cheap and nasty. She was not a person but a possession I wanted because you had her. I wanted to prove I was better than you at something.'

'Did you ever think of me when I was not there?'

'We shut you out completely from the private world we created for ourselves. It was a response to fear. We didn't want to think of the war around us. We created some security from our illusions. We couldn't allow your memory or any guilt to remind us of what was happening. I know what you are getting at. You are perfectly justified in thinking how bloody selfish and treacherous we were. What can I say? I am sorry about the impact it must have had on you.'

'No, no.' He holds up his hand to stop me from going on. 'You are wrong about the effect. It was minimal. The day I saw her turned out to be one of revelation. We were like mirrors for each other. It was very disturbing not to recognise ourselves. We realised how much we had changed. The awkwardness of our dialogue was a bewildered response to our altered circumstances. The political upheaval had dwarfed our private concerns into insignificance. We were too busy realigning our lives to a new order to indulge in recriminations. Even if you hadn't been there to complicate matters, I doubt if Shabana and I would have got together again. We had become strangers to our old lives.'

Another sad voice rings in my ears. The insights we gain into ourselves often have a converging point of commonality. They have so much to do with a struggle to understand all the strangers lurking within us.

I didn't think sorting myself out would be such an impossible task. This was the perfect opportunity to reach inside and drag parts of me out for prognosis. Not so simple! How was I to know that I would come up with all these restless strangers speaking in foreign tongues? I laughed when you grumbled about the forties being like a pack of cards with more than two jokers ready to reveal themselves at the most unexpected moments. I now know what you meant . . .

I ask him about the war and its aftermath. After the anger against him had subsided, couldn't he have done better? Governments had changed. There were opportunities to be grasped. I think of the unremitting greyness of his life in that grotty flat. Why hadn't he done something for himself? Had all his ambitions died? Was that possible?

'Can you ever understand? You, who have such a strongly developed instinct for self-preservation. You, who have never known anything but a life cushioned by your family privileges. You know nothing about the evils that can destroy a person and leave a lifeless stump in its place.'

I withhold a retaliation to blunt his accusations. What would be the point? They are only words, inaccurate to the extreme, flying around me like wild bullets. His misconceptions do not touch me the way they might have once. Our lives and perceptions are irreconcilably different. He doesn't mean anything to me now. There is no remorse in making that admission. Oh, there is some nostalgia when I think of the friendship we have known. Nothing unbearable. If only he knew that, like him, my priorities have altered, that I have ceased to strive for the lonely pinnacles of tangible achievements, that I have not used my family privileges. If only he knew that I, too, have known pain and sadness as I hobble along with my fractured life.

Naushad interrupts with a bundle of mail. Iftiqar flicks through the envelopes.

'More bills,' he mutters despondently. 'A court summons! What has he been up to now?' He tosses the letters on Zafar's table. 'You want to hear about my days with the *Mukhti Bahinis*? Let me tell you, war is the disease of the soul. You never quite trust yourself after you have finished because you have done the worst. You know that evil is a reality, that it is you. You are forever aware that there is a very dangerous force lurking inside you, capable of resurfacing again with an uncontrollable savagery. In the early days I was comfortable, enjoying life in Calcutta at the expense of the Indian government. But those final ten days at the beginning of December . . . '

'Yes?'

With restless steps he paces the narrow space behind Zafar's table. It is evidently a harrowing recollection, one he would rather keep in the darkness of his hidden misery. He looks at me with morose eyes, debating whether I can be trusted not to make a judgement which may justify the loathing he feels for himself. For him the war is not over. He keeps the experience hungrily alive, using it to punish himself without mercy.

'On the first day of December we were across the Jessore border. I spent most of the next day in a trench. The Pakistanis blunted our initial trust. We had to call for reinforcement. In the afternoon we moved again under the cover of air attack. I felt as if there were firecrackers exploding inside my head. Have you ever been afraid? I mean scared till you want to dig a hole and bury yourself in it? You begin to hear fear in every noise, see it in every shape. It slashes your insides like a sharp razor blade and reduces you to a cowering mess. We pushed forward. There were bodies on the ground around me. I would see a soldier running beside me. Then suddenly he was not there. You keep thinking, it must be my turn soon. I don't know how long I ran. There was only myself and a foreboding shadow beside me. I kept running. Running, weaving, ducking and firing. They finally surrendered. A group of weary soldiers filed out from behind a clump of trees. A captain waved a white cloth. We held our fire. A *jawan*, with his hands clasped behind his head, walked toward me. His cheeks were flushed with shame. There was smouldering hatred in his eyes. He was about seventeen, too young to be protective about life. They stopped when they realised we were not Indian soldiers. Perhaps they were intimidated by the revenge etched on our faces. There was a collective consciousness of oppression carved on that silent moment—the killings, the tortures, the rapes, the mutilations, the injustice, the ridicule, the humiliation. Years of accumulated anger was piled high. Tinder dry. Someone fired. The flat noise of the automatic rifle sounded almost innocuous at first. The *jawan* in front of me knew what had happened. He dropped his hands to his sides. The fiery defiance went out of his eyes. But his face didn't register fear. There was a flicker of confusion. It reflected a nonplussed resignation after quivering briefly with disbelief. That Allah should abandon those who willingly fought for Islam was as incomprehensible as death itself. The vision of Heaven must have bloomed like a summer flower before him. He laughed fiendishly, almost triumphant in the certainty of his destiny. He wanted to be a *Shaheed*. The poor fool! He began to recite from the Koran. Something about having faith in Allah and fighting for His cause. I couldn't bear to look at him. I was the one with the gun, yet I was the one who was afraid. He continued to shout about Allah forgiving his sins and letting him into the mansions in the garden of Eden. He called me a traitor and unsheathed a long-bladed hunter's knife. '*Haramzada!*' He cried and lunged at me. I felt as if I had been immersed in an ocean of iced water. I felt deserted. I had this feeling that my humanity had fled, leaving me stranded to empty the rifle in a narrow arc of death. All around me there were guttural expressions of tribal joy. I slipped away unnoticed. The trench was the only place of solitude. It received me with an indifference with which the earth swallows the dead.'

My voice is strange and distant to my ears. 'Does it serve any purpose to hound yourself with such memories? Killing is the heart of war. Without it there wouldn't be a beast.' I sound so awkwardly patronising. I can think of nothing else to say. He went willingly for a cause he passionately believed in. He chose to fight for the very expensive illusion of freedom without knowing what it entailed.

'I have never spoken to anyone about this before,' he says dismally, as though in a thoughtless moment of indiscretion he has exposed too much about himself.

'Didn't you ever want to talk about such a difficult experience? Even to some of those who fought with you?'

'Sometimes I was tempted. I couldn't bring myself to share their tales of heroism. That's what isolated me. I couldn't talk like they did. I was too ashamed of myself. There was too much guilt. The war had turned me into a moral pauper. It was much easier to hide than reveal.'

'Did you ever think of seeking professional help?'

'A psychiatrist? The symptoms were never bad enough. Or so I thought. I had no one to tell me. I didn't have nightmares or wake up in a cold sweat or anything like that. I read about the Vietnam experiences. I didn't react quite as dramatically as some of the American soldiers did. That's what fooled me. There was just this heavy pressure I had to live with. I was obsessed with all kinds of questions to which there were no answers. Was I normal? Why did I continue to pump bullets into that young man's body even after he was dead? What drove me to a desperate rampage the next day? I believe I was unsparingly barbaric. I tasted everything Evil had to offer. Everything. What made me go over the edge of a world torn apart by such inhuman savagery?'

We brood in a silence of mutual perplexity. Those experiences we do not understand often become a living part of us. They are the catalysts of change which alter our personalities and people's perceptions of us.

He laughs bitterly. 'So rest easy. The fact that Shabana and I broke up had nothing to do with your involvement with her. I had nothing to offer her any more. I couldn't feel for her as I once did. It was as if love and hate and the entire range of inbetween feelings had been drained out of me. There was nothing left. Without those vital emotions and the commitments they induce to give life its shape and meaning, I was condemned to a state of indifference. There I languish.'

'The relief work that you do. That is not indifference.'

'It's not done out of any moral conviction. It is something

to keep me busy. Your daughter's coming back. You are blessed to have such a child.'

Nadine's high-pitched laughter is a relief. It comes as a timely reminder of my uneasiness in Iftiqar's presence. I have to leave things as they are. The past cannot be rearranged for my convenience. Maybe that is a fair retribution for me. Every time I look back, there will be a measure of guilt and regret arising from the debris I can never sweep away from memory.

Outside the door we hear Zafar trying to calm an agitated Naushad.

I ask Iftiqar about the room with the dangling noose. I am saddened by what he has to say about Ajit Kumar. I remember the shy Brahmin and his clever political cartoons for the university newspaper. After liberation he worked for *The Voice*.

Soon after Mujib's murder, Iftiqar and Zafar were arrested by military police and bundled off to the cantonment. The interrogation lasted several hours. Were they communists sympathisers? Did they possess information about India's insidious designs on Bangladesh? How much did they know about the Awami League? What were their connections with India? They had to sign a document endorsing detailed guide-lines for future publications. That night they had to view a lengthy documentary on the army's role in liberating the country. Zafar was abused for pointing out that there was no formal army until after the independence of the country. They were lectured and then beaten; not severely but as a warning that the army was unwilling to accept any criticism of its political authority.

They spent a sleepless night on the floor of an airless and dark cell. Next morning an army jeep took them back to the office.

They found Ajit hanging in Zafar's room.

'Because he was a Hindu?' I ask glumly.

'And a member of the Communist Party.'

'It must have devastated Zafar.'

'He was distraught for months. They were very close, as you probably know. After the cremation Zafar vacated the room and had all the furniture removed. He placed a few of Ajit's personal belongings there. Even now Zafar goes into the room after work and sits under the rope for hours at a time. He says it gives him the strength to continue with the paper. We would have folded up ages ago without Zafar's will to keep it going. He keeps spurring us on, telling us that to give in would be to betray Ajit and everything we have ever believed in. It is idealism carried to a masochistic extreme. But it works. We keep going.'

Nadine breezes in, eyes glinting with excitement.

Behind her, Zafar is more subdued. 'There's an army truck parked on the other side of the road,' he announces laconically. 'They don't pretend any more.'

'Time we had a visit,' Iftiqar responds cheerfully. 'I was beginning to feel neglected. They have left us alone for several months.'

'What have you written recently to upset their addled minds?'

'Nothing? And you?'

'Would I dare do anything to upset them? I have to be on their side, remember?'

'Why not ask them in for a cup of tea?'

'They shall have to bring their own cups.'

'What shall we talk about?'

'The next coup d'état?'

'Ask their permission to leave the country?'

'Get a loan?'

'Seek their approval to change the paper's name?'

'What are the alternatives?'

'*Sound of the Generals, Khaki Voice, Cantonment Lies*. What will it be?'

'Let's ask the Australian!'

They both turn to me. 'You can choose!'
They find my obvious concern hysterically funny.
Zafar goes behind his table and breaks into song.

Bangali Babu *went for a long run,*
When he returned he was no fun.

Bangali Babu *has lost his old ways,*
He's now a foreigner, or so he says.

Stuffy Bangali Babu *thinks we are nuts,*
But that's because he's lost his guts.

Their flippant behaviour annoys me. Nothing ruffles them.
They sidetrack the seriousness of their situation with nonsensical banter and puerile humour. I have no desire to be here
when those army fellows walk in.

'You have been away too long!' Zafar chuckles at my
discomfort. 'You have lost that sharp edge of third-world
humour. What's life without its tests of survival? The ability
to flaunt adversity and laugh at it is the ultimate measure of
courage.'

'I am a coward then. I see nothing funny about being raided
by the army.' I nudge Nadine toward the door.

Zafar makes a great show of looking at his watch. 'Chow
time! Use the front entrance. You are perfectly safe. No jokes.
They don't have your photographs. You'll be passed off as
visitors. *White Lotus* is on the other side of the road. About
ten minutes walk. There's a table booked in my name. See
you in about half an hour.' He looks at Iftiqar for confirmation.

'Make it forty-five minutes.'

'Ifti, you are too cautious!' Zafar mocks. 'We will be rid of
them in ten minutes.' He turns to me. 'If we are not there,
call the police.' He edges close. 'I am a bit short on cash . . .'

'For . . . forget it!' I stammer with embarrassment. 'I'll
shout.'

'Shout? No, don't call the police yet!'

'My treat!' I say heatedly.

'Some things never change!' Zafar grins with approval. 'Sadly the humour has died, but you haven't lost your generosity.'

Outside we pause on the footpath. Nervously I glance at the truck. Two *jawans*, in battle uniform, lean idly on the bonnet of the vehicle. The driver sits rigidly in his seat, staring straight ahead. In the back of the truck, four *jawans* clean their guns with a loving thoroughness. Pedestrians show no curiosity. An army truck . . . a few soldiers . . . nothing to be alarmed about.

'That way, I think.' I grasp Nadine's hand. My palms are sweating profusely. 'The office is that way.'

TWELVE

Grief is an intensely private experience. Its solitude is a pallid backdrop inviting a random pattern of sentimental reflections. Memory obliges by throwing up a selective assortment of slow-moving images suffused with a glow of a previously perceived happiness. That in itself can be a cause of sadness, for to recall a dressed-up past often makes the present more unbearable than it is.

Memory can operate with the dexterity of a skilled surgeon. It removes the warts, smooths the bumps and covers the blemishes. What emerges can sometimes be far removed from the experienced reality.

My childhood surfaces without the cold shadows of fear or pain. I wander among its treasure coves, unafraid and unhindered, listening to the faithful voices which nurtured me and kept me company. They are still there, ageless and patient, forgiving of this heinous act of betrayal.

I have never considered the possibility of surrendering my childhood so abjectly. Had the breeding ground of my formative years been forcibly taken away by a governmental decree on the pretext of promoting an egalitarian society, I may not have embarked on this guilt trip. But to sell it so easily to make up for our negligence! Its vulgarity is insufferably odious.

There is nothing I can do to redeem my fallen world. I must

refrain from self-pity and not allow my grief to spill over in an embarrassing outpouring of excessive emotion. I am trained to believe that self-control is a prized virtue. It is a male imperative to be emotionless on the surface. I can only allow myself to hurt in private.

A dark, frothy anger buffets me like a turbulent sea. There is anguish and frustration, a frantic desire to claw and destroy the intruders and silence the cacophony of sounds which mock me without restraint. My sense of family propriety demands a restoration of the pristine order and the ancient cycle of life. I crave for the security I once knew.

You are trespassing! I long to cry out. *Leave things the way they have been! Please.*

Outwardly I remain calm and uncommunicative. The others have sensed my sullen aloofness and drifted away.

Hashim said something about a promised elephant ride for Nadine. Nadira went with them. Nafisa lingered for a time and then followed them after engulfing me in a hug, as if to say she understood my need for solitude.

I have distanced myself from the excited noises of bare-bodied villagers, their arms and backs the colour of a caramelised glazing, heaving and grunting as they strain to load a giant tractor on the ferry.

The ferry is a clumsy, alien presence anchored against the newly built platform around the bend where the river is at its narrowest. It is a hostile invader whose purpose is a stabbing reminder of a new life asserting a vigorous claim on my land.

More than the ferry, it is the murderous whine of chainsaws, from across the river, which has unnerved me. It is an unfamiliar sound for the villagers, a treacherous call to display an arrogant disrespect for the land which has nourished them and given them a life which is now to disappear.

I must not stand against progress, Hashim chided me when I expressed my reservations about the sudden reshaping of so many lives. 'You must think of the villagers first and not just your sentiments. Besides, you have come out of it rather well.'

I have avoided the engineers and the architects. One of them, Mr Azam was quick to inform me, had spent six years in Sydney. He is keen to meet me. All the more reason for me to stay here under the tree.

Their indistinct voices come from near the wall. They are hunched over a table, scrutinising their plans and making minor adjustments. Educated, modern men at home in a world of concrete and glass, adept at modelling a synthetic future.

'They moved in the day the contract was signed,' Mr Azam explained patiently when I mentioned the haste with which the machinery and the tools had been brought into the village.'Chaudhary *Shaheb*, you live in the West. You know what efficiency means. A shrewd businessman must squeeze every working hour from the available time. The secret of successful business is to find thirty hours in a day.' He spreads his arms expansively. 'Just think! The place of dreams will truly become a dream of the past. All this will be gone.'

It is impossible to avoid Mr Azam. He is everywhere, walking around with a bulging folder clasped to his chest. He has the magnanimous air of a man who has concluded a long-term arrangement with good fortune and does not mind sharing it with the less privileged. He has had nothing but favourable news.

Without a semblance of dissent, every able-bodied male in the village has agreed to be trained and employed in the refinery. Mateen has accepted an offer to manage the refinery workers after a clause was inserted in his contract, empowering him to promote or dismiss workers according to their performance. The village elders have been awed into silence by sums of money and promises of free accommodation. Shopnoganj is to be dissembled without protest. As for its replica, there was no need for it now since an amicable settlement had been reached.

'A most satisfactory arrangement, Chaudhary *Shaheb*!' Mr Azam gloated. 'Modern accommodation, subsidised schooling for the children, free medical care. It gives us great satisfaction to offer these people the benefits of the modern world.'

What were they planning to do about pollution control? Where were they planning to dump the residual waste from the refinery?

He brushed aside my concerns. 'Pollution will be an insignificant problem. We shall look into it in the future. We prefer to concentrate on the benefits to this community and the country.'

He was more interested in modernising the living conditions of the people. Were the villagers unhappy with the proposals? Had I heard of any complaints? Mr Azam was solicitous in his inquiry. Pukka buildings were a top priority. 'Self-contained flats,' Mr Azam declared proudly. 'With electricity and running water.'

Mr Siddique has been uncommonly generous. I cannot deny the impact of the ubiquitous uncle. His garlanded photographs have appeared in the village. Shopnoganj has a new benefactor.

It would be fun, we decided, to travel by bus and arrive unannounced. I was inclined to expose Nadine to the unpredictability of public transportation and to a raw slice of life experienced by ordinary Bangalis. Her experiences, ever since we arrived, have been monitored by my fear of exposing her to excessive culture shock. Her perceptions of Bangalis have been filtered and distorted because of her confined contact with an affluent minority. She is confused and disturbed by the glaring contradiction between her comfortable living conditions and the abject poverty she confronts when she steps outside the house. She is perceptibly more thoughtful now than she was about matters not directly related to her well-being. The misery she sees around her has shifted her focus from the unthinking, egocentric world of an only child to an uneasy awareness of a tottering society riddled with injustice and poverty. She is beginning to question the lopsided nature of a morally anomalous world. I can see the faint shadows of a sad wisdom in her eyes.

Under Nafisa's supervision and Nadira's discerning eyes, meticulous care was taken with our dressing. We scrounged around for old clothes. Ill-fitting shirts, old trousers, moth-eaten jumpers and well-worn sandals completed a credible image of city people taking a day trip into the country. I had to agree to live with the discomfort of a prickly stubble of beard after refusing to slick back my hair doused with mustard oil. Little could be done about Nadine. Her complexion and grey eyes could not escape a distrustful scrutiny.

We staggered to the bus terminal early in the morning to find it agog with an undisciplined energy of confusion. It emanated from that distinct brand of third-world inefficiency which converts the simplest of organisational routine into a laborious, time-consuming exercise generating a frightful clamour appropriate for a riot-stricken territory. Everyone spoke simultaneously and loudly. Porters haggled aggressively over the charge of carrying trucks and suitcases. Uptight travellers swore, abused and spat freely as luggage went astray to add to the chaos. Boisterous children had their ears twisted and their bottoms smacked. Irate passengers, frustrated by the inevitable delays, locked themselves into picayunish arguments.

There were several ragged queues in front of the rundown tin shed where passengers assembled to buy their tickets, check the delays and test their patience. Desperate latecomers, we learned from a young porter who insisted my backpack was too heavy for me to carry, could avail themselves of the services of a private entrepreneur in the back room of the grocer's store on the other side of the road. Buying a bus ticket from him was a risky venture. His refusal to share the profit with the police made him a regular target for harassment. We heard grim accounts of uninitiated travellers who suffered the misfortune of purchasing tickets at highly inflated prices, only to be stranded by police raids and lengthy interrogations about the illegal sale of fake tickets. What escaped the inexperienced passenger was the dubious nature of the white slip of paper, with a few faded words and a number printed in Bangla, which did not reserve a seat on the bus. It merely tokened a last-minute access to the roof-rack at the passenger's own risk.

Under the assault of angry travellers, the roughly constructed shed looked as though it were ready to collapse. Its sides were severely dented and the flat roof perched uneasily at an angle as if it were an ill-fitting hat that would blow away in the slightest wind. Impatient Bangalis expressed their annoyance by targeting the walls with stones, shamelessly drumming them with copious streams of urine and expectorating their contempt for the inefficiency of the bus services.

I volunteered to buy the tickets to escape Nadine's inexhaustible barrage of questions. A surly young man, in his early twenties, sat behind the glass window, issuing tickets with a contrived slowness. I glared and elbowed my way through to him. He took a long look at me. Despite my scruffy appearance, he decided I was worthy of his heavily accented English. He had been to university, he informed me as he fiddled with a roll of tickets. His sluggishness, I was tempted to think, was a retaliatory measure against a world which could do no better than to shut him up in a stifling cage from morning till dusk. He had lustreless eyes and seemed far away, perhaps dreaming of the accolades his university degree should have brought him.

In the dusty yard, an open-air bazaar had sprung up to tempt the traveller with everything from airline bags, transistor radios and blankets made in Switzerland to fly-ridden food and carbonated drinks of every conceivable colour. The competitive spirit of free enterprise was apparent in a tribal form of macho aggression. The vantage point was just inside the gateless opening to the ground. The old and the very young vendors were forced to set up their stalls in the shade-less centre and hope for a trickle of business from curious customers who might stray their way. The physical superiority of the more robust salesmen granted them the right to a sizeable profit at the end of each day. The competition was fierce near the entrance. The quality of goods was espoused with a polished precision. Pitch, intonation and timed pauses performed wonders for sales clichés and made the derisive remarks about other vendors sound more insulting than they were. Scuffles broke out frequently, my knowledgeable porter informed me. Knives flashed occasionally. Twice or thrice a day policemen entered the capitalistic arena for their share of the business gains in exchange for a display of harmless *lathi* waving and arbitration among the disputing groups.

The bus destined for Jamalpur via Shopnoganj was parked near the entrance, scheduled for departure at eight. We stood on the footpath and waited for the driver. A few minutes before nine he sauntered across the road, wearing a dirty safari jacket and a pair of black trousers. He looked sleepy and highly aggrieved as if his leisurely routine had been severely disrupted by a summons which required an unpar-alleled act of self-sacrifice. His sloven appearance slotted him inconspicuously among the hollow-eyed multitudes without the imaginative freshness to dream of a better future. With complete disdain he ignored the argument between the exas-perated bus conductor and an aggressively demanding passenger. Like a king ascending his throne, he climbed into the driver's seat with an air of regal aloofness and locked the door.

The raspy-voiced bus conductor, with the strap of a bulky

satchel slung around his neck, was engaged in a quarrel with an old farmer. The contentious issue was the status of a goat. The animal stood passively on the footpath between the feuding men. They were surrounded by a small audience vociferously supportive of the animal's cause. The heated exchange was accompanied by some deft footwork. The farmer held a clear advantage over his unarmed adversary. He held a folded umbrella with a pointed tin tip which he kept thrusting at the conductor's chest with an alarming vigour. The younger man parried the jabs by jumping sideways and backwards without the slightest intention of seeking a compromise.

'It cannot come inside my bus!'

'It is my luggage!' The farmer insisted. 'I do not have a trunk or a suitcase!' He glowered and made another lunge with the umbrella.

The goat was a sacrosanct barrier. Neither antagonist crossed the divide the animal represented.

'Luggage?' The conductor screeched beseechingly to the growing crowd. '*Eish*! This is too much!' He shook his head in emphatic disbelief before leaping evasively to his left. 'How can I admit a dirty animal into the bus as a piece of luggage? I have to think of my passengers!'

A matter of pressing urgency forced the wretched animal to break the deadlock and humiliate its owner. As if to justify the conductor's stalagmitic stand, the goat surrendered to a bout of enuresis. A trickle of pale yellow liquid splattered the footpath. The onlookers reacted with consternation. The circle widened quickly. People clapped. They whistled and exhorted the goat to a greater effort.

With spontaneous glee, Nadine joined the merriment. 'Go goat!' She yelled, with her hands cupped around her mouth. 'Go! Go!'

'You see what I mean?' The conductor appealed to a wall of grinning faces. 'Does a trunk piss? *Na*! Does a suitcase make such a mess? *Na*! Just think how smelly it would be inside the bus! *Eish!*' For emphasis he tilted his head upwards and pinched his nostrils with his thumb and index finger. With his other hand he fanned the air near his face.

In a frenzy of humiliated anger, the bearded villager kicked the goat and slapped its rump. 'Brainless animal!' He cried. 'Creature of *Iblis*! May Allah's curse fill your rotten body with filth!'

It was beyond anyone's anticipation that the Almighty would oblige so promptly and load the emaciated body. The curse had a spectacularly laxative effect. The goat bleated in protest and shed a load of small black pellets which bounced unevenly on the hard surface and rolled in every direction. People scampered for safety. The old man turned on himself and cursed his ill-luck. He began to weep disconsolately.

Furtively the conductor looked around to ascertain the crowd's dispersal. He glared at us as if to intimate that the public spectacle had ended. The occasion now demanded a private negotiation.

He placed a sympathetic hand on the farmer's shoulder. '*Aarey bhai*, we are all brothers in Islam. We must help each other.' He spoke in an undertone. He patted the old man with the generosity of a charitable victor. 'We should be able to arrange something.' He paused to adjust the satchel which hung in front of his crotch. 'Let me see . . . I am taking a risk. You understand that, don't you?' The voice dropped even further.

Nadine and I crept forward.

'It is possible that for a small fee we can find a space for your luggage.' He threw back his head and roared with laughter.

The farmer brightened immediately. He reached for the knot of his *lungi*.

A sharp-eyed vendor, carrying a bamboo cage crowded with noisy hens, pressed forward with money in hand. A milkman, carrying two milk buckets tied on each end of a sturdy bamboo pole, looked hopeful and decided to pursue his case.

Several satisfactory deals later, the conductor thumped the side of the bus with the palms of his hands. The side door hissed open and a mad scramble followed.

We were among the first to squeeze through the door to the front seats. Those with sizeable possessions struggled behind us. Live and inanimate belongings were crammed into every available space—under the seats, on overhead racks and in the narrow aisle.

A thick, glass window separated us from the driver. Without taking his eyes off the magazine which engrossed him, the driver beeped the horn and turned the ignition key. The door closed on a dozen or so passengers who were left waving their tickets in impotent anger. A drumming noise, like that of a freak hailstorm hammering a tin roof, pounded the bus. The conductor snatched an umbrella and strode belligerently to the rear window. A file of passengers were nimbly climbing the cast-iron ladder to the roof-rack. The agitated conductor exerted himself to force open the jammed emergency exit. He pushed and shoved, grunted and cursed. He pleaded for help. No one moved.

He turned his attention to the front of the bus. 'Monju Bhai!' He shouted. 'Open the door!'

I leaned forward to see what was engaging the driver's attention. Beside me, Nadine giggled. Her hand covered her mouth in embarrassment. The driver was captivated by the frontal topography of a dark-haired woman.

'Monju *Bhai*!' The conductor stumbled over boxes, holdalls, trunks, baskets and suitcases in a frenetic bid to reach the driver. 'Monju *Bhai*!' He yelled. 'Open the door!'

Through the illusory delights of erotomania, the conductor's voice must have reached him as a garbled signal to drive off. He sighed audibly. With parted lips he slobbered the photograph of the nude with the ardour of a reluctantly parting lover. I raised my hands in front of Nadine's face in a desperate bid to screen her from the wretched man's perversity. She doubled over and clutched her stomach. There were tears in her eyes. Hashim was shaking with laughter. Across the aisle, Nadira and Nafisa were straining forward, giggling mischievously.

I felt foolish and outraged. In a huff I collapsed on the seat. Nadine buried her head in my chest, her body heaving silently.

Suddenly the bus lurched forward as if invisible hands had given it a mighty push. Luggage clattered. Passengers were thrown forward and sideways. Those on the ladder panicked and jumped off. There was banging on the roof and screamed abuses.

No great harm resulted. The roof-rack travellers must have survived by clinging to each other for support. The only casualty was the conductor himself. Caught in mid stride, he lost his footing and fell heavily against a seat. He barely managed to grasp the bar of the arm-rest to prevent himself from smashing into a frightened little girl. Like a startled bird, the satchel flew up at an angle to his body, only to swing back like a pendulum and strike him in the groin. The flap of the satchel snapped open like a cage door, showering the aisle with notes and coins. A savage tussle for the money followed. Many took the opportunity to bump into him. Whenever possible, elbows, fists and feet punished him. He crawled toward the front of the bus and then sprang onto the lap of a newly married woman. His apologies and a rapid explanation gained him a small space on the seat between the forgiving bride and her angry husband.

The bus eased into the mainstream traffic. The scavengers were quickly back in their seats, pretending nothing had happened. The conductor made no move to recoup his losses.

We sat back for ninety minutes of a jerky ride.

The incense sticks burn quickly and shrivel into a few pinchful of ashes. My grandfather loved their aroma and stuck them in every corner of the house during *Shab-e-Barath*. They attract the angels, he would say. With a twinkle in his eyes, he then told a hushed audience of children how their fates for the following year had been determined in Heaven.

Despite my affectionate memories of Dada, it is the older grave, next to his, which draws my attention. It is cordoned off by a low cement wall, cracked and broken at the top and the sides. Weeds and grass sprout from the crevices.

The weathering and the destructive touches of vengeful hands make it difficult to read the faded engravings on the scarred slab of discoloured marble tilted at a slight angle to the head of the grave. I scrape the surface with a pocket-knife and blow away the grime.

ISHTIAQ AHMED CHAUDHARY
1850–1904

Allah has taken what belongs to Him

I rub my hand on the slimy surface and feel the rough edges of the carved letters. Whoever wrote the epitaph chose the words with a philosophical acumen. A wronged relative? A slighted village elder, perhaps? A holy man? I detect a warning for future generations. The most notorious of the Chaudharies, fabled for his wealth and arrogance, was no more than a possession, leased to life and taken back when his owner wanted him. The words have an emasculating effect on everything I have heard about my great-grandfather. I have never thought about the epitaph before. It was simply there. Words without significance. Now they assume a different dimension. I read them aloud several times. They deprive him of his legendary powers, turning him into a helpless mortal, humbled to the commonality of a resting place he shares with his lesser known relatives.

Suspicious eyes shadow me as I move among the neglected

graves. Moti Mia does not recognise me. The old caretaker remains stubbornly unconvinced of my identity.

'*Choto Babu* is not in this life,' he tells me.

I am supposed to have died years ago, on my way to a foreign land. Even the catchphrases we used as children, in our games of hide and seek among the headstones, do not evoke a flicker of recognition in him. In his more active days, Moti Mia was forever chasing us out of the graveyard for the disrespect we showed to the dead. No laughter. No noise. Those were his unbending rules. Only the wind and the birds were allowed to serenade those who rested there.

With a sharpened bamboo stick in his hands, Moti Mia sits under a tamarind tree and watches my moves as if I cannot be trusted among the graves.

I walk among the mounds with the smaller headstones. I pause near Shabnam's grave. I never really knew my volatile and rebellious sister. I squeezed some more details from Nafisa. A torrid romance led to a careless consequence. They were forced to announce their engagement. A week before the wedding, Shabnam walked into his flat unannounced and saw him with another woman. Her rage ended her life. He disappeared.

I bend down to light some incense sticks. Without any effort I manage a silent prayer.

Some of the other names bring back summer memories of a crowded house. KHALIDA BEGUM. ALIMUDDIN HASSAN CHAUDHARY. AZIZA BEGUM. ZAHOOR LATIF CHAUDHARY. MANSUR ALI CHAUDHARY. Then there are those who did not quite make it to adulthood. ANIS. SHAHEEN and IMTIAZ. Cousins and childhood companions who drift back into my consciousness as if they had decided to come out of voluntary exile.

I think of the vanity of it all. The preacher's words reverberate in my ears. Fading names and dates for the reposing bones. A catalogued family collection for the living mind to mythologise and recreate the past with gilded lies. I was told as a child that Muslims ought to be buried in unmarked graves. To keep grief alive by erecting any reminders was to dissent against Allah's Will. I relate to the idea of a finale which leaves no enduring traces of the mortal years. It fittingly negates the emphasis on recognition we crave in life. Here, among the bones, stones and memories, it does not take any inducement to ponder on the perverse motivators of earthly aspirations. A small graveyard, overgrown with grass and weeds, heightens the grim consciousness of lives trivialised by pettiness.

I have always had extraordinary difficulty in coming to terms with the concept of ending. The *mullah* drummed it into me. *Whatever lives is by Allah's Grace. It is His will to end it when He chooses. The end of life must not be mourned, for it is a destiny we all share.* The truth of such an inevitability has not blunted the piercing sharpness of fear implicit in the word *end*. It has a forlorn ring I associate with the silent sadness of a still night. My difficulty has been to give it a credible meaning which denies it the triumph of finality. The ability to believe in death as a transition and garnish it with hope is a gift I have denied myself. It isn't as though I have never made an effort to extract a meaningful satisfaction from its elusive vagueness. But my helplessness is like imagining a long passage through subtle shades of darkness and then attempting to describe it by using commonplace analogies.

The point is, I define myself by the awareness of my experiences. Will I be aware of death? For how long? Will I know, even for a speck of time, the point at which I die? Will it be a gradual dissolution of awareness or a sudden blip and then nothing? That is where I feel trapped and hopelessly inadequate. How do I conceptualise nothingness? It is an abstraction beyond description. Deep inside, I reject ultimate extinction. The possibility of losing the accumulated riches of knowing and feeling makes me resentful. Will that resentment turn into a nihilistic despair with old age? Is that what has happened to Abba?

Despite my fears, I am afflicted with a morbid desire to finish here, near the house of my birth. To be buried in a foreign land is an inordinately cruel ending.

An unknown graveyard under a murky sky. A black limousine ride for the coffin. A few people dressed in dark colours, huddled under umbrellas. Tears, sniffles and a discreet eye on time as a wet Victorian afternoon declines toward a wintery darkness. A *mullah*, I have never seen, mechanically reciting *surahs* to send me on my way. A short eulogy to make me sound virtuous and important. Boring, polite and necessary words to feed the living lies. He will never say what might have summed it up. *Here was a man who chose to be out of place.*

I bend down to touch the earth. It feels warm and hard. This is where I should end, among my own. There is a vain comfort in the absurdity of a posthumous identity. This is our place. The earth breathes our spirit here. There, next to my grandfather . . . there is room for three or four more.

This affinity with the land and the feeling of oneness with the surroundings may be an extension of my act of reconciliation yesterday.

Last night, for the only time in my life, I made Ma truly happy. It was a wondrous moment to see the amazement and the tearful sheen of joy in her eyes when I handed her the box of jewellery. We didn't speak. I held her and stroked her head as she clung to me and cried.

At my insistence Nafisa took me to the pawnbroker's shop. There was no difficulty in redeeming the jewellery. Mr Nawaz was a kind and honest man. He had never seen such exquisite craftsmanship in his experience. There was only one place famous for such skill. Bau Bazaar in Calcutta. He had guessed correctly. I was moved by the gentle manner with which he caressed the velvet-lined box before he handed it to me. Would I consider selling the contents? The jewellery wasn't mine, I explained. They did not belong to anyone. My mother was the present custodian. They were part of a collection that had a reverential meaning for us. Their value could not be estimated in monetary terms. No, they were not for sale. Mr Nawaz nodded his acceptance of what I said and took the bank cheque.

It shocked me to know how much had been spent on Nadine's *aqeeqa*.

'I would do it again for my grand-daughter!' Ma sobbed defiantly, as if she expected me to chide her for such a scandalous profligacy.

I did not understand her reckless generosity. I didn't say so. We have different ways of loving. Ma's selflessness was foreign to me. Her kind of loving is a rarity in a world where acts of benevolence are tempered by a measure of cautionary self-consideration. Had I been in her place, my inbuilt mechanisms for self-preservation would have prevented me from seeking Mr Nawaz's assistance.

Nadine is a privileged child. Some day I shall tell her about her grandmother's loving madness. I shall never forget the flushed look of disbelief on Nadine's face that evening. For a few unforgettable hours, she was transformed into a dazzling princess in a house of loving admirers. Ma made her the happiest child I have ever known.

We have been invited to meet Mr Siddique. He has agreed to stay for lunch.

'He will only be here for a short time. It will be an honour to be in his company,' Mateen said deferentially. There was an air of agitated anxiety about him as though he did not trust us in the company of his new employer.

From where I stand, I can see the wall between two tamarind trees. The table has been removed. The engineers and the architects have gone inside the house to meet Mr Siddique and give him their final report.

I stop to look back at the graves. My eyes sweep over them for the last time. I feel cold and shaken, as if I were standing on an empty plain at dusk, feeling a wind brushing me with strokes of mortality. Between the evening's growing blindness and my desolation stands the shell of remembrance glowing faintly with jumbled up memories.

Moti Mia looks at me dubiously. I am more acceptable to him, now that I have given him some money.

'*Choto Babu* left us many years ago.' His face carries the grave weight of an unpalatable conviction. 'He does not belong to this world. The dead never come back, *Shaheb*. Whoever you are, go in peace.'

Two young village men are leaning against the lichen-covered bricks, their arms folded militantly across their chests. They look at me with insolence as I approach the wall. One of them expectorates near his feet. He leans over to whisper to the other man whose eyes have never left me. Deliberately he dislodges a brick and tosses it near his feet. Then another. And another. They step on them and begin to sing the national anthem.

I avoid looking at them. I should like to think they are happy about being rushed into a new era.

Hashim and Nadine are near the jackfruit trees, undecided whether they should climb the branches for a better view of the other side of the river. Sitting on a log, Nadira is listening to Nafisa's account of the history of the village.

The ferry has almost made it to the other side.

'I assume we have also been invited for lunch.' Hashim pats his flabby belly. 'I've had a good morning's exercise. I hope Mateen has forgiven us for this morning.'

It is difficult to forget the look of disgusted shame on Mateen's face as we trooped into the house like a bunch of unkempt vagabonds. He was entertaining Mr Azam to a late breakfast. At Mateen's insistence we changed into *dhobi*-washed clothes. He was mortified by our indecorous irresponsibility.

'Fun?' He shrieked, wringing his hands nervously. 'It is an insult to the family to travel like commoners! This is not fun!'

Mr Azam was polite enough to turn his back to us and admire the arrangement of freshly picked flowers on a side table. Over a fresh pot of tea, he offered us his car for the drive back to Dhaka. 'Whenever you wish to return,' he added as an afterthought. 'No hurry.'

'There!' Hashim directs Nadine's attention to the other side of the river. 'See where the women are washing clothes? That was our crossing point. The water is shallow there. Beyond those trees was our playground. What fun we had! Would you like to go across after lunch?'

'Dad?'

'You two can go. I want to explore this side a little more.'

We look up. The minatory scream of two air force jets is like the pained howl of a wounded animal fleeing toward safety. The sky is pale and mute, its imperishable immensity blemished with flecks of mortal frivolity. Multi-coloured kites glide under the vaporous traces of the disappearing planes.

Then, just for an instant, for an infinitesimal grain of time, there is a dense primordial silence. It is an awed hush, as if a wayward world were returning to its senses. It is a fugitive moment of fragile quietness, quickly shattered as the noise begins again. My nerves jump as that dreadful buzz of chainsaws drags me back to the awful truth I cannot escape.

We begin to walk slowly toward the house. I feel as if I am an undertaker of a past which must be put to rest.

I stop to look back at the dark band of trees untouched by the early afternoon light.

Soon it will all be different.

'Things will change quickly once they get all the equipment and the building material across,' Hashim observes approvingly. 'We should come back in a couple of weeks. How about it, Nadine? We better have another elephant ride before the animals are taken to the circus.'

'We won't be here, Uncle Hashim!' Nadine's voice is vibrant with excitement. 'We are going home next week!'

Ahead of us, Nafisa quickens her steps. Nadira pauses to adjust the straps of her slippers. Hashim pivots around. I can feel his piercing gaze of perplexity.

I think of Michelle's cautious greeting on the phone. She wished me a happy birthday and offered to pick us up from the airport when I told her the date of our return. Bravely we agreed that there was much to talk over. Our mutual interest in Nadine's cultural experiences made it easier to bypass the serious problems which separated us. Toward the end of the call the conversation was flowing more easily.

I warm to the thought of a night out with Theo. I shall exaggerate the stories, simplify the experiences, censor the parts which cannot be laughed at. A great deal will have to be left out. I shall talk about *them* and *there* in a manner which will suggest unfamiliar experiences.

Then there will be a long afternoon with Claire. She is recovering from a minor stroke, Michelle informed me. I shall tell her that the womb was there all right, except I could not fit into it any more.

Now I know that the fabric of my life cannot be separated into their individual strands. They must remain interwoven in a complex texture. I shall never be able to close the sizeable hole at the centre of my life and shut out the view of that other world. I am destined to fret and pine, and endure the lonely burden of a dissatisfaction no one else will understand. I shall brood over what might have been. This is the way it must be. I have known too much to live contentedly.

There is a crackle of snapping branches. Then the reverberating thud of a falling tree.

So, this is where it all ends. And begins? And if this is to be a beginning, am I to go forward haunted by the regrets of spurned opportunities?

I listen intently for the fading echo of galloping hoofs. My imagination does not respond. The men-horses will not be returning, I guess. Nor the music or the dancing shadows.

The voices have been silenced.

Reluctantly I turn my back to the river.

Hashim's scowling face confronts me.

'I meant to tell you earlier.' The hesitant voice is distant, and does not sound as if it is entirely my own. 'We are going back next Thursday.'